# Bloodaxe

## The Demise of Saxon Wessex

## Annette Burkitt

Privately printed in the United Kingdom in 2025
on behalf of the author
by The Hobnob Press,
8 Lock Warehouse, Severn Road,
Gloucester GL`1 2GA
www.hobnobpress.co.uk

British Library Cataloguing in Publication Data
A catalogue record for this book is available from the British Library

ISBN 978-1-914407-18-5

Typeset in Adobe Caslon Pro 11/14 pt.
Typesetting and origination by John Chandler

*Illustration of the eagle and crown by Tom Charlesworth.*

*For Patrick and Joanna*

*Then out of the sea I saw a beast rising. It had ten horns and seven heads. On its horns were ten diadems, and on each head a blasphemous name... The beast I saw was like a leopard... The whole world went after the beast in wondering admiration. Men worshipped the dragon because he had conferred his authority upon the beast; they worshipped the beast also, and chanted, 'Who is like the Beast? Who can fight against it?'*
The Revelation of St John, 13 vi-4

*Let's take a trip, on my time machine, my time machine, you know What I mean....*
Mick Softley, 1971

Also by Annette Burkitt:
Kings of Wessex Series:
*Flesh and Bones of Frome Selwood and Wessex* (Athelstan)
*The Gorge* (Edmund and Elgiva)

Articles:
With Tim Burkitt, '*Badon as Bath*'in Popular Archaeology, April
1985
With Tim Burkitt, '*The Frontier Zone and the Siege of Mount Badon: a
Review of the Evidence for their Location.*'Proceedings of the Somerset
Archaeological and Natural History Society, vol.134,1990

*'Your majesty, when we compare the present life of man on earth with that
time of which we have no knowledge, it seems to me like the swift flight
of a single sparrow through the banqueting-hall where you are sitting at
dinner on a winter's day with your thanes and counsellors. In the midst
there is a comforting fire to warm the hall; outside, the storms of winter
rain or snow are raging. This sparrow flies swiftly in through one door of
the hall, and out through another. While he is inside, he is safe from the
winter storms; but after a few moments of comfort, he vanishes from sight
into the wintry world from which he came. Even so, man appears on earth
for a little while; but of what went before this life or of what follows,
we know nothing. Therefore, if this new teaching has brought any more
certain knowledge, it seems only right that we should follow it.'*
Bede, A History of the English Church and People.

Edwin holds a council with his chief men about accepting the Faith
of Christ. The high priest destroys his own altars (A.D. 627.)

# Contents

# Characters

Characters are historical, unless otherwise stated.

**Aelfgifu,** wife of King Eadwig.

**Aelfgifu of York,** first wife of King Aethelred.

**Aelfhere,** Ealdorman of Mercia, died 983, rival of Ealdorman Aethelwine of East Anglia.

**Aelfthryth,** third wife of King Edgar, mother of Aethelred. Stepmother of Edward the Martyr. Died c.1000.

**Aethelwine,** Ealdorman of East Anglia, died 992, rival of Ealdorman Aelfhere of Mercia.

**Aethelwold,** priest, a leader of the reform movement of the church, Bishop of Winchester, died 984.

**Ahmad Ibn Fadlan,** diplomat and traveller, born Baghdad 879, died 960.

**Algar,** fictional novice monk at Frome and Glastonbury. Friend to Nonna.

**Anlaf,** Norwegian, king of Dublin and Northumbria at various times. Also known, in Ireland, as Amlaib Cuaran and in England as Olaf Sihtricsson. See Timeline for more information. Born 927, died 980. Another Anlaf (Olaf Guthfrithson), died 941/2 was formerly king in Dublin and York. Olaf Sihtricsson was his cousin and succeeded him. In this story the two men become one single Anlaf to avoid confusion.

**Aethelred,** king 978-1013 and again from 1014-1016.

**Athelstan Half-King,** Ealdorman (not King) Athelstan of East Anglia from 932. His father was descended from the West Saxon royal family, holding extensive estates in Somerset and Devon. Athelstan and his brothers wielded immense power throughout England. He fostered the aetheling Edgar. His family home was probably at Upwood near Ramsey on the edge of the fens. Was known in later years as 'Half-King' because of his enormous responsibilities during the reigns of Athelstan, Edmund, Eadred and Eadwig. He worked with Queen Eadgifu and Dunstan particularly during the reigns of Eadred and Eadwig. His family were as powerful in the tenth century as the Godwins in the eleventh. He retired, or was pushed out of court circles, in 955, after the death of King Eadred, and became a monk at Glastonbury. It is not known when he died.

**Bica,** fictional servant to Eadred.

**Dunstan,** Abbot of Glastonbury, Archbishop of Canterbury (from 959), leader of the monastic reform movement, died 988, aged about 78. Became a saint.

**Eadgifu,** queen and mother, by King Edward, Alfred's son, of Kings Edmund and Eadred and paternal grandmother of Kings Eadwig and Edgar. Great grandmother of Edgar's children, Edward, Edith and Aethelred. Lived through much of the tenth century.

**Eadred,** king 946-955, died in Frome, Somerset; younger brother of King Edmund (died, probably assassinated, at Pucklechurch, near Bristol, in 946).

**Eadric Streona,** aide and chief minister to King Aethelred. Achieved the epithet Streona 'the greedy' and marked down in history as a traitor to Wessex.

**Eadwig,** eldest son of King Edmund. Ruled after the death of his uncle Eadred. Died in 959 at age of nineteen.

**Edburga,** saint, daughter of Edward the Elder and Eadgifu. Predeceased her mother. Nun at Nunnaminster, Winchester and buried there.

**Edgar,** younger son of King Edmund. Ruled after the death of his elder brother, Eadwig. Died in 975 aged about 30.

**Edith,** daughter of King Edgar by his second wife. Became St Edith of Wilton.

**Edward the Martyr,** son of King Edgar by his first wife. Died in uncertain circumstances at Corfe, Dorset in 978.

**Egil Skallagrimsson,** Icelandic fortune-hunter, mercenary, poet and farmer.

**Emma of Normandy,** second wife of King Aethelred.

**Eric Bloodaxe,** king of Norway, Orkney and twice king of Jorvik (York).

**Gunnhild,** Eric Bloodaxe's wife, 'Mother of Kings'.

**Hersfig,** fictional servant of King Eadred.

**Nonna,** fictional clerk at the Wessex court.

**Oda,** Archbishop of Canterbury.

**Oswald,** nephew of Oda, a leader in the monastic reform movement. Bishop of Worcester.

**Swein Forkbeard,** king of Denmark 986-1014, king of England 1013-14, father of Cnut (king 1016-1035). The placename Swainswick, near Bath, records his camp, from which he harried south-west England.

**Wynflaed,** maternal grandmother of Kings Eadwig and Edgar.

**Wulfstan,** Archbishop of York from his appointment by King Athelstan in 931 to 952. Died in 956 at Oundle, a monastery founded by St Wilfrid of Ripon, near Peterborough, Northamptonshire.

# The Bird

IT WAS YOUNG, adventurous, fearless; barely out of the nest, a male, its tail feathers still brown, its exuberance at its own majesty and size unquelled.

The white-tailed eagle, as it would be, pointed its left wing-fingers to the heavens, its right to the sea, earth and cliffs below. Hartland Point lay crisp in the dead of winter; grey-green January seas surged and swelled back and forth, back and forth, against the jagged rocks.

The eagle soared over the cliffs, watching for plunder cast up by the waves. There was plenty in this wild place; St Nectan's church was under construction, not yet functioning. The farming folk had not yet claimed the woods and furze of the cliff-edge, preferring to leave them to the hunting creatures of the coastal strip and sea. Gannets and seagulls filled the air below the eagle. From high to low, the hierarchy of birds took their natural places as they fed and flew.

There were other places to explore besides this forbidding shore, but never far from the sea, always in sight of the sea. The eagle called to reassure itself and to repeat to the world, its world, that it existed. It flew up on a sudden thermal, and wheeled north-eastwards on a fast westerly wind, following the edge of the waves. Before long, high up, it spied the peninsula below, a short, jutting piece of land which stretched tentatively into the sea, reaching for the opposite shore. Brean Down, the ruins of its temple visible to the bird, hosted a nest of hares. They scattered through the frosted grass across its sides as the eagle swooped and caught one of their brethren, screaming as it was hoist into the air, pierced by the yellow claws.

Crook Peak lay just inland, the western edge of the Mendip Hills. The rocks on its summit rose like an eagle's talon above the marshy Levels, a willing partner in the game of dismemberment. The eagle pitched there with its prize and there devoured it. The debris of past meals was scattered about, the bones sparkling in the frost.

The winter sun, forging past the banks of mist and cloud, revealed, as it ate, the chief features of the landscape; sea, high hills, flooded flat lands. Brent Knoll and Ynis Witrin, Glastonbury Tor, the isle of glass, its tower and church as yet unbuilt, dominated the low clouds. Having consumed its kill, the eagle left, to explore the north. Returning to Wales, where it had begun life, it began to grow the first of its white tail feathers. The path to maturity had begun.

## Monastery of St John, Frome, Autumn 988

IN THE STUPOR of the sick room my friend and tutor Nonna sits in a low chair, his feet on a stool, a blanket over his legs, asleep. His mouth hangs open. A sleeping face looks so much like death.

He is often this way, these days. He is old, after all, not so much ill, as worn out. Should I wake him? Will my extreme youth offend him? Might my presence enliven him? I sit beside him, stroking his veiny hand with a finger.

'Algar, is that you?'

'Yes, Nonna. How are you?'

Nonna opens his eyes. They are sparkle. Perhaps sleep has energised him. He points to a mug on a nearby table. I pass it to him. He drinks, just a little. Now he can speak.

'I was dreaming about you, my friend.'

I am aware of the value that my learned brothers bestow on their dreams. They have often been turned into prophecies which send armies to war. Archbishop Dunstan's dreams have that effect. He writes them down and uses them as teaching aids.

'Have you the strength to tell me about your dream, Nonna?' I am really interested. This old man has educated and surprised me with his recall of events and people. He has spied on them all, kings, bishops, nobles, concubines and wives. He is a living diary of this time before The End. I mine his precious memories, hoping to survive, in time, to tell others.

The old man rolls onto his side and sits up. The blanket falls onto the floor. The tiles where it lands are marked by a potter's fetid imagination; sgraffito dragons with claws as large as their heads, impossible crowns and snarling cats, in bright yellow and brown. This is the floor of the caldarium, where gloomy things are banished and healing powers, of tradition, kingship, ownership and pets are displayed, if you look down to your feet, downwards to hell. In these days, upwards and downwards have assumed new significance. I have to be careful where I place my eyes, in annoyance or impatience, to the sky, in humility or in shame to the earth. I pick up and replace the blanket, arranging it neatly on Nonna's knees.

'Thank you, my boy. A small amount of care travels the longest way, they say. Yes, about you. You know, my dreams are not to be taken seriously, as others are. I dreamt that you and I were walking in a high place in good weather along a stony track between walls, descending to a village – a fishing village, I suppose, by bright blue sea water. There were gulls crying overhead, there was an air of contentment, of summer calmness, like the feeling one can get when observing a line of washed clothes blowing in a breeze. A sense of a task achieved, a time of relaxation. Do you know what I mean?' Nonna coughs and spits.

'I think I do, Nonna. But what were we doing in this place and what do you suppose the dream means?'

'My boy, it means that I have dreamed, of you and I, that is all.'

Nonna notices my disappointment. He sighs. 'Well, it might mean that you and I are on the right track... that there are sunny times ahead... that the small, utilitarian place that we are destined to come to eventually will suffice, though it is on the edge of the world...perhaps we may go so far as to say that the coming millennium fantasy will not be as dark as some suppose; that we will adapt and reach accommodation with a refreshed state of being...but you are tempting me to say more than can possibly be imagined. Your face! Do not look so worried, my young friend. Father Dunstan may feel the need to go into the streets each night to wash them with his prayers, but, as you can see, I do not. All will be well, Algar, all will be well.' Nonna cups my face in his hands. His hands are cold. The caldarium's warmth does not reach all parts.

'This matter of the dark and the light, Nonna, it does trouble me so.' It has not been his intention to frighten me, I know, but sometimes after waking, people say things which are better not aired. I should give him longer to return to the living world, in future. The time which my old friend takes to come fully to his senses is becoming longer. He will soon be more asleep than awake. 'But never mind. The archangel Michael will see to matters of a serious nature, I am sure. I am glad that we walk together in sunny paths, Father.'

Nonna closes his eyes, savouring something, the dream, perhaps. 'You called me Father. I like that.' Nonna smiles. His face creases like old linen.

I know that he has children of his own, that once he was married, but that was long ago and his children are far away. 'I shall call you it again, then.'

Nonna drifts painlessly back into his dreams of the past. I squeeze his hand lightly. Will he be able to tell me more before he goes to join the angels?

'Father, you were going to tell me about the queen. You have told me much about the kings of Wessex, but what about Eadgifu? She was old when she died, was she not? All that I know is that she was Edward's queen and that she was young with the new century. What was she like? Father?'

But it is too late, for now, to get more from the old man. He snores.

There is the bell for vespers. After that, there will be supper. My voice is required in the church. How much longer can I sing with a treble voice? They want me back in Canterbury to be assessed, but Nonna needs me here.

'Father Nonna, I must leave you now, the bell has rung. I will see you again in the morning after Prime. Goodnight, my friend.'

Nonna's eyes open a little and close. He is dreaming. His lips twitch. Who is he speaking to?

Will I see life in his bright eyes tomorrow? Will one night take Father Nonna, my father, from me to the gates of heaven?

# Part 1
## Eadred 'Weak-in-the-feet' and Eadwig 'The Fair'

## After the Witan, the Palace of Winchester, late August 946

EADGIFU STRODE THE long hall past the feasting fireplace. Her long skirt dragged dust and crumbled tiling grout. A large tabby cat followed her, with murder in its heart.

The carved and stacked chimney of stone, half-way along one wall, lay empty of flame; huge iron firedogs at its sides, their jaws apart, ate the air in anticipation of autumn gatherings to come, their ears and curling tails collecting the webs of hopeful spiders. The yellow, forbidding light of early autumn descended from high windows, providing illumination but no joy. It failed to probe the dark recesses of a palace in mourning, or to lighten the atmosphere of the centuries of human fallibility it had witnessed. The ancient stone walls held and nourished the memories, the secrets. The Wessex dynasty had plenty of those.

There were no other women of note in Winchester, the capital. Eadgifu's freshly-dead son Edmund's wife Elgiva died years ago, though she was a saint and therefore, in theory, living. Eadgifu was the only breathing queen of the royal Wessex dynasty. Edmund's second wife, Aethelflaed of Damerham, having proven herself to be barren, had been sent home to her father. The girl's male family members had been more active in promoting themselves than in contributing to the general well-being of the nation. It was unfortunate, but the girl would find another husband soon enough, away from the business of the court and the royal imperative to breed. Eadred, who became king after Edmund's untimely death in May, had signed a declaration that he would not marry. No loss, Eadgifu thought, to him. He had little interest in women, or they in him.

A king without a queen was not uncommon; caretaker kings did not expect to breed valid heirs themselves. Athelstan had not. The bloodline needed to be kept clear of pretenders and by-blows. There were enough problems with legitimate heirs, without quarrels about succession from other sources. Leofa's son had been a case in point. Whether he had intended to assassinate or not, Leofa's return to England at Pucklechurch had ended in the death of Edmund. That bright May morning three months ago had been a severe jolt for his mother, Eadgifu, and for Wessex. England would recover, with Half-King's help, and Dunstan's, but the kingdom was now in the hands of Eadgifu's younger son, the ill-starred and sickly caretaker heir, Eadred.

She doubted his competence. His health was not good. She had heard it whispered that he had been called "Weak-in-the-feet". What was wrong with his feet? There was only a slight shuffling motion, with bowed head when running, that looked slightly odd. Young boys could be cruel. Edmund had once noted, aloud, that his brother, younger by only two years, had thin ankles. There had been a slight accident when jumping from a horse which had led to noticeable bandaging around a lower limb. The comment had stuck; Eadred's weakness became a court joke. Kings had nicknames; Hairy or Bald was common; Eadgifu's sons were handsome creatures, not tending to any description which the court could bestow on them, and they were, by and large, popular. Nevertheless, nicknames could not be avoided. Eadwig, his nephew, her grandson, would become king after him, when he was of age, but there were doubts about him, too. At the age of eight, he was more than a handful, but at least he was called 'the fair'. Time would tell if the epithet referred to his personality as well as to his golden head and beauty.

Problems, problems. But when had any reign gone smoothly? Mourning for Edmund was now at an end; the first witan of Eadred's reign had been held; it had not been memorable, but it had not been a disaster. The cobbled-together nation of England would go on as before; it had to. External enemies defined it and gave it unity. Internal enemies, which every nation had in abundance, divided.

Eadgifu muttered as she marched, her earrings swinging in time with her slightly crab-like gait. She winced as she felt a stab of pain in a hip. Managing the men in her family was a full-time, troublesome career, steering youths from cradle to kingship. There would be rest, in a convent of her choosing, in time; meanwhile the management of Eadred's reign and the training of her wayward grandson Eadwig was a full time task. Pain was not only felt in the hip, but in the head, and the heart, too, with all that she had to do.

*Got to keep on, keep on buggering on.* Her mother had been a stoic as she approached her demise. She would be, too.

The queen-mother had lost little of her vitality since the tragic disaster of her eldest son's demise. She was perhaps a little thinner, perhaps more lined about the face, chin and eyes, but the determined mouth and carefully constructed wimple around the locked-in hair, together with her energetic demeanour, gave an air of complete command. She would change the world, not it, she. Despite her advancing years, her back was still straight. She could still balance on her high-heeled shoes which brought her up to the level of the shoulders of the tallest men of the witan; she still had the pick of the jewels and ornaments of the royal household. The grey mourning clothes of recent months had been discarded; today she was resplendent in orange and purple. She was the only queen Wessex had, or needed.

Eadgifu was on her way to a conference with Eadred and his secular advisor, Ealdorman Athelstan Half-king. Dunstan, representing the church, would be making his way from his duties in the New Minster and would meet them in the robing room of the palace, she had been informed. She paused near the far end of the long hall to mutter a silent prayer and to shake out her aching leg. The cat sat behind her. Starting off again with a limp, approaching a heavy door, she passed the tattered banners of war limply hanging above an intricate wooden shrine, on which a candle burned perpetually as a reminder of the glories and sacrifices of Wessex and English warriors. Her brother and father, lords of Kent, were commemorated there. Memories, memories. She turned and looked back along the length of the hall.

Throughout it, in dust-filled corners high and low, lurked trophies of war and hunts and heavy, antique oak furniture. The latter displayed the ingredients of an imaginative pagan past: carvings, crude as well as intricate, of beasts and half-human animals, defenders and attackers of former realms. Between and below the banners and flags there were assorted mirrors, polished metal shields and plates, tapestries and embroideries emblazoned with heroic feats in bright colours or scenes of capitulation and sorrow. Revenge and self-seeking were the themes of the past; now they were beginning to be outmoded. Forgiveness, allied with strength of arms, the mark of a resolved and firm god, these were the new watchwords. The hands of an executed thief, dried, surounded by herbs and propped on metal spikes near the fireplace, served to remind those who saw them of the justice and mercy of the crown. The soporific memories and customs of deep ages of Saxon rule over southern Britain were etched into these mighty walls and into all the ancient palaces of Wessex. Sometimes it felt, to Eadgifu, that the golden times of the Saxons were behind and not to be found in the future. Holding on to power was harder than achieving it. She expressed her fears to Dunstan when they were alone. He, likewise, who had also witnessed the events of their century, felt the urgent of need of a shakeup, for reformation, of society, of the church, of every individual. The past was holy, like its saints and relics, but change was afoot and was necessary. The millenium rapidly closed, with pressure on those who had the leisure to think and terror for those who did not.

Eadgifu sighed and turned to face the door. The palace had become a mausoleum. There were chairs in which former kings had sat, which could not be discarded. Broken swords which they had held at barely remembered battles lined the walls; fusty animal heads, stuffed and now anonymous, like the kings, dotted the high places. The glancing summer light entering through windows at shoulder height threw everything into relief or shadow. There was always dust, dust everywhere, in the air, on all the surfaces, dust to which we will all return. Was Edmund's spirit dancing in the motes which descended upon her as she paused before the door to the royal chambers? Could he see and hear, through her, what his councillors would say and do?

She passed through the heavy tapestry curtains which decorated the studded door at the end of the hall. She picked up an ornamental sword which hung on a hook beside the door and used it to give the wood a sturdy blow to announce her presence. A guard looked through a small metal grill and pulled open the door into the royal apartments. He bowed as the queen-mother passed through into a narrow passage. The door swung closed behind her as she entered the very male domain. The cat, shut out from the coming conference, retreated and concentrated its attention on the spider population in the hall.

Eadgifu was half-way along the stone-lined corridor which led to the robing room when she heard the door open again behind her. Male voices were talking determinedly. She turned. Dunstan and Half-king were approaching. They saw her, stopped talking and bowed.

The two men were as chalk and cheese. Both were middle-aged and a similar height, but the soft-living world of the abbot and artist betrayed itself in the tapered hands and tonsured brow of Dunstan. He had put on weight in the months since becoming Abbot of Glastonbury; the loose priest's garb could not disguise the wealth and high-living of his new calling. He had responded well to the crisis caused by Edmund's death; drama suited him and he had literally grown in stature. A paunch swelled his cassock. Half-king was, by contrast, a dark-browed warrior, a soldier first and foremost, with the determined look of a man continually on campaign or preparing for the next. As Dunstan's hand lay almost permanently on the cross around his neck and dangling from a richly ornamented necklace in the centre of his chest, so Half-king had a tendency to handle the snake-embossed hilt of his own personal help-mate and comforter, his dagger.

'Good morning, Madam,' they said together.

'Good morning.' Eadgifu did not curtsey in response to the bows. No need. She was rapidly assuming new responsibilities in this new reign. She may not be acknowledged as regent for her grandsons, but her influence with a flexible and none-too-well son was growing and the court was aware of it. Battle lines were being drawn. A woman's place was not necessarily only in the sewing room, but there were limits.

Eadgifu pressed on, picking up her trailing skirts as, ignoring her hip, she skipped up a step to enter a second, unguarded door. It pushed open easily, revealing Eadred inside, pulling a heavy embroidered tunic over his head and coughing as he did so. Dunstan and Aethelstan Half-king paused before entering the room, allowing the personal greeting of mother and son to be completed.

'Mother.'

'Son. How are you? I have not seen you for so long. What... are you not ready to receive us?' Eadgifu frowned. Eadred looked more material than man. He had inherited his mother's small stature. The ceremonial witan robes he had been wearing, which were handed down from his older brother, swamped him. The king's height, or lack of it, was another point of humour amongst the less compassionate of courtiers. To be short had more disadvantages in kings than in the ordinary populace. Like his mother, though, Eadred was aware of another inherited gene, that of determination. Mother and son were alike; they both knew it and were learning how to be careful of each other. Neither was yet adept.

Bica, Eadred's dwarf servant, was standing on a table, tugging the tunic up. Eadred's head and arms were invisible. Seeing Eadgifu's brow deepening to thunder and fearing an unwarranted expletive of anger at his act of possession of the body of the king, Bica yelped and jumped down, retreating to a wooden chair beneath a high window, in shadow and partly obscured by a large relic cabinet. The heavy gown fell back down over the king. Eadred touched him briefly on the head as he went, a reassuring gesture as to a small child.

'Mother, I wish you would be kinder to my servants,' Eadred did not wish to highlight his awareness of his mother's single-minded hatred of Bica. 'There is no need to frighten everything in your path.' Softening, he replied to her enquiry. He had intentionally steered clear of his mother in recent weeks. 'I am well. The sickness has not returned. The cough is nothing.'

Dunstan and Half-king entered the room. They bowed. Eadred checked his irritation at his mother to greet them. The atmosphere of male dominance in the room was restored. It had been in danger of adopting a shrewish flavour. He straightened his robe and walked towards them, deftly sweeping the over-long tunic and cloak to one side with a kick of a foot. On the move, he seemed more assured than when seated or standing; he had some of his mother's impressive vigour about him. Energy showed, too, in his hair, which he wore, as Edmund had done, in a tied-back Viking style, but with a long, thick strand of blonde waviness falling across his forehead. It covered his eyes, giving the viewer the impression of a peering hound. Beyond the masking curtain of his hair lay a discerning mind, learning how to be a king, a caretaker king, his mother's son.

Eadgifu surveyed him. He had charm, though not in abundance, like Edmund, but he would do. The queen-mother was not uncontent, regarding her son as he approached the others. If only that dwarf Bica was not always present, like a bee about him. Like a wasp about her.

'My lord Athelstan Half-king and my lord Abbot, welcome. The witan went well, I think.' Dunstan coughed. 'Or perhaps not so well?

Come and be seated. It is a little hot inside this robe, but perhaps I will keep it on for a little while longer. Bica, you may go. Send in Hersfig to serve us wine.' Eadred turned to Dunstan and took his arm. 'He is my fool, you know.'

Bica scurried out of the room. Hersfig entered from a door which led to the kitchens, bearing a tray of goblets and a jar. Half-king, Dunstan and Eadgifu sat on sheepskin-covered stools at the single large table in the room. Eadred joined them at its head, standing. The crown, which he had worn at the witan, was in the centre of the table next to a platter of bread and cheese. He picked up a silver filet from a nearby dressing bench and placed it around his head.

'That's better.' Eadred was learning how to project kingship. Symbols mattered. They were visible signs of authority; dress was important. Headgear conveyed status. Clothing displayed wealth and superiority. He might be hot and uncomfortable, but his guests would be impressed. Crowns and gowns, jewels and relics, these were the ingredients of diplomacy and power. There could be enjoyment in the burden of the wielding of power.

'Dunstan, what did you make of the drama back there?'

'Your highness, there was no unwelcome drama, you can be sure. There is no opposition in the ranks of the witan nobility to your right to rule and those who murmur are the few who have foolishly nourished some dreams of northern independence. They are now silent, or gone from Winchester. Your maiden speeech will have been heard by well wishers. But what do you mean by "your fool"?' Dunstan looked into the shadows under the window. Bica's comfortable chair, its cushions crushed, indicated the presence of someone, other than the king, in permanent residence.

'Bica?' Eadred looked at the empty chair. 'Well, if I have no opposition in court - and that I am not altogether sure of, despite what you say, lord Abbot - then I am certainly needing some at home. Bica will provide me with that other point of view which is needed - an alternative way of seeing things. Every man loves flattery and positivity, but I have learned from the fate of my brother that it is wise to contemplate the possibility of failure, as well as success.'

'Why do you call him "fool", my lord? I see no fool, only a small man.' Half-king had looked across the top of Bica's head as he disappeared. A fyrd commander could only note the space in the air where a waist, shoulders and head should be. Bica would be of little use in his warrior ranks, except for picking things up from the ground.

Eadred called his servant back into the room. The door to the kitchens opened again as Hersfig retreated and Bica returned. He stood with his back to the wall in a corner of the room.

'Bica, speak up for yourself. You are present in this room with the rest of us. Forgo the shadow, let them see what role you can play, as my fool, in this world of make-believe that is the court of Wessex.' Eadred flourished a copious amount of regal cloak and kicked his over-long shift in the direction of Bica, who danced around it and then stood on the dark material which flowed in ripples several feet beyond the king. He took up the position of a supplicant, on his knees. He pretended not to notice the guests. He was with his protector. He was happy to be called a fool; he knew that he was much more than that. He smiled and played his part. It had been rehearsed.

'My lord, have a care, I pray. I am but a small man and a simpleton. From the worm's point of view I can see the world upside down. I can see up into the nether regions and nostrils of the great men who tower above me and see the hairs and constitutions which govern their lives; with the small creatures of the world I can pick up the rumblings of the earth and detect the storms of mankind as they trample in haste to make war upon themselves. I can see the actors as they play upon the stage and point out that their hats are askew and look ridiculous. Some need to be shown that they are naked, when they think they are armoured. Look at these hats. Hats of the costume cupboard!'

Bica leaned over to a table of hats and filets next to Eadred and snatched up a piece of headgear which resembled a cat, with a long striped tail. He put it on his head, back to front. 'Now hats are very fine things for swelling heads. Foxes and bears grin at us lowly mortals from the heights of a noble's head. Dead animals on felted hoods, their eyes looking out at you in conversation, put you off your stride. I hope they do not piss on the prince's hair, though that would perhaps enable a new fashion to be brought about.' He paused. 'A cast-off like myself has his uses, though I would not presume…' Bica whipped off the cat and chose a hood with a ferret's head perched on its peak, its teeth agape, and put it on, grinning at Eadred as he did so.

'Indeed, Bica, that is enough. I think my guests have seen you at your best.' Eadred laughed and tugged at his cloak, sending Bica toppling over, scrambing up on his short legs and giggling. 'Go to the bedchamber. And close the door behind you.' Bica backed, bowing, towards the bedroom door behind him, did a pirouette and deftly reached for the handle of the door, stretching as he did so. He couldn't quite turn the handle. He looked plaintively back at Eadred, then grinned again as the king crossed the room to usher him out, bowing himself. The little man skipped through the door. Eadred closed it behind him. From inside the bedroom, Bica could be heard barking.

'He thinks he is my lapdog and pretends to do my bidding.' Eadred turned to his mother.

'What a performance. He calls this a costume cupboard! I am surprised that you let him behave… but no matter. Well…as long as he does not sleep on your bed at night…' Eadgifu had noted that Eadred had begun to show signs of eccentricity in recent months, but had not appreciated the changes in his personality since the death of Edmund and the imposition of responsibility onto his shoulders. 'Bica will have to mind his manners around me and will especially have to be careful of my cloak when he treads behind me, or I will have him fed to the ravens who are waiting for the next prisoners to be dismembered.'

'Mother, don't worry, Bica will be careful of you. We all know we have to be careful of you. And this room is a bit like a fancy dress cupboard, don't you think? Have some wine. Cheese, anyone? Witans make me hungry.' Eadred chewed on a crust. Half-king looked questioningly at him. There was an empty plate beside the cheese and bread which would later be filled with Eadred's leavings. He called it his 'ort plate'. The unchewable portions of Eadred's meals were the horror of his guests, as was the sight of his struggle to swallow.

Eadred, in the few sentences he had shared with his mother in recent days, was begining to be able to compromise with her. Bica gave him strength. Together they might make a team to offset the worst of his mother's and the witan's criticism. Two small men, if they stretched themselves, might make one giant. He turned to Dunstan and Half-king, who were examining, from their seats, the variety of ceremonial hats and crowns on cushions. There were hats for leading the hunt, hats for prayer, crowns for feasting, filets for dancing, feathered, furred and jewelled caps for winter wear, embroidered riding summer gear with matching gloves. Every hat which could be imagined, furry and feathery, was on display on trays, on stands, on modelled clay heads. Each season in its relevant colour code and every activity suitable for a king was represented, gathering the same dust as in the main hall, being added to daily as the court seamstresses and tailors laboured to expand the items of regal choice or took in or up Edmund's robes to fit his smaller brother. Chests and wardrobes around the room, their lids and doors up or open, showed recent interest by the new king in the sartorial arrangements for government. Clothes make the man, it seemed, to Eadred. They give the impression, at least, of making a king. Eadred glanced at the rows of tooled leather shoes and boots arranged along several shelves. The new pairs would be examined later. He sat on a cushioned chair, placing a half-eaten crust on his ort-plate.

'Do you have any news of Wulfstan, our friend in the north?'

Irony was beginning to be understood in court circles. Puns were Bica's forte; irony was Eadred's. Dunstan and Half-king looked at each other. Archbishop Wulfstan had shown himself capable of duplicity in the past. He was no longer regarded, except by a few, as a friend to Wessex. There had been imprisonment and escape, followed by forgiveness, unaccountable and unecessary forgiveness, Eadgifu thought. Little contrition had been shown by the old man. Dunstan was more ambivalent. Archbishops who had been monks claimed admiration from those who were merely abbots. Elgiva, Edmund's queen, had had something to do with the survival of the northern leader who looked towards Bamburgh fortress in Northumbria for secular authority rather than Winchester. Dunstan assumed the responsibility to answer for his compatriot of the church.

'He is travelling from Ripon, my lord and will no doubt be late for the feast. He is making a special effort.'

'To be the bad fairy - again. He has already missed your first witan day.' Half-king's gruff voice was an octave lower than Dunstan's.

Eadred pulled off the garment with which he had been wrestling and threw it on the floor. 'Both of you- tell me again why I should not send yourself, or a few taller men than me to insist upon his staying in the south on a permanent basis? I know he is a deeply religious man, attached to his northern archbishopric and that he has a troublesome leg which prevents him from travelling often, but I would dearly like to interview him on a regular basis, particularly in light of recent events. I hear he has been bedding with his Danish friends in York.'

Half-king, who viewed the northerner, indeed, all northerners, as an enemy of the crown, felt entitled to comment. He stepped forward in front of Dunstan. 'Not only Danes, my lord, but Norse. His sentiments are with the north, as we know. He has done great harm to Wessex and to England with his support for the Danish of Northumbria. He gives them hope for independence which would ruin our dreams of holding this country together. When -if- he arrives in the south, he should be locked up, in my opinion.'

'Not so fast, my lord.' Eadred was uncomfortable with attacking a prelate, even if he was one who had proved perfidious in the past. 'Wulfstan was put in place by my brother Athelstan. He has had to dice with the warlords from Scandinavia. Anlaf was a persuasive liar. Now that he is off the scene- he has returned to Dublin, has he not- we may find that Archbishop Wulfstan, as he has promised, will be able to convert any Norse newcomers in York. Christianity will have the effect of tempering their bloodthirsty ways. Dunstan, what do you think?'

'I agree with that. If anyone can convert the Norse, it is Wulfstan.'

Half-king grunted. 'I don't see why we tolerate him in his position of power, despite being appointed by King Athelstan all those years ago. His value then was in holding the north together and under our dominion, but his actions in recent years have been less than helpful. He did not travel to the Pucklechurch meeting. Do we not suspect that he had something to do with Edmund's death?'

Eadgifu crossed herself. Each person present, except Dunstan, had witnessed the stabbing of Edmund at Pucklechurch, had heard the cries of pain and experienced the raw muddle of unfettered emotion. Dunstan could include himself in this category; he had received a vision of the king's doom as he rode towards Pucklechurch. Eadred muttered a Hail Mary. Dunstan said 'amen'. Half-king grimaced. It was clear that traitors should meet a traitor's death, to him. Why was no action taken against this priest? Anlaf might be gone, but snakes fill empty nests. There would soon be another pirate in York's palace hall.

Half-king opened his mouth to begin to speak again but Dunstan moved forward, giving him the slightest of nudges as he did so, and made the point he had planned to air.

'My lord, it is likely that Egil Skallagrimsson and Anlaf were the main perpetrators of the scheme to depose and kill Edmund, your brother. Archbishop Wulfstan may have had a hand in it, but there is no proof of that.' Dunstan felt a threat to the Church's authority. Archbishops should be protected, whatever they had done, or not done.

'No proof? Since when has a king needed proof of traitorous intent?' Eadgifu gasped. She felt the threat, any threat, against her person, her children or gandchildren as physical assaults upon her corporeal body. Tremors made her sweat at night; the idea of an injury to her young Wessex clan produced nausea during the day. The longer she lived, the larger the numbers of her family, the more intense she felt the psychic blows of malcontents and malicious innuendo. Her face reddened, her eyes flamed.

Eadred decided that it would be better to reserve any discussion of Wulfstan to a time when his mother would not be present. 'Half-king, how is my nephew, Edgar, faring?'

Half-king closed his mouth. He had been staring at the queen-mother. Eadgifu could be less than diplomatic in her opinions, though he held her in high esteem. He had seen her courtly skills at work over many years and had admired her back-room support for Athelstan, the king with the same name as his own. She had acted as regent in his absence on wars in the north without stirring envy or jealousy; her birth as a Kentish noble's daughter had assuaged that region's sense of isolation. He wished that the Mercians could be similarly pacified. Their resentments were already more than half a century old. How long did it take a nation to accept that it had lost autonomy? Written histories, which were now in vogue, did not help. They perpetuated grievance. He resented the requirement to read and write. Soldiers were better able to fight on barked command when they had not to read their orders or to check their inventories. It was different for kings. Eadred had to make readable laws which must be adhered to. The courts had a simpler task, now that the written word was becoming common, though the justice system was slowing due to the requirement of record-keeping.

'The aetheling Edgar is a very bright lad. He is soaking up both scripture and learning in general. Already he can read latin and play a simple flute. He is attracted to wooden weaponry and though these are early days, I think he will make a fine ambassador.'

'Good.' Eadred waved a finger in the direction of the queen. 'Mother, I think I would like Eadwig present at the next witan. I know that you think he is too young and Edgar certainly is, but

Eadwig is old enough to comprehend the importance of events and people. He is as old as Alfred was when he went to Rome. You know how impressed he was by the Pope and by the clothing he was given, let alone the items of kingship. Winchester is not far from Glastonbury, not as far as Rome, at any rate. When he is out of mourning, I should consider it a privilege to have my heir sitting by me for at least some of the major decisions I shall have to take on his behalf.' He corrected himself. 'We, I mean, the Cupboard Quartet.'

'Is that what we are called?' Half-king let out a roar of laughter. 'Well, I suppose, since we creep into this small room, beyond the hearing of all but Bica - do you hear me Bica...?'

There was a low 'woof' from behind a door.

Half-king continued. ' – then we of the intimate cupboard should be able to accommodate the occasional visit of the aetheling Eadwig, don't you think, my lord abbot?'

'There might be some difficulty in interrupting his studies at Glastonbury, where Aethelwold is hard at work tutoring him personally, but I see no reason why he should not attend witans which occur nearer, in Somerset; Frome and Cheddar, for instance. My lady?' Dunstan turned to face the queen.

Eadgifu had calmed down. 'I see no harm in it. But Edgar should stay where he is for now, as he is doing so well in Ramsey with you, Athelstan. I agree, Eadwig should be exposed to more eventful, though tiring, witan work now that he is seven years old, within limits. He should learn patience. See to it, would you, Dunstan.'

Eadred gave a tug on the shoulder of his voluminous under garment, which was slipping. 'I am glad that he saw my coronation in Kingston. He will remember that.'

Eadgifu nodded. 'And look forward to his own in the future. I shall have to begin to think about a wife for him. One from Kent, perhaps.'

'Or from East Anglia – or Mercia - my lady, perhaps?' Half-king tried to shift political interest north and west. The south-eastern kingdom of Kent was a waning power, its noble families rich enough.

Dunstan coughed. 'We should be preparing notes for the next witan, not yet marrying off our princes. Bring in Nonna. He will record our business.'

Eadred caught the look between his mother and Dunstan. Some distance was growing, there, at last. He stood up. The robe slipped further. 'The witan members are gathering in the New Minster nave. Prayers will be being said. We should kneel for our own. But first let me show you something.' Eadred crossed the room and beckoned his companions to a tall relic cabinet which stood in a dark corner. 'I have a new relic which will be of interest to you. My sister Eadburh came by it in The Nunnaminster, where she has been put in charge of the haligdom.' He took a key from his belt and unlocked the cabinet's heavy door, taking out a leather boot-shaped reliquary. He placed it on a small oak table which served as a mobile altar and lit a beeswax candle in an ornate holder. He stood back for the others to examine the newest trophy to fall into the hands of the Wessex clan. 'Behold, the foot of St Wilfrid of Ripon.'

Eadred dramatically waved an over-long sleeve at the relic and ushered the others towards the precious object. They approached the shrine. The relic shone golden in the candlelight, its surface tooled with minute holy figures and animals pertinent to gospel stories. Delicate silver-gilt hinges on its side, tooled to resemble straps, indicated where the holy bones and flesh could be accessed.

Eadgifu, Dunstan and Half-king immediately knelt. They were in the presence of something magical and potent, as important as the relics of St Oswald and his contemporary St Aldhelm. Relics of Wilfrid, the seventh-century saint of the north, were held in awe. They were key to power over Northumbria. The south understood the totemic powers of northern holy heroes. Cuthbert occupied the highest rung of the northern heirarchy of saints. If parts of Cuthbert could be brought south, or perhaps the entire corpse, the might of the north would be forever eclipsed. The monks of Lindisfarne, however, at their temporary base of Chester-le-Street, would never allow that to happen, not for any price. Here, in the form of a foot, was an emblem of learning, forebearance and achievement, a reminder of the golden age of the early Anglo-Saxon kingdoms, before the dust of indifference had covered it over. The reliquary of the holy extremity cast its spell over the praying members of the cupboard quartet. Its corporeal partner and the other relics of Wilfrid were held by Ripon monastery. In time they might become available by negotiation or other means; the economic value of a prophet lay in the slow dismemberment of his, or her, body. Eadred could profitably yearn to unite the parts of the northern saint. It would be expensive, but possible. The weakening of Northumbrian hopes required theft, as well as blackmail. It had been done before.

Dunstan had had dealings with northern monks. 'If you can believe the provenance. Perhaps Oundle Monastery would like to house it. It was Wilfrid's foundation. They have a satisfactory guard.' Hearing the bell for None, he stood up. 'I must leave you for a short while, my lord, but I shall return after prayers. I will bring Nonna with me.' He bowed and went out.

Eadred, Half-king and Eadgifu continued discussing matters raised at the witan. Eadgifu was particularly interested in affairs relating to relics. St Aldhelm, St Oswald and now St Wilfrid would back the cause of Eadred against the north, against the growing threat from Norway. The archbishop of York, Wulfstan and now a new Norwegian aspirer to York's throne, Eric, were flexing their muscles. They wanted severance from England, an independent Northumbria. From the point of view of Wessex, York should not be allowed to become a major trading town of the viking world, from where an attempt could be made to take over the whole of England, with its ports and southern trade routes. Eadred, praying, could call on the potent national saints to assist him to keep the lands which Athelstan his brother had won and Edmund had almost lost. Only St Cuthbert was missing from the relic collection now in Wessex hands. Cuthbert, the personal saintly aid of his grandfather, Alfred, had been summoned in spirit to aid Alfred to win his war with the Danes.

He had saved Wessex from annihilation. It was Cuthbert who had sustained Alfred in the sea battle at Swanage. Without the corpse of Cuthbert, or parts of him, could Wessex rule in peace and strength, relying on the weakened spiritual forces of the denuded north?

The Wessex collection of relics was extensive. Eadgifu had, or thought she had, the head of St Radegund. St Elgiva lay entire at Shaftesbury. St Aldhelm lay, for now, at Malmesbury, though Dunstan had plans to remove him to safety and greater splendour in Canterbury. St Oswald was similarly in southern territory, but at the Mercian centre of Gloucester, which might in future be problematic; it all depended on keeping the former midland kingdom sweet. Much of the expenditure of the nation's coffers at witans was dependent upon this matter of trade in relics, in some form or other, through land grants or gifts of treasure, or marital arrangements.

One other item of relic importance sustained the new king in his frequent sleepless nights. In times of doubt, which were often, he could call upon the aid of the relic of Athelstan's which he, like his brother had done, wore around his neck: the small portion of the true cross, encased in rock crystal. And by his side, encased in a strapped belt-pouch, the reminder of the Word: Athelstan's psalter. In his head and by his bedside, ready to be consulted in the dead of night, lay the Consolation of Boethius as translated by his grandfather, Alfred. A piece of Cuthbert: that he did long for. How it could be taken or bought, he would have to consider. The Archbishop of York might have a role to play, but would he willingly weaken his own northern territory? Much depended on the character of this new upstart, Eric, and whether Wulfstan would openly support him against Wessex.

There were relics and words enough, it should be thought, to guarantee success. If only Eadred's stomach did not hurt. He was becoming convinced that a relic of Cuthbert would be efficacious to his own healing. If the nation could be healed by Cuthbert's presence in the south, so might he. Later, his visitors gone, he paid one last visit to his guard-robe before an early bed. He was not nervous, only ill. Kingship made his bowels growl.

# The King's Bedchamber, Winchester.

I T WAS GROWING dark in the sleeping-room. The high windows would soon be shuttered. Nonna and Bica sat on a dressing bench in the cosy room, which was largely occupied by a wide bed with ornate bedhead and canopy. Eadred was in it, the coverlet high under his chin. He was looking, and feeling, green. Like the bench, the bed had dominated its space for more than a hundred years, slept in by more than a dozen kings. Eadred himself had been conceived and born in it. The stone walls, ceiling beams and most of the hanging tapestries had absorbed and memorised the cries both of royal copulation and childbirth, ready to disgorge their store of royal human experience to any willing to listen or able to hear. Mostly, with the external sound of owl hoots, it stole into dreams, mercilessly reminding the bed's occupants of bloody battle, revenge and jealousy. They had no memory of death; kings and queens had met their maker elsewhere. War deaths, deaths by poisoning, accidental death, murder or assassination, all had been contrived to happen, with the help of the watchful saints, beyond the confines of the royal bedroom of the palace of Winchester. The bed and the room, therefore, in daylight hours, were redolent of creativity and hope and breathed out reminders of past acts of courage and success, which did not pass unnoticed by its latest occupant and his immediate circle. Eadred felt safe in his bed. He would be safer still, one day, if he could obtain a relic of Cuthbert to keep under his pillow.

'Well, Nonna, how do you think that went?' Eadred had discarded most of his outer clothing. He was not untidy or dismissive of the ritualistic clothing which had been as relevant to the day's proceedings as they had been at the coronation in Kingston a few weeks before, but sickness brought about shortcuts. He was feeling a little better. The thought of Cuthbert comforted him. He sipped a concoction from a blue glass beaker. The green face began to gain colour. The silk and embroidery layered tunics and cloak had been hung up with the assistance of Bica, in a closet designed to house the designated duty wear of royalty. The heavy jewellery and tokens of kingship, studded with symbolic gems and designs, had been put in a chest by Hersfig and carefully locked away. The keys to many royal treasures and their sartorial accompaniments jangled at Bica's waist. 'Nonna? Speak up. You know how I value your thoughts. We are the closet parliament, now, the mightiest beings in Wessex, not Mother, not Dunstan, not Athelstan Half-king.'

Bica roared with laughter. 'The witan would love to hear you say that!' He looked at Nonna, who arranged a scroll and lifted his quill, ready to take notes.

Eadred grinned. 'I thought I would join you, Bica, in having a go at the establishment. I find, learning from you, that it is quite refreshing. Nonna? Don't mind Bica. Bica, be quiet. How did I do?'

Nonna was becoming used to the arrangement whereby Eadred and Bica bantered and parried in the hour before sleep, when he would often be called to take notes or report on conversations overheard in the court or witan. His notes and his memory had been relied on by Athelstan and Edmund, in their reigns. They and it had not grown less useful or less sharp with time, as yet.

'Lord, you were a young child when I first beheld you, a blonde, mop-headed, shorter version of your brother. Like a sapling growing in the shade of a greater tree, I saw how you retreated from the possibility of spreading your own branches wide. Your leaves remained pale and sparse. Many thought that you would not thrive, that you would need to be plucked out to allow the greater tree to flourish in its soil, but I have noted over the years of my, dare I say it, close acquaintance with you, especially in the palaces of Frome and Cheddar, away from the hothouse of Winchester, that the possibilities of your personality, honesty, humour and doggedness, might one day be allowed to come to the fore. So they have. Today you were magnificent. Your voice was clear, resolute. You chose your words well (I assume that Bica had something to do with that), not too many, not too few. You restored a sense of momentum and courage, suggested the direction in which we are going as a nation, comforted those who need war for their sense of being and those who do not.' Nonna paused.

'Wordy,' Bica elbowed Nonna, 'but right.'

'Go on, Nonna, if you can. Was there anything wrong with today? Be brief, if you can, my nerves can take a little criticism.' Eadred sipped again.

Bica interjected. 'Only a little, mind. I do most of that work.'

Nonna continued. 'Wrong? Nothing, Lord, your words were spare and to the point. They roused us all from the gloom which had come upon us after King Edmund's untimely death at Pucklechurch. But if I may be bold, I could make one or two suggestions which you might consider for the next witan, to be held at Dorchester. As time goes by and you progress to other centres, the interests of a region under your sway will need to be addressed. Southern central Wessex, near the sea, will have an interest in the navy. Wareham, Swanage and Weymouth will be represented in the court sessions. It will be a good time to address the needs of your fleet and of course, the fyrd. You will recall that your grandfather won a decisive battle against the Danes at Swanage; your family has since learned much from the prowess of those sea-farers in terms of man-power, boat building and sea-going. If I may suggest it, a visit to Noden's castle on the coast before the witan would give you first-hand knowledge and understanding of your navy's requirements in this new era of Norse influence. The Norse are, if anything, better skilled and more wide-ranging, in particular at warship building and use, than the Danes are. Their dedication to conquest is greater, their desire for domination formidable. Nothing was wrong in what you said today, Sire, but details next need to be addressed. Leave your ministers to deal with the trials and courts; my information on their group meetings is that they are capable and that the devolvement of civic taxation is working well.' Nonna stopped. Eadred raised his hand, absorbing the elements of Nonna's advice.

'Good, Nonna, details, less generalisation, at the next witan. The Norse warships need to be copied. We need bigger, faster ships. Get a navy commander to see to it. Issue an order to fell mature oaks in Selwood. Bica, you can close your mouth.' Eadred raised his hand. 'I have heard, there is no need to say anything. How about the Church? Did I cover enough to please the bishops? And no need to be so formal, Nonna.'

Nonna began again. 'As you know, Lord, I stand between the Church and state on matters which affect both. I observe the direction in which both travel and try to steer my king to a path between. Perhaps, not steer, that is for others to do, but to suggest, based on the knowledge which I and my fellow clerks can discover.'

'And Bica, hiding under tables with the children, can overhear.' Eadred found the business of diplomacy as wearying as his brother Edmund had done, but recognised its necessity. Spying was an art at least as important in controlling a kingdom as bribery and sanctions. They were the more acceptable face of a court hoping to function successfully in an otherwise negative milieu of imprisonment, torture, exile and excommunication. 'What is the current state of leadership in Church hierarchy, do you suppose? Do I need to cow-tow to any fresh reformers? Are there any favourites of my mother who need land or support for their monasteries?' Again he raised his hand, with pointed forefinger, to indicate that Nonna should continue and that Bica should hold his tongue.

'It is clear, Lord, that there is a greater emphasis among those who have power in the Church today on the subject of reform. Not reform of the arrangements of the kingdom, but of themselves. A great deal of navel-gazing has been underway since your brother appointed Dunstan as Abbot of Glastonbury. Of course, for both of them, the drama of the cliff-top hunt at Cheddar triggered important decisions. They saw what was necessary for the realm, for its right ordering. Some thought that Edmund became too much influenced by the Church as a result of cancelling Dunstan's exile. In the years since the event at Cheddar Gorge, much has been done and written by your Archbishop Oda, Oswald, Dean of Winchester, Aethelwold of Abingdon and of course Dunstan. They all wish fervently to restore the golden age of the Church, a time of education and order. As you are aware, your mother wishes to assist them in this.' Nonna paused. He could not quite relax in the company of Bica, he was not sure why.

'Mother has suggested that Dunstan should be made Bishop of Worcester and that Aethelwold should be kept from going overseas to Fleury. He says he has had enough of tutoring princes. Edgar is doing well with Athelstan Half-king at his manor in Huntingdon. What do you think?'

'There is no doubt that the three main protagonists of reform, Dunstan, Aethelwold and Oswald, should be encouraged, in my view, to continue their work, as long as the secular state is not impeded by their progress. I would counsel, though, against the enforcement of priests, where they are married, to divorce their wives. It would cause much dismay and possibly lead to insurrection. Chastity may come, indeed, it may be a relief for many in the evenings of their lives, but to be forced to remain or to become virginal, will not be popular. It is said, though by heretics, that even Jesus Christ had a wife and children. There is also the problem that a monk or priest must be seen to be above improving their personal wealth.' Nonna paused again. 'Dunstan, though, has his detractors. The Queen...'

'Thank you, Nonna, I see what you are getting at. But why so formal? I have known you for many years. Relax.' Eadred indicated to Nonna that he should sit. 'The Church has its own battles with its own kind, as I do with some of the nobles. In a tug-of-war, I suppose, a king must of necessity refrain from taking sides. Perhaps Edgar will benefit from Aethelwold's firm views as it appears Eadwig has not. Where does the Archbishop of York stand in this tussle over reform?'

Nonna paused. Wulfstan's position on most matters relevant to the affairs of Wessex were difficult to fathom. The former advisor to Queen Aelfflaed, Edward's second wife, whose sons might have reigned instead of Athelstan, was a Northumbrian conundrum. He disliked travel. York was so far from Winchester. It was easy for an older man with a bad leg to complain that the witan, any witan, held further south than Dewsbury was too far away for comfortable travel. As the witan was never held in the northern towns of Mercia, but always well within the confines of the bounds of Wessex, he rarely made an appearance. 'Wulfstan? Lord, Wulfstan is married and has seven children. He has a large palace at Ripon. He is unlikely to abandon his current affiliations. He is concerned with converting the Norse into any kind of Christianity which they will accept. We should leave him be. Now to lighter subjects.'

Bica squeaked and laughed. 'A former monk, with seven children? Is his woman a wife or a concubine, I wonder? I can't imagine a monk taking a wife in a marriage ceremony. If so, it indicates his personal flexibility, I suppose. The northerners are a strange lot. No more heavy subjects? Good, I want to be able to sleep this night.' Bica was already lying flat out on a pallet beside the royal bed. His peevish, disembodied voice broke into the discussion and thoughts of the king and his clerk.

Eadred, recovered from his sickness, threw back the bed cover and jumped out. He stretched his whole body. 'That's better, the pain has passed, as it always does. We go to Frome tomorrow, for the hunting. I have put out my new riding gear and my feathered hats. Which suits me best, Nonna? The peacock or the sparrowhawk?' Eadred went across the room to a chest and picked up a hat, flourishing another. He juggled them as if they were balls in the air.

Bica snorted from the pallet. 'Choose the feathered hat which will tickle him most, Nonna. He needs punishing for keeping us up so long. Goodnight!'

# The Shadow of Edward

I T WAS BEFORE dawn. Nonna had been summoned by Eadgifu to her room not long after he had left Eadred and Bica. He was not perturbed; the night office of Lauds was becoming a favourite ritual of his, being more of a night owl than a daytime lark. Besides, he needed to get up for the pot at that time anyway. More plans were developed and decisions taken were made at this hour, he had found over the years, than at any other time of the day or night. He could snooze during the daytime. He was at the height of his powers and experience as a court clerk. Unobtrusive and unremarkable in appearance, he blended easily into the shadows and shapes of the world of information exchange. He quickly donned his day cloak over his shift and hurried along the corridors of the monastery, out across the yard between the palace and monastic buildings and past the guards at the palace gate, who knew him well. The moon, a harvest glow, shone full and yellow.

Eadgifu was herself no stranger to the early hours of the day, particularly in summer. The cocks in the stable yard behind the palace would soon be up and about, their noisy presence ruling the outhouses, rousing the grooms. She was learning to follow the Benedictine order of prayer; the day would soon come when she would retire to holy orders, or become, as her friend Wynflaed had, a secular vowess. It was only a matter of choosing where she would go to live out her days: to Wilton, like her predecessor as queen Aelfflaed, or Shaftesbury, like her dead daughter-in-law Elgiva, now a saint, or here in Winchester, at The Nunnaminster, where she could keep a close eye on the doings of the court and hear about the progress of her grandsons. The queens and princesses of recent years had ensured that their retirement, as widows or divorcees, would be comfortable. In any event, she was a wealthy woman, endowed by her marriage to Edward and by gifts from her stepson Athelstan and sons Edmund and Eadred. She would secure more, in time, from her grandsons.

Whichever place she eventually chose, she would be guaranteed a welcome. Her popularity and reputation as wife, mother and grandmother of the Wessex clan ensured that she would enjoy the best of facilities and attention; she had taken a keen interest in the construction of new guest suites in several female monastic institutions as well as physical improvements at many of the royal palaces. Cheddar had become a popular venue for the witan; its improved facilities for exacting noble families as well as witan members had become expected throughout the realm, though some old-fashioned centres resisted the queen's plans for modernisation. They were the last bastion of the old ways, the soldiers' quarters, where the environment was almost exclusively male and a woman's presence was considered an inconvenience, except as a servant or prostitute.

Edward, her husband, had felt most at home in these more manly palaces, but then, he had had little leisure time during his reign to enjoy the softer pursuits of culture and convenience, even if he had wished to. Since his reign, the atmosphere of so many palaces had changed, softened by her influence, as well as Dunstan's creative artwork and encouragement of continental culture. Crudity was being banished; social attitudes were changing, too, with a move towards curbing the worst excesses of lewdness and blood feud. She, Dunstan, and Aethelwold, who had the education of her grandson Edgar well in hand at Ramsey in Athelstan Half-king's household, were sowing the seeds of a cultural revolution. In artistic terms it meant fewer beasts, more flowers and leaves as decoration. The inner world of the mind and soul might be populated by these animals, but the world of mankind should no longer be ruled by non-Christian symbolism. The forces of darkness revealed themselves in the minds of men, if not countered by correct thought. Dunstan was clear on this matter, and so was she. It only needed complete control of the treasury to produce a major shift away from expenditure on resisting Vikings and focussed investment to produce a new golden era of Anglo-Saxon financial, religious and cultural might, an example to the world of a well-ordered and competent state. The price of a cultured peace, though, was high, higher even than for war. Prayer indulgences could deliver those extra taxes. Stone, replacing wood in building, required expensive, skilled craftsmen and all the wealth that a promoted interest in relics and worry about the length of time spent in purgatory could provide. Stone provided permanency, settled order. It symbolised immortality. It showed the futility of resistance. Stone was the future; palaces, cathedrals, halls; bigger, better, more permanent structures would secure the legacy of Wessex and England.

Eadgifu, waiting for the arrival of Nonna, felt satisfied with the current state of conditions at the start of the new reign. Eadred was more likely to do her and Dunstan's bidding, to accept their ideas and to implement them, than had been Edmund. He had been too headstrong, too quick to anger, too quick to dismiss Dunstan, particularly. The near-death experience at Cheddar had revived their plans, but Edmund had remained difficult to persuade, obstinate, like his father.

Never mind, all that was now in the past. Having reminded herself of her husband, dead so long ago, she found herself thinking about him. Nostalgia was becoming more comfortable a bed as the years sped by. She began to muse on her brief marriage to Edward. If she had had time, she might have been able to help him to relax, to take a book down from his father's dusty shelves, and to practice reading, which he had done as a child. His first wife, Aelfflaed had given up trying to calm him down during her marriage to him; he often said that he wanted a sword in his hand, not a book, that action spoke louder than any written fancy. It was his body which had a memory, he had told Eadgifu as a young bride, having put Aelfflaed into Wilton Abbey. *I am a warrior, not a wordsmith. Do not expect me to change*, he had said. He left the recording of his doings and others to the scops and scribes. That was their job; his was to ensure that Danish ambitions were controlled, to make history, not to record it. Besides, the scops did a good job when recounting their poetry. He liked to hear the words hanging, dramatically, in the air.

Edward was not certain that a written record of his reign was necessary. Memory and law were enshrined in the repetition of bards' words. Boasts of success and failure, of wars won and lost, were hammered into the minds of the elite sitting around hall fires. He was wary of legal red tape; an old-fashioned oath was surely enough to secure a promise. In his reign, he told Eadgifu, he could report how close the nation of Saxons had come to being made slaves, as in earlier centuries the Saxons had made the Britons their servants, in their own lands. Dumnonia had been transformed. It was now Western Wessex, a significant portion of southern England, with ports, cities and monasteries of value. The woods and forests of the south-west were providers for the timber industry so necessary for burgh, palace and ship building. Hillsides and islands were quarried; Ham Hill shrank, Portland became honeycombed. The Church grew wealthy, swelling its ranks of timber and stone naves, building bigger, building better, building more. Dane-ravaged monasteries were being restored in the east and the middle shires; Aethelwold now had their progress in hand. The British Dumnonians had gradually become, albeit lower-class, Saxon citizens. Their language was heard less often at the markets. As the Catholic Church's influence and clothing fashions had altered the outward shape of the nation, binding Danish immigrants in the east and British farmers in the west, people had learned to speak the common language and to live together. New taxations had ensured that surplus crops and livestock were produced by the peasants, which had boosted the growing market towns. Cash to buy items was being produced at new mints. Only the accents and languages, spoken in pockets of the north and west, of the conquered Britons remained as reminders of former foreignness, of a different approach to life, of antipathy to the Saxon way. Edward had lived in interesting times. A pity, it was, that he could not see all three of his sons upon their thrones. But that is the fate of kings. All this, he had achieved, like the soldier he was, without any requirement to write it down.

The wergild and gold with the king's head on coins, developed by Edward and furthered by Athelstan, was the market currency of a growing economy. Eadgifu had watched as Alfred's dream of a united England had become a reality, approving most of Edward and, later, Athelstan's efforts. Weapons, armour and cunning, along with wealth, were Edward's tools, effective against the onslaught which might come again, who knew? Moveable objects, relics and land, were in the gift of the king. Hides of land were gifted here, exchanged there, consolidating ownership and power, developing a code of loyalty and honour which would take a considerable effort to dismantle. Three reigns after Edward, the structure of state which he had done so much to establish was now hers, the widowed Queen Eadgifu's, to enjoy and protect. She was determined to do so. No son or grandson would get in the way of her plans, reformed since Edmund's death, to safeguard the wealth which the nation now enjoyed. Dunstan held the keys to the treasury. Eadred would do her bidding, she was sure. Edward's legacy, now hers, would be cast in stone, like the churches and palaces now being built and enlarged throughout the realm.

Eadgifu, marrying Edward at the age of twenty, knew that hers was a marriage of convenience, a buying of support from the Kentish nobles for the Wessex king, a subordination of her folk to the greater powers rising in the west, the defeaters of Guthrum's Danish army. Her husband was by this time a grizzled veteran of constant war and planning for war, approaching fifty, active, fit but doggedly sceptical and often ill-humoured. He was ruthless, relying on his own decision-making for the most part. He was toughened in youth by the treason of his cousin Aethelwold as he took the throne. He competed with his sister in Mercia in her last years as leader of Mercia against the eastern and northern Danes, to rule the midlands. He forcefully removed her daughter Aelfwyn on her death. He was prepared to act in what he regarded as Wessex's interest and did not care what was said of him. Eadgifu, her own eyes opened early on to the necessity for and tragedies of war by the death of her own father at the battle of The Holme before her birth, could both admire and appreciate the fatherly decisiveness of Edward, and the subtlety of mind which lay behind his choices. He could have been a scholar, if the times had allowed, but he much preferred the war-room. He became her father, as well as her husband.

And in the bedroom, he was her lover. She had found Edward to be ardent, though brusque. She liked it that way. She felt dominated, safe. Now, she began to remember those times when he had been tender, as well as tough, those few occasions when, a battle won and men discharged, he could unwind enough to say to her how much he appreciated her beauty, her youth, her fecundity, her willingness, her mannerisms. She could remember a few times when he had meant to flatter her, the last time being when she had announced her fourth pregnancy by him in five years of marriage; he had gone onto his knees, taken her hand as she told him, having already brought him two sons and a daughter, and told her in a low voice, alone in what was now Eadred's bedroom, that if there was such a thing as love, then that is what he felt for her. He had found it difficult to express affection; she could appreciate the effort. It was as near as any woman, married as a political convenience in those recovery days after the Danish wars, could expect of a bloodied and wearied soldier. He had thanked her for their children, had promised that they would have a role in the governance of the realm in time and would take preference over their half-siblings by Aelfflaed. He would make sure of that in his will.

But he had not made a will. He was not a man of words, spoken or written. Within a few months, campaigning in the Midlands after the death of his sister, the Lady of the Mercians, with his sword in his hand and no pen or a scribe nearby to write for him, he had died of a sudden fever, leaving his vast brood of children to fight over the succession. Eadgifu's children were babes in arms.

They could not rule. Their half-brother Athelstan had become king, a thirty-year-old. No child younger than fourteen could be allowed to rule, without the aid of a competent regent. She had, over the following years, as a queen in essence at Athelstan's court, become that competent one, aided by Dunstan and Aethelwold. Edmund had competency at eighteen when Athelstan had died, tired out. Now Eadred, at twenty-four and reasonably well disposed towards her and Dunstan, was able and willing to take up the reins of power. She, along with Dunstan, had steadied the realm, made sure of the succession. It was unfortunate that her grandson Eadwig was proving to be an unwilling scholar, as his grandfather had been, but Edgar was doing well with Aethelwold as his tutor. The two boys, the one destined to be king, the other his heir unless Eadwig produced a son, could perhaps be made to complement each other. In Glastonbury, the whip as well as the carrot were useful tools to be used for an unwilling student; they usually succeeded in making a child compliant; they had made Edmund, a fractious child, like his son Eadwig, into a passable reader, writer and even poet; they could turn the temper of an unwilling young pupil into a well-informed, pious but warlike decision-maker in his teen-age years, or so it was to be hoped. If the medicine and learning of Glastonbury and Dunstan's tutorship failed, there would have to be plans to split the kingdom or even…but no, that could not be thought of, not yet, or perhaps at all.

There was a knock on the door. 'Madam, I am here, Nonna.' Nonna's voice was faint as he stood in the stony corridor outside her room. He was trying to alert her while wishing not to awaken others. Nevertheless, a cock on the dungheap outside heard him and began to shout, though the dawn had not yet arrived.

'Come in, Nonna.'

Nonna pushed the door open. It creaked and the cock cried again.

'Madam.'

'Sit here, Nonna.' Eadgifu pointed to a chair near her. Her hearing was not improving as she aged; it was the only physical ailment, deafness, which she truly feared. Two cats, wrapped up in each other's embrace on the bed, stirred, yawned, and sat up.

Nonna sat down and waited for the queen to begin.

'It is late, or early, whichever, I do not care and I know you do not either, Nonna. But I will spare us both any niceties. What do you know about the latest relic of Eadred's?'

'You mean the foot relic of Wilfred, Madam? It has been put with the other most precious relics in the haligdom here.'

'Of course, it is a stupendous find and one that will bring honour and riches to Wessex. But I wish to know more about how it came into our possession. It is a northern border guard of the highest order, like St Oswald's relics. It is not the sort of object which would come naturally to my daughter Eadburh in Winchester, whose life and background are not commercial. Eadred thinks it came from her. Bearing in mind your involvement with the Cuthbert saga in Chester-le-Street– yes, I know about that, I wormed it out of Eadred - I wondered if you might know anything about its former ownership? Its provenance might have a bearing on the display or use of the object.' Eadgifu stopped short of revealing any interest in the relic other than as a religious focus. There were limits, even with a discreet servant.

Nonna's antennae were as acute as ever. The control of relics, particularly totemic guardians of the nation, was ever in the mind of his masters, and mistress.

'I believe that my lord Half-king may have bought the relic from the Ripon monks.'

'Bought? Brought? Took? I know that he has no love for Archbishop Wulfstan and would have him unseated.'

'I believe that a large sum of money was involved, Madam, though whether the sum went directly to the Ripon monks…'

'Taken, then. Wulfstan benefits, I suspect. No matter. The relic is here with us, now, and closely guarded, I hope?'

'Yes, Madam, it is with the most valuable of the relics and treasure. Dunstan has it safe with the main chests. He holds all keys to the chests of the treasury.'

'They are becoming difficult to move. Is there a plan to make a permanent treasury or are we forever to have to cart our riches with us wherever we go?'

'There are suggestions, Madam, for a permanent treasury here at Winchester, and a fortified haligdom for the most important relics at Canterbury.'

'And Dunstan will have charge of both?'

'Yes, Madam. He also has plans for a guarded haligdom for some items at Glastonbury.'

'Good. Near Edmund's tomb. His soul will appreciate that. But the gold and silver coin will still travel with us from palace to palace?'

'That is the case. Wherever the king goes, his coin treasure will go with him. It will be a suitable separation of the wealth of your family, I think. The more important relics will remain under guard at the archbishop's palace, or here at Winchester, or at Glastonbury and the spending money for secular purposes will walk on its hind legs, like the army and navy which it represents, travelling with the body of the king, always ready to be dispensed as necessary.'

'Or counted. I see. Regarding Wilfrid's foot; I should like to see it again before it goes off to Canterbury and becomes lost in Oda's relic-room. Inform Abbot Dunstan, would you, that I will see it now. That will be all.'

Nonna bowed and retreated. Dawn and the office of Prime were coinciding. Dunstan would not be available for a short candle's time, but he knew where he could find him, on his knees, praying for the guidance needed to steer the new king. There were two Half-kings in the pay of Wessex, now. But this second half-king, Dunstan, was already receiving his future in glory from another master, far away in Rome.

# The Sanctuary of Ripon.

## St Wilfrid's Monastery, Ripon, Yorkshire, September 946

I T WAS MID-MORNING, between the offices of Terce and Sext. Rain splattered on the crumbling flags of the cloister, its roof under repair, beyond a stone-walled room where three men sat around a table. The table groaned and creaked under the weight of leather-bound books, jugs and bowls of ale and food and the substantial bodies of the three men, who leaned across it to conspire.

There was much to discuss. The Archbishop of York, trained by the monks of Ripon but a proponent of secular priesthood, in post for fifteen years, sighed and leant back in his chair. This was heavy weather, getting foreigners with poorly spoken English to understand the finer points of Northumbrian diplomacy. The two men opposite him were indifferent to his interest in the Benedictine reform movement of the south. They were indifferent to most things to do with the south, apart from the numbers of men in its fyrd and navy. They were Scandinavian. One of them was slim and tattooed, the other stocky and bearded. The belts of both carried finely-worked leather and metal fittings for a sword, a long knife and a lightweight axe. Archbishop Wulfstan raised his quill and dipped it into ink.

Eric, King of Norway and Anlaf, King of Dublin, were allies of a sort; it was becoming clear that Ireland and York were difficult to control as one nation; Strathclyde and the Irish Sea divided them. The Northumbrian Saxons had been happy to take the older man, Anlaf, as their king as long as he was successful in war, as long as he represented their interests against the southern Saxons, but the battle of Brunanburh in the north-west had sown a seed of doubt. The losses had been heavy. The later failure to grasp the opportunity of taking the south with Leofa's return from exile had smarted. Wessex's Edmund had been killed, but the dynasty had quickly recovered from the blow. Nevertheless, it was yet to show its ability at enforcing rule under Eadred. Viking children who had been orphaned in the rout at Brunanburh had since become men. There was a new generation of resentful Norse immigrants and Northumbrians with Danish ancestors, anxious to flex their inherited muscle of war and with the temperament to launch a fresh offensive, or at least a rebellion, against rule from Winchester. Wessex had had its way for too long. Its arrogance was insufferable. Besides, its heirs were proving to have feet of clay. Wulfstan had heard that Eadred was reluctant to cross into Mercia, let alone Northumbria.

'Eadred's nappy does not allow him to ride across a saddle, they say.' Eric raised the image of the Saxon king, sitting side-saddle like a woman.

'It's probably not as bad as that, but I hear he vomits a lot.' Anlaf, sturdy and hale, had noted the tales of Eadred's disabilities. 'The whole of England fears having to eat with him in case they are showered with the contents of his intestines.'

'Don't believe everything you hear.' The archbishop paused. This irreverence towards the line of Wessex, even if true, annoyed the Northumbrian. There was a vestige of sympathy for the princes of the south; they were likely to have to meet their doom, soon, at the hands of one or both of the vital young men with whom he now supped. 'So, we think we can compromise, do we? Can I write down what we have just agreed, and will you both sign it?' Wulfstan, Northumbria's representative at this table of power, began to write his name at the end of a list of land-holdings and power-sharing. Gifts and silver flowed across the page; this to this man, that to another. The nation's carving in physical form echoed the requirements of the archbishop: Eric and Anlaf would kneel before him to pray and be baptized. The neutering of Scandinavian plunder-culture was a prize worth paying for. They called themselves kings, these men, but in reality, they were bullying pirates who had had good luck. Their boldness was worthy of admiration. Wulfstan envied their freedom to create their own worlds. If turned towards Christianity, they could be a force for good.

'I can do that.'

Anlaf shot a look at Eric from under bushy eyebrows. 'And I.'

The value of the ability to hold a quill and an understanding of the binding nature of a readable signature on a semi-permanent document was becoming realised by the pirate kings. Documents, forms of agreement, charters and wills were fast becoming essential means of the transfer of wealth, to be countered by exile and forfeiture. The right hand, or the left, was learning to make its mark as a matter of course. Gone were the days when a ritual swearing would do; in any case, what would the Norse Vikings swear upon, and to who? Thor or Odin would not answer. Stick-like runes might look fine on the side of a rock on an island in the Baltic, but would not seal a charter's right to claim a kingdom. Not, at any rate, Northumbria.

# The abbot's room, Fleury Abbey, Orleans, France, March 947

S PRING LIGHT VENTURED through the latticed panes of round-topped windows, casting distracting beams onto a pile of letters and plans heaped on the abbot's desk. With his back to the insistent call of nature's beauty, Oilbold tried to concentrate his mind on the tasks before him. A large candle behind glass burned before him, illuminating the carefully penned documents of the business of a major European abbey, where the written word had become a commodity in itself. His scribes had been busy recently, at a decade-long court of jurisdiction; an argument about land entitlement, as usual. Heirs were entitled to rage, but Fleury needed to claim and to prove what was rightfully theirs. Time was on Fleury's side.

The new Abbot of Fleury gazed with some trepidation across his desk. There were long letters from the east, letters from the south, a few from the west, all demanding assistance and offering little reward to the helper. Lesser monasteries and abbeys, bishops and abbots, repeatedly begged Fleury for help: not of a financial nature, nor of a spiritual kind, but something in between: the influence of a successfully reformed Benedictine monastery, one cleansed of its sins and wealthy enough to demonstrate to others, particularly kings, that reform could mean an improvement to income as well as moral performance of a nation's citizens. Sometimes requests came from nunneries, but their paperwork, in neat handwriting, formed a small pile of letters, kept separately at the far end of his desk, held firmly in place under a fossilised sea-creature. One day, he promised himself, he would look into the matter of the age of the earth, if he was spared. Abo might know something of it. He should ask his opinion. But not now.

Oilbold took up the letter which was on the top of his heap and which he had studied before; it was well thumbed. This one was from the north. It was from Dunstan, Abbot of Glastonbury. He knew the place; he had visited it as a youngster in the train of a former abbot of Fleury. He read again the distinctive lettering and floral language of the English abbot. There was no mistaking Dunstan's style. He had not met him, but could see him in his mind: a man who would be neat, circumspect, careful, diplomatic, possibly pedantic, still young enough to want more than merely to rule an abbey, still hopeful and hungry for improvement to monasteries in England. Dunstan, like so many other plaintiffs, would be mindful of his, the Abbot of Fleury's potential influence to make the sweeping changes which were necessary to achieve the Church's goals. There were studied hints of Dunstan's own intellectual powers and influences: Bede and Aldhelm were quoted in the body of the letter.

Dunstan was ambitious. It was clear that he wanted to make England's religious houses an important part of the empire of Christianity which reached in all directions from Rome, seat of the papacy. He wanted to make Glastonbury the equal of Fleury. The world map of the edifice of Christ, as exemplified by the seventh century Benedict of Nursia, was woven into the minds of children and novices throughout Europe as they sat in their classrooms imbibing the missionary spirit of their times: peace, order and above all, control. The history of times when chaos had been dominant was taught to all who came within the confines of Fleury to learn and to become its adherents, taking its objective of illumination forward, like ants in a nest, onwards through the centuries, undimmed. Since the founding of Fleury in the seventh century, the steady grind of intellectual pursuits, mathematical, cosmological and historical had honed its willing workers and stunned them with its library, the finest in western Europe. And now it had the heart of a beating engine of reform: the sacred relics of St Benedict of Nursia himself, rescued from the Lombardic incursions from his home monastery of Monte Cassino. Like a fiery beacon, Fleury had risen in stature since the translation of his bones, become recognised by satellite kings and monks alike as a stream of encouraging power, as illuminating as the sun, as bright as the beams of light which now allowed the abbot to interpret the lettering of his English counterpart.

This was another begging letter, but one with a difference: things were evidently in hand under a determined character; money was not the requirement, only a ray from the beam that was Fleury, in the form of a teacher. Dunstan wanted a piece of Fleury to come to England, he said, to show his compatriots in the reform movement how to go about altering the mindset of the secular clergy. By the corporeal example of one closely associated with the monastery which preserved the relics of St Benedict, the house of Wessex could be persuaded, finally, to do away with laxity and permissiveness in the monasteries and nunneries of England. Dunstan was clear: he had the permission of the new king, Eadred, and his mother, Eadgifu, to seek help to clear the way for monastic reform. The Vikings had destroyed much, particularly in the east of the country, he said, but there were several sites which could, with the money provided by pilgrimage and royal revenues, be rejuvenated. Relics had been appropriated: saints' parts were in ready supply and miracles were noted daily; all that was needed was a Fleury academic who could galvanise the remaining reluctant nobles to let go their attachment to married priests and to focus wealth and interest on the monasteries of Wessex which were now beginning to return to their former glories. *He means Glastonbury,* the abbot thought.

The abbot read on. The language was full of praise for Fleury, understandably so, and for himself as abbot. What could Dunstan know of himself? The man was a natural diplomat, it seemed. If a visit from himself, the esteemed driver of the Benedictine heart of Europe, could not be managed, then perhaps a second-in-command would be able to cross the English Channel, to teach in both Glastonbury and at court. The king and his mother were willing to listen and would act as examples to the nobles and other reluctant courtiers. It was tempting to imagine himself at the Wessex court, addressing a willing king, his eyes wide as he listened to the learning which he could shower onto the walls and floors of monasteries and palaces, spreading like sparkling liquid to the very feet of every gaudily dressed gentleman and lady of the land, soaking up through their woollen capes and silk dresses to their skin, infecting them through their eyes and ears with the words of St Benedict. He could imagine how a portion of the relics of the great saint himself could be carried to the English court and make the viewers bow down, to kneel and cross themselves, so powerful had Benedict's saintly stature become. He would dearly love to witness the birth of the reform movement in this new country called England and bask in its adulation of Fleury's achievements and example at the renowned brightness of the Wessex court, but there were problems at home which needed him here.

Could he leave his monastery for a few weeks, could he trust that his deputy would hold together the fragile status quo of the monastic orders which threaded throughout the religious houses of western Europe, even here, in Fleury? Violence had been known to erupt, monks had been known to wield sticks and lances, to protect their dearly-held beliefs, not against non-monks, but against their own brothers in Christ. What were these beliefs? That a man should be able to have a wife, or not, that nobles should be able to have influence in monastic communities. That priests could have possessions, could even be rich. This was the heart of the problem: secular versus purist Benedictine requirements. Dunstan was clearly doing battle, along with others (Aethelwold and Oda were mentioned in his letter) to rid the monastic world in England of its tendency towards noble interference, and was well on the way, having persuaded the former king, Edmund, apparently by a miracle performed at a gorge somewhere, to back him. King Eadred and his mother, it seemed, needed no miracles to persuade them of the merits of his case.

How tempting it was to witness this new regime, to give it a boost in its infancy, to help to bring it in line with mainstream

European thought, to expand the allegiance owed to Rome. But no, he could not afford to leave Fleury at the moment. His deputy, however, could be sent during the summer months to encourage and observe the new reign and to report to him the progress of reform, of power shifting from king to pope.

Yes, he could send Reginald. Dunstan should have his man, and perhaps could accompany him back to Fleury for instruction on management of a successful monastic unit, furthering the knowledge and experience required to progress the religious movement. These were heady moments in the life of the Church; an empire of Christ required the ablest and most diplomatic skills and minds to drive their plans forward. The coming millennium event would be a test for all men; reform was a necessary prerequisite to be saved from the fires of hell. He, the Abbot of Fleury, and Dunstan, evidently realised this; it would take persuasion and publicity to coerce others, and perhaps a relic or two of Benedict.

Oilbold began to write. England, that young kingdom which suffered from perversion, would be earmarked as a place of mission, not of Christianity but of Catholicism. It would be ruled by his master in Rome. Dunstan would be the architect of change. Kings would come and go, but the present king, Eadred, seemed to be willing to accept the example of Fleury. 'Weak-in-the-feet' and his energetic mother, Eadgifu, would allow the mission to take root, that much was clear.

# A farmstead in Orkney, March 947

THE AIR WAS sodden with rain; the thatched farmhouse dripped mould, moss and bird excrement into puddles which were becoming lakes around the exposed foundations. A patch of sea pebbles near the main entrance provided dry footing for a few yards, but beyond that, the sky and sea melded into one grey morass of colourless hell. The rain obscured views; it obscured thought, casting a gloom of grey on living things and dead. The sculpted rocks of the shore wept wetness. Even the dark seaweed, draped like dispirited creatures on them, lacked lustre as it waited, waited for the tide's return.

'Take me back, Eric. At least in Norway we had winters which were dry. I understand snow. The ice and mountains are friends.' Gunnhild shot a look at her husband. 'The cold I can beat with furs, but this continual rain, this flat land, this wilderness of sea and greyness, I cannot cope with.' The wife of the king of the Norwegians and Orkney stamped her foot, not from cold but from annoyance. Theirs was an equal partnership made in the sight of Odin; it was Odin's will they were destined to carry out. The bargain was this: Gunnhild produced sons and Eric produced wealth, and, most important, power. The team of man and wife, mutually disposed to take what they could in a life which would inevitably be short, felt dispirited. The Orkneys, after Norway's charms, though often lethal, were small and far from any kingdom which could be called such. A queen deserved better.

Scandinavian power, the power to rearrange the ownership of lands to the south of Norway, as well as those of the island of ice, to do the will of Odin, to bend others to the burgeoning trade, slave and otherwise, of the northern world, was yet to be recognised by the peoples of the south. The people of the warmer lands had had it their own way for long enough. Norwegian fish-eaters and pirates had become self-proclaimed kings. From Jorvik to the Arctic Circle, the fair-haired peoples of the world of perpetual winter were born to rule, to be kings among other peoples, to command the seas and waves, to terrorise into submission those who would not recognise their might; to lay the sword-wielding hand of enforced peace upon the land, any land, which could be taken, plundered and subjugated to their will.

But to settle for a miniscule kingdom in Orkney? It would not do. Jorvik, called by the English York, and the satellite fiefdoms around it, that would be a prize. It would be drier there. It was a plum worthy of a king, and queen; if not plucked by Eric and Gunnhild, it would be another. A Viking had always to watch his back in case some other upstart adventurer, with Odin's help, refused to retreat in his bid for power. Like the stags of the forests at rut, challengers to the head of state came thick and fast. So far, Eric had smashed the minds and bodies of young bucks who thought that they could be king in his place; who thought that they could carve a nation out of the islands and mountains of this many isled country of Britain. He had left countless adventurers and many of his own brothers bleeding on the cobbled floors of their own abodes, ruing their attempts to challenge him; none were clever enough, or ruthless enough, to overcome him. Harald Fairhair had bred many sons, only one of which, it was Eric's contention and rule in life, could satisfactorily carry out the will of Odin, capricious though he sometimes was, to unite the Norwegian colonies of settled lands under one king. That king was Eric, in Eric's mind, and Gunnhild's. The rune-covered sword of Stainmore, a present from the king of Ireland, Anlaf, and blessed by the Christian archbishop, Wulfstan, charged with magic and washed with holy waters, combined the powers of the gods who were available to an ambitious Norwegian king. Gunnhild had produced her part of the partnership; she was pregnant with their fourth child, another son, no doubt. Mother of kings, they called her. They would learn what it was to rule and control the English nation, what it was to strut in front of cathedrals and monks, to throw English kings of Wessex into their own cesspits and dungeons. She picked up a wrap and threw it around her shoulders. Eric looked away. Good, he had noticed.

Meanwhile nothing changed. The miasma of damp gloom pervaded their hall. The team of husband and wife sat miserably for a few moments, considering their contract. A child wailed. A piece of furniture, perhaps a rotting floor joint, creaked somewhere in the byre which was being used as a nursery. There were no books or hangings to teach the young sons their destiny as in Saxon homes; weapons of war and personal protection, the magic of Odin and the poems of scops were all they needed. They played boisterously, learning how to fight, with wooden toys brought from Norway. Wooden swords, shields and helmets, metal-wheeled toy carts with metal figurines resembling cargoes of slaves, boats made for a three-year-old to float on the puddles outside the door and in the rock-pools, cemented their future as fighters. Their mother's strong-willed insistence on self-sufficiency, their father's example of ruthlessness, their own backsides sore from chastisement, that was all they needed to grow into the toughened men they needed to be.

'You will not have to put up with this place for much longer, Gunnhild. I have told you, the archbishop will have us in Jorvik soon.'

'And you have promised him something in return for his help, I suppose?'

'Of course, there is always compromise in these matters. I come as a conquering king, but the will, as well as the flesh, of the nation must be broken.'

'Will breaking the will of the Northumbrians give you the country as you desire it? And what is the compromise?'

'You know what that is. It is a simple matter of removing Odin's requirements- and you know I have been having my doubts- and paying heed to the Christian god.'

'He wants you to be baptised? Like Anlaf and Ragnald? Can

you really give up everything you have believed in? What about going to Valhalla? A Viking must go there, or to a Christian hell.'

'Anlaf and Ragnald were baptised. It is a meaningless ceremony. It didn't stop them from offering to Odin as well.'

'So, suppose you give lip service to the archbishop and do as he says, and become Christianised. Is that all he wants from you in return for support from the Northumbrians?' Gunnhild could hear the cries of a brotherly tussle coming from the byre. Eric seemed impervious. If she wanted to finish the discussion of their future, she must question Eric urgently. He was the sort of person who could disappear, exit from the porch in his weather oilskins, push out a sea trader with a few compatriots and be gone for several months. On his return, he would claim victories, throw jewels at her feet and take her to bed to make yet another son. They were named by her in memory of the victories and lands he had told her about. One day she would have a daughter, named for Freya, or perhaps, like herself, Hild. Eric was tapping his foot. He had heard the boys fighting. Their voices began to rise above the sound of rain and wind. Their nurse shouted at them, adding to the cacophony. He moved towards the door.

'Don't go out! Don't go…tell me more.' Gunnhild could see the dislike in Eric's eyes, not of her, but of childhood memories. 'At least they are all your own children and you know who their mother is!'

'All my sons will be kings. They will be your sons, no other. I will spend time with them when they are men. Meantime, I have work to do.' Eric grabbed at a pile of skins and raised the latch of the door. The sound of rain and wind drowned even the yells from the byre. A crashing wave thundered against a nearby cliff-edge.

'You will have much work to make yourself a Christian, I can promise you that. You will have to learn to read…'

But Eric was gone. The grey wetness had swallowed him up. Was it day or night? He would return sooner or later, he always did. But in the meantime, she had no idea of where he was going or much, when he described his trips, about where he had been. But someday, it seemed, Jorvik, a city in the dry south and away from the storms of sea, would be her home. A stone-built palace and meals with an archbishop, an easier life, for her and her children. A place where a daughter could be brought up with the prospects of marriage to another king. The mother of kings, she was, potentially, as Eric told her as he was begetting a child on her, and the mother of queens, too, if she could steer her daughter, perhaps the child she was carrying now, who knew? The goddess Freya had told her it would be another boy, to add to the raucous shouting matches in the byre. But Freya could sometimes be wrong. Perhaps if she prayed to the Christian Mary, as Eric seemed determined to do to the Christian god, she might grant her a female child.

Yes, what was the harm in trying?

# Borg, Iceland, April 947

A TRADER, FLAT bottomed and slower than a fighter, its sail down and oars out, entered Brakarsund at the north end of Borgarfjord. It brought a small but significant cargo of one man, besides the rowers: Eric had come to visit Egil Skallagrimsson at his home farm. The trade, in this instance, would not be of materials, but of information.

Skallagrimsson himself was at the harbour of Borg to meet the arrival, one of many ships entering or exiting the Brakarsund, but the only one with the flag and eagle-prow of Eric, King of Norway and Orkney. A visitor with well-known ambitions, more than the usual amount expected of a Viking seafarer, gave rise to consternation. A pony scout on the coast at Yngvar had alerted the settlement of the approach of the most respected Norwegian chieftain of his generation; Eric, at thirty-seven, was not merely a hero of the Viking world; he was a legend.

Skallagrimsson was himself unafraid. He had survived years as a bodyguard in the court of Wessex, had gained valuable experience in the art of diplomacy, had joined with others interested in supporting as well as destroying the Wessex domination of England and been paid well for assisting both King Edmund and his northern enemies in York and Dublin.

The waiting host was ugly, but he was charming. He was a large figure. He looked and acted like a formidable force of controlled aggression. Controlled, that is, until he sometimes chose to be a berserker, which he did less often in recent years; his sons were taking over that role. Asgerd Bjornsdottir had produced plenty of those, enough to bear his legacy, his poems and accounts of the English court, for centuries to come. He was equal, in semi-retirement, to any king, and if they wanted to see him and to pick his brains, they had to travel to him.

Which is what Eric, the younger man by fifteen years, had chosen to do. Age earned respect, particularly for one so experienced. Egil had been present at both Athelstan and Edmund's court in England. Eric wanted to know the details of the characters he might encounter, particularly the depth of the involvement of Eadred in his own martial affairs. Weak-in-the-feet might have unrecognised strengths; small men could be vicious. It would help to know where to aim, when the time came to make an assault on the south. Would the head be as weak as the body?

Egil was wrapped, head to toe, against the wind which blew from the north. The pony-skin cloak, tanned and softened by many hours of female labour, was decorated with boar's teeth about the shoulders and leather-sewn with designs in red about the armpits and wide hem. Egil's bare forearms shone in the midday sun with arm-rings. A lizard in blue clambered up the rough skin of his neck to his ear on his left side; on his right, a cross and hammer marked his religious affiliations. The Christians had made his head wet, but not reached any other parts. He, like Anlaf of Ireland and Ragnald of York, godsons of Edmund, was a born-again pagan, and proud of it. There was more than one god, in his view. If he was not to go to Valhalla, then to Heaven, though the feasting would be better, he thought, in Valhalla. Why not give gifts to both? Hopefully there would be many more years to ponder his ultimate fate in the skies. The Norns had foretold at his birth that he would be grey and wizened when the time came for him to depart this world. He would eventually be the oldest man in the Viking world when he died at ninety-one, Heaven and Valhalla being unable to decide for many years which should have him.

Eric, having stopped off for refreshment and an exchange of news at Lerwick and Thorshaven on his journey north, had learned of Skallagrimsson's intentions to breed ponies in Iceland in retirement and to write poetry. He was bored, the islanders had told him, of life in the halls of others; he now wished to dedicate his efforts to establishing himself as a leading light in the Thingvellir parliament in Iceland. His reputation had grown as tall and broad as himself in the year since he had returned to settle in the land of fire and ice; his prowess with his tongue as well as his battle sword had given his farmstead the aura of a palace. This was no mere horse breeder, and the visitor knew it.

Eric, unlike the older man, was lightly clad. As the ship was pulled onto the shore, he jumped into the gravelly shallows and splashed his way towards Egil, who was unmistakeable in size and appearance. Egil put down his hood.

'So, the new king-in-waiting of England comes to call. I will put my kettle on to boil.' Egil extended an arm, welcoming Eric. Thick-set, dark but balding, Egil contrasted with the fair-haired lighter man, whose arm-rings clattered and clashed with his own.

'Not yet king, my friend,' Eric noted the height of the man standing opposite him and now walking by him uphill to the farmstead. 'There is Northumbria to settle first. A toe-hold will turn into a fist-clench in time, but there is the small matter of Eadred and Athelstan Half-king to consider. And perhaps there are others that I should know more about? You can tell me much that I wish to know. A battle is won with the head as well as the muscles of the arm.'

'And with cash. I presume your lockers are well-filled?' Egil would not be giving away information without a commitment by Eric to enrich him.

Eric had come prepared. He rattled the purse at his hip. 'There is gold enough in here to prise the words that I want to hear, even from you, Egil Skallagrimsson.'

'Then let us sit by my fire and dry your feet, young scallywag. You shall tell me about your sons and I shall tell you about mine. My wife Asgerd will feed you and provide you with entertainment brought from the slave-holds for the nights that you are with us. Settle your crew at the dockside. I assume you will want more than a fleeting visit to hear all that I have to tell you; but first, I must know,

Has Gunnhild forgiven me?'

'She will never do that. She is a vengeful woman. Her brothers were dear to her. The death of close kin requires revenge. You know that. Your killing of them will never be forgotten, though my sons fill the gap in her need. Forgiveness? You can forget that.'

'Then I take it she doesn't know that you are here. Very well, I do not expect people that I have wronged to vouch for me with the gods. I cannot win all my wars, I know. I am long in the tooth and regret some of the things that I did in youth, but not all.' Egil gave a glance sideways at Eric.

'No, Gunnhild does not know, but I will tell her, when I return, of your hospitality. I take it I am welcome?'

'You have gold.' Egil slapped his visitor's thigh, making his heavy purse chink. 'Why not?'


A peat fire was burning in the central pit of the farmhouse. Egil lay across the open sleeping closet, his pony-skin cloak still around him. His large feet with long toenails emerged into the main part of the hall. Eric sat opposite on a bench, with the fire dividing them. Asgerd, Egil's wife, sang to herself in a nearby storage room, hunting for pickled condiments.

'She sounds content.'

'Eh, oh Asgerd, you mean? She sings away to herself day and night, day and night. When she is not whistling, that is. She is pregnant again.'

'As is my wife, but she is not as content as that.'

'Content? No, I would not call Asgerd content. I am always here, she says. It was better in the old days when I was away in England for much of the time, she says. I have too big and cumbersome a body, she says, and I take up too much room. Particularly in here. She says she thinks that I am still growing. Well, perhaps she is right.' Egil slapped his stomach, drew his feet under his body and sat up. His head emerged from behind the bed closet curtain.

'I would not wish to flatter you, but your personal beauty does not improve the grace of your rooms.'

'You know I like to be flattered, Eric. I love a good insult, too. You score well. And as for yourself, well, what can I say? The North Sea salt is ditched in you; you look like the steel of the waves. There, in your cheek-lines, there is the mark of the eagle, and in your eyes, too. And your nose…hooked like the predator I know you are. Did they carve your ship's prow with you acting as model? But enough of our charms. Tell me about the northern archbishop. How is he? What did he say?'

Eric ran a finger down one of his pronounced cheek furrows. They used to lead to dimples, in his youth, but now they were ravines of experience. He was folding up on himself. He imagined himself in his coffin, lying in his eagle-prowed boat someday. The furrows of age, if he lived that long, would produce layers of skin, neatly piled on top of each other. The fat of his arms and the weight of his arm-rings, under gravity, would reveal a thin skeleton of bone on the top of a pyre. One day. One day, when he was as old as Egil, perhaps. But perhaps he would have a sea-eagle's death, caught by another, younger bird, torn with talons stronger than his own, ravaged by the quest of youth for the power of a former generation. Then the sea would be his grave, feathers scattered on the waves, floating endlessly on the surface of the sea, his soul restless within, or gone to bang on the doors of heaven, hell, or Valhalla, there to knock forever in purgatory. He had spent too much time listening to Archbishop Wulfstan. He was confused.

'The Archbishop of York is an indecisive man. Wulfstan cannot make up his mind between supporting us or Wessex.'

'I would have thought that his time with Anlaf, being besieged in Leicester and their escape from Edmund would have convinced him to side permanently with us. Is it a matter of money? The minster of Jorvik and the monastery of Ripon will be short of funds. The traders from the north bring wealth, but not necessarily to him.'

Egil stretched his legs, got up and came around the fire pit to join

Eric on the bench. 'I am warm enough, now. Hark, the singing has stopped. Asgerd will soon be bringing us some food.'

'No, not money. He genuinely believes that his religion can be acceptable to us. He thinks we should both be able to be Christians as well as pagans, to share the north as leaders. His plan is to establish Anlaf in the west, in Ireland, with me in the east. This is what he wants, in return for his assistance in taking over the Northumbrian kingdom. I tell him that we will do this anyway, whether he likes it or not, but I go along with his bible tales. He seems to like Anlaf personally, but like the rest of the Irish Norse, he has become untrustworthy. He has been baptised. This Christian religion weakens our culture, Egil. Did you not feel the pressure to become Christian, during the years you spent with Athelstan and Edmund?'

'Yes, but my thick head was interested in making a living.

'You sold yourself.'

'Never mind what I did. It is what you will do which interests you, and me. You will fall out with Anlaf, I predict. Since when did two Viking commanders share power? One will go, or be helped on his way. It might be you.'

'It might.'

'And to the highest bidder. Look what I have now. The runes say I will live for another forty years. I have my skin-warmers, my ponies, my sons and my wife and visitors like you, wanting advice. Words, I can produce in great flow. Each one has a silver penny attached.' Egil kicked a sack protruding from under the bed-closet. 'You see, I sleep soundly over the fruit of my thoughts.'

'As you are going to live so long...,' Eric glanced around the hall. There were no trophies or weapons on show. He felt his own dagger and moved a hand over his arm-rings. No Viking could wish to die in a bed, surely, even one with such wealth stuffed below? 'You may feel the need to recompense my wife for her brothers' deaths. You may have regrets about that affair which need to be settled on this side of Valhalla's door. Who divines for you?'

'I did it for myself. Valhalla yawns for all men and I will willingly go there, or to the other place, when my time comes. It will happen at three o'clock in the afternoon, the skald says. I shall have had excellent pickled herrings for my lunch. Would you like some?' Egil slapped his wife's bottom as she passed the men on the way to the kitchen fire. 'A plate for the King of Norway, wife. And herbs, and bread. Beer, too, with cups, if you please. No horns. This is not a drinking party.'

Asgerd turned, wiping her hands on a decorated apron. 'Really, Egil? You are slowing down in your old age.' She retreated to the kitchen area and could be heard assembling food and drink, whistling while she worked.

'Your wife is very free with you.' Eric would not countenance such a remark from Gunnhild, in public. Would his wife tell him if he had many years, or few, to live? She was an expert at foretelling. Eric examined Egil's feet. They were huge, and hairy, like his hands.

Egil chuckled. 'My features are my blessing. Asgerd looks after me. She bites my nails for me. What more can you ask of a wife? We have excellent partners, you and I, by all accounts, but perhaps yours has a tongue which rasps. My spies have heard her slamming doors and seen your burning ears. But never mind the behaviour of our women. So, Gunnhild has not forgiven me yet?'

'She never will. Bardr didn't deserve to be killed…'

'It was an accident. I could not help it; he was so small and I am so large.'

'And then you plunged yourself further into the mire by killing Gunnhild's brothers. She meant them to get compensation from you, that's all.'

'They came to me with knives in their hands. I gave them what they deserved.'

'Then you deserted Norway, having set up a horse's head against us. There are difficulties in forgiving you that.'

'And yet you are here. Let us move on. I take it that you wish to know more of England's king?' Asgerd abruptly entered the room and slammed a plate of food onto a table. Egil sprawled across the bench and picked at fish and bread. 'You see that she has little finesse, but she lays well.'

A gust of wind brought the smell of rotting fish from the shore, laying flat the flames of the fire. Eric stiffened. Could Gunnhild, far off in Jorvik, overhear his conversation with her enemy? Did she know, through her magical means, that he was here in Iceland? He recalled the line of shags he had seen on the ship posts, drying their wings after diving for fjord herring. Could one of them be a courier for his wife?

'Your wife, she is a good lay, is she? Makes you forgive her for her less propitious ways? Here, fill your cup.' Egil threw back his head and emptied his beaker. Eric, uncomfortable with any discussion of the merits of his wife, did likewise. The effect was instantaneous. Both men relaxed, laughing.

'Queen Gunnhild has her own very special ways of making a man happy. That is all you need to know.'

Asgerd, still in the kitchen, began to sing a song, shared among Icelanders, who had no king or queen, about a fair maid who wished to be married to a prince. She trilled loudly in Norwegian which was becoming heavily accented as generations lived apart, in Iceland, from their motherland. Nevertheless, the song, which ended in tragic death for the girl who would be queen, was understandable to Eric. It ended in a piercing high note.

'Enough, Asgerd! Stop that noise. Take yourself off. Go and stone a cormorant or skim a pebble.'

Asgerd threw off her apron as she passed through the hall, shuffling off her knitted slippers and putting on pattens. 'You will find me, when you want me, in the Faeroes, singing to the seals. They will appreciate my noise. I may marry a merman and bring him back here to share our bed. But I forgot: you may like the idea of that, so I shall not. I shall keep him to myself.' Asgerd opened the door, her hair flying back from her face, and stepped out. She could be heard, singing the same song, as she marched down to the sea-shore. A shower of small pebbles rapped on the door.

'She is only making her presence felt. She pretends that she is coming back and would like the door to be opened for her. She likes me to get up from my bench to lift the latch for her. You see, she is short, whereas I am tall and this hall was built to suit me. I do not do it, but she tries, over and over, each time she goes out or wishes to enter alone. One day she will want help to open the door and I will not respond. She will have to stand outside in the cold.'

'But you never chastise her?' Eric was astonished at the openness of this pair. They could insult each other, it seemed, without caring what they or anyone else would think.

'I would call it horseplay. She likes it. Now that you have had some beer, tell me what you want.'

'I want as much as you can tell me about Eadred and Athelstan Half-king. I understand that he is a seasoned fighter.'

'Half-king I know well. We fought together at Brunanburh in 937.'

'You were fighting on the Wessex side?'

'They paid me in gold. The official enemy then were mostly Cumbrians and Scots, though, I have to admit, there were Irish Norse.'

'But not Icelandic. That might have changed your affiliation?'

'I don't suppose so. The Irish are mean. Half-king is your chief problem. He is an experienced and charismatic warrior, a leader in Athelstan and Edmund's armies. And, you know, he is Ealdorman of East Anglia, a very wealthy man. He will support Eadred in any battles to come. He will fight hard to prevent the north from falling into your hands. I take it that you wish to expand the kingdom of York? Aren't you being a little greedy, having Norway, the Orkneys and York?'

'You fought for gold. I fight for possession of land.'

'Yes, you want an empire of the north. A terrible ambition, my friend.'

'Nevertheless, it is my ambition. And if not me, there will be others. Think of it, a Viking empire spanning the waves, with access to subject peoples for the slave trade as well as endless treasure from the monasteries which they are beginning to build again.' Eric leaned forward. He wanted to pick the brains of this contented, retired mercenary. It was impossible to fathom how a Viking could be without ambition, particularly one who knew he had so many years in which to be idle; but then, there were the domestic battles with Asgerd to enliven long winter evenings.

The two men refilled their cups. The beer was good. Before long, Eadred, Eadgifu, Half-king and Dunstan had been described in detail to Eric. He felt he knew them personally. 'And then, there is the archbishop in York. Wulfstan has already said he will help me.'

'Wulfstan. Now there is a wolf in sheep's clothing.'

'A wolf worth his bite, I think.'

'His fangs are polished and well-used, in the name of Christ. And like a cat, he has already had several lives, aided by that so-called sacred ring around Ripon to which he can retreat.'

'The sanctuary, you mean. I don't understand why the Saxons think that a boundary which is only in the mind can be effective, and yet they let him stay there, unmolested.'

'Yes, that has always puzzled me. But their holy ideas, like the praise and idolatry of their saints' relics, has always been peculiar. It goes back for centuries. Bones of ancient holy men and women rule all their thoughts and dreams. These untouchable places or relics, beyond bounds, seem to dominate their lives. They dare not cross them or touch them, except for their touch-relics, for fear of being swept off to hell by their devil. A mad proposition, and one which I observed at first hand while I worked for Athelstan and Edmund, particularly Athelstan. And he would not marry, either; a strange man. I hear Eadred is going to stay single, too.' Egil paused. There were so many contradictions in the English viewpoint of life, and death. Nothing was straightforward or honestly manly. Could Eric, who had little experience of the English way of thinking, understand this? And yet he needed to, if he was to rule. 'There are many inconsistencies in the Wessex approach to life. All of the

Saxons, from south to north, have this strange fear of the afterlife, in particular of the end of what they call the millennium. This thousand years after their god's birth has a stranglehold on their imagination.' Egil continued. This would be an expensive lesson for the would-be king of England. 'Death holds no fear for us, eh? And what is a thousand years when your god has no date attached to him? Today is what matters, and perhaps tomorrow. Drink up, King Eric, I promise you that you will be ruler of England before one year's end, before the last of the winter snow in our fjords in the coming year. Tell the shag on the post outside, who is probably in your wife's pay, that though I am not forgiven, I will cast runes, make poetry and foretell that Eric, son of Harald Fairhair and killer of his own brothers, as I am killer of his queen's brothers, will prevail. There will be a new Scandinavian empire and its emperor will be Eric Bloodaxe, yes that is what I shall call you. Bloodaxe.'

Eric repeated the name. 'Bloodaxe.' He laughed. It was a better name than Hairy-cheeks, which Uncle Grim was given, or Hallbjorn Half-troll, or Olaf Peacock. Bloodaxe conveyed intent and fear. The nick-name of Olvir Hump, another relative from the misty past, did not have the same ring.

Eric Bloodaxe, king of many places, conqueror of mountains and soon, fertile plains and woods of England. What would he rename the country? The kingdom of York, expanded, perhaps. The Northland empire? Perhaps. Ericaland? But that could be regarded as temporary. How many years would he live to enjoy his fame? Would one year, or two, be enough for glory? How many years would his wife grant him in her dreams? How many years would the superstitious English give him, counting the fingers of their relics, the toe bones of saints rattling on their stone floors? What would their starling murmurations say of this son of Scandinavia, come not merely to their isles to plunder, but to stay, to rule?

Eric was brought back from his daydream by Egil's voice. The words were charged. No Viking could resist.

'But, then again, the runes and Norns may decide differently.

After all, the odds are stacked against you. Athelstan Half-king may prevail. I'll lay a bet. You won't be able to take the crown of England. I will bet a sum of a thousand silver pieces. The Wessex gang are too cunning and determined to hold onto their kingdom. And why not? They have the right of centuries' possession.'

'If I cannot take the crown, I will pay you two thousand.'

'Two thousand silver pieces? Just checking. Today will only cost you five hundred. A down payment, perhaps?'

Eric nodded. Arm rings chimed in unison as the two men sealed their deal. The die was cast. A new king, willing and able to do what he needed to do, would sweep down like a sea eagle from the cold north, bringing death in its talons to Wessex.

There was only one small matter to deal with: Wulfstan's fondness for the Irish Anlaf, whose ample behind was firmly on the throne of Jorvik. It would take more than a sharp talon to prise him off the seat which led to the conquest of England.

There was a thump on the door. 'Asgerd has returned from confiding with the shag.' Egil heaved himself up from the bed and lifted the latch, revealing a wet woman and wet scenery. She scooted inside, shaking herself like a dog, and disappeared into the byre. 'One more point, my friend. You will have learned to mistrust your enemies already. Beware your friends and associates, too. As we both know, relatives and friends can be the most vicious of enemies.'

# Frome Monastery, May 947

THE RHYTHMICAL SOUND of sawing filtered through an open window. An early summer warmth was on the land. Swallows and martins had returned to the farmyard on the hill above the church; the tithe barn on Behind Town was empty of its winter store of hay, waiting to be filled again.

'The swifts are not here yet, are they, Grandmother?' Eadwig was easily distracted from his studies. If a cloud passed overhead, darkening the room, or if it rained heavily, or if it snowed, Eadwig would instantly react to the voice of the natural world.

'Ssh, Eadwig, attend to your work. Dunstan will be here soon to test your Latin.'

Eadgifu was not a gifted instructor; she had been able to teach herself most of the written English language and had had help from Wynflaed of Charlton Horethorne when she visited court. She could just get by with the increasing amount of documentation which needed to be perused, in order not to be swindled by a subtle point of law in matters of landholding, in particular. The clerks did the work, but they needed to be checked. Dunstan was increasingly absent, supervising works at Glastonbury, and Aethelwold was at Cerne Abbas, learning more about the priesthood and what was expected of him as a potential bishop, though what they could best teach him, Eadgifu thought, might be humility. Aethelwold could be priggishly superior, but Dunstan regarded him as his right-hand man, a coming man, as they say. Partners in crime, some thought.

Footsteps tapped along the corridor from the church nave to the schoolroom. Dunstan and Eadred were on their way to view the scholarly achievements of the heir to the throne. Would this be the day that he matured into a compliant child, one who would be ready to hear the basics of what made the character of a right-thinking king, to conform to the wishes of his elders? Ideas of what was required of him in future were laden with confusion, to the child's mind; he must be strong, bloodthirsty, even, towards his enemies, who would be chosen for him by others, yet he must practice Christian patience and forbearance and always aim for peace. Peace. It seemed to Eadwig, young as he was, that that could only be won with blood-splattered war. Contradictions surrounded him, annoying his mind, like the fly buzzing on the windowsill, desperate to escape to the outer world. Too stupid to sense the nearness of an open window, it reminded the boy of the sons of some nobles who sometimes shared his classroom; they repeated what they were told, believed everything Dunstan said. Only he, Eadwig, knew of the contempt his father had once held for the now mighty abbot. Edgar, his brother, had gone down in his estimation when he had said, on the last occasion of their meeting, *everyone knows that God and Dunstan have magic powers, except Eadwig.* The fables of the pagan visitors to court were more appealing to Eadwig than the bible tales of far-off lands and their dusty heat. What had deserts and palm trees to do with England's lush meadows and oaks?

The schoolroom door opened. Eadwig stayed on his high stool, sighing over his latin grammar and dramatically heaving his shoulders, breathing heavily as though he had just run a race. He looked round at the visitors. Eadgifu walked towards them.

'He is quiet, but not enthusiastic, as you can see. Be gentle with him.' Eadgifu eyed the bunch of twigs which Dunstan had brought.

'I shall not submit to you; you need not use them,' Eadwig shouted at the abbot of Glastonbury. 'You cannot cane a prince and Grandmother will not let you. Nor will you, Uncle...will you?'

Eadred looked at his mother. She raised her eyebrows. Eadwig did this often. He had a knack of singling out, and appealing to, the soft-hearted in any room to save him. He had succeeded as a small, charming child with inattention or misdeeds for too long by this method. Uncle Eadred was king, higher in position than anyone else in the room or in the nation. The king would let him off this awful requirement to obey, surely, as he had before?

Eadred was learning, late in life, however, that children who must fill an important role in life, who must support the survival of the house of Wessex, must be made to harden themselves to the idea that though their position was to be envied, their choices were narrow; they could not think to do as they liked, when they liked. He had an idea.

'Eadwig, come with me, my fine fellow. I have something to show you.'

Eadwig looked at his grandmother and then at Dunstan, then hopped off his stool and took his uncle's outstretched hand. Eadred had become his protector since Edgar's departure for Half-king's manor in East Anglia. He had, indeed, taken over the role of father, in place of his own. The two looked like father and son, as they passed through the schoolroom door into the sunlight, their fair heads shining.

'He will be spoiling the child, again,' Eadgifu muttered.

'But there are signs, Madam, of improvement in him.'

'Not enough.'

'Eadred himself is becoming more decisive, do you not think, Madam?'

Dunstan had been trying to recover his old intimacy with Eadgifu. They had once considered themselves more than friends, though that was in the days of Athelstan, a king almost forgotten. They moved together, almost touching, to observe, through the window, Eadred and Eadwig as they walked towards the sawpit where the topman slave was singing as he drew the long-toothed saw through an oak log. The beat of the saw and song was echoed by the grunts of the underman in the pit below.

Eadred took Eadwig to within a few yards of the labour-intensive operation. There were lessons to be observed here, without the need for a desk or instruction.

'See, Eadwig, the effort being put into the sawing of this tree of the forest. It will become a beam of a house, or, more likely, a number of planks for ships. We Saxons know how to turn the living product of our land into articles of use, and not just for war. Wood from our forests is a main staple of our culture. We are the men of the wood.

'So, Selwood Forest is not just for hunting, Uncle?'

'You may call me Father. No, not just for that. It is a good source of large trees. Here is the limb of one of them. But what else do you see, besides the wood and the men, labouring to turn the tree into an article of use which will last for a hundred years or more?'

Eadwig listened to the singing, and sawing. His adoptive father released his hand as he moved closer to the pit, watching the methodical movement of the saw. The top man continued to bawl, his voice deep and bell-like, even though the effort of pulling the double-ended saw through the dense wood was evidently tiring. He looked into the pit. Standing in wet sawdust with bent legs and puffing, a younger man folded and straightened as the saw descended and rose. More wood-dust fell on him with each stroke. His hair and face were covered with fine powder. His clothing was indistinguishable from chippings. Only his strapped leggings could be discerned, from the calf to the knee. His feet were lost in the caked remains of past oak limbs. Eadred stepped to Eadwig's side and again held his hand.

'You see how it is, Eadwig. These two men are like Wessex and Mercia, like yourself and your brother Edgar. The top man is called the top dog- you see how the wooden dogs hold the branch in place- and the other is the underdog. The top dog rules his work; he guides the saw and dominates proceedings.' As he spoke, the top man stopped singing and shouted an order to the underdog. The saw was reaching the end of the branch. An adjustment needed to be made.

Eadred began again. 'The top man, or dog, is free of sawdust and able to sing. Look how the lesser slave has to toil in filthy conditions and relies on the guidance, eyes and good sense of the man above. When the time comes, one of you, yourself or Edgar, will be king of Wessex and England after me. Edgar will rule in Mercia, if the Mercians are willing and if he survives to manhood. Now, you must decide: are you willing to work hard, to achieve competency at kingship and to be the top dog? Because, if you do not want it, Edgar will take your place and you may spend your life in the pit.' Eadred squeezed Eadwig's hand. The boy took a step back and shook off his uncle's hand.

'I shall be top dog, Uncle-Father. I know what is required of me, but Dunstan is so harsh and Grandmother is so insistent on learning particular things. She seems to think that her Kentish works must be studied. Dunstan wants me to study Aldhelm. The subjects bore me. Kent is part of Wessex, now, and Aldhelm was so long ago. His writing is tedious. I want to look forward, not backwards.'

Eadred took the boy back to the classroom. Was a lesson learned? There was so much for an aetheling of Wessex, particularly in a time when reading and writing had become essential, to know. Edgar was doing well at his learning, according to Aethelwold. The young brothers were likely to offer different talents and personalities to the nobility when the time came to anoint a new king. The elder boy could not be guaranteed the superior role. Circumstances, character and the will of the courtiers would play a part in deciding who would be the aetheling most desired by the English people. Dunstan would arbitrate between factions. The strongest might not win the prize; the most competent, or the most compliant, would take the crown, or whoever looked the more likely to live.

But this was all in the future, which Eadwig and the Wessex kin had to try to foresee. Dunstan was known to be able to peer into the future, but angels and devils populated his visions. What use were they, Eadred wondered, to a future king, or to himself?

# The Norns

THREE BIRDS, RAVENS, flew from the Tor of Ynis Wytrin, where they had scavenged at the remains of a rabbit, to the questioning stone finger of Crook Peak on the wall of hills to the north. Early summer light was held back by a heavy lid of grey cloud. Somewhere beyond the solid dullness was the sun and a bluer sky, but wind and a shower of rain were needed to sweep the curtain of high pressure away. It would come, but not yet. Cart and army tracks remained rutted and dry after a hot April; roads which were normally muddy and impossible to use were unexpectedly available for marching warriors. Mankind reviewed its options for war. Wessex and Northumbria, in particular, considered their fates.

Athelstan Half-king, Archbishop Oda of Canterbury and Eadred were in discussion, seated in the main chamber at Cheddar palace on the edge of the wetlands below the hills. The views and cultures of East Anglia, the Danelaw and Wessex ran in their different gene-pools.

'Should we bring in Dunstan?' Oda felt the need for another voice representing the Church. He was still, after all these years, having to atone for his Danish forbears' aggression. To be a recent convert from Odin's thrall in a land anciently Christian was no easy thing. One had continually to prove one's loyalty. It was wearisome. Dunstan had been won over; Oda supported his planned reforms wholeheartedly.

Half-king's voice was razor-edged. 'No need for the present; when we have decided how to act, we will consult him on the payment of the troops. He may interject too often; we need to make our decision today. Now is the time to invest in the thrashing of Northumbria.' Half-king stood up and put his hands on his hips, challenging Oda. Eadred and Oda stood with him. Oda was the taller of the three; the Scandinavian genes gave him some authority. A moment of tension passed. Half-king sat down again. 'Apologies. It is difficult for a soldier to come to terms with a committee.'

The three men settled down again. Oda and the ageing fyrd general Half-king, keen to make a last attempt to do what Athelstan had asked him long ago, to finally unite the realm under Wessex, looked again at the younger man. The unlikely king, Eadred, despite his physical difficulties, had an air of calm optimism.

He doesn't understand what it is to be a soldier, Half-king thought.

He doesn't understand what it is to need to promote peace as a Christian king but to make a decision to fight against pagans. The Norse will turn us into Woden-worshippers if they are allowed to, Oda thought.

Eadred was not stupid, whatever else he might be. His stomach disorder, his leg-muscle weakness which made him drag his right foot as he walked, his almost toothless mouth, none of these had put to sleep his wits. He was his mother's son. As yet, resentment at others' dismissal of him had not become paramount. His head was healthy. His acute hearing, and the ears of his mind, could pick up thought.

'My lords, I may have feet of clay- no, I know that you are both aware of my limitations, but so am I...' Eadred was coming to terms with his strengths and weaknesses. 'I propose that Half-king does what he wishes and takes our troops north. The roads are good, I am told, and the uprising is current. The Northumbrians are thinking of coming south on their own soil; we cannot have them crossing into the midlands. The five boroughs are under threat again. My lord Oda, what is the state of the leadership in York? I hear the Norwegians continually change their minds about who should be king. Is there any gain which might be made on the basis of their indecision?'

Oda coughed. He was uncomfortable, after many years of having accepted the supremacy of Wessex, with the idea of invading the northern territories which contained so many of his Danish kin. But many had changed side and allegiance recently; Mercians favoured Wessex leaders and the Welsh favoured them too; Norse and Danish soldiers fought with the southern king as mercenaries. In Northumbria, the Danish settlers of the last one hundred and fifty years were wary of the latest incomers, the Norse. Without Anlaf and now Eric, calling themselves leaders, there had already been indecision about who best to follow. The north wavered, looking to its archbishop to guide its choice. Anglo-Danish Northumberland, carrying, in addition, the resentful ghosts of its own British inhabitants, the descendants of Elmet, Deira and Bernicia, was a complicated mixture of peoples, with clashing cultures. Would it be the sharp taxes of the southern king or the biting sword of the Norse kings of Dublin or York who would win their allegiance? It seemed better the devil they knew, or, rather, two devils. Anlaf and Eric were both successful pirates and plunderers, both had large families of children. From the southern Saxon point of view, it was to be hoped that the broods would kill each other, as Eric had reportedly killed some of his own kin in Norway. It was difficult for Edmund and Eadred to come to terms with a brother, Eric, of their own foster-brother, Hakon of Norway, as the fratricidal murderer of his kin. The climbing of the greasy pole of the Norwegian dynasty had involved blood in plenty. Harald Fairhair might rue his fecundity. Wessex had taken note of other families' difficulties over succession; theirs was a more pragmatic way of deciding who should be king. Their own pole was slippery, too, but tempered by the, at times, pragmatic fairness at the heart of Saxon religious thought.

There had been a breaking down of barriers in the rush to unite and to exploit the full area which could be called England. Differences were crushed, languages reigned in. Beliefs and customs were curtailed, or encouraged according to the state's need. Compromise was rewarded in the courts, blood-feuds discouraged. Theft and revenge were outlawed, by common agreement and by heavy fines and public rebuke by churchmen. Trees of once-remarkable forests were being felled. Ancient sites were being plundered of their building stone to make the imposing new halls and cathedrals which were the visible signs of power of the burgeoning state. Trade had become important for church revenue, its taxes bringing in more than could be taken by Rome. The state coffers were doing well; The chest of treasure which Dunstan had started to take with him on each progress to the various palaces required eight men to lift it. His heavy shell, he called it. A separate, much smaller, chest, travelled with it, full of the paperwork by which Dunstan carried out his taxation deliberations. He had a finger in both state and church finances; war could be good, or bad. It was as well that he was not at Cheddar to take part in their current deliberations. The pace of change required fewer irons in the fire, not more. Dunstan's role was as the treasury accountant of plans. Those present considered that they were the chief instruments of action. Dunstan and Eadgifu were feeling the force of the door closed against them. No matter, they would be given gifts, of land or gold, or reliquaries, which would assure their support in the witan.

Half-king interjected. 'I understand that Anlaf is the current king in York, though there is unease about his split loyalty. The kingdom of Dublin requires his attention often and there is the matter of trust; it is said that the Irish are trying to oust his deputy there.' Half-king waited for Oda to speak; his mouth was open, but he carried on. 'The Norse will never let Dublin go. There is too much investment in the slave trade. They are still mining the Irish hinterland of its heathens as well as expanding their activities to warmer lands. Anlaf will probably return there soon.'

Half-king looked at Oda. The slave trade was an area of embarrassment for the archbishop. On the one hand, slaves were necessary to all the cultures and societies of Europe; on the other, it did not seem right to encourage or to condone the capture, sale and use by coercion of another man, let alone his soul, though there were exceptions: heathens and pagans, if they were unwilling to become Christian, must be forced into accepting God's word. If uprooting, manual labour and persuasion could assist them to Heaven, then slavery could be justified. Children would benefit, it was thought, from being removed from their backward societies.

Oda had his nightmares, as those born of one culture and successful in another, must have. 'There is the matter of Archbishop Wulfstan. I fear that he is again stirring his proteges into action. Anlaf is one; but I hear there is another.'

'Another pirate who would be king?' Eadred was beginning to lose his composure. This was more serious than he had thought. No wonder Half-king had been pressing him to move troops to Northumbria.

Oda continued. 'The Archbishop, I fear, has been receiving, as his personal guest at Ripon, a king, or former king, of Norway.'

Eadred gasped. Sometimes the person who should know of events is the last to be told. He was aware that Viking pirates could become kings overnight; there was no lengthy successional procedure as with the making of the heirs of Wessex. So, another upstart had come onto the scene. He might disappear as soon as he came, or he might not. 'How serious is this development? And why does our own archbishop support these adventurers at the cost of our nation?'

Half-king could guess the answer to most of the puzzle. He had long ago discerned the growing jealousy between Dunstan and Wulfstan at the witans, in the old days when Wulfstan had regularly attended. The Church had its own dividing lines; Benedictine reform and the old ways. Wulfstan had a Danish wife and was a Northumbrian. There were going to be no favours given between the two. The old king Athelstan had appointed Wulfstan long ago to rule matters in the newly acquired north; during the years since, the king-maker of the Northumbrians had accepted his fate and allowed the overpowering might and trading acuity of first the Danes and now the Norse to take the name and position of king in York. But would he be in favour of letting them be satisfied with the north alone? He took items from the corner of the table and started to rearrange them as if on a map.

'The kingdom of Jorvik, as they call it, now encompasses not merely York. Anlaf and Wulfstan control the whole of the area north of the five boroughs. It is only a matter of time before they raid, or decide to try to take, those cities. We must act, Lord.' Half-king thumped the table. Oda looked convinced. Would Eadred be? He was known to recoil from physical confrontation. His years with a hot-tempered brother and a strong-willed mother had trained him in inaction.

Eadred looked actively thoughtful. The smacked fist had not been necessary; he was awake to the danger. He leaned back in his chair. There were a few seconds of silence. Oda and Half-king waited. 'My Lord Ealdorman Athelstan, the time has come. Will you undertake, for me, the journey north, with half our army, to threaten Northumbria to submit to our rule? There is evidently no time to be wasted. Take to the roads, Athelstan, with my blessing and the good will of the whole of Wessex. Take Edgar with you, if you will, to witness the actions you take. My nephew will learn much from seeing men in action. It may only need a little sword-waving to bring the northerners to heel. As for Wulfstan, well, his position is under review. The archbishopric given to him by my brother can be taken away by me; Wulfstan lives too long. I know that Dunstan would wish to have him replaced with one more to his liking.'

'But a southern bishop would not be acceptable at present, Lord. It would be better to come to some agreement with Wulfstan as he has so much support. I fear that a Benedictine as archbishop would only enflame the northerners. They are easily offended.' Half-king had a fair grasp of church politics. He intended to retire to a monastery someday, though he was in two minds about whether it should be pro-reform or one of the older, more relaxed institutions. Another ten years at court, time to let Edgar grow into manhood, and he would be glad to be shot of the intrigues and manipulations. He had his eye on Oundle monastery, or Glastonbury. Perhaps Dunstan would not go too far with his reforms. Plenty would stop him, if they could. Guests might still pray alone in a comfortable room, without being required to attend all the monks' offices, presumably? Old soldiers must rest somewhere. If one is to die in one's bed, it should be attended by healers, and they were all monks. The hospital at Frome was good, too, but the monastery there was ramshackle and in need of investment. No, the modernised rooms at Glastonbury would be more comfortable. And Cheddar palace, nearby, would afford some contact, if he still wanted it, with the royal family.

'And you might not wish a Benedictine to benefit?' Oda was torn between the old and the coming ways, despite recognising the rising star that was Dunstan.

Eadred made up his mind. He startled the listeners with his words. 'Summon Wulfstan and Anlaf to a meeting at Tanshelf in Yorkshire. Do your heavy threatening, Half-king, and do it well. Be violent if you must. When you have made the arrangements for a fresh treaty of submission, I will come to Tanshelf to witness it.' He stood up, ending the discussion.

There was a knock on the door. It opened before the occupiers of the war cabinet could prevent it. Dunstan entered, his skirt swirling.

'My lords, I understand that heavy matters are under discussion. May I intervene?' Dunstan looked at the faces of the men at the table. His swinging skirt and heavy cross settled. It was too late to have an input. Eadred faced him, with a flushed face. Rightly or wrongly, he had cast a stone into a pond. The ripples would alter the legacy of his reign. He was not just a caretaker for Eadwig, or for Edgar. This was his show. He may not be capable of leading a charge in war, but he could delegate the task to others. The treasure chest was brimming with coin; loyalty of those others would be bought. As long as Dunstan pushed reform and pedalled purgatory for the masses, the coin would continue to increase.

Now to concentrate on the payment for the enterprise. 'Dunstan, come with me. We will discuss the work that we must do.'

'Which work, my lord?' Dunstan was unused to being told after the event of a major decision by the Wessex line, and he had had no vision, on this occasion, that matters were so far on in discussion.

'The invasion of the north, my friend. We will plot our armaments and costs. Take me to your room. I need to have fresh accounts and projections of coin to come.' Eadred put an arm around Dunstan. The Abbot of Glastonbury overcame a fleeting feeling of being patronised and recognised that his meticulous work as accountant for the country was an essential part, but not the whole of, the running of Britain. They went together, one man dragging his leg, the other shuffling in long skirt and sandals, along a corridor to Dunstan's cosy treasury, to spend happy hours counting, sorting and assessing.

# St Wilfrid's Monastery, Ripon, Yorkshire, June 947

ARCHBISHOP WULFSTAN DOZED. He was ageing and knew it; he had not been a young man when put in charge of the north, in 931, by Athelstan. Sixteen years of receiving instructions about what to do north of the Humber from the far-off southern court, sixteen years of being berated by the Danish and Northumbrians, their demands emanating from the edifice of Bamburgh, had taken their toll. Long years of bowing to southern instructions, visits from the priests at Durham and Hexham urging him to stand firmly against the sweeping tide of reform and his own Danish wife requiring reassurance that she was not to be cast aside, along with their mongrel children, had been wearying. Most English Northumbrians ate two mouthfuls of differing cultures with their bread. Most insistent was the meat-filled diet of the pagan Danes, rife with ancient tales of long-ago gods and goddesses and bloody heroes. On their plates was also the saving bread and body offered by fervent Celtic Christianity, which, since the Viking depredations of the last century, had become an underground activity. The newer Catholic Christian ways which were replacing them were insistent; they were clamouring to become the only fodder consumed. The uptake in relic requirement and the popularity of pilgrimage had taken hold of the popular imagination. These were not the old Britonnic ways. So much had changed. Hilda, Abbess of Whitby, turned in her grave.

*Probably right over, and stayed like that, on her face,* Wulfstan thought. He had to admire, despite his despicable character, Wilfrid, who had opposed the strong-willed Hilda at the Synod of Whitby three hundred years before. He had been a reformer, like Dunstan was now, and achieved a great deal in bringing Britain into line with Rome, but only to a certain extent. Wilfrid had achieved sainthood;

Hilda had not. And after all the troubles with the north/south, English/Danish divide, then came the Norse, with their own outlook, thoroughly pagan and ruthless. The attempts at conversion had all to be done again. No wonder he needed a nap. Janus with his mere two faces had had it easy.

In dozing, Wulfstan could think the unsayable. Even to his wife he could not explain the tussle in his mind between loyalty to the crown, his Northumbrian identity and the need to placate or convert the newcomers, who were determined to rule. So often it had seemed that he was to choose between the lesser of two evils; the Wessex dynasty who had little understanding of the requirements of Northumbria and the Viking pirates from Ireland and the fresh, red-cheeked, energetic and ambitious newcomers from Norway via the Orkneys. Who was most likely to cut off your head, or your arm or to poke your eyes out? Would it be disgruntled southerners or the Norse who liked, by all accounts, to witness a slow execution? Balancing the factions, state and religious, was a fine art. Souls and gold weighed heavy on both sides of the scale. Which problem was the most acute at present? He tried to play the sides on a daily basis as the demands came, from the Norse, from Dunstan, from Northumbrians.

*Curse them all,* the devil on his shoulder said. *Try to find a common ground,* whispered the angel on his other shoulder. *Wilfrid, help me, please.*

Another voice suddenly surfaced in his mind. It was female. 'Wulfstan'.

'Who?' Wulfstan woke as a sunbeam, glancing off a copper vase, played on his face. His eyes half-opened. 'Who spoke?'

'Wulfstan, I am here. Hilda. Of Whitby.'

Wulfstan's jaw dropped. He shook. 'No, Hilda, you are dead. Don't trouble me, I beg you.'

'I must. You and your kind have forgotten how to be close to the land and sea. You have forgotten how to use your senses to hear music in the wind, to smell lime blossom in the air in summer, to bathe in rock pools amongst the sea creatures. You have forgotten how to dance, how to love, how to be free.'

Wulfstan recovered. Visions between sleep and wakefulness were not unknown to him, or to any churchman. It was only a matter of deciding, later, their validity or usefulness. 'Free, Hilda? We cannot be free; we are hedged around with rules, with laws, with requirements. You know that our lives in this modern age are restricted. We must obey the rules of a new set of fellows from the south; kings and priests send emissaries to tighten the belt around us. Northumbrians must sing a different tune in these days, dear Abbess; these are not the times of formerly, when the Northumbrians could make their own way in the world.'

'My monastery on the cliff-top requires rebuilding, Wulfstan. Men and women should live there again as they once did, in harmony worshipping our god, mindful of the natural world, praying for balance in creation.'

'Yours were simpler times. Your world bridged the old requirements of the Britons and Northumbrian English. You spoke a different language but the sea had not severed your connections; you had many things in common. Now I have to deal with Danes, English and Norse, with their different ambitions.'

'And Bamburgh does not help you?'

'You ask me a question; therefore, you are not spirit, or you would know the way things are with me.'

'I know.'

It was another female voice which had spoken, a much lower voice. It repeated.

'I know.'

Wulfstan had not had visitations by two voices at one time. Old Edith, the wooden knob atop the archbishop's seat at York minster, sometimes argued with him in a low tone, but this voice was not hers. 'Who are you?' This was an unfamiliar, powerful woman's voice. It was not unlike his wife's, guttural, comprehensible but veering from far off in sound to close at hand. There was a screech like a banshee in his ears. Wulfstan felt the force of centuries. He covered his ears. The screeching sound subsided. A heartbeat pounded. Was it his own or another's?

'My name is Cartimandua. Do not look at me. You will have heard of me, though your people have forgotten my battles to save this nation. Once Northumbria, as you call it, was owned and ruled by me. It was Brigantia, then.' The voice faded, waiting for a response. The ghost wanted, needed, to be recognised.

Wulfstan's mind raced. Was he asleep? Was he really being visited by ghosts of the long dead, by a queen who gave her nation away to the all-conquering Romans and handed over the British leader Caractacus? But he might have something in common with this queen of the raucous voice. She might have a message for him. He shut his eyes and waited.

Cartimandua seemed able to read his thoughts. Was she inside his head, or an external spirit, tormenting him or offering advice in the only way that she could? The searing threads of time danced and wavered before his eyes. She spoke again. 'Yes, I gave away my land to the mightier nation and saved my people from famine and destruction. Then, the rebellious south suffered from the ravages of its conquerors, but Brigantia flourished. Our partnership with Rome allowed us to live, to enjoy peace, to pay taxes, yes, but to grow our crops, to eat, to sleep, to bring up our children. You are being made to compromise, too.' The voice was certain of its choices made centuries before. It had no hint of regret.

Wulfstan had studied the effects of the Roman empire on his motherland. There were lessons to be learned from deep history, circumstances which repeated themselves. 'You sacrificed the resistance leader of Britain to the Romans and had him taken to Rome in chains and paraded there. Were you not ashamed to be a traitor to your own people?'

'Not my people. Southerners. They were seeking to take my land from me, to turn Brigantia into a client state. I did what I had to do and ensured that the north was free of southern interference until this day, but now you must rid Northumbria of two sets of foes who have besmirched the northern peoples. The British hide in the hills, a beleaguered and backward people, my people, still speaking my language. They hear me, but they are few. The Angles have taken their farms and brought their new faith into the land, separating the people from the earth. Their faith makes their minds value another holy land, but it is not here, amongst the green hills and the grey sea. I have learned to accept that the Saxon invaders have come to be the dominant tribes, but I cannot tolerate these new interlopers who grab and smash their way into our territory and with blood, and the threat of blood spilled, take with ease what it took centuries to build.'

'You mean the Danes, or the Norse?'

'They come from the same place. They are foreigners and pay no attention to the culture on which they squat.'

'My wife is Danish.'

'I have noticed. But you are Northumbrian. Your mother was British, one of my kind.'

'So, what do I do? You will know that I must meet with the king of the south soon, at Tanshelf.'

'And the foreigner, Anlaf, is to go with you. You have made a tricky bed to lie on, Wulfstan.' Cartimandua's voice screamed again. 'No compromise, no more!'

Wulfstan opened his eyes. Seeing the monster might make the voice go away. Standing erect on the other side of his room, by the lectern which he used for prayer and in front of the relic chest, was a tall woman, dark hair blowing in the unseen winds of past time, her mouth firmly closed, her garments a ripped shroud waving across her body. As Wulfstan looked at Cartimandua, her image dissolved. There was a stillness of the early summertime in the room. Light took the place of the dark past.

Still the low voice of the queen of Brigantia echoed in his mind. *'No compromise'*. What would Hilda want? Was it time to resist the requirements of the south, to try to make a last stand against the house of Wessex, which would not rest until everything was under its power?

At Tanshelf, with Anlaf, there was a chance to preserve some independence for the north. He would try to wave his sword, or rather, Anlaf would. But it had been tried before. Wessex would win out, again. Or would it?

Wulfstan feared the loss of unique northern history and culture; the foreigners, the Danes and Norse, were here to stay. They were the known devil. If Wessex were to fight them, Northumbria would be the battleground, his mixed-race people would suffer. And he would suffer, too, at the hands of Abbot Dunstan.

# Ladies in Waiting

'HE IS MORE likely to be in a director's role than that of a leading man.' Eadgifu could be open and frank with her old friend. She opened a door and ushered in her friend.

The two royal grandmothers, Eadgifu and Wynflaed, entered the room and sat on a window seat in a small sitting room in Winchester palace. The queen's room was a refuge in style from the masculine great hall; hangings and embroidered cushions softened its stone walls; woven patterns on curtains reminded of gardens, not wars. A ginger cat, one of two occupants of the room, lay asleep on one of the chairs. It opened an eye as the women began to speak.

'But your son Eadred has many fine qualities. He has overcome his disabilities and seems determined to make the most of the position he is in.' Wynflaed was naturally disposed to make the best of a situation. There were no other sons of Eadgifu who might have given the family a choice of king. Children and women would not do; even regency was considered more than a woman was capable of. But Half-king and Dunstan were significant props, props which had become pillars and buttresses in the last few months, if not the entire edifice. 'A trinity of leaders might do better than one person alone. Eadred will grow into his role.'

'There is comfort to be had in the characters of Half-king and the abbot,' Eadgifu did not like to mention Dunstan by name, 'and at Tanshelf they will be necessary in deciding the arrangements for the north. Edgar will be a witness to the discussions.'

'And Eadwig?'

'He is staying here.'

'Ah, pity.'

Eadgifu frowned. 'Not so. There are important things to

be learned here. Aethelwold is travelling from Cerne to be his temporary tutor and will take him to Glastonbury for a full year of instruction. He is behind Edgar in his reading.'

'But doesn't he dislike Aethelwold? I thought that you had agreed that he would have a secular teacher?'

'Likes and dislikes do not come into it. He is eight years old. I was betrothed at that age.'

'But then unbetrothed. Things change. The luck which brought you marriage to Edward may strike Eadwig at some stage, make him wake up to his responsibilities. Give him a little time.'

'There is no time. And miracles do not occur. I fear that he is not aetheling material.'

'Such a shame! And he the older boy. What will you do? There may be enmity, such a destructive emotion.'

The cat jumped off its chair, meowed to let the women know that it was passing and scratched at the door. Eadgifu stood up to let it out. The thoughts in her head sounded loud, as though the room was full of them.

'What are you thinking, Eadgifu? What can be done?' Wynflaed was as fond of her grandsons as Eadgifu, but she had her favourite, as had her compatriot grandmother. Had she chosen the wrong one? 'What will become of Eadwig?' She saw, suddenly, that the eight-year-old was being marked for failure. 'He is original…'

'Wessex does not require anything original. The kingdom has been constructed. It now needs steady hands.'

'And you think that Dunstan and Half-king are those steady hands. Yes, I see. But Eadgifu, is it your intention to allow Eadred to marry?'

'He says he would not wish to. He says everything he now does is for his nephews, that there will be no heirs of his own to challenge them. He regards himself as a caretaker.'

'But he has been anointed as a king. He may go on for many years as ruler.'

'The abbot and Half-king will make most of the decisions.

Eadred is not a fool, but you know, he is not well and not likely to live long. I just need him to last until one of the two boys comes of age.'

'Eight years into the future? What will England look like then? Eight years ago, Edmund came to the throne. Things were so hopeful, then. Now we are dowagers, mourning our children, you, your son, me, my daughter. Who know what even one year will bring.'

'We must hope for time, Wynflaed, enough to settle our frontiers and send the northern insurrection to Hades where it belongs.'

'Yes, what is happening? Are we in Wessex threatened?'

'Not yet. The Archbishop of York has been consorting with the Dublin Norse and Anlaf and now a new creature has emerged from the waves of Norway. A Viking called Eric has arrived to muddy the waters. It is Half-king's plan to set all three conspirators against each other. The Northumbrians themselves are in a muddle of indecision about where to look for leadership; one day they declare for Anlaf, the next for Eric. Wulfstan himself must be like a headless chicken, trying to decide which of the blood-thirsty Norse to claim as leader for his people. He will have a hard job persuading the Christians amongst them to accept either.' Eadgifu walked to a table and picked up an orange.

'So Eadred must assert his rights over the north, which were lost.'

'Yes, lost, but only recently. So much seems to depend on the character and strength of the personalities involved. Half-king thinks that he will be able to persuade Wulfstan, finally, to back Eadred as over-lord and to throw out the Norse upstarts. He will make promises to Wulfstan which he cannot refuse. That is the carrot.' Eadgifu proffered an orange to Wynflaed.

'And if he does refuse?'

'Then Wulfstan will suffer the consequences. You know about the sanctuary of Ripon? It protects the cathedral from secular interference and robbery as well as shielding Northumbrians from

Viking depredation. Even they will not cross the Ripon boundary. Wulfstan has a home inside the sanctuary gate, where he hopes to build his power-base. He thinks that St Wilfrid's monastery will be untouched, as it is within the walls. Abbot Dunstan has suggested that the walls of the sanctuary could be demolished and the right of sanctuary be dissolved. That is the stick.'

'And so Edgar will witness the discussions at Tanshelf. He is so young, but I suppose he will soak up the skills of persuasion that must be used by aethelings if they are to become successful leaders. I wonder if Eadwig will have the benefit of this kind of learning, too? Or is he really to remain in the south, where the problems are not as great?' Wynflaed thoughtfully peeled her orange and swallowed a morsel. 'This is bitter.'

'Eadwig stays here to finish his education. His learning is coming to an end. He prefers to be in the field with his friends, fighting. Perhaps the time has come to let him have his head. In a few years more, he will be married.'

Wynflaed choked. 'Dear me, married! But surely, Eadgifu, that will create more difficulty, won't it? Or perhaps you have plans which will allow an easy choice between the lads and any family they may have?'

Eadgifu did not smile. She did not nod. She had plans. Her favourite for the throne had been decided upon.

# Eadred travels North

GALES BLEW, RAIN threatened. Trees leaned, as did the travellers who were witnesses to the history which was about to be made.

The northern border town of Tanshelf was less than inviting as a place to camp; it consisted of low buildings of wood, shacks, more like, comparing badly with the stone structures which housed a king and sheltered his foreign dignitaries and guests in Wessex, but it would do as a frontier meeting-place between Mercia and Northumbria. It was positioned on the south side of the river Aire which tumbled down to the mighty Humber mouth, the natural route inland of so many Danish and Norse immigrant arrivals. This was Mercia's northern frontier. The Humber had gobbled the newcomers greedily, filling itself and spreading its gorge to the lands on either side. Scandinavian languages and accents were the noises most made by the relentless human tide; the culture of the Britons, their language and songs, preserved until recently, was in retreat. They cowered and resentfully clung on in the deepest valleys and tops of western dales.

A man emerged from a latrine shed, adjusting a heavy robe over his shoulders. Archbishop Wulfstan was a man, as other men; his needs were the same.

'There is the married monk.' Dunstan pointed Wulfstan out to Eadred and Edgar.

'He does not have horns, or does he?' Edgar carefully observed the despised and disgraced archbishop.

'No horns, Edgar, but see his burning ears.' Dunstan barely recognised the ageing archbishop. It was many years since he had regularly attended the court of Athelstan. 'He must have worried himself into old age. Beware of fretting and grudge, Edgar. It is better to act decisively and to perhaps regret than to dither and allow others to determine outcomes.' Dunstan enjoyed bestowing advice to the aetheling. Like the Humber, Edgar swallowed whatever was put before him; none of it was wasted. It was a policy of Dunstan's to limit access to the boy. Half-king was trustworthy; and his wife. Who it was who held and pulled the strings of the kingdom was becoming clear.

'And here comes the other one.' Eadred pushed Edgar behind him and into Half-king's protection. Edgar took the hand which Half-king held out. Half-king's sons, Aethelwald and Aethelwine, stood on either side of Half-king and Edgar, like young bookends. *Stand up straight,* had been the chief injunction of their lives. Their father, the army commander of east Anglian forces, hardened by years of dealing with Danes in his earldom, knew the effect of brazen confidence. It was the first requirement of his soldiers. The second was to fear God.

Anlaf, 'the other one,' strode towards the Saxon group, being joined by Wulfstan, limping as he came. Edgar tried to hide behind Half-king, but he held him firmly. Dunstan and Eadred stood firm. Eadred resisted an urge to touch his stomach. Anlaf was impressively large in stature.

Dunstan spoke first. 'I see that you are alone, as instructed. I take it that there are no archers in the woods?'

Anlaf replied, after looking at Wulfstan. 'We are honourable men. I take it that I am addressing the Abbot of Glastonbury? A monastery with fine buildings, I am told.'

'And like to be better. The investments have been made. It has not been ravaged lately.' Dunstan could afford some irony.

'Has Glastonbury ever been ravaged, Uncle Athelstan?' Edgar was new to the world. His history lessons were not yet complete.

Half-king whispered in response. 'No. The English thought at first to do so, but that was many years ago, before we had learned about Christ. Dunstan is trying to discomfit the Norseman, to embarrass him. It is a useful ploy.' Half-king winced. He had seen Anlaf's reception of his comment.

'You will be pleased to know that we barbaric heathens no longer destroy your Christian citadels or kill your monks, or babies, either. You will also be aware that I have been willingly showered with your holy water. It has driven out the many devils which beset me, so I am told.' Anlaf widened his eyes and stared at Dunstan. 'I will speak with the king, alone.'

Eadred shuffled forward. He was not afraid, but his body let him down on these occasions. If only he had been taller, his disabilities would not have disadvantaged him as much. But he had youth and his mind and that might be enough to challenge this Norse interloper. 'I will speak with my archbishop, and only him.'

Wulfstan murmured something in Anlaf's ear. The Norseman retreated one step. Wulfstan moved forward as did Eadred. The limping man and the short man with weak feet moved together, their cloaks becoming intermingled. They were one shape of heavy, dark cloth.

'So, we meet at last, Archbishop. I see that it is true that you have a bad leg. Your excuse for travel to my court can be forgiven. I myself have difficulty in travelling so far. You do well to cross your bridge into my territory.'

'Northumbria is yours, but I see your difficulty. This bridge,' Wulfstan indicated the wooden structure behind him which had been used by invaders, conquerors and tradespersons for centuries, 'has seen some events of historic note. This is one. I may retreat across it and defend it if necessary. But against what? Northumbria is yours. Anlaf will bow to you. But you have had the courage to meet us here. I do not regret my past actions which have all been to preserve Northumbria against the Norse for your united kingdom. You must see that my task here has been next to impossible.'

Dunstan leaned forward to try to hear the conversation. He could only grasp a few words. The wind took away the words of his king and the archbishop. 'Nonna, you may be needed. Go forward and ask if you may be of assistance.' An impartial clerk might be allowed to get close enough to record the intents of the chief actors of the drama.

Nonna, his eyes and ears attuned to the requirements of recording Saxon events and aware of his king's limitations, physical and mental, moved towards the king and archbishop, coughing as he went. It would not do to surprise the men who were evidently deep in conversation, but Dunstan was right; these matters required noting. Nonna stood a yard away from the men, downwind. He could hear most of what was being said. Perhaps the preambles were over and the heart of the matter was under discussion.

Eadred and Wulfstan both looked briefly at Nonna, who stood with his arms by his side, motionless, but leaning slightly backwards as the wind gusted. His shoulder-length hair covered his face. He was as unobtrusively invisible as it was possible to be under the circumstances. He was like a small tree, bending slightly in the movement of air. They continued their confidential talk, aware that outcomes, at least, would be recorded by the clever clerk's memory and later written down. So be it. This was the age of such things. Wulfstan had his clerks, too. The management of Northumbria could not do without them, the growth of trade and coinage had grown in recent years. The Vikings had brought chaos initially, but riches as well, which required counting, storing and guarding.

'So, you agree, do you, Wulfstan?' Eadred was aware that the archbishop was well known to Nonna. The clerk had been present at the inauguration in Wessex by Athelstan of the new archbishop of the north, his right-hand man in the newly-Danish lands. Nonna had taken notes at the granting of the Sanctuary of Ripon, too. Nonna had been present, as a silent tree, or as a cat beneath tables, or as a child sitting, reading in a dark corner, or as a lily pond, listening to the acts of moment in the reigns of so many kings. He heard the assent, saw the decisive shake of hands, saw Anlaf, standing apart near the entrance to the bridge with its toll house, smile.

# Glastonbury Abbey, January 948

THE ABBOT OF Glastonbury, in his element and within earshot of his stained-glass workhouse, strolled with his king across lawns by the scaffolded church of St Mary. A centuries-old graveyard of monkish bodies and kings to their right, marked by wooden and stone headstones, punctuated the green sward. Pigeons sat on the wooden posts, defecating onto their owners' carved names. Moss and ivy had not yet begun to creep onto the upright stone slabs; but it would.

'I have in mind to employ ten gardeners in our enclosure.'

'How many do you have now?' Eadred appreciated talk of structures and gardening. He would have chosen, if he could have, to work in a monastery garden for all his pain-racked days. That, or to sail on a trading barge along the sun-filled shores of the southern coast of his country. But it was not to be. A day's visit to Glastonbury Abbey while staying for a hunting party's sojourn at Cheddar palace would have to suffice.

'Three slaves, near the end of their usefulness. Not enough. We can afford more.'

'You know best what the abbey, and the state, can afford. Talking of which, do you have the treasure here at the moment? And the relics?

'All is in safe keeping. I will show you the treasury. Come this way.' Dunstan felt for his abbey keys. *Different pouches for different jobs; things were becoming complicated.* He would be staying at Glastonbury for some weeks, to oversee the works at the church; there were no particular requirements for him at Cheddar or Winchester, now that the northern affair had been settled. The pouches of office, containing different keys to the haligdoms of

Wessex, hung on hooks in the hall of Winchester Palace, each marked with his own, Dunstan's name and guarded by three armed men. The Abbot of Glastonbury had become a title to be respected, to be feared. Laws regarding theft had been tightened, at his suggestion; a convicted thief could expect to lose a little finger, a whole hand or foot and in some cases to be scalped. The growing treasury of the king and others needed continual protection; physical marks of rejection of the Christian code of commandments were needed to deter. If a man who had been tried and convicted of theft had his life spared, he could be grateful. The courts were not unwilling to be magnanimous. Dunstan's thoughts ran on.

*But some thieves are not recognised by others.*

A voice drifted through the winter mist from the direction of the graveyard. There was no one there. Ah, yes, a single gardener, bent over, hacking at the greenery against a hedge, may have uttered something. Who was he? He was too far away to tell. A layman, probably, employed by the abbey manager. No-one in particular. Dunstan dismissed the voice. No monk or lay-brother would have dared to speak within his hearing. Was he becoming too sensitive to a critical voice? Perhaps he had too little sleep last night.

The abbot and king wandered on into the block of outbuildings which were awaiting restoration. A single stone-built barn with a solid roof and stout wooden doors lay straight ahead, marked out by a guard. He bowed as the men approached.

'We wish to enter. Stand aside.' Dunstan had his key for the heavy padlock already pointing forward in his hand. He removed it and swung back the doors, closing them behind. The January gloom of the barn was enlightened a little by high, cross-shaped windows. After a short time of adjustment, the men could see. They crossed the well-swept floor to examine the trunks and chests piled at the far end. Individual items, reliquaries which were too large or heavy to be encased, sat on top of trestle tables.

'Is St Wilfrid's foot here?' Eadred had a particular reason to ask, his own feet being deemed by many to be less than perfect conveyors of the human body. A touch, or a prayer, might be of some benefit.

'Yes, My Lord, awaiting a new casket. Over here, my lord.' Dunstan walked to a low table. The tooled leather relic casing of a foot sat on its own with two unlit candles on either side. It was the latest in the collection of treasures to be hoarded by Wessex and so given special status in the royal haligdom.

*Ah, it is the left foot. Mine, also;* Eadred muttered to himself, then recovered. 'Are all the Wessex relics now collected here, Abbot?'

'Nearly all, my lord. The Exeter collection of Athelstan, as you may know, has been taken there and your brother's will has added to them. But what remains is still the finest collection of relics, marking the accession of Christian saints throughout this land and Europe. Here you can witness the glorious rise of Christianity. The holiness in this barn surpasses the collections of all others.'

'But we do not have a relic of St Cuthbert.'

'Of St Cuthbert, no. He is the only saint of worth who is missing.'

'And of whom I have most need. Oswald and Wilfrid, they are of value, but the northerners may still wriggle off their promises and commitment, if we do not have at least a part of the body of the holy Northman Cuthbert.' Eadred had seen the smile on the face of Anlaf, at Tanshelf. It was unmistakeable. There was little intention to honour an agreement. Archbishop Wulfstan could make promises, but he had offered nothing to guarantee his word.

Dunstan struck a tinder and lit the candles beside the portion of Wilfrid. The tooled reliquary blazed golden and shining, but repair was obviously needed. There were worn parts and stitches missing. The leather was cracking. Inside, the foot would be as good as new, its holy nature preserving it for ever, to be re-joined on the day of judgement to the leg of its former owner, but its man-made outer covering, if the object was to be used for public perusal or as a touch relic, was in need of restoration.

'Abbot, I would like to see the foot, to touch it.'

'Now, my lord?'

'Now.'

'Shall I order a reliquary priest to remove it?'

'I shall do it myself. I see the strapping which encases the leather at the back. I will not damage the reliquary further and as it already needs repair...'

Dunstan hesitated. The Wessex treasure was his responsibility and there was a growing sense of ownership, if not by himself but by the Church who would inevitably share in the wealth being accumulated by access to the relic. He looked sideways at Eadred, who was already removing his own shoes.

'Do you wish me to leave you, My Lord?'

'What? No, Dunstan, that will not be necessary. We both have investment here. But if you will, pray for me and for Wilfrid while I address the saint.' Eadred began to unstrap the outer covering of the relic. He eased it apart with his long-nailed fingers, murmuring prayers as he did so. Dunstan sank to his knees on the hard clay floor, clutched the cross at his breast and shut his eyes in prayer.

Inside the leather cover was a wooden structure containing the foot. As the leather was removed and carefully placed on a low table, there was a small gassy emission which mingled the aromas of tannin and fetid flesh.

*Behold, the left foot of the saint.* Eadred muttered prayers as he saw the uncorrupted white member, veins passing along the top of the foot, blue and lively as though still living and still passing the blood of its owner to his heart. He touched the cold flesh with his hand, his own pink skin throbbing with desire, the desire of the ill to be whole, to be at one with the holy and uncorrupted. It was not idolatry which he felt; the foot and the saint were not what he worshipped; it was the idea. He was not sure what the idea was, but knew it would have an effect. Three hundred years of incorruption; this was what marked out the holy from the ordinary man. Eadred raised his left foot, and then his right, to brush the foot of the saint. Stride for stride, the saint's foot was much smaller than his own. Eadred walked, in his mind's eye, alongside the great man. He saw the open wastes of the north, saw the heights of the Yorkshire Wolds and dales which harboured his enemies and the lands beyond, where Wilfrid had been abbot and held sway. Hand in hand with Wilfrid, he strode along the road between the east coast and the west, seeking out the highest point, a wild place, which he knew was to figure in his future; how, he did not know.

Eadred lowered his foot to the clay floor. Dustan stood up. The sanctified dreams of both faded. Eadred wrapped the foot in its outer covering and blew out the candles. He crossed himself and recovered his shoes.

'My Lord, what did you see?'

'I saw what you saw the other night, Dunstan, a lonely, windswept place high on the hills, green and brown heather, emptiness. I saw a man there, his horse beside him, sagging to the earth, a blade in his heart. Who is this man?'

'I saw no man, My Lord, only the heath. Wilfrid has shown you that this scene is in the north. Stainmore is the name, of the man or place, which I heard an angel say.'

'The place I saw may be called Stainmore and it has some significance. I have heard of it. Find out what you can about it.'

Stainmore. A place stained, with what?

With blood, but whose?

# Cheddar Palace, the next day.

THE BOY, EADWIG, and Eadred his uncle prepared in the king's room for the hunt. Leather jerkins and linen shirts and trews cross-strapped took time to assemble and to put on correctly; the leather buckles of the outer layer of protection and the heavy belt carrying both dagger and sword took effort to arrange. The young prince was going on his first boar hunt in the gorge. He was excited.

'When I am king, I will do this all day, every day.' Eadwig tussled with his strapping. Hersfig came to his assistance. 'Leave me alone, Hersfig, I can do it.'

'When you are king, IF you are king, you will have other duties as well as pleasure, nephew.' Eadred enjoyed seeing enthusiasm on the face of the eight-year-old, but felt sadness for him, for the disillusion which would inevitably come. How could a king feel solace for the disappointments which he must endure, for the rearrangement of his dreams as he grew into the awareness of his responsibilities? The saints, of course, the holy ones, the relics which were now housed at Glastonbury, would assist. He must take the boy there. 'We will go to view the treasury tomorrow'. He was feeling positive about his legs and feet after the visit to his relics. He was still mesmerised by the thought of the lonely northern moor and the dying man who had appeared to him. He was wondering whether his wish for the nation to have a relic of Cuthbert was not more important than his personal hopes for strength in his own limbs as bestowed by Wilfrid's foot. Indeed, in the light of day and after a good night's sleep, his personal wishes for his health paled by comparison. Wilfrid's vital relic had been attained. Only Cuthbert was missing from the Wessex collection. Cuthbert was the saint he, as king, needed, to see, to touch. 'We have St Wilfrid's left foot, you know, kept safe in the treasury.'

'St Wilfrid? Isn't that the relic that Grandmother has been talking about? She says that the head of Radegund and the foot of Wilfrid will do much to protect us from our enemies. But what about our friends? Do we not need protecting from some of them, too?' Eadwig gave up trying to strap his trews and allowed Hersfig, who had been hovering, to finish the tying. 'Do I have to see Dunstan if we go to Glastonbury?'

'He has the key to the haligdom, so, yes.'

'Uncle, how is it that there are so many body parts of holy people in our barns?'

'They are all at Glastonbury.'

'All the moveable ones, yes, I know. Does Dunstan have the only key?'

'Yes, for now.'

'And the barn at Glastonbury holds all the treasure as well?'

'Yes, it is heavily guarded.'

'There is something which I asked Grandmother which she could not answer.'

'There is another question coming. Go on, Eadwig.'

'I asked her, why it is, when we believe that on the day of resurrection, we shall all stand entire to be judged, that the most holy men and women of history have been dismembered and distributed, stolen or sold to so many places in our land? What happens to them on the day of judgement and why were so many carved up into little tiny pieces like a jigsaw?'

'You should have an audience with the Pope. He could answer all of your questions. Perhaps I should send you with the next chosen Archbishop of Canterbury when he goes to Rome to collect his palium. Then you can ask him as much as you desire.'

'To Rome! Like Great-grandfather Alfred?'

'Yes, like him, and at your age, too. I am sure that many questions which he had were sorted with the pope of his day. Perhaps you should go as soon as we are able to secure you a safe passage.'

Eadred began to see a way forward for the headstrong prince. His enquiries about church doctrine were endless, and not necessarily supportive of the ideals and order which the church propounded. He might learn much and come to terms with the ideas which must be accommodated by the prince, if he were to encounter someone mightier than himself as king.

Eadwig put on a hunting cap. 'But not with Dunstan, Uncle? I could not bear to journey to Rome with him.'

Eadred waved a finger. 'You have allowed a misconception of your tutor to grow, Eadwig. He is a worthy man, an excellent priest with much foresight. You would do well to accept him.'

'Grandmother keeps telling me that, too. But I do not like him.'

'He is your teacher. Often teachers are disliked, because they must inform us while encouraging and controlling. You do not like to be controlled, that is understandable, but later on, you will appreciate Dunstan's knowledge and wisdom.'

'I don't like Aethelwold, either.'

'I fear no teacher would be your equal in the strength of feeling which you display, Eadwig. You must learn to accept knowledge and wisdom from those who are older than you, who have experience of life.'

'I listen to you, Uncle, and I would have listened to my father, or mother. But not Dunstan. He makes my blood boil.'

Eadred sighed. 'Well, I am ready for the hunt and I see you have chosen your cap.' He put on a feathered huntsman's cap. 'You asked me a question before I sent you off to Rome in my mind. Ah, yes, saints' parts. Perhaps I can answer this question without the need for a long trip to Rome. Long ago I wondered the same. I remember now, I asked Archbishop Oda what he thought of this matter of the body arising on the day of judgment, and also what became of saints. As I recall, he said there was no difficulty for the holiest of flesh; each head, eye, hand or foot, each hair, limb or heart contains the entire grace. The parts will be joined on that fateful day; the saints will be whole again. So said, apparently, a Greek theologian, Theodoretus, and he should know. He was a fifth-century bishop. Are you satisfied?'

'Well, but if all the parts of a saint retain the grace of the entire person, won't that make the unified saint rather overburdened with grace?'

'That's enough for now. The boar awaits.'

# Frome Palace, May 948

E ADRED WAS IN 'position one'. That was what Bica, his manservant and fool, called it. He was in a comfortable chair, seated
and backed with goose-feather cushions, and accompanied by a stool
on which another thick embroidered cushion and the king's aching
leg were resting. It was a bad day, bad for Eadred and bad for those in
attendance on him. The sun was out, the hunt in Selwood had gone
off without its king to lead it and the cure obtained by the touch of
St Wilfrid's foot had not been sustained. It was clear that something
else was needed.

Bad temper and grumbling had surfaced in the young king; it
was unbearable to have to stay at the palace, even in the luxurious
surroundings which he enjoyed at Frome. A human, whoever he
was, still had to get up and go to the latrine occasionally; only he
could do that for himself. Hersfig attended him like a persistent fly
in the background, bringing warm damp cloths for the leg and hot
drinks with 'nourishment' in them, honeyed vegetables and meat
broth in alternate visits. The cloths did not do more than soothe and
the drinks necessitated more trips to the latrine. Hersfig's nursing
abilities were not good; despite his efforts, he served to remind
Eadred that he was not a well man. There was little to smile about,
for Eadred. The rack of shoes and hats on the wall opposite his couch
were an added reproach to a usually well-shod, well-turned out king.

Even Bica was dismayed by the downward spiral of his master's
mood. This miserable creature, this so-called king, was wrapped up
in woollen blankets, his head peeping out from a silk velvet collar.
Eadred was his meal-ticket, gloomily forecasting his own demise in
the near future. *He's standing by his own grave, waiting to fall into it*
was how he described Eadred to Hersfig, when they were alone, *'and*

*he rather fancies the idea to happen sooner, rather than later.'* The pall of despair filled the chamber where the monks of the hospital had earlier tried their best both to relieve Eadred of physical pain and to lift his mood. It spread its pale tentacles through the hall, the stables, empty now of the great hunting horses and most of the companions of the bedchamber and court. The grey miasma of gloom crept out into the courtyard and kitchens, into the schoolroom and into the ladies' room, where a few matrons were repairing sheets. Creativity was at a low ebb; seamstresses and embroiderers increasingly removed themselves to the popular palace of Winchester and to the Nunnaminster, where the nuns were well-fed and cheerful. Wilton and Shaftesbury Abbeys, too, were the resort of the hopeful and optimistic. The courtiers of a similar age to Eadred, who were staying for a two-day witan visit to Selwood and to sign into being some land laws, were off in the depths of the oak wood, celebrating their successful chase of the hart and rejoicing that there was some respite from the requirement to listen to the verbose king's chancellor, Dunstan, and lift pens to mark their names on deeds of transfer. The pen felt heavier than a sword, to some, though it was said to be mightier.

'There will be venison tonight at the feast, at least, My Lord.'

Bica had recently been appointed to a new position in the private entourage of the king, much to Queen Eadgifu's annoyance. The Keeper of the King's Secrets, unlikely to attract anything other than scorn from the more distant members of the intimate circle of the king, some of whom had been placed in that position by Dunstan, was highly favoured by Eadred. He was someone who was less well-liked than himself. Attempts to overcome the revulsion of the more physically active members of the elite, young men and women who revelled in their youth and strength, by giving gifts and wan smiles, had failed. Two years into his caretaker reign, Eadred was in danger of being rejected as king.

How to cheer up a young man in pain and beset by gloom was Bica's chief concern. The happier the king, the more generous he would be. On the other hand, Eadred paid handsomely, when he felt less well, for anyone or anything which could claim to offer pain relief, however temporary. Bica had provided a multiplicity of healing potions and travelling doctors, who, it had become apparent, were more mouth than knowledge or cure. Each claimed to have a magical arrangement of medicine which could provide comfort and, after a day or two of relief provided in the main by pleasant words or a soothing hand passed over the brow, retreated to the path to other manors and great houses to sell their wares to others with pains in the back, pains in the head, pains in the heart.

Nothing worked. Prayer assisted. The Abbot of Glastonbury, becoming closer to Eadred as the months wore on, created extravagant services and prayers to distract him. During prayer and in consultation with an important relic, part of his treasure, Eadred could feel support, could forget his pains and growing discomfort with the responsibilities of leading a kingdom, which became more complicated with every passing day. The nobles resisted taxation, they howled at the idea of changing the time-honoured way of appointing abbots and bishops which had involved their relatives and improved their land-holdings; they complained of the necessity to read and even more of the requirement, increasingly apparent in court circles, to write. The Church demanded order, which the written word provided, and the cream of the results of taxation, that which did not go towards defending the land. It was nearly impossible to reconcile the opposing interests of Church and state and there was growing unrest. Without the nobles' backing, Eadred could be deposed. Without Church backing, he was in danger of the clergy's suspected ambition to make his mother regent, and one of his nephews king. Might they favour Eadwig, his adopted son, or Edgar? Could they insist on the division of the nation into north and south, would the nobles, or perhaps the Church, threaten to take England backwards, to have it split into Mercia/Northumbria and Wessex once again?

Eadred groaned. Even with Half-king's advice, who was always ready, whatever the expense, to send troops into full-scale war, he could not commit to a course of action. Thankfully, the future was decided for him by circumstances, as they often are when indecision causes inability to act.

There was a knock at the door. A guard opened it and stepped into the room.

'I said there was to be no interruption. I am busy.' Eadred sat up. The cloths and coverlets fell away.

The guard cast his eyes around the room. It was momentary, but the look was noticeable. This was a new kind of busy.

'Well, what is it?'

'My Lord, Lord Dunstan is outside, wishing to speak with you on urgent business.'

The damage had been done; Eadred had been seen in his worst state.

'Show him in, no, wait a moment.' Eadred shouted to Hersfig and Bica to clear the room of debris and to smarten the bed. He would not have time to dress; Dunstan would have to see him in his undergarments. He reached for a dressing-gown and threw it around his shoulders as Bica and Hersfig, having taken platters and mugs from the table, retreated into the corridor leading to the kitchens. 'And stay out of sight. Bica, you may wait behind the door.'

By the time the abbot entered the room, its mood had lightened. Eadred appeared alert, though his hair was dishevelled. Some order had been restored. Eadred pushed a glass bottle behind him as he leaned forward from the edge of the bed. Its heavy curtain swung across as he released its tie. The battleground of many sleepless nights was obscured.

'You wanted to see me, Abbot?'

Dunstan bowed slightly. He was a man on a mission with no time to spare. 'My Lord,' he noticed the top of the sack bottle peeping though a gap in the curtains, 'there have been reports of violence in the north. Eric Bloodaxe, as I understand he is known, and Archbishop Wulfstan are gathering men and arms and are threatening to annex Northumbria. Eric has declared himself king in

York, with Wulfstan's blessing, it seems.'

'Eric? Not Anlaf?'

'It seems that there has been some disagreement between the Norse leaders. Anlaf has returned to Dublin. Eric now presides in your city of York and commands the whole of Northumbria, with the willing support of the people. The sanctuary of Ripon has become a training ground for a mixed bag of mercenaries.'

'It seems that the mongrel race, the Danes, the Saxons, the Britons, the Welsh of Cumbria and the interlopers from Norway have set up a new flag of independence. It was not unexpected.' Eadred stood up. A last cloth fell away from his leg and sank, wet, to the floor.

'I am pleased to see your lordship looking so well, and so animated,' Dunstan knew what was needed at this time; he and Half-king had already consulted on the latest news. Action needed only to be approved.

'I have been better, but now I shall be well. Bring Half-king to me. We must make plans.

Sometimes an event drives action in response. Eadred, the caretaker king, began to see things afresh. War makes leaders, or destroys them. There was little to lose.

# Ripon, July 948

THE AIR OUTSIDE the monastery of Ripon was hot; inside the stone walls humidity was lower and in the cloister with its glass windows and green sward a man might feel he was in a blessed environment.

Archbishop Wulfstan felt less than blessed. He sat, sweating, on a low chair, his hands bound in front of him. At least Eric had got away. He would be back, no doubt.

'Tell us where he has gone.' Half-king was becoming frustrated. He had asked the question many times and each time the archbishop had declined to answer. There is only so much a fyrd commander can do to an archbishop of the realm to force him to reveal useful information.

Dunstan stepped forward from the back of the room. 'We cannot feel assured of your loyalty while the hideous personage of evil in the form of Eric Bloodaxe is at large. You have a reputation, My Lord. And it is not helpful to my king.'

'Of England.' Eadred limped towards the archbishop and leaned against the chair's back. If it was not required that the interrogators should stand and the interviewee be seated, he would have requested that he should have the chair. The room was bare of other furniture. 'It is England which you have threatened by your friendship with the upstart of Norway. Your position is now irredeemable. You must relinquish your post. Are you not ashamed?'

Still Wulfstan said nothing. His bulk looked uncomfortable on the chair, but his will remained defiant.

'Should I apply a little more than words, My Lord?' Half-king put a hand on the knife at his belt. 'Blindings have been known to induce the tongue to wag.'

'No, no, not for now.' Dunstan could put himself in the archbishop's place. This was a man of God that Half-king was proposing to wound. Dunstan himself had ambitions. He would not like to think that such a person could be subject to military justice meted out summarily, and in a holy place such as this, the monastery of St Wilfrid. Canterbury itself might then not be sanctuary to prelates of such aged dignity. And Wulfstan was certainly looking aged.

Archbishop Wulfstan shifted on his seat. He felt that his life was forfeit, but he had escaped retribution before. His days of escaping on horseback from Leicester and from Edmund's wrath were, however, over. Silence was perhaps his only choice. He called on Old Edith and Wilfrid for advice and help. Beneath his robes, a slither of the true cross and a finger of the saint himself moved on their fine chain as he leaned forward to wretch.

'Bring a bucket.' Dunstan could feel for the prelate.

Half-king looked around for a slave or monk to fulfil the duty. There was no-one else in the room besides the four men. 'Too late.'

Wulfstan emptied the contents of his last undigested meal onto the floor. The stench was revolting in the heat. Flies immediately found the vomit.

'Leave him be. We will discuss this outside. Perhaps his time incarcerated with his own production will cause his tongue to loosen. If not, there may be other ways of dealing with him.'

Eadred cast a look of disgust at the archbishop. This is how a man who is robbed of dignity looks; just like others who have been found out and incarcerated. Yet there was something defiant about Wulfstan, something which he, Eadred, wished to possess. Was it experience? Was it wisdom? A silent man may not appear to be wise, and yet Wulfstan had something of that about him. Great intelligence? Cunning? It was clear that Wulfstan, at birth, had been given skills which ordinary mortals could not hope to obtain by payment or example. Growing up, Eadred had met him often at Athelstan's court, where he had been a popular figure, but in the years since, as Wulfstan had avoided coming to court, the man had changed. He had had to. In his defence, Eadred thought, he has had even more difficult a role than myself or Edmund in Wessex.

Half-king, Dunstan and Eadred retreated into the cloisters. A guard locked the Archbishop of York, still folded double over his vomit, in his cell.

In the quiet cool of the cloister the three men discussed the Affair of the North, as Eric Bloodaxe and Wulfstan's attempt to take over the part of England north of the Humber had come to be known. It was audacious. It was a nearly-successful challenge to Wessex and to the south of England, to Athelstan, Edward and Alfred's dream of England. Had he succeeded, the new king of York would have made the whole of England bow to the lands of ice and fire. York would have turned the nation to face north. Winchester would have become a haven of Norse and Danish merchants, with foreign voices speaking from its hallowed throne.

'It is the sanctuary which must go.' Half-king looked at Dunstan. Would he agree? 'It has given too much security to the would-be kings of York. Anlaf and Eric have been hosted here by our friend who now pukes his finest meal, his finest wine. It should go.'

'The sanctuary of Ripon? It would rip the heart out of the so-called kingdom of York.' Dunstan might have need of its sanctuary himself in time. There was evidently no security in the title of archbishop alone. What if the sanctuary of Canterbury, of any other bishop's sanctuary or that of minster churches or abbeys or monasteries could be revoked by a soldier's whim, or a king's?

'Exactly. We must desanctify this place, so that it does not become a refuge for criminals in future.' Half-king waited for Eadred to agree.

Eadred looked at both the other men. His role was to straddle and balance the needs of the Church and secular state. Dunstan nodded. Ripon was far away from Winchester, Canterbury or Glastonbury. Eadred needed to be clear. 'Criminals? You mean the Norse? Only them?'

The abbot had made up his mind. 'Them as well as others who have defected to their ideology. Potential heathens. Recidivists.' Dunstan was in no doubt. The loop was closing. 'But Wulfstan may have finally learned his lesson.'

'You are not thinking of freeing this viper?' Half-king's whisper exploded.

'Then do that. Lord Abbot, I agree that the archbishop is our best hope to calm these pirates. But desanctify Ripon. Remove the reliquary containing St Wilfrid. I will take it south with me. Remove any relics which the archbishop is concealing about his person. I will have them, too. He will have no help from the saints, if it can be prevented. Take away his hope. Let him rot in this cell, in this constructed nation of his own making.' There would be other decisions to be made in time, but Eadred felt man enough to decide on destruction of a holy place. Would he be cast into hell as a result? Eadred now became aware of the experiences of great responsibility. What had Athelstan and Edmund been through? Was it similar to this? Sleepless nights would ensue, but that would be nothing new.

At last, there was someone who was in a worse state than he, Eadred thought. It was ignoble, but the desire to avenge his physical ailments on another creature was strong. 'Burn the monastery, too. As for York itself, the trade of the city should continue. I will appoint a new archbishop, one from the south, who will oversee the business of unifying the kingdom. There will never be a Northumbrian-born archbishop of York again.'

Dunstan looked at Half-king. This was a decisive Eadred, one they were not used to, but one which both felt they could deal with. The destruction of a monastery, any centre which acted as a mission for the outreach of Christianity, particularly among the heathen Norse, would be a step backward, Dunstan felt, but the associations of Ripon monastery with the pirates of the north, the terrorists, was too much to fail to expunge. The rats' nest would have to go up in flames. Half-king evidently agreed.

'I will give the order to set the monastery afire. The prisoners will be taken south to gaols in Leicester where they may rot. '

'Where is Edgar?'

They found the Child-who-might-be-king, as the troops were beginning to call him, sunning himself, sitting on the back of a cart with a guard, watching the parade of soldiers as they marched and sang round and round the mile-wide sanctuary of Ripon, a bunch of Norse prisoners, distinctive by their clothing and hairstyles, shuffling, dejected, along with them.

'My Lord.' Dunstan and Eadred stood by the cart, shading their eyes. The prisoner group passed them by. Northumbrian peasants and burghers of the town crowded around the gates, observing the passing of their former, temporary masters.

'They don't know whether they are coming or going, whether to cheer or wail, their masters have been supplanted so many times.' Dunstan hated chaos, loved to see resolution.

'Edgar, are you hungry?' Eadred was and could think only, after his exhausting decision, of the pleasure and comfort of food. 'I think the fun is over. We must begin to think of returning south.'

'Uncle. Abbot. Yes.' Edgar jumped off the cart. He had seen the army march by a number of times. He was beginning to recognise the chief commanders of his uncle's forces. Names were being put to faces. 'What has happened to the archbishop? Have you gouged out his eyes?'

'He retains his eyes, for now.' Eadred winced. His brother Athelstan had survived an attempt to blind him and prevent his accession to the throne many years before. The loss of eyes was a certain way of ensuring that a man could not reach his potential, or be used as a pawn in king-making. A man's life was spared, at least. He could have his uses elsewhere, in a monastery, for instance. The monasteries had many such men in their kitchens and gardens, criminals, mostly, but some were the unfortunate sons of aspiring thanes.

Edgar would learn, in time, of the requirements of kingship and self-protection. Meanwhile, the monastery kitchen, while it still existed, was producing bread. The smell of loaves baking became apparent as a sudden gust of wind brought dried leaves from an unswept corner and the signal, better than a bell, for the midday meal. After the meal, there would be preparations of a different kind. The visit to Ripon had been effective. Eadred was now secure in his position as king in Northumbria as well as everywhere else south of the Humber. The threat of Eric Bloodaxe had been removed. Perhaps Eric had been killed; he looked exactly like all the other infidel Norse, bearded, hirsute, tattooed, insolent. Perhaps his body, like the others, lay outside the sanctuary rotting in the midday heat. Perhaps he had escaped. Time would tell. What was clear, to Eadred, Half-king and Dunstan and now to the Child-who-might-be-king, was that Archbishop Wulfstan was in no position to bring about a further insurrection. He had learned his lesson.

Or had he.

# On the road south from Ripon

THE HEAVENS HAD opened; the glaring heat of July had come to a sudden end with a storm. The Wessex army, retreating from their successful foray to York and Ripon, where they had suffered few losses, were drenched. Thunder clouds studded the high moors. Rain drove from west to east in heavy sheets. Vision was obscured. The marching fyrd bent forward under oil-skins, where they possessed them, or rough sacking if they did not. The misery accompanying the wetness, was, however, mitigated by the successful outcome of the endeavour. There would be financial rewards; each soldier would be given a coin, or more, according to his status, with the king's name emblazoned on it, to keep or to use to buy a sheep, or cow, or to purchase land or buy freedom. There were fewer slaves in the fyrd in these days; mercenaries outnumbered the willing freemen. Half-breed Danes, serving the highest-paying masters, had taken to selling themselves as support to the Saxon king. Birth allegiance counted for nothing. Men and horses slipped and slithered their way slowly south. The old stone road from Eboracum, York, to Lagentium, Castleford, was slick with mud, as were all living creatures venturing upon it.

The boy Edgar, sitting on an exotic carpet in the back of his covered waggon, peered through a scudding rain curtain to the town they had recently left. He could just see the smoke of the burned monastery of Ripon, the foundation of the great saint Wilfrid. Wilfrid's reliquary casket travelled with him, taken from the crypt where it had lain for three hundred years. The monks who had for so long guarded his remains had melted away. There it was, a small, primitive, planked coffin with little decoration along its sides, behind him. He leaned back on it, its worn oak edges gouging into him.

The boy pulled at a discarded cloak and placed it at his back to make himself more comfortable.

How the monastery church, built entirely of wood, had crackled, how the flames, born of the embers from the kitchen fires after their last meal, had shot up in the July heat to envelop the ancient abode of the monks. The church was razed to the ground within an hour, like a tinder-dry woodland. A physical reminder of the Northumbrian fickleness in their loyalty to Wessex, an abode of pirates and their supporters, would no longer host the ideas or aspirations of a mongrel hegemony. Something else would rise in its place, perhaps, but not until after a decent time of adjustment and re-education, particularly of the seemingly remorseful Archbishop Wulfstan, who had been freed of his chains and allowed to creep on his unworthy legs to York.

At a witan in Tanshelf, Eadred had secured the written submission of the northerners, a promise to obey their southern overlord. Sealed over the corpse of Wilfrid, it was thought that any oath-breaking would not be serious or long-lasting. The army could turn around and return to admonish again, though Half-king would be reluctant. Better to crush completely. He had argued with Dunstan and Eadred against Wulfstan's release. They countered that the fear of reprisal would be too great. The lesson, much more than a mere slap of the wrist, had been given; the king of Wessex, Weak-in-the-feet, was not, after all, a king to be ignored or played with. Wulfstan would still have a role, he had sworn, in converting and pacifying the pirates of the north.

The large crypt, the heart, of Ripon minster remained, its columns supporting nothing but a stone ceiling, empty of its cultic attraction; its revenue from pilgrimage destroyed, its will shattered. Retribution for the outrage of a northern peoples' daring to choose its own, foreign king, had been brought. The sense of satisfaction among the wet marching army was palpable. Even in the rain, with full stomachs and coin in their pockets, returning to their families and fields, ready to be harvested, joy, despite the soreness of every foot and the sogginess of every shoulder, was to be had. God was on their side.

Most of the Saxon army had crossed the narrow bridge at Castleford, entering Mercia and home soil. Suddenly a trumpet alarm sounded. As the first part of the horsemen and waggons gathered on the south side to wait for the remaining baggage, the back-markers were ambushed from the north by the enemy. Eadred, Dunstan and Half-king, already safely across, wheeled around. Edgar was in one of the carriages under attack. The rain had stopped. Rising cloud allowed them to see what was befalling them.

'Traitors,' Half-king shouted. 'They have broken their oaths!'

'Hell will be their abode.' Dunstan, an expert horseman, having travelled many miles across the hills and valleys of Wessex on his masters' business, spurred his horse towards the bridge over which he had just passed. It was not a substantial bridge, only wide enough for two men and a narrow cart. Beyond it, as he squeezed past the men now hurrying to cross, he could see a pirate hoard bearing down on the rear phalanx of troops. They were completely vulnerable. The main body of troops had already crossed and could not go back to help the last men.

'Anlaf! It is Anlaf! Anlaf comes! Retreat!' A commander, accompanying his men at the rear, shouted to the forward troops, who now turned around to face the bridge. The men still on the bridge came towards Half-king, who had galloped back from his forward position.

'Anlaf? But he is in Ireland, surely.' Eadred grasped Dunstan's arm in alarm. 'But all Vikings look alike.'

This was serious. Whether it was Anlaf, or Eric, or someone else, the assault was deadly and well-organised. About one third of the marching army was vulnerable to the hoard which now descended on them at breakneck speed, swords flashing. There was no chance that the troops would be able to defend themselves, being weighed down with baggage. It took more than an hour to put on defensive jackets of leather and two for any thane to divest himself of riding gear and don chain-mail.

'If it is Anlaf, and not Eric, then he will regard himself as outside any treaty which we have made with Wulfstan. Eric is no longer our foe; here is a new one, or rather, one which has returned, regrown, like the snake's head that the Norse are.' Dunstan felt for his own sword, hanging in a scabbard on the saddle. It might be used, he felt, this time, though his abbot's skirts would be a hindrance. He had never fought in battle before, but it would not do to refrain in the presence of Eadred, Half-king, or, for that matter, Edgar, who had jumped off the halted waggon which was halfway across the bridge and run to the two men.

'Uncle, Abbot, what is happening? Have the Northumbrians broken their word?' Edgar was about to witness slaughter. There was no way to shield him from the sight of men being murdered. Perhaps there was no need; an aetheling must harden himself, or be hardened.

Dunstan replaced the half-withdrawn sword. The rout had begun; no help could reach the rearward part of the troops captured on the wrong side of the bridge. Men screamed as they were hacked at by a superior, determined force. A few Scandinavians, if that is who they were, fell from their horses as they were rushed by a few brave Englishmen. They may have been attacking other men whose origins were in Northumbria, other Englishmen, but in these times of changing fashions, conspiracies and mercenaries, it was difficult to be sure, by visible means, of any man's allegiance.

It was simplest to explain hate. Eadred, panting with excitement, shouted at his nephew. 'The north has broken its promises. They have a choice of two kings; Eric and Anlaf, both Norse, who the Lady Mary seems to love, today. Tomorrow we shall have our revenge, never fear, Edgar.'

Eadred was surprised at himself. He could comfort an aetheling, he found. His own reluctance at taking on the mantle of kingship had melted away; he had become the tough-skinned character which his mother never thought he could be. Disappointment and the understanding that men lie through smiling mouths, cheat and fight for themselves and their own interests, despite what their faces say, had at first led to despair and then to determined resolution. Trust no-one. What had to be done, would be done. The baggage train, under heavy attack, managed to clear the bridge, leaving a few stragglers to face slaughter. There were casualties, but for the Northumbrians, there would be many more. The slap on the wrist would be delivered again, but this time it would cut deep. Chasing the remnants of the attackers, Eadred turned northwards once again. A few hours later, Northumbria capitulated.

Wulfstan clutched at Old Edith's head on the armrest of his throne in York minster, rubbing his hand over her wooden brow, desperate to receive some wisdom from the carved oak, the oak of old Northumbria. The archbishop's seat, once a safe place in the minster of York and now surrounded, like the rest of the choir, by filth and market waste, was where the archbishop expected that Eadred would return, along with the dreaded Half-king, deaf to the complexities of rule in Northumbria. He waited, becoming more anxious as the sound of hooves at the minster door came to a halt. There was the sound of men dismounting, many men. The west door opened.

Eadred, Dunstan, Edgar and Half-king approached, kicking aside a pig's head in the centre of the nave. The archbishop remained glued to his seat. He must acknowledge his allegiance to this southern king. Eric had fled. Anlaf was back. A new treaty was there to be made; new oaths must be taken.

Could he, Wulfstan, survive intact? Would he retain his eyes? Surely no abbot would countenance physical damage to a man in holy orders, one whose being was at one with Wilfrid, Wilfrid of the north, whose body the south had made their own.

*Do what you need to do.* The combined voices of two women spoke on his shoulders as the men approached, looking determined. *Use your charmed voice to persuade, show how difficult and dangerous is this place. Reserve your right to rule, to do their bidding, then turn and face northwards again; they will go south, back to their comfortable beds and fat, licentious lives in their palaces and monasteries. You, you have the more onerous task. Promise them silver, promise them gold, but keep the north free of these men who want to own you, want to force Northumbria to bend to England's will.* The voices of Hida and Cartimandua rose to a high note, like a chorus of banshees, and trailed off.

*You are too shrill.* Wulfstan muttered under his breath. *If I survive, it will not be thanks to you, but to my own will.* He felt Old Edith's head under his hand. There would be words which he could find, words of promise, of compromise. Eric had gone and Anlaf had returned. The Wessex king and his coterie could be placated; most of the men who had died at Castleford had been northerners. The losses were less to Wessex and more to Northumbria. Some of the men had been Danes. Eadred would not mind a few less of them.

'Welcome to York, your city of Northumbria, my lord.' Wulfstan bowed.

For now, welcoming was all that he could do.

**948:** *Here King Eadred raided across all the land of Northumbria, because they had taken Eric for their king; and on the raid then the famous minster at Ripon, which St Wilfrid built, was burned. And then when the king was on his way home, the raiding army which was within York overtook the king's army from behind at Castleford, and a great slaughter was made there. Then the king became so angry that he wanted to invade again and completely do for the country. Then when the council of the Northumbrians heard that, they abandoned Eric and compensated King Eadred for the act.*

Worcester Manuscript of the Anglo-Saxon Chronicle

## The Orkneys, August 948

SHIPS WERE PULLED up onto the upper pebbles of the beach. Last winter's seaweed, brought high by storms, lay still drying on the gorse bushes growing beside rounded rocks. Neither land, nor sea, could entirely rid the other of a continual attempt to grow or succumb to each other's might. The scraping sound of other battleships and traders, further along the beach, being parked high with the intention of a lengthy stay, was a background noise accompanying the seabird calls. Eric turned away from his ship. He was tanned, filthy, but happy. There had been an adventure. He had learned much. He would be back, back to the York which he knew could be taken again. Wulfstan was willing. Anlaf could be bought.

'You weren't there very long, then.' Gunnhild folded her arms as she surveyed the handsome sailor who was sometime king of Norway, of Orkney, of York. The survivor. 'I think you will live forever.'

'No, that will be Egil Skallagrimsson.' Eric loved to travel and to win battles and booty, but he was also glad to return to his wife. 'I see you are just about to drop another son for me.'

'A daughter, this time.' Gunnhild called for her young sons to come from the back of the bothy, where they were annoying small animals. 'Leave the goats alone. Come and greet your father.'

Three scrawny, fair-haired boys ran out of the enclosure behind the cottage towards the beach. They were bare-footed. The youngest stopped mid-run as he contemplated the man, called Father, who he barely recognised. Ships were one thing to be excited about; they brought interest and sometimes gifts, but this man, staring at him, had more presence than the traders. And he was wearing a metal band around his head.

'What is that?' The child pointed to his father's head.

'This?' Eric took off the crown. 'This is the crown of York. This is what kings wear.'

Another of the brothers addressed his father. 'But you are king in many places. You have never worn metal around your head before. You told us that a sword made a king. An arm-ring gives power and magic. What does a crown give?'

Eric laughed. 'We say that when in Rome, a man does what Romans do. The English wear crowns. I suppose it is better than a ring through the nose.'

The third boy, the eldest, snorted. 'Perhaps it shows that their brains are in a harness.'

Eric laughed again. 'Yes, you are right, it is a harness, of sorts. But the heart knows no harness, it is Viking, it is Norse. Come here, all of you.'

The boys ran to their father. It was good to touch this charismatic hero, to know that they were part of him, sired by him. Gunnhild, rueful but also pleased to see him, brought her stomach to nestle against her husband's oily side. The smell of a Viking man was overpowering, particularly one who had been at sea for many days. Salt spray, grease, fish, sweat, improved her view of a man's personal magic. The beard, unkempt, would provide her with many hours of combing and plaiting, intimate times of murmuring and explanation, of tales of overcoming beasts and men, of assessing the outlay and practicality of yet another conquest in the future.

Conquest; there would inevitably be another one. Eric was forever planning. Planning to beat, planning to avenge. Some would call it dreaming, but Eric's dreams had so often come true. Her husband was Eric, Eric Bloodaxe. A name to fear, a name to remember. He would soon be off again, on his adventures. And she would soon be in Jorvik, ruling there as queen alongside her king.

# Milborne Port, near Sherborne, Dorset, February 949

THERE WAS A carpet of snowdrops, spreading as far as the track below and up to the sky on the summit above. Eadred got off his horse and led it through them, trying to disturb as few as possible. Streaks of light and shade from the beech coppice plantation wove pathways through the lower slopes of the hill.

'Bica, Hersfig, wait here. I will go with Eadwig to the cottage.' Eadred motioned for Eadwig to jump down from his pony. 'Adjust your clothing, Eadwig. Use a portion of your cloak to cover your face. We do not want to be recognised.'

'There's little chance of that, Lord, you look just like one of your slaves, though they are better dressed. Perhaps you should act in one of the court dramas.' Bica had schooled the usually natty king in how to look unattractively poor. 'Here is the purse.' Bica handed Eadred a small leather purse.

'Will this be enough?' Eadred looked at the purse's contents. He never handled cash and was unfamiliar with his own coins.

'More than enough. They are the old king's coins and lighter in value than your own. You will find that Mother Herne will accept anything. She might even see you for nothing.'

'Why should she do that? As you are so convinced that she will be able to give me back my health, she may deserve more.'

Eadred gazed up at his saddle. Perhaps this was a bridge too far; a visit to a British witch at Bica's suggestion was, for a Saxon king, one mindful of the teachings of the Church, and in particular Dunstan, as bad as facing Viking hoards. His soul was in peril. Dunstan had not been advised of this trip, nor would he be. The abbot was quietly engaged with his plans for the reformation and rebuilding of Sherborne abbey in honour of its founder, Aldhelm, who would be celebrated in ten years' time, two hundred and fifty years after his death. The rebuilding would be splendid and was necessary. The old missionary monastery was not fit for the modern world. Planning its works would keep Dunstan busy for several days before the court returned to Cheddar.

'No, you will not need more. Nor will you need an interpreter. She speaks English.' Bica knew how his master hesitated when attempting something new. 'Pretend that she is a new hat. You must try her on to see if she will fit. Go, now. Climb the hill. She will not come out to greet you. You must knock and enter when she calls.'

Eadred looked at Hersfig, holding the reins of his horse and Eadwig's pony. 'Are you sure that I am disguised?'

'Go, Lord. You must explore what this person can do. The monks have failed. She may be able to help you.' Hersfig gave Eadred a gentle push on the shoulder. As the king's official Pedisequuus, the one who follows the footsteps of the king, he was officially able to encourage, or to dissuade. Bica, too, shared this role and had done for many years. It had its own rewards. They had both seen Eadred's will, indeed, had helped him to make it.

Eadred ran a hand over his balding head. He spat out a clove which he had been sucking to relieve his constant toothache. His stomach was better this morning, but the ailment was not, generally, improving. It never would. Grandfather Alfred had had the same trouble. It had not stopped him from achieving great things, but would he have consulted Mother Herne in the woods if she had been available? Eadred considered that he might. It was possible. There was a British witch in every wood, it seemed. Medicine had advanced since Alfred's day; the witches and warlocks had perhaps improved their abilities to cure.

Eadred made up his mind. 'Come, Eadwig, we must climb this hill, this mountain. We must listen to what this old woman has to say. You may have my disability, though you do not look as though you do, but they say it may run in families. Stay quiet, for once, and listen.'

The ten-year-old Eadwig nodded. This was a long way from the Church's remit and teachings; practical wisdom, of British origin, was something which his grandmother had spoken about, but warned against; poisons were what interested her, which the magicians of the British race could inform her about. They had their uses, it seemed, in curing, as well as killing. Dunstan and Aethelwold would not have approved of today's exploit, he was sure, if they knew of it.

'Yes, Uncle, let us climb.'

'Mind the snowdrops.' Eadred grasped his nephew's hand and they both made their way to a stone-built cottage half-way up the hill. As they approached, the front wall appeared to sink into the cliff behind. It was, in effect, a cave, with a shambling facade. There was a door and one window. The window was a hole in the rough stone wall; a wooden shutter lay open at its side, propped by a branch. A variety of skulls sat on a wooden bench below the window, ranging from small to large. 'Hare, fox, badger, wolf, beaver…' Eadred named the creatures with which he was familiar, 'and this one, bear.' He knocked gently on the door. Eadwig peered through the open window. Another skull dangled on a cord through its eye sockets from above. 'Monkey, or something else…' Eadred compared the hanging skull with his nephew's head. Surely not? This might be a hermitage; in appearance, it was, except for the outlandish decorations.

'No need to try to see what can't be seen. You have met my ancestors. Come in. I know who you are and I am expecting you.' An elderly female voice called. The man and boy pushed the door open. Inside, in the gloom, was a woman well past child-bearing age, sitting in what appeared to be a pile of sheepskins of different hues, some brown and white, others green and red. Drying herbs hung from a chimney breast, along with damp clothing. An aged cat and a dog, of indeterminate breed, lay on another moth-eaten fleece on the floor. 'Come on in where I can see you.'

'There is no light.' Eadwig pushed his uncle through the door.

'You will adjust. Step in. Do you want broth? I have some. There is no meat, only vegetables.'

The unexpected offer of sustenance from a stranger took Eadred by surprise. She seemed to guess that he would not wish to chew on anything. 'No, I do not wish to eat, or drink,' he noticed that the old woman had started to pour a yellow liquid into a wooden bowl.

'Nothing to eat or drink. Very wise, considering.'

'Mother Herne, I have come to consult you.'

'I know, and despite what you look like, I know who you are.'

'And then you know who I am, too,' Eadwig came forward. 'I am the heir of Wessex.'

'And more besides. You are fair, but you should beware of vanity.'

'You may not speak to me or my nephew in such a way…' Eadred took a step back. Women, even his mother, were never so bold.

'This is my house, I have offered you food and drink, you have refused. Do you want my help? I may refuse it.'

Eadred stepped forward again. 'I am here to ask your advice. I have coin.'

'That may not be necessary. I am only paid by my results. They are always positive, so I am told. I see what you require. The boy, too, he needs help with something, though it is less clear what that may be. Perhaps a cure for pride.'

It was Eadwig's turn to be offended. He yelped, but Eadred put a hand on his arm. 'Eadwig, we must be patient. We have come a long way to see Mother and we must hear what she has to say, even if it is unpalatable.'

'Sit.'

Uncle and son looked for a place to sit, but saw none.

'There, on the skins in the corner, opposite me. Let me examine you.' Mother Herne got up and lit a candle and moved towards the man and boy who had squatted on the fleeces, crossing their legs in front of them. 'No crown on, today, I see, but plenty of wrinkles. The wrinkles of care, I'm sure. Responsibility does no one any good. You are lucky not to be dead yet, by the look of you.'

'I am only twenty-five. I wish not to hasten to my death. What can you do for me?' Eadred peered into the face of the woman. She was obviously old but remarkably unlined. 'I see you have had few responsibilities or cares.'

'I live simply, rely on myself, owe nothing to anyone and drink rainwater only.'

'And yellow, foul-smelling herbal remedies,' Eadwig was holding his nose in disgust. 'Uncle, should we go?'

'Stay. I can do you some good, but I cannot promise a cure. Here is a bottle of hair unction, and one for your teeth.' Mother Herne reached for two pottery jars which she seemed already to have to hand. 'You can pay me for the jars. The contents you can have for nothing. Perhaps you can pray for me. I am old, much older than you and I need help, too, sometimes.'

Eadred took the jars. They were sealed with wax and linen and would survive a horse-ride. 'My legs, my feet?'

'You have been blessed with legs which carry you and feet which can stumble along. I will consult with my helpers and you will find ease in a few days' time, but you must adjust to your circumstances, as we all must.'

'Your helpers?' Eadwig could not contain his curiosity. 'Who else is here?'

'No-one that you can see, young man. You are Saxon. I am British. I belong here, whereas you…'

'Enough, Eadwig. We have troubled the good lady enough. Madam, I shall leave coin outside the door. Perhaps your helpers will pick it up. I thank you for your assistance.' Eadred took Eadwig's hand. 'And I shall certainly pray for you, and for your soul.' The two retreated through the door into the snowdrops outside. Eadred put his purse on a log which appeared to be a seat. He took out a coin. 'Not the gold one, I think. I am not sure that she has a soul.'

The old woman shouted through the window from the interior. 'You may put your crown back on now, my lord. And watch for my helpers on your way down the hill!' She laughed. 'And you can put the gold coin back!'

'Whatever you do, do not tell anyone about our visit here today, or about the old woman. Eadwig, do you understand?' Eadred and Eadwig ran down the hill between the trees, trampling flowers.

'Not even Grandma? She would be interested.'

'Especially not her.'

*...the king himself, prostrate at the feet of the saints, devoted his life to God and to Dunstan, by whose admonition he endured with patience his frequent bodily pains, prolonged his prayers and made his palace altogether the school of virtue.*

William of Malmesbury

## Somerton, Somerset, Easter 949

THE WITAN HAD been in full session. Men had crammed into the hall for four hours in the sultry heat of the afternoon; now there was the urgent need for release. Eadred, wearing the Easter Crown which Dunstan had designed for him, turned right out of the main door and began to run for his private quarters. The witch had effected a temporary cure, like the foot of Wilfrid, but there had been a recurrence of the old illness. The pressures of the witan had not helped. Travelling quickly from Amesbury where his mother Eadgifu had insisted he visit her had contributed to his anxiety. The leaves and flowers of his temporary crown fell down onto his shoulders as he reached the safety and comfort of his quarters.

Eadred could hear Mother Herne calling after him, in his dreams and daily as he awoke. She inhabited his dreams. *You can put back on your fine clothes, and your crown, if it will stay on...bring me more gold coins next time you come.* There would not be a next time. Eadred would have to rely on the monks and their prayers. Dunstan had insisted, on discovering the visit to the witch (Eadwig had inadvertently revealed it during his lessons at Glastonbury to a classroom friend, who had told Dunstan), that the most efficacious treatment for Eadred's illness was in prayer by monks. Nuns could also offer their prayers, but the monks were more likely to be heard in heaven. Perhaps nuns' prayers worked for women's ailments, Eadred thought. He fingered the charm bracelet which he wore at his wrist and the hair necklace of Radegund which his mother had given him at Amesbury.

As he disrobed, Bica and Hersfig assisting, Eadred ruminated on the revelations discussed in the witan. There had been much to cover; no wonder the session had been so long. News has arrived of the Scottish king's raids on Northumbria. He had come as far south as the River Tees, perhaps in support of Anlaf, who had displaced Eric as king in York. He was tolerated as a client king. The Northumbrians had at least rejected paganism. Anlaf had shown himself to be influenced by the Irish and had become a student of Celtic Christianity, the wrong sort of Christianity, but it was better than Eric's half-hearted attempt to pretend to adhere to Roman affiliations. And there was that witch-wife of Eric. Gunnhild would never be acceptable to the Christian Northumbrians.

'Are you feeling better, my lord?' Hersfig looked at the Easter crown with disgust. It dropped leaves and petals onto the floor as he took it to a waste basket.

'I shall be, in a moment. Bring me my robe'. Eadred pointed to his early-evening shift which indicated that there would be no more appearances in public that night by the king.

'Already retiring?' Bica brought Eadred a pair of well-worn slippers. The familiarity of his vestments soothed the sick king, like old friends. Eadred sat on a chair which travelled with him and put his feet up on a stool, which had been his grandfather's. Connections. Comforts. These were becoming more important as the years and months passed.

'You may convey to Half-king that I shall not be present at the feast tonight. He may lead the toasts. Bring Abbot Dunstan to me.'

'Here?' Bica looked around the room. It was ornate, its woodwork intricate. The hangings were suitable for the most modern of royal hostels, but clothes were strewn around and relics poorly displayed. They had arrived only the night before and Eadred had wanted rest after his travels; there had been no time to arrange the room to receive guests.

'Yes, here. Dunstan will not mind the mess.'

Bica considered that the abbot, known for his fussy and fastidious nature, would notice and dislike the disorganisation which had been growing in the king's private quarters recently, but said nothing. He went to find Dunstan. He knew where to look; the abbot had use of a splendid red tent, lent to him for this occasion by a vowess of Shaftesbury. Glastonbury Abbey was becoming a repository of gifts from nobles anxious to catch Dunstan's eye. The king had him constantly by his side. He would find him in the tent, no doubt, copying out his notes on the witan meeting.

As he thought, he found Dunstan and Nonna hard at work. 'Lord Abbot, the king requires you.'

'Now? There is much to do.' But Dunstan knew he would have to go. It was not far to the hall and private quarters, and it was not raining. 'Nonna, continue with the notes, will you?' Dunstan drew on a cloak against the damp air and stepped outside with Bica. 'Go ahead. How is the king? We had a long session this afternoon.'

'Tired. But his mind is active. He seems agitated.'

'Leave us, when I have joined the king.'

'I am the keeper of the king's secrets!'

'You may be the nearest thing he has to a friend, but you are not mine! You will leave us, as I request.' Dunstan raised his voice and widened his eyes to intimidate Bica, then lowered his voice and closed his eyes to slits as he finished his sentence. The dwarf took a step backwards to distance himself from the abbot. They were, after all, and probably for ever, mortal enemies. Briton would forever resent Saxon; Saxon would forever regard Briton with suspicion.

Bica opened the door to Eadred's room and retreated. Dunstan entered, discarding his cloak on the dishevelled bed on which the king, in a heap, lay reading. 'My Lord, you wanted me? There is much to do to record this afternoon's business…'

'Thank you for coming, Dunstan. I want to discuss a matter of some urgency with you. Please join me over here.' Eadred waved to the sputtering fireplace and two chairs on either side. One had clothes on it and some petals; the other was free of detritus. Dunstan took the unencumbered chair and waited for Eadred to begin. It would not be long. Unlike some members of the royal family, Eadred was able to deliver his thoughts with alacrity and clarity; and he was improving.

'It is this business of Anlaf and Wulfstan which is bothering me. Should I object to Anlaf being in power in York once again? What do you think?'

'Wulfstan seems to think that Anlaf is the more sincere Christian. We should perhaps give him time to establish how popular Anlaf will be with the Northumbrians. You know that they favour the Celtic Church. It may be that things will settle down better with him in charge than Eric.'

'So, Eric is gone, back to the Orkneys, presumably?'

'Yes, so I am told. With his wife.'

'That has to be good, I am not in favour of witches ruling the court, not any court.'

'Of course not. But Wulfstan is here, my lord. He arrived late this afternoon. Would you like to interview him?'

'Not tonight, Dunstan. Let him rest for now. But you should see him. Try to get out of him what he thinks is the best course of action for returning Northumbria to our control. He is a wily bird and will no doubt spin a tale of hope and promise. Apply some pressure. Get to the heart of what the North thinks it wants. Bring me news of your talk tomorrow at dawn. I shall be awake; the damn birds will alert me, no doubt, despite the thickness of these walls. I wish I was in my own bed in Winchester palace.' Eadred caught a look of disapproval from Dunstan. 'Now tell me about the afternoon's witan session. Did Eadwig understand the business?'

There was a knock on the door. 'Who is it?' Eadred and Dunstan both spoke together.

Bica's voice came clearly through the grill, sounding aggrieved. 'Nonna wishes to know when the abbot will return to his tent. Archbishop Wulfstan wishes to talk with him.'

'Let him wait!' Eadred and Dustan both shouted together.

# Frome Palace, Autumn 951

ADGIFU SHIFTED THE cushion under her leg. 'The monks in
the hospital have a name for it. Whatever it is, it is painful.'

'I have something similar on occasion. I remember I had it at
Eadred's coronation in Kingston and later, when Eadwig visited with
you at Glastonbury and we were celebrating one of the saints' days, I
forget which.'

Wynflaed and Eadgifu were lounging, sewing, at one end of the
great hall, by the fire which had been recently lit. Smoke tried to find
a suitable way out of the building. It spiralled upwards and formed a
cloud high above their heads.

'It would be better to be outdoors, but at least we are private, for
a while, until the hunt returns.'

'With your leg and my back, we cannot go with them to hunt
any more. We are widows who have lost our usefulness except as
willing listeners to the excitement of youth. You can be sure that they
will all return with some thrilling tale, which they will embellish.'

'And some venison, I hope. The cooks here know how to spit
roast hart, but little else. And we are not useless, Wynflaed. You
produce your horses for the hunt and I... I have my ear to the politics
of the day. I am an advisor, perhaps not officially so, but I am still
allowed my opinion, and it is heard.'

'By Eadred?'

'Yes, by him and by Dunstan, of course. Eadwig is a wilful and
obstinate boy, but he will come round, in time.'

'Yes, our grandson has plenty of character. What about Edgar?'

'I hardly see him. He is in Half-king's household. They tell me
that Aethelwold has him under instruction and he is obedient.'

'Ah, obedient. That must be good.' Wynflaed resumed her

embroidery. 'What is in that cushion? Does it do any good?'

'It is stuffed with the hair of many saints. I myself embroidered it.'

'It is externally accomplished and beautiful. I presume that it has the hair of Radegund?'

'Of her, and others. There are nail-clippings, too. They say hair and nails will aid bone formation and repair. I have my hopes. If you ask whether it is effective, they say that I must perform Hail Marys at certain times of the day and when the moon is full for a complete cure. I have not managed to do all that the old woman asked, so I suppose I should not expect to have a full cure. In any case, the trouble usually leaves me after a few weeks.

'Old woman?'

'A British witch. She lives near Milborne Port. Dunstan told me about her. He had warned Eadred not to go near her, but Eadred pricks up his ears at anything to do with illness. He imagines he has every bodily pox that the monks in the hospital here can tell or show him. They pickle diseased parts in jars as a cook will pickle beans. He has his own favourite maladies, poor boy, and they are not improving. His teeth are very bad. He does not need to imagine more. If ever I cannot find him here at the palace, I know that he will be with the hospital monks, standing over some poor sick creature, assessing what is wrong with him, questioning the leprous slaves close to death, asking them what it is like to be standing at the gates of heaven. Edmund had his temper; Eadred has his hypochondria.'

'Our children seem like aliens, Eadgifu, sometimes. That is one of the curses of motherhood. The strange creatures which we spawn grow away from us.' Wynflaed bent further over her work. There were sadnesses in old age, as well as great joys. A child could be a friend when it was young, but the adult was often wayward, unrecognisable from the bright hope it once had been.

'I tell Eadred of the unfortunate Alfred, his grandfather. He had stomach troubles, too. It is in the line. Eadwig may have it. I saw him doubled over in pain at Glastonbury when we were last there. It is to do with his digestion.'

'Such a shame!' Wynflaed could not bear to think of the enjoyment of food to be removed from such a young prince. 'Do you think that there is a curse on your family?'

'The Black Stick? No, I don't believe in such nonsense.' Eadgifu readjusted the cushion. 'That's better. Now tell me about your latest tapestry hanging. What is its theme?'

'It is a short hall tapestry, recording the battle of Brunanburh.'

'Plenty of red in it, then.'

'Yes, my girls are fond of bloody scenes.'

'One of our successes against our enemies. There aren't too many of them. I look forward to seeing it.'

# The Great Thorn Hedge of Oundle

ETHELWOLD SURVEYED THE remnants of a hawthorn thicket which partly surrounded the old missionary monastery of Oundle. Not far from the reinvigorated monastery of Peterborough, it had decayed not merely through pagan Danish depredation but through encroachment by the growing township. Money had flowed to Peterborough in recent years; Athelstan had started the process and Edmund and Eadred had continued it. The east of England was a challenge; it was to be reclaimed for Christ, but, like the three-hundred-year-old monasteries in the west which Aldhelm had founded, this ancient monastery of St Wilfrid was in severe decay. It would take much manpower and coin to make this again a worthy place to host pilgrimage.

St Wilfrid's foot had to rest somewhere in the south, and where better than this quiet spot, where the Danes had become Christian, where the restoration works at Ely and Peterborough were going apace? Abingdon, too, would rise again. Starting from scratch, the restoration of these places which were sanctuaries of holiness at the time when Saxons had first become Christian would become his, Aethelwold's, remit in life. Glastonbury had taught him much. He would have liked to study further abroad, but Eadgifu wanted him to remain in England. *There is time to study more when you are an old man, Aethelwold,* she had said. She needed him here, for the improvement of the east, for the education of Edgar. Indeed, there was much to occupy him and he enjoyed her confidence.

Aethelwold sighed. Oundle monastery was in a dreadful state. Could Aethelwold manage to rekindle the light which had once shone here, in those early years of Saxon enlightenment? St Wilfrid had died here. The place from where he had passed to heaven needed to be honoured. A small shrine would not be enough. In recent years, the ownership and commercial value of relics had determined the fate of some early monastic edifices. Would Wilfrid be able to attract southern pilgrims to provide a comfortable income for a small group of monks dedicated to his memory?

Economics were not Aethelwold's chief interest. Dunstan was clever at assessing value for money. He would be able to calculate the investment needed, on Aethelwold's reporting to him. What would be required, as well as a chapel and dormitory for pilgrims, would be a sound set of rooms to hold northerners who might be required to stay for lengthy terms; renegade archbishops, perhaps.

# Winchester, Eadred's bedchamber, an afternoon in winter 952

EADRED LAY ON his back, staring up at the embroidered canopy of his bed.

'He thinks the pretty stars will help him. The angels have let him down.'

Bica stood, with crossed arms, in the doorway to the room. Hersfig, carrying a ceramic bowl, paused on his way out to confer. The patient was not well, again.

'He's fallen into a gloom. Even the Christmas festivities failed to brighten him, this year.' Hersfig continued out into the passage to a window and threw out the contents of the bowl. 'Get the servants to bring more water. We're going to need it tonight.'

'Tell them yourself. Look at him. He lies in his bed with both hands over his heart.' Bica waved a hand in disgust towards the prone figure of his king.

'Is there something wrong with that, too?'

'What is not wrong with him? We may pick up our inheritances sooner than we thought.'

'Perhaps he is praying. They say that the Friend of Faith leaves us last.' Hersfig wiped the bowl with a rag and placed it on a table covered with medical instruments and supplies.

'Our king needs all the friends he can get. His mother is tired of him and tells him to pull himself together. The abbot and Half-king are forever in conference, mostly, it seems, trying to find a way to get him to act. Act? Pff. He can hardly get out of bed.'

There was a knock on the door.

'Someone to see him? Tell them that the king has taken to his bed for the foreseeable future.'

Bica stamped his foot. 'Tell them yourself.'

Things were unravelling at Winchester. Dunstan would have to wait to tell Eadred in the morning that the usurper Anlaf had left York and Eric Bloodaxe had returned, with his wife and a hundred sons in attendance, and now again sat on the coveted throne with Archbishop Wulfstan standing, and no doubt grinning, by his side.

The many-headed serpent of Norway had reared up, its snarling beak more vicious and ambitious than before.

*At the time of Aethelwold's period in charge of Abingdon monastery, he invited King Eadred, his retinue and some Northumbrian guests to dine, and the king ordered in a good supply of mead. The king ordered all the doors to be locked, so that no-one could leave. They all drank heavily throughout the day, the supply of mead hardly decreased, and the Northumbrians became swinishly intoxicated.*
Aelfric's biography of St Aethelwold.

## On the road North, May 953

ALF-KING, DUNSTAN AND Eadred led the small army. The sick king jiggled about in a waggon alongside some of the important relics of Wessex which would be required at the necessary oath-takings. It was more like a large retinue than an army; Eric Bloodaxe had sent word that he would welcome the southern king to York.

'Upstart Viking,' Half-king grumbled.

Half-king had shouldered responsibility for the travel arrangements. To his mind, a battle was necessary to remove the growing menace of the dynasty now sitting comfortably in the Northumbrian capital's palace in York. 'How many sons has Eric got? One for every year of marriage, you say? As well as the by-blows that the Norse seem to count as legitimate? There must be hundreds. Diplomacy will only take us so far.'

'Like the stars that Eadred counts on his bed canopy every night, so I'm told. Countless. Kill one and another takes his place.' Dunstan looked weary. Travel north was not as attractive as movement south. There was much to do in Winchester, besides all the other works to which he had to attend. His income was stretched and the king had become more careful of his personal finances and that of the nation in recent years. Illness had the effect of making him more frugal. Expenditure was everywhere checked. Aethelwold was still rebuilding at Abingdon and Ely, but work had stopped, for now, at Glastonbury.

'What caused this latest flare-up of Eadred's? It is most inconvenient.' Half-king had known few set-backs of a personal nature; God and the angels had given him strength and his parents had gifted good genes. Illness was for him a stranger and he had little understanding or compassion for those afflicted. 'We have to keep stopping. The journey is long enough without waiting for the king to empty his bowels at every tree and bush.' He growled. The king's carriage had come to a halt yet again and the figure of the king jumped out and rushed to the side of the road.

Dunstan groaned but said nothing. The emergency would be over soon, as it always was. The king returned to his seat, smiling and waving.

'It is soon over.' Dunstan spurred his horse on.

'Was it the feast last night? Edgar told me that Eadred locked the door of the hall at Abingdon and insisted that the Northumbrian visitors played High Cockylorum and Bumpety Buckets. I think they broke the record for mead consumed in one night. He should have been resting for this journey.'

'He has been feeling well in recent days. His confidence has grown.' Dunstan allowed himself a sigh.

'We should be looking to bring on Eadwig to take his place. Eadred may only have months to live, since nothing seems to cure him, not even a visit to a witch.'

'The visit to a witch?'. Who told you that?'

'The manservant -the dwarf- told me. Sometimes he gives me information, if I pay for it.' Half-king moved his horse into a trot to vary the pace. Even if only for a few yards, it felt as though progress could be made. The same landscape stretched out before them, freshly green and beautiful, but boring.

Dunstan shrugged. Eadred had been a better king in many ways than his brother Edmund, but his physical disabilities were becoming a burden. His own hair, like that of Eadred's, was falling out. He wondered how long both of them in partnership had to achieve their tasks. Kings could not entirely be controlled; each new monarch had his own foibles and strengths; each had to be trained by the able and experienced. Him. He looked back at the retinue of soldiers and courtiers behind. There was the fourteen-year-old Eadwig, riding well and confidently. What would the future bring? Eadwig looked like an aetheling, but inside that golden head and behind those fair features was a young bear, untamed and potentially untameable. Suddenly, Dunstan knew what to do.

'Divert to Ripon.'

'Not go to York?' Half-king drew up his horse.

'To Ripon we shall go. The intemperate Archbishop is not expecting us. We shall beard him in his lair.'

# The Palace of York, May 953

G UNNHILD STROKED AND brushed her luxuriant dark hair. It was the longest in York, she had had it confirmed. Along with pride in her sons, she enjoyed an abundance of beauty. Despite the births of so many children to Eric, she still gave the impression of youth and vigour. Some said that her beauty was produced by witchcraft. Eric had been heard to joke about his magical wife and her talents. She had adopted the new faith at Eric's request, but the decoration of her person and speech marked her out as a Norse pagan, and proud of it. Eric was dubious of the effectiveness of Christianity; it felt as though there were too many considerations to be made before an action could be taken, but, at forty-four, more thought and more leisure should be undertaken before assault, it seemed to him.

Eric, lying on a bed, watching his wife preen herself, ruminated on the impatience of his brood. Three sons were approaching warriors in full manhood; the others were chaffing to be allowed to maim or kill humans as well as creatures. It was their birthright, to fight to climb above others. The Christian god was armed like them; he would fight for what was right. Eric's kingship was right and after him would come his sons, sitting on a variety of thrones across the Viking world, from The Russ in the east and the Black Sea in the south, from Miklagard to the ocean shores of the unknown world beyond the west. They would rule, like the stars he had heard that the sick southern king counted on his bed canopy. The boys were all tall and strong; none had died or become ill in infancy; all limbs, all heads were as they should be, blessed by some god or other, destined to rise above others by fair means or foul.

Foul. There were those who had their own sons, who wished for them to continue their bloodline, just as ambitious to establish a legacy as himself. Eric thought of Anlaf and grunted.

'You thought of Anlaf.'

'Eh?'

'You grunted. You don't do that unless you are thinking of your opposition. Eadred is not a problem. Wine, beer or mead will see to him. Anlaf is not so easy to manipulate. You thought of him. Anlaf.'

'No need to remind me of him; or of your magic powers. But you are right, darn you. Maccus is coming to the palace for the greeting.'

'Anlaf's son? All the way from Dublin? I thought that he preferred to lay low until his father was dead like a good son. Not like yours, I am pleased to say.'

'Not like your sons. A noisy bunch of pirates, so I'm told they are called.'

'Our sons. Yours and mine. And, yes, pirates. Also, kings to be. I ame the Mother of Kings.'

'And Queen of the Best, The Bloodaxe.'

'But The Bloodaxe is getting old, like a worn-out plough ox who will soon slump to the dirt.'

'Come here, witch, I will show you how old I am. There is life and blood in me, woman, and you have magic enough to cover us both with your hair. There is time before the feast.'

'Time to make another daughter, perhaps, one for the fair city of York?'

'One for York, to marry Maccus.'

'Or King Eadred. I would be Mother of Queens, too.'

'There's no chance of that. Maccus will have to do, or Eadwig, who is coming to York with his uncle.'

'Yes. Eadwig. I shall have him myself. He is fourteen, isn't he?' Gunnhild laughed and flopped on the bed next to Eric.

'He is too young for you. You would kill him.' Eric began to cover himself in the dark hair. He peeped out beyond its folds to examine his wife's face. 'Crow's feet. Too old.'

'A child needs instruction. I shall teach.' Gunnhild pulled her hair aside. The feast could wait.

# Ripon, May 953

THE KING'S RETINUE rode past the damaged bell tower of the monastery of Wilfrid. The remaining upright posts of a wooden fence around the ruins, ineffective now against intruders into the sanctified space, stood like blasted trees after a wildfire.

'No bell to summon us. No guard to challenge us. No buildings to harbour the old devil.' Half-king relaxed in his saddle and waved to the following soldiers. There was little to alarm. 'Where will he be hiding?'

The leading group of riders including the king dismounted. Dunstan walked to the church, the only part of the monastery buildings which had retained most of its roof. He pushed at an open door and examined the dark interior. He returned quickly to report to the others waiting outside.

'There's nothing left, nothing of value. The crypt wall paintings are the only undamaged things.' Dunstan turned to Eadred. 'I ordered full destruction. It was the only way. A symbolic removal of power. Wulfstan would only take notice if we removed his sanctuary and took back what Athelstan had gifted him when he appeared to have loyalty to Wessex.'

Eadred stroked his leg. Riding, in the carriage or on horse, for so many days, had been hard. He was feeling better than in the first stages of the journey. 'Look into nearby buildings. Wulfstan won't be far away from his beloved Wilfrid.'

'I thought that you brought most of Saint Wilfrid south with you last time, uncle?' Eadwig dismounted and surveyed the damaged entrance to the crypt which had once housed the relic of the saint. The steps were worn from years of pilgrimage, but otherwise there was no sign of recent human use. There were no blazing candles, no chanting monks, no incense burning, nothing which might remind one of the presence of a holy spirit, unlike the chapels and churches of Wessex, unlike the splendid mausoleum of saints in Winchester, divided between the Old and the New Minsters. The colour, sound and smell of those houses of the dead was overpowering. Here, there was the sense of a cult destroyed. 'Uncle, had you thought of building a church to Saint Cuthbert?'

Dunstan replied to the boy. 'We have in mind a new sanctuary and cult centre in Wells. The design has been done. I will show you on our return.'

'Yes, Saint Cuthbert will be our main focus. Saint Oswald is safe at Gloucester and Wilfrid at Canterbury. In the west of our nation we need another centre of pilgrimage and Saint Cuthbert, or part of him, will grace our new building near the church of St Andrew, away from the waters which fill that place in winter. Wells is to be our latest venture, a town which will host pilgrims all year round, not just in summer. It is the coming thing.'

'And beneficial to the public purse.' Half-king examined the crypt door at the bottom of the steps. 'And to you, Eadwig, and your uncle. There is a growing industry in the making of remembrances for pilgrims to buy. They will then go on to Glastonbury to stand by the graves of your family, including your father.'

'So, Wells and Glastonbury are to be major centres of pilgrimage?'

'The revenue will benefit the nation. The most notable saints of our history will all be housed at centres in the south. I need not explain how that will benefit the English nation.' Dunstan had his back to the main church door. He swung around as footfall and the sound of a crutch came from behind.

'You stole Wilfrid. You stole Wilfrid from me, you, you... tyrants.'

'Archbishop! We expected to have to search for you. I see your leg has grown worse.' Eadred hobbled towards the older man. Wulfstan limped forward. The old and younger man, matching in lack of vigour, looked comical to Eadwig's eyes.

'So, this is the famous traitor, Abbot. I see he is as ferocious as you said he was.' Eadwig sniggered.

'Thieves!' Wulfstan shook his crutch wildly, overbalancing. Eadwig ran to him and caught him as he fell. He lay on the dusty stones, feebly muttering.

'Not thieves. Restorers of the kingdom. You are the thief, my lord.' Dunstan stood over the prostrate priest. Wulfstan dribbled. 'The shock of our arrival has done you no good, my lord. Come with us, we will accommodate you. Come now.'

Eadred surveyed the wreck of his Archbishop of York. Thieves should be punished, according to the laws of his forefathers. Northumbria had been in revolt, conquered by the help of this man, willing to have a new king, any king, which would free it from Wessex shackles. A pirate had been invited in; the Norse had had two kings on the throne of York. Could he put this man to death, this pitiful creature, worse off than himself? Wulfstan had not long to live; he was already in old age and his health brought the view of the swinging gates of Heaven nearer at hand.

'Come, Archbishop, this is no longer a sanctuary for anyone. We will take you south, near to your beloved Wilfrid.' Eadred helped to lift Wulfstan and restored his crutch. The archbishop hobbled towards the broken door. Half-king steered him by the arm towards a carriage.

'He is fit for monastic incarceration and no more.' Half-king waved at the guard to let the archbishop and Eadwig through the remains of the sanctuary and towards the waggons. He was loaded as if he was a reliquary chest, but with little ceremony, onto a heap of carpets at the back end of a covered cart. 'He will be comfortable, at least, with any parts of Wilfrid which we will uncover here. There will not be much; a patch of cloth or hair, perhaps, which we can sell.'

'They will fetch a good price. We will take him to Dewsbury overnight and then south to Oundle to see out his days.' Eadred turned to Eadwig who looked questioning. Wulfstan groaned as he arranged his legs. 'Oundle is a Wilfrid foundation. This mad old man has done us damage, but he is the archbishop of York and has been for many years. He will die in that state.'

'It won't be long before he relinquishes that office, by all the saints.' Half-king aired the obvious.

'Will he be a prisoner, our prisoner, Uncle?'

Dunstan replied. 'No, we will not call him that. There is the dignity of the office to consider.'

'And what about Eric in York? Will we now go there as we had planned?' Eadwig enquired. He was fast becoming aware of the machinations of his own office. His uncle Eadred was not long for this world, either.

'The Northumbrians will see to Eric.' Dunstan supplied the answer. The nobles from the north had pledged to uphold their allegiance to Eadred at the rumbustious game in Abingdon before they had left the south. 'It seems that our long-drawn out journey with your uncle has not been in vain.'

'No more tree-stopping on the way south, then.' Half-king whispered to Eadwig, smiling.

*King Eadred had Wulfstan imprisoned in the stronghold at Iudanburh*
*because he had been frequently accused to the king;*
Anglo-Saxon Chronicles

## The Prison, Dewsbury, Yorkshire, May 953

I T WAS A hexagonal room. Wulfstan's mind spun as he again
counted the corners, waiting like empty plinths for effigies of
saints. His platter of bread and cheese was uneaten beside him on the
settle in one of the corners near the door; his ale had lost its foam. A
half-eaten apple had browned around a single bite. The sun had sunk
behind late-evening cloud; twilight had begun. In an hour's time, the
darkness would be complete.

Around the edges of the room he went again, in his mind. It
was a disturbing, repetitive loop. The five empty sides, unfurnished
and unadorned, fell into shadow. The remaining light of daytime
fell onto him alone, revealing, if anyone cared to look (and no-one
did), a hunched, pitiful figure. The archbishop of York had finally
been adjudged a traitor and awaited his fate at the mercy of the
lieutenant of Yorkshire, Dunstan and the king, not one of whom was
sympathetic to his plight, though mindful of his position. Bringing
an archbishopric into disrepute was no easy matter. He had heard it
said, during the early stages of his incarceration, that the office might
be abandoned altogether, ending a tradition of metropolitan oversight
for the north of Britain, a position which had been in existence since
the first early days of the church, since before Wilfrid, even.

There was one hope: Eric Bloodaxe, his gaoler told him, was
still on his throne of York and was said to be making reparations to
aggrieved Northumbrians who had jibbed at his nepotism. Eric's sons
had been given freedom, by their father, to pilfer and raid far into the

countryside. Waiting longer than they cared for extensive gifts from their father, the young men of Eric's family had first acted together and then against each other as they vied for power and wealth. Eric, in a bid to control them, had at first imposed punishment and then fines to stem their assaults on the common people. Anti-Nordic sentiment had become rife amongst the Danes of Northumbria, who had steadily converted to a form of Christianity which suited them and had developed their own laws, independent of the southern king's system, with his blessing. The Norse way of doing things and the language of Norway, however, was not theirs. The Danes had been taken over by a newcomer, a pagan, and his wife, the witch Gunnhild. The Nordic king's sons were like rats, everywhere to be found, scoffing the easy pickings of Danish farmers' crops and their daughters.

The last shaft of light snapped down on Wulfstan's room. The corridor outside was silent; the gaoler had gone to bed. The short night of early summer would be long, longer than Wulfstan cared for. Five nights he had been here, five nights and days to contemplate his personal fate and that of his persona, the archbishop of York. This was not what he had intended when Athelstan had made him archbishop for the north in 931; he had been a stripling of 35 years, then; experienced in theology and at ease with his Northumbrian royal relatives; he could accommodate the Christians who held onto Celtic ways and could gently coerce them to move towards the orthodoxy of the Roman Church. Athelstan had quietly reminded him that, since nearly three hundred years had passed since Wilfrid's successful argument in favour of Roman Catholicism at the Synod of Whitby, it was time for the nation to act in unison with, not against, the Pope. Indeed, his own palium was given by the vicar of Rome to him in person. Travel to Rome was a chore to some archbishops, but more often a delight and all expenses paid. He had enjoyed the lengthy visit to the heart of Christianity and revelled in the glories of the sights and sounds and the repasts, platters of plenty which filled his dreams and delighted his heart; he loved his food.

Wulfstan looked at the bread and cheese. He had lost his appetite. Would he lose his life? Agnes and the children would be looked after by his relatives; he had no worries on that score. A mouse looked out from a loose piece of mortar nearby. Its whiskers twitched as it made plans for its later assault, when the man's foot had lifted away from the platter and onto the string bed. It retreated, judging the moment not yet right, as Wulfstan groaned loudly.

*So, this is what it has come to. They do not mean to starve me, only to deprive me. They must see that I have been torn; between so many factions, not merely north and south. The different Christian traditions, required by differing peoples, the conversion of the Danes, the interference by the Norse, the requirements for Benedictine reform – doesn't Dunstan understand that we are only just getting the monasteries up and running again in the north after so many years? Has he not heard of the ruins that they are in? Of the gold and silver investment which is needed to reinvigorate monastic life in the north, let alone try to force it into a pattern of theology which is foreign to it? Apart from Wilfrid's Ripon and Hexham, none of the northern monasteries, when they were in existence, followed anything like a strict Benedictine path. And then they only continued in that vein until the Viking onslaught which brought everything to a halt. Wilfrid was a strong character, with an iron will; he, though, grew unpopular and took refuge in the south, away from the arguments and abuse hurled against him by his converts. He pushed them too far. Anlaf and Eric, taking over rule in the north, provided a certain freedom of worship for the Christians here who wanted their own style and they offered freedom, too, from the laws and taxes of the Wessex court. Was I wrong to take their side? My ultimate aim was to ride out the kings' requirements, whatever they were, and to bring Northumberland gradually into a union of Britain, perhaps a union which the Danes, Saxons and Britons living in the north could accept, a workable compromise.*

He sighed again. He had done what he could. It was not enough. No-one was satisfied and now he was chained to this bench, away from his beloved Agnes and her fine cooking. He looked again at the drying bread on the floor. The mouse could have it. He took a sip of the stale ale. As he replaced the wooden mug, the last light of day slipped away. The night came in like a sheet across his face. Nothing stirred, not even the mouse, waiting until the human should be snoring.

'You should have done more.'

'He did not do enough.'

Wulfstan must have dozed off. There were voices, people, with him, in the room. They were female voices, dissatisfied shrews, not like the soft tones of Agnes.

'Agnes, have you come?' Wulfstan spoke in his dream. No, not a dream. He felt his dry lips moving. He opened his eyes.

On the other side of the bare room there were two figures, indistinct shapes, occupying the corners, shrouded in silvery cloth, one tall, the other short. One wagged a bony finger at him. Hilda had come to visit him again.

'You should have done much more to persuade the Northumbrians to fight against Rome.' The finger loomed out of the darkness. Its bony nail and arthritic joint jabbed at Wulfstan. He could feel it piercing in his chest. Could a woman, three centuries dead, make him feel pain? He felt it.

The other shape, the tall one, wailed. Wulfstan felt the sigh and groan of his own throat. He had awakened these remonstrances. He must bear what they had to say.

'Ohhh, he should have done the bidding of the southern king sooner, instead of prolonging the agony. Wessex will have this land, sooner or later, as Rome had Brigantia.' Cartimandua wailed again. The queen of the Brigantes could not, would not, be quiet.

The women, tall and short, shapes of cloth and hair, began to argue one way and then another. From their positions, which, thankfully, thought Wulfstan, they seemed unable to leave, they fought with strong words to berate each other and the archbishop. Each had valid points. Northumbria was in a mess, summed up by his own position here in this gaol. There would never be a Northumbrian archbishop again.

A male voice spoke, breaking into the wails of the women as they wound their voices into a crescendo of screams.

'Be quiet, women. You both did what you thought was right. Britain lost her right to self-government long ago. It was you, Cartimandua, who gave me up to the Romans, you, Queen of Brigantia, who signed me over to end my days in the house of the high priest of Rome, where they offered sacrifice to strange gods. Never again did I see my homeland. You were the traitor who allowed the forces of the south to rule here and throughout our land. You are to blame for the success of the pillaging of Britain.' Caractacus flared out in colourful glory, his anger displayed through the centuries, steeped in vengeful remorse, glowing from his plinth in another corner of the room. The ghost of the former leader of the Celtic Britons subsided into a pile of rage and rags on the floor, its light gone out. The women grew quiet. Seagulls, flying late to roost, screamed as they flew above.

Wulfstan said nothing. These were the arguments which he had tussled with all his life. The betrayal of Caractacus by Cartimandua had troubled him from childhood. Briton betraying Briton, Northumbria betraying Wessex: revenge was at last being taken, was it not?

Another voice spoke up, more cheerful and hopeful than the first ghosts. 'I did what I could to reconcile the north to the south. I succeeded, for a while.'

'Wilfrid!'

The male shape, dressed in the long silk robes of a wealthy man, spoke from his own plinth, two corners away from Wulfstan on his bench. He appeared to be near the ceiling, on a pedestal of some sort. Wulfstan dropped from his seat to kneel on the floor.

The ghost called Wilfrid, seemingly gratified to be addressed, spoke above the fading chatter of the others. It was not a cacophony, but had the sound of a piece of music. Wilfrid was the over-arching organ sound, booming deep. 'I brought Rome to Britain, I defeated you, Hilda. The north rejected my teaching and banished me.

Retribution will follow all those who reject the teachings of the Pope. Your fate was in your hands. The pagans took you in, they gave you what you thought was the power to dismiss the kings of Wessex. Look where you are now!' The ghost of Wilfrid, like that of Caractacus, subsided into colourless gloom.

There was a pause. Wulfstan, child of the Christian centuries, the mixed messages and allegiances of the north, the mixed peoples, with its destroyed monastic sites, its pagan background, for a few moments felt the chastisement of the ages. He was to blame for the ultimate failure of the land, which had once been the greatest and most powerful of the nations in the island of Britain, to retain its independence.

Another male voice, deeper than the last, spoke from the remaining corner of the room, next to Wulfstan, who was kneeling on the floor. The voice boomed over him, coming in waves of authority and softness, admonishing and soothing. 'Wulfstan.'

Wulfstan groaned. 'Cuthbert.' He prepared to be told by yet another figure of the Northumbrian past what he should have done, what he did not do. Wulfstan would confess. He was going to hell. What chance had he of passing through the gates of heaven?

Cuthbert spoke. From the time before Hilda and Wilfrid, from the earliest Christian time in Northumbria, the time of pastoral missionaries, when the glorious nature of peace brought by the word of God, illuminating the sparrow-like lives of the pagan Saxons, living in darkness, his voice, which had spoken to so many in the noble houses of kings and the humble huts of peasants, roared and retreated.

'Once there were Christians in this land, who built great monasteries, who enlightened their folk by the pastoral duties of visiting communities, who shrove themselves in the salt waters, day and night, winter and summer. You know, Archbishop, how we suffered to conquer ourselves and to act as examples to the wretched around us, exhorting simplicity and courage. You know, Archbishop, too, that I fought to maintain our ways in Northumbria, how we led the rest of Britain in our endeavours to convert and maintain a Christian way of life. You know, also, how, ultimately, I failed; there had to be compromise, once Kent had acceded to the Romish ways.' Cuthbert's voice faded.

The liminal time had passed. Full darkness came. The plinths emptied. There was no hope for Northumbria, that was clear. Wulfstan felt the might of the cacophony of words, berating like weighted lashings on his shoulders. He lay on the floor. What was left to him? Only to beg for time, for time to retreat, to be conscious of the loss of the north, to bemoan his fate, to contemplate his time in purgatory, or worse. Where would it be? Here? Or in some monastic institution of the south, not of his choosing?

In the morning, he would know his fate. He struggled onto the string bed, the chain around his sore leg chafing. There would be no more words from ghosts tonight. They had said their piece.

The mouse heard a snore and took its chance.

# Glastonbury Abbey, September 953

A THIN RAIN fell on to the hooded figures standing by a stone-lined grave. The students of the abbey, about to become novice monks, listened as their master and teacher, the renowned Abbot Dunstan of Glastonbury, courtier, diplomat and treasurer of the king, regaled them yet again with the stories associated with their abbey school. They shifted closer to him as banging repeated from the scaffolding surrounding St Mary's old church, where the thatched roof was being replaced by stone tiles. Three workmen raised tiles in a leather basket from other labourers below, shouting as they did so. It was difficult to maintain peace inside the monastery buildings in a working environment, which is why Dunstan had decided to take his oldest group of students outside for a lecture. He could compete with the workmen's labour here, while interesting his charges in the history of their school. They would soon be passing into the refectories and churches of Wessex and perhaps further afield, to repopulate the old monastic sites of the midlands and north which were beginning to recover from Viking depredation; they would take the ideas of Wessex dominance and progressive thought with them to these benighted sites.

At fifteen or sixteen years of age, the lads, despite their youth, had been trained to encumber themselves in cloth which was sombre in colour, reached to the ground, winding often about their legs in high wind, and to cover their heads as required by Dunstan, when in public. In the choir, they could sing like the free birds of youth which their bodies demanded they recognise; but in the dormitory and refectory they were subject to the new Benedictine rules. On the whole, they were delighted with their well-ordered fates. For now, they would live, eat, work and pray in relative comfort, doing the good which multiple prayer could do, doing the will of the abbot, in the richest and most comfortable monastery in the land, richer even than Malmesbury.

Or so Dunstan hoped. Restoration works had been undertaken to preserve the older buildings of the monastery, and new buildings, accommodation, kitchen and church were being built or planned. The monastery enclosure wall needed attention, too, but fencing and thorn hedging worked reasonably well to ensure that anything undesirable was kept at bay and the temptations of the world were not easily available to those within.

'And so, the last of the British kings, Geraint, was buried here, alongside the earlier general of the British, known as the Bear, Arthur.'

'Is this the resting place of the kings and queens of Dumnonia, then?' A short boy, standing at the back of the group, piped up.

'Of some of them, yes, I believe so. It is said that Arthur was buried here, at least. This is the tomb which is said to be his. Of course, there are claims that the early Christian fathers came to this place and some stayed, but, in any case, Glastonbury abbey has been an important place of worship for hundreds of years, long before our forefathers came to this land.'

'Was this not always a Benedictine monastery, Abbot?' Another, taller, fair boy felt empowered to speak. The abbot was not unapproachable and liked to be asked about the history of his monastery.

'No, the Irish monks were the first to establish this site as a Christian monastery and they, of course, had a different understanding of our religion to ourselves in modern times. But Inys Witrin, as they called it, may have much older connections, deep into the past.' Dunstan waved his arm, indicating the bare hilltop which loomed over them from the north. 'The Tor has many legends attached to it. Men have come here to pray to their gods for aeons. They were wrong to do so, we know that now, in the light of Christ, but they knew no better, long before the coming of Our Lord.'

The boys looked up to the Tor. One threw back his hood, the better to see through the mizzle. It was always there, the magical hilltop. Some had climbed it in their childhood, before they had been given by their parents to the monastery.

'A pagan past, a Christian present. It is all here, then, Lord Abbot?' The fair-haired student had a deep voice. He was mature, for his fourteen years.

'Yes, Eadwig, and a Christian future.'

'What happens at the millennium, Father?'

He could not avoid the question. It was the one uncertainty in his mind, which no dreams or prayers could satisfactorily answer, but Dunstan responded immediately.

'We shall all be judged. The good will sit at God's right hand. The bad will be dragged to hell, that is clear.' Dunstan turned back to the monastery buildings. 'It is time for Sext. The bell is ringing. Follow me to the church.' He led a straggle of slightly wet young men towards the scaffolded church. Two stayed, lingering, at the back of the group.

'Your father lies here, does he not?'

Eadwig put an arm around the hooded boy, the shorter of the two. 'My father's tomb is yet to be built. He lies in the church, near the altar, for now, beneath the stone floor. I suppose I shall join him there, one day. Aelfwine, what do you suppose will happen on the Day of Judgement? You and I may be alive at that time; we will not be very old. The abbot would have to be as old as Methuselah to see the time he talks about; Brother Aethelwold is convinced that he will be alive then, but I do not think so. I am sure that he does not deserve to be. He tells Edgar what he thinks will be a good life for him, marrying once and for ever, obeying the laws of both the land and the church and answering to him and Dunstan for any misbehaviour. He has him in a spin. But he is only twelve years old and is ignorant of the ways of men.' Eadwig, aetheling and student, was approaching the end of his formal education. He would be announced as co-king of Wessex at the next meeting of the witan.

'It must be a burden, looking back at your family's past and ahead to the responsibility of defending what they have gained. You have to be strong in body and mind, at all times.' Aelfwine clutched the taller boy's arm. 'I would not like to be in your shoes.'

'Must be strong in body? You know I have some weakness in the stomach, like my uncle. But I am not afflicted often, or for long. I can overcome the pain, though not by prayer. I have some medication from the witch at Milborne Port which helps me at such times. Look, we must catch up with the others. They are going into the church. Aelfwine,' Eadwig ran with his companion, 'don't tell the abbot what I said about the witch. Nor that I am going out tonight.'

'Going out?'

'Beyond the sacred walls! It is shocking, isn't it, to think that one of the illustrious students of Glastonbury should want to escape his confines for any purpose except to honour God or his holy mother. You may come with me, if you care...'

'You are a king's son. I am not. You have different rules. But I won't tell the abbot, you can be sure.'

'I know that you won't. I trust you, Aelfwine. You have something about you of wisdom and ability. I hope that the abbot appreciates you.'

'He does. He has praised my singing voice and wants me for the choir in Canterbury.'

'I might want you for my aide, in my new role in Wessex. Would you stay with me?'

Aelfwine looked at his friend, panting, as they approached the church door. Which was his future, with the secular king-to-be, or with the monks and choir of the great St Augustine in Canterbury? A life circumscribed by worship and prayer, or a life supporting and acting as aide to the young man whose future stretched ahead?

'I will be with you to the end. To the millennium, if need be.' Aelfwine squeezed his friend's arm again. Eadwig slapped him on the back.

'Forward, then, to the millennium, whatever that may bring.'

Singing flowed from within the church as they opened the door. They took their places, in their last few days of being boys. In two weeks, they would pass into the world of men.

# York palace, October 954

'I TELL YOU, Osulf,' Eric had spittle on his chin, 'you will be forever at the behest of the southern kings if you reject my offer. You have little sway with that court. With me and my connections, you know that you will have ample opportunities to become independent, to rule yourselves.'

Eric was becoming angry. Osulf, the earl of Bamburgh was being intransigent. An over-confident English earl, full blood scion of the Angles, considered that he had leverage. Granted, his forefathers had for long held sway in this northern land. But Wulfstan was gone; what hope in hell's chance had the Northumbrians of ever becoming a separate kingdom again? The idea was idiotic. As part of the empire of Norway, York and its hinterland could hope for effective influence. York was a successful western centre for the Norwegian empire.

Eric wiped his chin. 'You have tried this before. Anlaf, you despised. Dublin was too much for you. I offer you the treaties, best of all the northern world, with Norway and the islands. I am your best hope of retaining hegemony. Besides, I have many sons who could all become kings in the north, become a dynasty to look after your affairs. A dynasty to rival Alfred's. Look at my fecundity! Look at my energy! Would you throw this away for the sake of a dubious English bloodline of your own?'

'Dubious!'

Eric had gone too far. His wrath was equalled by the coldness of the Earl of Bamburgh. The worm was turning. Osulf had little to lose; he was old; death had little in it to frighten him. He could see a way to independence for the north; his dreams led him to imagine that it was still possible, before the ill, possibly dying southern king could be replaced by a determined youngster. He had to seize the chance. His own sons and Eric's adversaries in Dublin, with whom he had quarrelled, were of the same mind. Anlaf was unlikely to want to return to the palace of York; he, too, was growing old and wished to retire to a monastery. It was now that Osulf must act. If Eric would not go willingly, he must go forcefully. He held Earl Maccus in reserve. The shadow of Anlaf's son stood between the two men. His name was never mentioned in Eric's hearing.

'I do not relish a Norwegian dynasty, nor the ties which a pagan empire will bring. We are a Christian country. Ah. I know,' Osulf raised his hand to prevent Eric from protesting. 'I know what you have said to Wulfstan. I know how you pray daily on your knees. I wonder who it is that you pray to. Self-serving prayer alone will not suffice to convince me or my followers that you intend to lead this nation towards a Christian future. I see many trends returning it to a benighted pagan place. Your wife...'

'My wife?' Eric put a hand on his dagger. He could take insults against himself or his sons; they were no better than they ought to be, but Gunnhild was sacrosanct.

'Put your knife away. I will not utter words further about the queen. A woman is not responsible for her actions. You, Eric, should have controlled her. Apart from her hospital ministries, she does not form the ideal character of a queen of a British nation, Dane or English. The Britons in the west have little liking for her, either, though they are a small minority in any case. No, your time has come. You must go.'

The sound of many footfalls echoed through the courtyard outside. The door of the audience room burst open. Two tall Norwegian guards fell backwards as they were pushed inside by heavier men.

The Earl of Bamburgh was surrounded by men in his livery. To Eric, the small audience room appeared to be full of grim-faced soldiery not his own. This was no time to decide to defend his liberty; at best he could hope to kill half-a-dozen before succumbing to a bloody fate. His tongue had got him where he was; it could get him out of trouble as well as into it. Eric had a plan, an escape mechanism from just such a scenario. It had, after all, been coming. Gunnhild had foretold that there would be trouble. What dynasty, being overcome by another, was ever willing to roll over onto its back?

Eric quickly backed to a curtain behind the main chair, a huge throne from which he conducted his affairs. Its solidity acted as a shield against others in the room, who would be reticent to be violent towards a former victor. He pulled the curtain aside and in the moment that the Northumbrian earl and his coterie were waiting for a surrender, he slipped through a narrow door and closed it with a plank behind him. The soldiers ran to it, but were too late. Eric was along the narrow passage and out of the palace grounds through a metal grill hidden behind bushes, by the time the door in the audience room had been forced open. A passing nag with its owner stepping briskly to market allowed escape.

'Bring Earl Maccus to me.' Osulf would make the shadow into a man. Eric must be stopped, or, like so many Vikings before him, he would turn up again, perhaps with several heads. How do you catch and kill a successful Viking captain? You employ another Viking. Before long, Maccus, son of the former king of York, Anlaf, would be in pursuit, with an army of followers, to sweep up Eric Bloodaxe and to send his sons packing, back to where they had come from, back to the distant Orkneys. His wife? She could fly on her stick to the icy lands and rule there, for all he cared. Her child-bearing years were passed. There would be no more self-indulgent young princes born of that womb, at least.

**954:** *Here the Northumbrians drove out Eric, and Eadred succeeded to the kingdom of Northumbria.*
Anglo-Saxon Chronicles

*...he was killed by a certain Earl Maccus in a lonely place called Stainmore.*
Roger of Wendover

# Frome Palace, Christmas Eve 954

'AND BLOODAXE MET his end, so they say, on Stainmore.' Wynflaed looked blank. Eadgifu continued. 'Somewhere in the bleakest part of Yorkshire. He was trying to escape, like a rat. Earl Maccus and a few Northumbrian housecarls chased him on horseback for many miles, but the Viking's horse flagged. He was killed by a single blow. They say he stood to receive it. Valhalla has another occupant.'

The queen-mother could enjoy this Christmas. Things were going well; twenty years on from the celebrations at Frome with Athelstan, she could relish the achievements of her brood: her son Edmund, former king, her son Eadred, now king, her grandson Eadwig given responsibility in Wessex and his brother young Edgar likely to receive responsibility in Mercia. Northumbria was back under Eadred's sway. Archbishop Wulfstan was still safely imprisoned in Dewsbury, having resisted attempts to move him further south. Yes, there was much to celebrate. God had looked on the nation kindly.

'But I hear that Wulfstan may be being brought south?' Wynflaed took a sip of mead. It was almost as good as her own make. The waters of Frome made good ale, but the mead was not superior.

However, it was pleasant to join the court at this special time, despite the long coach journey from Charlton Horethorne. Eadwig and Edgar had arrived that morning from Glastonbury and Ramsey and it was good to see how they were growing. Their smiles lit up the court, contrasting with their uncle's pinched face. The grandmothers were slightly in awe of the young men which they had become. Eadwig, in particular, was strikingly handsome. At fifteen, girls were looking at him and he was looking at them. Edgar, at thirteen, had not reached this stage. He was shorter and plump, but he would alter, as Eadwig had done, in the next year or two. He would also be a handsome youth, though perhaps not as tall as his older brother.

'Yes, they are transferring him to Oundle. He might be there by now.'

'To Oundle? Isn't that an old monastery of St Wilfrid's?'

'St Wilfrid, yes. Eadred cannot bear to kill Wulfstan, though in my opinion he deserves death. He says he meant no harm. No harm! Eadred has gone soft. Dunstan has advised him, on religious grounds and because Athelstan chose him as archbishop and because he is related to the Northumbrian royal family, that incarceration behind the thorn hedge of Oundle will be the best place for him, away from Northumbrian influence, but comforted by the ghost of Wilfrid.'

'To taunt him perhaps? Didn't Wilfrid die there?'

'Yes, and Wulfstan will be offered his cell in the tumble-down monastery. He is not long for this world. He has complained for many years, you know, about his health.'

'I thought it was just his leg…'

Eadgifu waved her bread. She had lost interest in what happened to Wulfstan. The past had been successfully dealt with. Eric Bloodaxe was dead, Archbishop Wulfstan was mentally and physically crippled. All was well in the south, in Wessex.

Except for one niggle, or perhaps two. There were always niggles. Eadred was eating too much, desperately trying to put on weight. His clothes hung on him. He had had to spend time in the hospital here. The royal rooms were being cleaned and fumigated. The feast on the previous day had been something of a disaster; Eadred had vomited publicly. The monks had him under observation; this had happened many times before. Eadred was only thirty-one, he would recover, as he always did, but the hunting party would miss his presence tomorrow and perhaps for several days. Eadwig was capable of filling the social space left by Eadred, but this was not entirely satisfactory. The young man was beginning to see himself as sole ruler, beginning to plan changes which were not beneficial to his grandmother. Dunstan was despised. Aethelwold would suffer. Eadwig was also taking too much interest in an older woman, she had been told. Who was she? She would speak to Nonna. He would know how the king was, whether he could hold down any food, and whether Eadwig was likely to be in trouble. Sons and grandsons; they all grew away from her. None were perfect. All needed her experience, her wisdom. It had been long in the making.

Eadgifu sighed as she prepared her gown for the feast of Eve. The procession would weave its way to the church of St John, past the hospital where Eadred lay, no doubt groaning, poor man. He would hear the choir. The prayers would be focussed on his health and well-being. Her prayers would be heard by Saint Radegund. She fingered her relic box, hanging from her belt and hidden by the many folds of her garment. Radegund would relieve his pain, surely. The perfection of the saints could be relied upon.

'Are you ready, Wynflaed?' Eadgifu regarded her friend. Wynflaed brought her veil down across her face. They had seen many things, many mishaps, in their time in Wessex. Children who had uncontrollable tempers, children who died from the world, pleasant surprises, too, children who were unexpectedly raised to sainthood. There had been triumphs. Tonight, they must enjoy the present, be grateful. Eadwig was going to announce his betrothal at the Christmas day feast. The young man could be a father, himself, and she a great-grandmother, by next Christmas. She shook her head. What came on the morrow could not be foreseen, except by exceptional souls, such as Dunstan. If only he and Eadwig could get on...

Wynflaed was ready. Unlike Eadgifu, resplendent in multi-coloured layers of silk, she wore her vowess clothing. The blackness of the robe and the transparent headdress which covered her face marked her out as a semi-religious. Eadgifu saw her friend gradually retreating behind the cloth. She was becoming distant. Wynflaed was less often at court. The travelling troubled her, she said. Her days were becoming quieter, she said. Eadgifu feared that she was losing her, to solitude and the end of life which inevitably comes.

'Hold my hand, dear friend.' Wynflaed took the proffered hand. 'This is a time to celebrate all that we have, all that we have lived through. Tomorrow Christ will be born. Tonight, we shall follow the star. Our star of heaven.'

They walked together, hand in hand, from the palace to join the Christmas Eve procession. Eadgifu, not willing to concede to the grim reaper, had more battles ahead. Her friend had made her peace, she would peacefully go where her maker wished. There was no need to say anything; wisdom had come, at last.

# Frome Palace, Christmas morning.

'Nonna, I don't want my mother to know. Or my uncle, for that matter. That dwarf of his would make much of it. Keeper of the King's Secrets, what a laugh. Spreader of court calumny, more like. Not a word, got it?'

Eadwig was displaying character. Dunstan would not approve, but then, Dunstan seemed never to approve of anything that Eadwig did. Nonna could sympathise. He had been young, once.

'There is no need for this to be reported. You had some ale, you summoned a woman to your bed, there is little evidence of her presence…' Nonna looked around the bedchamber. He had been told by Dunstan to check on Eadwig. The court would need him to be in full control, of himself as well as them, on Christmas day. It was unfortunate that Eadwig should choose this night to bring in his mistress and worse still that the lad had not covered his tracks. The serving man would know. Nonna decided to tidy the room himself. He scrabbled around the youngster's bedroom, picking up the remains of a meal, an item of clothing.

'Right, Nonna, that's enough. How is my uncle? Will we see him today?' Eadwig jumped out of bed and splashed his face at the basin which Nonna had brought.

'He is still with the monks. The prayers of last night do not seem to have revived him.'

Eadwig pulled his outer tunic over his head and adjusted the sleeves, edged in gold thread, for maximum effect. His bride-to-be, Aelfgifu, had sewn them and would look for them later on, when they met again. He fingered a brooch, given to him by her mother. Should he wear it? He decided he would.

The young man was soon fully robed, as much as he cared to be.

Dunstan, Aethelwold and his grandmother favoured longer tunics on royalty, but he had good calves and liked to show them off. Long gowns would come in time and on formal occasions. Christmas day was not one of them; there would be speeches, of course, but no law-making today. The court would be joyous and mostly too drunk to care about the length of a tunic or robe.

Nonna studied the co-king of Wessex. If things continued as they were with Eadred, this lad would soon be full king of all England, including the freshly re-won kingdom of Northumbria, or, rather, the earldom of Northumbria, as it was to be called. Eadwig was even better looking than his father had been; his eyes brighter, his hair fairer. He was taller than the gangling Athelstan in his later years. No wonder he had his pick of the ladies at court, young or old. Nonna had no doubt that he had been introduced to the pleasures of the flesh at an early age and by more experienced, and probably married, ladies; the lithe body and slim hips would have been too tempting. The young body had already seen experience and learned much about love-making, but the head? The head was one, sometimes, of an imbecile. The hot-headedness of his father had descended with his genes; Eadwig was not stupid, but he was inclined to jump off cliffs of his own making. He had landed safely on his feet so far, but there would be occasions in the future… Nonna picked up the last shreds of evidence of coitus and arranged the sheets. He offered Eadwig a comb. His hair was the last part of the co-king to need attention.

'Thanks.' Eadwig brushed vigorously at his locks and began to plait the golden streaks which fell forward from his forehead. 'Send in a woman. I need help.'

'A woman, sir? Will Hersfig be able to help you? He has no-one to assist at present, with the king in the hospital.'

Eadwig cast his eyes around the room. 'Alright, send him to me. He can follow my footsteps for a while, if he likes.' Eadwig paused. 'But not Bica. I don't want him around me, under any circumstance.'

Nonna retreated, taking an armful of clothing and food waste.

Not Bica. What would the Keeper of the King's Secrets do if his king were not to survive? Hersfig could dress anyone and adapt to follow a youth as well as an ailing adult; he was trained to serve; but Bica, what would be his fate as mocker of the court beyond the bedchamber of Eadred? A dying Eadred?

# St Wilfrid's Monastery of Oundle, near Peterborough,

## Christmas Day 954

THERE WAS SOME comfort, as well as discomfort, in the guarded retreat which Wulfstan had been allowed. Allowed or granted? He was not sure whether his request to end his days at a monastery of his beloved St Wilfrid had been fully taken into account. Whatever he had done, or been judged to have done, he was still the archbishop of York until death. He had argued for Hexham or a rebuilt Ripon to be his last home, when he suggested he would be happily incarcerated and content to pray in the saint's presence, but they had brought him south, away from Northumbria, to spend the rest of his days behind the scabby thorn hedge of the monastery of Oundle.

They would not be many. He was already an old man of fifty-five. He supposed that Half-king, whose estate was nearby, would feel able to keep an eye on any suspect visitors who might wend their way here. The abbot of Ramsey had taken on the task of vetting any priests with northern accents who passed south to visit the ancient monastery; the church was still in good repair but the Viking wars, as with so many religious establishments in the east, had left the monks' main buildings in disrepair and little had yet been done to restore roofs. St Wilfrid's rooms and the refectory were still whole, but the dormitory and kitchen were part destroyed and ivy had grown over the walls. The great thorn hedge was overgrown and, in some places, had become a small thicket, past which only dogs and thin, determined clerics could squeeze. Only a few monks, mostly older men, now serviced the prayers and satisfied the appetites of the inmates; but Wulfstan could take some pleasure in his circumstances;

he was ever an optimist. He missed the conversation of his northern people, even the excitable banter which he had become used to with the Vikings who had come to York to rule, and to take. They had been open about their ambitions; he could deal with them. Now he was in the south, the motherland of deception and tongue-twisting.

There was a knock on the door. 'May I enter?'

Wulfstan was surprised. Christmas day in a monastery, albeit a rag-taggle one, was not a time for social calls. He got up, with difficulty, from kneeling on a cushion which had been provided for his sore leg. He gave thanks, once again, for the wound which had developed into an ulcer many years ago; it had often provided a good excuse for his refusal or inability, as he preferred to call it, to travel south to the court of Wessex. 'Who is it?'

'Aethelwold. I have come from Peterborough to see how you are faring.'

Could Wulfstan be glad of a visitor? Could he be glad of this particular visitor? Aethelwold was not fond of secular priests or archbishops with wives. But, in Oundle, Wulfstan had renounced women and all others. It might be amusing to hear how Dunstan's plans for reform were progressing and what news there might be of Northumbria. He remembered Aethelwold as a young upstart, training at Dunstan's suggestion, late in life, at Glastonbury, enthusiastically robbing the state's coffers to rebuild churches and monasteries in the east of England. Aethelwold was a new breed of disciplinarian; he had been known to insist on a wayward monk's hand be thrust into boiling water, to learn a lesson. He would have outraged Northumbrian monks, where subtlety of word use were the means of control. He would not have understood St Aidan, or St Columba or even St Cuthbert, who worked their miracles of conversion by persuasion, not torture, and they would not have tolerated him.

'Come in.' Human company, welcome or not, was a challenge Wulfstan could not refuse. There would be little of it in the days or months ahead, whatever was left to him.

Aethelwold entered the room. To his eyes, it appeared suitable for a prelate of the church in distress. The furnishings were plain, not ornate, there were drab but serviceable curtains at the windows to cover drafts, a table and chair to sit at and write, books enough to entertain. A brown-coloured ewer contained a few stems of grasses and a single, dead rose. That was unnecessary decoration. He frowned. 'Archbishop.'

'Father Aethelwold. How do you do? I am sorry, I have only the one seat. Do take it. I have my cushion here.'

'I will not stay long; I shall remain standing. I am as you can see, busy. I am on my way to the court in Frome, a long journey and I will be late for the festivities, but I hope to arrive by twelfth night. Is there anything that you need, that I can do for you?' Aethelwold eyed the famous leg.

Wulfstan was airing the ulcer, letting it dry. He covered over the wound with his robe. 'There is nothing that I need, more than can be arranged for my health in this place. The monks are kind, they bring me food and enough drink. The ale is good. May I offer you some? Perhaps you can tell me a little about my home?'

'Your home? This is now your home, Wulfstan. The king has spared you to live out the remainder of your life in prayer. Northumbria is no longer your concern. Forget it.'

How can a person, who has been born in and lived all his life in a land, forget it? Like the salmon who return to their place of birth in the streams of the north, Wulfstan felt his soul was attached by an invisible cord to the open moors, hills and great rivers of Northumbria. That cord was stretched, to the limit. He hated being in the south. But this was a last enterprise of faith, in a life which had been made more difficult than most by the influx of immigrants to Northumbria and their quarrels over who should take the prized position of king. Perhaps it was just as well that there would never again be a king of York, or Northumbria. The book of the glories of that land was closed, the story over.

There was no point in arguing against this representative of the south. He would not understand the longing for place which Wulfstan felt, or the longing for a wife's company. 'Yes, I shall forget. I pray that I will forget. Then my pain may be lessened.' Wulfstan felt a tap on his shoulder. A voice hissed in his ear.

'You will not forget me!'

'Or me!'

'Or me!'

The voices of Cartimandua, Caractacus and Hilda screamed in his ear. He started and began to speak. 'No, not now...'

Could Aethelwold hear them? No, by the look of unconcerned impatience on his face, he could not. Such a man would never be vulnerable to the voices of the past, or of different peoples or persuasion. He was indoctrinated and drunk on the rise of the Wessex house and church. He was probably making plans at this very moment for the rejuvenation of Ely. His legacy was what mattered to this man, and extracting money from others for his schemes.

'There is one thing which you could do: divert a little of your church monies to restoring this place, not for my comfort, but for the sake of Wilfrid.'

'There is little point in restoring the missionary churches and monasteries of the past. There is much to be gained from resources being aimed at developing a future of monastic prayer in new foundations or a few of the larger establishments. Resources are scarce; the old monasteries which serve as hospitals, such as this one, are not my remit.' Aethelwold opened his mouth to continue, but, realising that the archbishop would never be on his side in any theological or political debate, he closed it again.

There was little to say to a man who believed in pastoral work, who prayed less and talked more, who loved to be with the poor and to speak their language, the language of family and work. A man who Athelstan long ago had liked for his worldliness and love of hunting, who liked women and fine clothes. Aethelwold turned back to the door. He could report that the archbishop was unchanged, that he was sad to be separated from his beloved north, that he appeared to have voices in his head who chastised him.

The archbishop, he considered, was in the right place. Wilfrid would sort his conscience, as no gaoler might do. To be chastised by a saint of the catholic persuasion, in the place and the very room where he died, was comfort enough to those who might have had him executed, or blinded, for his renegade resistance to the requirements of Wessex.

This Christmas day of 954 had brought considerable gifts; the prize of a settled Northumbria, the greatest of all. Its last champion was now an incarcerated madman.

# Twelfth Night, Frome Palace, 955

THE ONCE-FRESH GREEN decorations over fireplaces were beginning to sag; some thegns had already left the court to celebrate the occasion of twelfth night in their own halls. The Wessex family was allowed some privacy to relax, with just a few diplomats from across the waters to entertain in the evenings. They would be leaving the following day. The extended family could renew its self-knowledge and self-awareness.

'We haven't seen each other for so long, little brother. I have almost forgotten what you look like. Tell me about yourself. What is it like, living with that brute, Half-king?' Eadwig was lounging on a wide windowsill. He could see out across the lazy Frome river, spreading in flood, past the fog in the valley to the large oaks on the hill to the north. Rooks were beginning, even as early as January, to fight for their nesting sites. Eadwig watched them as they flew up and down again. Hazel catkins waved their arms just outside the window in a slight breeze. 'The fog will soon lift. We shall hunt later this morning.'

The cautious younger brother, in awe of his sibling's mature form and demeanour, was reticent to correct him. As one king to another, though, he felt bound to defend his defender.

'He is not a brute, Eadwig.'

Eadwig shifted his position on the windowsill, raised a leg and positioned his long arms around it. He was on the higher ground. Edgar sat in a cushioned chair, attending to a game of chess.

'It is your turn. Why do you call people whom you do not know by such terrible names?' Edgar sat back and stared at his brother. How he had grown! Would he catch him up in the coming years? He looked at his pudgy arm in its linen finery. There was no sign of a muscle beneath the material. 'Come on, brother, come down here and play your queen. She is looking distressed.'

Eadwig took his time. There was something challenging about Edgar; he was too knowing. After a long minute, he jumped off the windowsill and joined Edgar at the chess table. His hand hovered over his queen. He felt that Edgar had an advantage; he couldn't see what it might be. He moved the queen.

'Ah, pity.' Edgar took the queen with his white bishop. 'Sorry.' The chess piece sat in a pile of pawns and a knight. 'Perhaps you should think more before you move…'

'Perhaps you should watch your bishop.' Eadwig took the white bishop with his black knight. They were almost equal.

'Anyway, Half-king has done well for us, for Uncle Eadred. He has brought back Northumbria for Wessex. We couldn't do without him. Matters which have been troublesome for a long time have settled. Dunstan says that taxes will flow into the treasury again from the north. We shall be able to travel to York in safety, if we wish. There will be a new appointee to the archbishopric. We will all speak the same language.' Edgar, at thirteen, was becoming a master of the nation's affairs, Eadwig granted him that. But there was one thing which he had experience of, which, as far as he knew, Edgar had not. Sex. The older boy had the advantage there.

'Do you wish to know what it is like to lie with a woman?'

'Not particularly. I suppose I shall find out for myself in time.'

This was not the response which Eadwig required. 'An older woman?'

Edgar looked up from contemplating his next chess move. 'You mean the lady Aethelgifu?'

'How do you know that?'

'I am cultivating my spies, as I am sure you are.' Edgar moved a pawn forward. He was closing in on the far side of the board.

'There is so much to know about you, little brother, I am sure. You are so experienced. Should I instruct Nonna to follow you about, to check on what information you are gleaning? And why?' Eadwig's hand hovered over the board.

'There is little to know about me, Eadwig, and nothing which should concern or worry you. Grandmother would tell you if there was anything amiss. Are you going to move that pawn?'

Grandmother. A queen to consider. Eadwig had lost his queen on the board. He feared that he had lost his grandmother's affection during his puberty. But it could not be helped; she and Dunstan had exercised too much control. He moved the pawn. Again, Edgar attacked and took it. The pile of conquered pieces on his chair arm was becoming embarrassing to behold. Couldn't his brother – his bother, as he was beginning to call him, play a little less well? 'I hear that you are to take charge of Mercia.' Eadwig had little choice but to recognise that the small chubby boy was becoming an equal partner in the realm.

'Aethelwold and Dunstan – and Grandmother, think that I am ready. And you know how ill Uncle Eadred has been.'

Eadwig thought that Edgar was ready, too ready, for his liking. Now there were five in a camp who might disturb his plans; Edgar, brainwashed by Aethelwold to be holy, Dunstan who he heartily disliked, Half-king who had adopted Edgar and gave the impression of favouring him as more than just ruler of Mercia, and Grandmother, who had fussed and talked about her "golden son" throughout the Christmas period. What was he, Eadwig, if not golden? But he had grown to be a man and was therefore no longer a cherub. He could admit to himself, he was no angel. But to be forced into a shadow by this imp was unacceptable. The sooner he was back in Ramsey, the better, with Aethelwold. He made a bold move with his king.

'Checkmate!' Edgar had won the game.

# Frome Palace, November 20, 955

'HE IS WORSE. Look.' Hersfig removed the cloth from the pot. Bica recoiled. The time had come. 'Dunstan was here yesterday. Did he spend long with the king?'

'About an hour. Nonna was with Dunstan.'

'The scribe. They were writing something, probably the will. We shall have what Eadred has promised us, at last.'

'I wouldn't be too sure. A dying man may change his mind. You have not gone out of your way to endear yourself to Dunstan, or to the queen, for that matter.'

Bica pushed the proffered pot away. 'The king has always told us he would do right by us. I know Nonna. He is brought in for important business and when Dunstan is in too much of a hurry to see to matters himself. Where is the abbot now?'

'Gone to Winchester and after that he said he was going to Glastonbury. He took a fast horse instead of the usual waggon.'

'I mean, Nonna. Is he in the monastery?' Bica began to jump up and down.

'How do I know where he is? Go and look for him, if you want him. I have work to do. The herbalist will be here soon and I need to tidy things.' Hersfig threw the contents of the pot out of a privy window onto the midden below.

There was a moan from the bedchamber.

'I've got to get back to him, poor man.' Hersfig ignored the anxious-looking Keeper of the King's Secrets. What price the secrets of a man when he is dying?

Bica spit out one more question as he opened the heavy door. 'Where is Eadwig?'

'Probably in Cheddar, hunting. I don't know.'

'The queen is in Winchester, indisposed. I suppose he would not want to be there.'

'No.'

It was the last exchange, in Eadred's reign, of the Keeper of the King's Secrets and He who Walks in the Steps of the King. There was panic, but also hopefulness, in the air. Change is welcomed by some.


Bica found Nonna at a desk in the monastery library, writing. Several sheets of parchment lay on the floor at his feet.

'The king has sent me to ask you how the writing is progressing. He wants to sign the disposition of his estate by nightfall. May I see?'

Nonna raised his pen. Another smudge of ink. He would have to start that line again. Bishop Aelfsige of Winchester would be annoyed to know that his written name was spoiled by the intrusion of the lord Bica. Another piece of parchment fell to the floor.

It was, in Nonna's consideration, less than ideal that the lord Bica should view a work in progress, particularly a will, but this was the king's closest companion, who held a prominent position in the private affairs of Eadred. He put his pen into its inkwell and allowed Bica to view the writing. It was half-done. The name of Aethelwold, Bishop of Winchester was repeated several times, in conjunction with several gifts. Nonna had included Dunstan in the will, of course. Eadwig's name was not visible.

'I want to see the notes. There may be discrepancies.'

Nonna protested. He had no view on the secret-keeper's discretion or lack of it; he had learned long ago that court officials were wise to bow to favourites of any king. But this was a private matter, entrusted to him by Eadred and Dunstan. 'The notes, my lord?' Nonna moved a wax tablet aside. Bica would have difficulty reading his hurried writing, but it would be best if he did not have a chance.

Bica peered at the tablet. There were many names of household servants, but his own was not one of them. He flounced off without another word.

# Glastonbury Abbey, November 21, 955

A SHORT PERSON, in a colourful cape and a feather in his hat, sporting expensive riding boots and astride a carefully decked filly, rode casually up to the main gate of the abbey. Frost was on the ground still, at the end of the day. Both rider and horse snorted with the cold. The morning ride from Frome had been pleasant, but hurried. It was not a race, though there were other competitors in the field, not far behind.

Bica spoke to the guard, a housecarl. He was not known at Glastonbury, as yet. He hoped not to be recognised, but his size and wealthy appearance would advise some, who were aware of his abilities, who were behind him.

'I have come from the king. I am the Keeper of the King's Secrets, the lord Bica. I wish to see the prior.'

Bica had done well for himself over the years and had not lost the powers which had endeared him to Eadred. On this occasion, however, his apparel and brooch, made of silver and gold, and his authoritative, deep voice, overcame any obstacles or misgivings on the part of the guard, who opened one side of the iron-topped gate and let him in. In these days, there had been little reason to doubt the veracity of wealthy visitors; they would have, anyway, to pass through several doors to gain entry to anything of importance.

Abbot Dunstan, as far as Bica knew, was still in Winchester, conversing with the royal family. Plans were being discussed. The reign of Eadgifu's second son was rapidly drawing to a close; Eadwig was the rightful heir, but not a popular choice with the family. Edgar was too young to take over full power; would Queen Eadgifu have a second chance at regency, denied to her at Edmund's death? The grandmother would fight for what she considered her rights.

Her strength, in her mid-fifties, had not diminished. She still wore her high heels across the palace tiled floors, clack-clacking her determined presence as she went.

Bica had been promised much by Eadred, but Dunstan was not his friend, nor was the queen. *I will make you rich, one day.* The words had rung sweetly in his ears. Now Eadred was very ill; there had been a loaf too many, taken soaked in dark ale. It was as if he wanted to kill himself. Perhaps he did. Bica had donned his finest gear, some of it borrowed from Eadred's wardrobe, and taken a favourite horse from the stable. His thighs ached; he was not used to long rides. He looked for a mounting step. He found it behind the gatehouse and dismounted, with only a few steps to walk, with difficulty, to the refectory.

A bell sounded, summoning the prior's clerk.

'I have come from the king. He has asked me to fetch him a certain relic.' Bica handed the clerk a written note. The king's stamp in wax hung from its edge.

'I will bring you to the prior. He is at the midday meal.' The clerk eyed the great brooch on Bica's shoulder and the small stature of the man. The voice was commanding from such a small frame, as authoritative as Athelstan Half-king's, but this creature was not a soldier, nor could ever be. Besides, his dark hair was greying. He could be fifty. He was an usually wealthy Briton, one who had succeeded in a Saxon world. The clerk's mother was British. 'Welcome to Inys Witrin,' he said. He ushered Bica into the prior's room and asked him to wait.

After some moments, during which Bica rehearsed his speech, which was intended to unlock the haligdom of Glastonbury, the prior entered, wiping his mouth with his sleeve. He could be a Briton, too, thought Bica.

It was surprisingly easy to convince the prior of his need to view the haligdom. The king's seal was enough. Had the abbot been present, there would not have been any hope of success. It was enough to have confirmed that the king was ill, that he needed a particular relic to comfort him, that Bica, the lord Bica, who was known to have an important role as assistant to the king, should be sent to fetch it. Within moments, the prior found the key to the barn containing the bulk of the treasure of the realm as well as its most precious relics and ushered Bica in to find what he wanted.

Abbot Dunstan, meantime, in Winchester, had similar orders from Eadred, this time bona fide. The king wanted all the gold bullion brought to him in Frome. He did not trust those around him. His earlier, unsolicited promises might have spawned dangerous covetousness. Dunstan was on his way to his abbey, on horses much faster than Bica's, but the roads were knee-high in mud. It would take him at least two days to get to mid-Somerset, plus the time taken to speak to the king in person at Frome on his way. The king's mattress would be supported by gold. The treasures of the realm were being gathered in with the aim of supervising distribution. Trust had left the palaces of Wessex; the beaks and snouts of greed were being sharpened.

# Frome Palace, November 22, 955

'HE RALLIED FOR a while. They found that he could not take bread or ale.'

'Then the water will be killing him.'

'He takes wine and mead. He has no teeth left with which to eat solid food.'

Nonna consulted at Eadred's open door with Hersfig. Dunstan panted along the corridor behind him.

'How is he?' Dunstan was covered in mud. He had lost weight in recent days. His eyes were ringed brown. He pulled a small gold-covered wooden relic chest from a leather bag strapped around him. 'Take this and put it under his pillow. It is precious.'

'There is not much room…'

'Make room, and double the guards. Let no-one in other than yourself until I return. I must go to Glastonbury, but will be back tomorrow.'

'Shall I order food and drink for you, my lord?' Hersfig hoped to hand over responsibility of the care of the king to the abbot, but Dunstan was already turning away. Eadred was presently asleep, but his body seeped liquids which needed constant attention. Hersfig had not before seen death in a bed; was this inconvenient agony the way of all those not killed in battle? If so, the plight of those with an hereditary illness was one which could not be soothed away by prayers. When conscious, Eadred had begged the angels, the saints and God for mercy from his bodily pains; no relic or prayer had brought about a cure. Faith had left him; only his cries and terror told him that he was still alive, or was this already hell?

Hersfig thought of the legacy which would be his and returned to his king, still king until he was a corpse. He placed a plank across the back of the chamber door. The palace bedchamber of the king was now a fortress of the treasury of the nation.

*For his part the man of God, wishing to repay his love in all sincerity, used often to name the king as dearest of all men to him. In this spirit of trusting affection, the king handed over to Dunstan his most valuable possessions: many land charters, the old treasure of earlier kings, and various riches of his own acquiring, all to be guarded faithfully behind the walls of his monastery.*

The Life of St Dunstan, 19.2

# Between Frome and Glastonbury, 23 November 955,

S t Clement's Day.
The covered cart creaked eastwards up the hill towards Doulting. The carthorse from the abbey was not used to long journeys; usually it worked around the grounds, moving building materials. Dunstan and a guard walked beside it as it trudged, bearing the heavy load of much of the nation's treasure. A thief had disturbed the hoard of assembled gold, which Dunstan had not had time to fully tally. Items were missing, he was sure; the heap of loose jewellery had not been so small before. An assessment of what exactly had been taken would be made, later. For the time being, half of all that was important to the wellbeing and order of England was here, behind the heaving backside of the horse, including manuscripts of land holdings, the production of a reign of taxation as well as the accumulated wealth of former Wessex kings.

The cart reached the top of the hill and began the flatter onward journey to Frome. Other carts would be coming on the long journey from Winchester, bringing the remainder of the accountable treasure to the palace where the king, sick but lucid, lay waiting, waiting for an angel to save him from death, or another to take him to the heavenly realms. At such times, it was difficult to know whether to pray for release or to retain the ability to manage the kingdom's affairs. This was a task, to collect the nation's treasure, which Dunstan could have done without, this demand of the dying king, fuelled as it was by panic, but it was, he recognised, necessary. He brushed aside the thought that Eadred might have doubts about his own trustworthiness. Eadwig was the problem, not himself. On hearing of his uncle's likely and sudden demise, he would be hastening to his bedside, waiting to catch the crown as it fell from his uncle's head. The treasure of the nation must be distributed amongst Eadred's friends, or it would fall into others' hands. During Eadwig's time at Glastonbury, he had made contacts, allies unfavourable to himself, Dunstan, and the queen.

The carthorse was whipped along in a reluctant trot and descended into Frome late in the day. The contents of the cart were unloaded into a large barn and placed under guard. Dunstan had to return for the other half of the treasure in Glastonbury and to assess what had been pilfered, if possible.

'How is the king?' He had time to take bread and cheese and sip ale before the return journey. There was not time enough to visit the stinking bedchamber; that would have to wait until the next evening. The gathering in of the treasure was an imperative.

'No better, no worse.' Nonna viewed his lifelong companion. At forty-five, Dunstan was entering the respectable era of seniority of years; his will was becoming the stronger of the two aspects of man: the body and the mind. There was a little more round-shoulder in the frame and the hair was becoming sparse and turning to white, but hair was not a matter which an abbot could afford to mourn and Dunstan was not a vain man, whatever else he might be. 'Your friends have arrived. Bishop Aelfsige has been notified of the king's illness and he is on his way, as are the queen and lord Half-king.'

'Edgar?'

'He is with Half-king, travelling from Ramsey. He will be here tomorrow.'

Tomorrow might be too late. 'Is Eadwig here?'

As Dunstan was making his enquiries, the palace gate opened and a tall young man rode in, alone. Dunstan and Nonna both watched him through a window. The young man was in no hurry. He led his horse to the stables and emerged after handing it over to a groom. Cien, his father's horse, was still a decent ride for Eadwig.

Nonna and Dunstan watched him cross the cobbled courtyard. 'Make sure no-one apart from yourself is allowed into the king's bedroom. I will be back as soon as I can. No-one. Get Hersfig out of the room.' Dunstan pointed at the slim figure of the aetheling Eadwig. Did he know of Eadred's sudden illness? 'Do not tell anyone of the king's condition. We must buy time.'

Dunstan quickly mounted a fresh riding horse and rode out of the courtyard by another gate, following the cart. There was no time to be lost. The journey back to Glastonbury would be quicker, after the steep rise out of Frome's valley. He joined the original guard and began the ascent.

They made good progress along the road. At Shepton Mallet, the cart was overtaken by a king's messenger from Frome. He shouted at the abbot. Dunstan drew up his horse and signalled for the cart to stop.

'What?'

'The king has taken very ill. His clerk wishes for your hasty return.'

Dunstan reviewed in his mind what he must do. A large amount of the nation's treasure was still at Glastonbury. Much was now at Frome, stacked high in the king's bedroom, waiting for distribution, if the worst befell the king, to its rightful beneficiaries. If Eadwig managed to get to the king before Dunstan, there would be great difficulties. Should he return to Frome at once or go to Glastonbury to collect what he could?

He turned his horse and the empty cart around. The king would need his prayers, and his help. His own position might be in peril. He looked at the sun, hovering weakly in the south. It would be at least three hours back to Frome. The clouds parted, a shaft of bright light fell onto the path before him and a large bird squawked from a rowan tree to his left. Dunstan was becoming harder of hearing, partly as a consequence of close quarters with heavy bells, but he heard the bird as a high-pitched voice.

'The king has died.' It spoke to Dunstan, and flew off the branch into the air towards Frome. The abbot pulled violently on the rein, causing his horse to rise up and then fall, injuring itself, though not its rider. It lay there, thrashing in pain. The guard dismounted and rushed to assist the abbot, who had been thrown clear onto a grassy verge.

'My lord! Can you walk?'

Dunstan, winded but otherwise unharmed, shouted. 'The king, the king, he has died! The bird…an angel has told me. Look, the heavens have opened to reveal it!' He knelt on the grass and raised his arms upwards. Another vision had come. The drama of the occasion confirmed his status as a seer. This had happened before; he had seen Edmund's death, too. None of this was hindsight; one day a biographer would write of his saintly abilities. Eadred had been a reasonable client as king, one who would accept advice and pliably apportion wealth between the state and the church. But now he was dead, or close to death, Dunstan felt fear in every one of his potentially saintly bones. He must return in haste. There would not be many willing to care for the dead king; there were things which only he could arrange. Eadwig, once he was aware that there was a corpse and not an uncle in the palace bedroom at Frome, would take the crown and hold a feast, a gathering for all his supporters, not Eadred's. Or his, Dunstan.

*Hence the departure of the man of God Dunstan…with the task of*
*bringing back to the king what he had stored for safe keeping. When, some*
*days later, laden with the king's riches, he was coming back the way he*
*had gone, a voice from heaven spoke to him: 'Behold, now King Eadred*
*has passed away in peace.' At these words the horse Dunstan rode was*
*suddenly struck dead, for it could not abide the presence of the sublime*
*angel.*

The Life of St Dunstan 20.5

*Unfortunately Dunstan's beloved King Eadred was very sickly*
*all through his reign. At meal times he would suck the juice out of his*
*food, chew what was left for a little and then spit it out; a practice that*
*often turned the stomachs of the thegns dining with him. He dragged on*
*an invalid existence as best he could, despite the protests of his body, for*
*quite a long time. Finally his worsening illness came over him more and*
*more often with thousandfold weight, and brought him unhappily to his*
*deathbed. So long had he been ill that he felt unsure of living longer. He*
*accordingly sent round everywhere to collect up his property, so that he*
*might dispose of it to his kin, while he could, freely and in accordance with*
*his wishes. Hence the departure of the man of God Dunstan, like other*
*trustees of the royal treasure, with the task of bringing back to the king*
*what he had stored for safe keeping.*

The Life of St Dunstan, 20.3

# Frome Palace, evening, 23 November 955

NONNA WRUNG HIS hands. Dunstan had returned and gone
again, this time to Winchester, having exhorted him to tell
no-one of the king's death. But the truth would inevitably get out,
surely? Apparently, Dunstan wanted a few days in order to gather

in as much of the treasure as he could under one roof. In a few days the corpse would start to rot; a passing nose would notice. Dunstan wanted it known that the king was sick, but not dead. A few days…Nonna liked the aetheling Eadwig; would the young man not understand what had happened, or at least suspect it? But Dunstan could hold that responsibility and take it to heaven, or hell, with him. Eadwig had not stayed long at the palace at Frome; he had gone hunting, he said, at Zeals, with Wulfric the huntsman. He would be gone several days.

Standing outside the door of the king's bedchamber, now deserted except by the body of Eadred, Nonna considered that he had not known as difficult a time in his experience at the court of the Wessex kings. He had been there when Athelstan had 'entertained' the Scottish king in the very same palace in 934 and again when Edmund had been stabbed by Leofa, his friend, at Pucklechurch in 946. He had witnessed the shenanigans of family members of the Wessex dynasty with their relic obsession and the attempts by his compatriot, Dunstan, from Glastonbury schooldays, to climb the greasy pole of power through the church. He had seen how truth could be bent, how history could be rewritten, and made the notes for both kings and priests on which to base their versions of it. The application of hindsight, combined with a position of superiority, produced much which was pertinent in the chronicles of the times in which they lived. A Saxon kingdom which had expanded, suffered under Viking attack, shrunk and then recomposed, felt the defensive burden of maintenance of its history. As the dreaded millennium approached, was this the end for the dynasty of Alfred, or the beginning of something fresh, rejuvenated, with the onset of a new reign by a sixteen-year-old, Eadwig?

Had Eadwig guessed that Eadred was dead? Nonna had heard the young man entering the main hall, calling for food and drink, on his return from Glastonbury, from a hunt at a friend's home or perhaps from Bath Abbey, where he often went. The careless young man was well aware of his role as the eldest son of Edmund and therefore likeliest to made the king of England after Eadred's demise.

Eadred had been unwilling to recognise the possibility of his own death. Like many, he had assumed that his life would be allowed to continue, in pain, often, but, like his illustrious ancestor, Alfred, who had died at the age of fifty, he had assumed that his bodily pains, though bad, would not cause him to be taken to the heavenly gate of paradise, at the relatively young age of thirty-two. Eadred rarely looked at himself in a mirror. Frome's palace had been stripped of them, except in the queen's quarters. If he had seen himself, he would have noted how his years of illness had altered his once youthful looks; his hair had gone, his teeth likewise and his cheeks were sunken. His furrowed brow creased even when meeting ambassadors. His toothless mouth grinned, the loose skin folding in waves towards his jutting ears. Eating in public had become a nightmare; the food loved by feasting courtiers had been difficult to chew, even with the help of a bone false tooth specially shaped to crunch cooked flesh and vegetables. Ale, even the ale made of good Frome water, renowned for its healing properties, made him want to wretch. Soft bread, removed of its husks, could be swallowed in milk, but even that had become a source of pain. In recent days, he had given up eating or drinking anything, watched by Hersfig his loyal servant, who had tried to persuade him to take something, anything. Eadred had given up. The Lord could take him if he wanted. In heaven there would be no pain, no problem with food. Eating had become a worse enemy that even Vikings.

But the Viking question in the north had been settled. Wulfstan was safely hedged in at Oundle. The North had acquiesced to the Wessex kingship. For now, despite their waving of the holy cloth of Cuthbert and holding his body at Chester-le-Street, it had had its fill of Viking kings and the disruption which they could cause. Eadred had overseen a period of instability; peace had come; he could relax and be at one with his soul.

But the soul was contained in a body, and that body needed food, if it was to remain in this world. Dunstan had been too busy to note the king's recent descent into lassitude and starvation. Prayer by the monks in the decrepit monastery nearby the palace of Frome, few as they were, would not, even though Eadred had been taught that prayer would assist the sick, be enough to cure or to bring him to a state of hopefulness. Eadred was despairing, of life, of health, of success. He no longer cared, except for the treasure.

As he felt his health deteriorating, he had exhorted Dunstan to bring all the main items of treasure belonging to him and to England to Frome. He had hastily made a will, gifting much to Dunstan and his mother, Eadgifu, as well as the Bishop of Winchester, Aelfsige, his household priest. Prayers would do little to comfort him now; only the safe gathering of the royal treasure to a heap beside his bed would suffice to soothe the anxious king.

*Dunstan, that man of virtue, now demonstrated indeed his good faith and true loyalty, offering to the dead what he had offered to the living. For while all others turned away and disdained to attend the king's exequies, Dunstan and his men took the body, now mere earth, back with him and gave it decent burial.*

Adelard of Ghent, Lectiones in Depositions s.Dunstani

## Winchester, 26th November 955

RAIN FELL HORIZONTALLY across the stone-paved area in front of the Old Minster. The bowed, exhausted form of the abbot of Glastonbury, the well-padded Bishop Aelfsige of Winchester, Aethelwold in dark blue robes, Half-king and the aetheling Edgar, freshly ridden in from Ramsey, accompanied the aged queen mother, who had lived through the deaths of her husband and two sons. She had her favourite grandson, Edgar, to comfort her.

Edgar was a pleasant-looking thirteen-year-old. She had not seen him for a while; his tutor Aethelwold had him under instruction at Abingdon and she had had regular news of his progress. It seems he took after his uncle; there was pliability in his makeup, unlike Eadwig, the older boy, who reacted negatively to authority of any kind. Edgar was also free of the family tendency to anger; his father's emotional genes had not passed to him; his mother's saintly nature seemed uppermost. He was a sweet cherub, thought Eadgifu, as she surveyed the chief mourners from beneath her dark wimple. The puppy fat would go, she knew, the man would emerge with all the vices known to men, but indoctrination was already well in hand; Edgar would be a worthy ruler of Mercia, in a few years from now. With Aethelwold and Dunstan to watch over him, he would do what was right; what was right for her and for the kingdom. Eadwig, however, with his outrageous ideas and obsession with sex, was not… perfect. And yet he would rule England, by right. There were clouds around Eadwig which grew denser each day; he rejected the advice which she and Dunstan offered. He had chosen and taken a wife, without her involvement. She remembered choosing Edmund's wife for him; the matter had been settled on a political basis, as it should be.

Eadgifu was suffering from an emotion new to her: jealousy. She had been beautiful, now she knew that she was viewed as just an old woman bedecked with jewels. She was surprised at how strongly she felt; the antipathy which had been growing towards her eldest grandson had doubled since he had started to consort with a woman much older than himself. She hated Aethelgifu, a noblewoman of Mercia. If she had been the wife of a lesser thane, it would have been an inconsequential affair; young inexperienced men had been known to be attracted to older women, usually prostitutes. This was different. Not only was Aethelgifu darkly beautiful, she was well-educated and said to be amusing in character. As a merry widow, she was corrupting the young, in Eadgifu's assessment; her young. Eadwig had consorted with her for about a year, her sources told her. He would ride out from Frome or Cheddar, or Glastonbury, wherever he was hunting at the time, and seek her out when she stayed at Bath Abbey. The chasing of deer and hunting of fowl had given way to the pleasures of the flesh. And there was Aethelgifu's daughter. How could a mother allow her daughter to move in public as she did; the lines of her body could clearly be seen through the light clothing which she wore. In theory she was covered, as expected at court, when she appeared in the company of her mother, but some women had a way of overcoming being swathed in cloth; their desirability overcame their disguise. Aelfgifu, the daughter, had already a reputation for turning men's heads. At fourteen, this was not acceptable. At fifteen, and safely married, she would be dismissed as comfortably claimed and probably pregnant, but this was a girl who expected to attract by desire the richest prizes and the most obvious catch available, Eadwig. She had heard that the girl was hoping to exchange her wimple for a crown. A crown! Even she, Eadgifu, had not been granted that item. Jewelled headbands held her hair and wimple in place. No women of the Wessex dynasty had ever been accorded the status of crown-wearing, despite being called Queen. The consorts of the kings in recent times had been just that; breeding companions and providers of legitimate heirs.

The New Minster bells rang. The coffin bearing the body of Eadgifu's second son, dripping with the autumn rain, was borne into the nave and placed on a bier. A flag was draped over the coffin and the crown of Wessex placed on it. The service of thanks for his life and achievements began. Eadgifu knelt to pray, alongside Athelstan Half-king. Dunstan, who had arranged everything, led the prayers. Aethelwold and Oda, the archbishop, took their places at the altar. Ealdormen and thegns sank to the stone floor. Edgar shuffled on his cushion. There would be many occasions when the royal family had to kneel, though the cushions, as time went on, were plumper and more decorative. Where was Eadwig?

Late again?

Worse than that. Absent.

*When the thousand years are over, Satan will be let loose from his dungeon; and he will come out to seduce the nations in the four quarters of the earth and to muster them for battle, yes, the hosts of Gog and Magog, countless as the sands of the sea...*

Revelation of St John 20, v7-9

*But as for the cowardly, the faithless, and the vile, murderers, fornicators, sorcerers, idolaters, and liars of every kind, their lot will be the second death, in the lake that burns with sulphurous flames.*

Revelation of St John 20, v8

## Monastery of St John, Frome, Autumn 988

'B UT WAS HE shriven? Nonna? Did he really die alone?'
The old monk had fallen asleep again. Algar poked his shoulder. He needed to know the answer to his question.

'Eh? Where was I?' *Who am I?* Nonna opened one eye. The other was gummy. 'Ah, Algar, I was telling you about the king who died in Frome, was I not?' *Of course, I was. How could I forget what I was saying? I shall soon be following Dunstan to the heavenly Gates, at this rate. But my notes and books will be left in capable hands.*

'King Eadred, yes. You told me that the palace was in a panic and that Archbishop Dunstan was travelling backwards and forwards from Glastonbury to bring the treasure to him, but who shrove the king? Did it happen? What if it didn't? His soul would be in torment, in that dreadful place...with the beast...' Algar broke off. His child's imagination had studied and benefitted from Dunstan's doom in the church and the shapes and colours of glass in the windows. The walls of the palace were festooned with the heroic tales of love, life and particularly death, but not the afterlife. Hell and heaven were left to the church to portray. It did it well.

'Calm yourself, Algar. I will tell you what happened, as well as I can. Give me my rag.' Nonna wiped his eyes. 'That's better. Is it suppertime?'

'Nonna!'

'Ah, yes, was the king shriven. You want to know, do you, my young friend?'

Algar shrugged with impatience.

There was a long silence as Nonna took his old and now feeble mind backwards in time to that awful day, as bad as the day of Edmund's killing at Pucklechurch, when Eadred died alone, except for Hersfig, his man. Had there been a priest at hand who had assisted the king in his final throes of life? The death had been expected for years by all but the king himself; the signs of decrepitude were obvious, but the suddenness of the actual demise had taken everyone by surprise.

'I was not a monk at that time...' No, he had not been persuaded that he, himself, at that time had needed the protection of the church by Dunstan, or by Aethelwold. Especially not him. Nonna was silent. Was Eadred really alone at death, unaccompanied by a priest? He had not thought of that before, but then, the last rites by a priest had not been commonly done in those days. In recent years it had become essential for all good Christians to be shriven, thanks to the teachings of Oda, Oswald, Aethelwold and Archbishop Dunstan. Would there be a turning back of the clock to simpler requirements, as has happened in Eadwig's reign, he wondered, now that Dunstan was dying? But the end of the millennium was near. No, there would not. The panic in Frome palace in 955 at Eadred's death was as nothing to the panic which was throughout the nation in the present. King Aethelred was even now hosting a summit to discuss paying off the second great wave of Viking marauders. They were the sign of the end of times. The invaders would punish the nation for its sins, just as the Saxon forefathers had punished the Britons.

'It's sins.' Nonna muttered.

'Whose sins? The king's? What sins?' Algar touched Nonna's shoulder again. He was drifting back into sleep.

Nonna opened his eyes and sat up. He remembered the doctrine which he had learned from Dunstan. 'We all sin. You will sin, Algar. It cannot be helped. The king was a sinner, as was even the archbishop. None of us is perfect.' He stopped speaking for a few seconds, drawing a deep breath. 'We are all alone. Was he shriven? Perhaps it makes no difference, I do not know. Perhaps he was abandoned. His friends left the palace where he died. Was this right? Should it have been so? I do not know. All I know is that it was so.'

Nonna shut his eyes. Troubling theology was wearying. Did it matter if he were to die without the presence of a priest? At any rate, there were plenty at hand to smooth the way.

# Kingston-on-Thames 7 January 956

'BUT IT'S NOT your birthday. You told me that you were born on the twelfth of January.' Aelfgifu chuckled.

'It's near enough. I want my birthday present. Come here.' Eadwig grabbed at the folds of silks of his young wife.

'You would tear my dress? Unsheathe my hair? After all that has been done to bind it? You will be late for your coronation.'

'This day will be memorable for more than the wearing of a crown. Besides, I have been king in all but name for years. Uncle was incapable.'

'And you are capable?'

'I am king and of age. Of age for a lot of things. Come here, wife.'

Aelfgifu could not resist. She had become the official mistress of Eadwig at the Christmas celebrations. Today she would be called queen, if Grandmother Eadgifu would allow. There had been other queens in her time, but they had died. Grandmother would be the next to go, she was so old. And then she, Aelfgifu, would be the only one, unless disaster happened... but looking at her husband, vital in his nearly sixteen summers on earth, there would be no disasters, not for many years. Eadwig had spent the Christmas period here at Kingston buttering up the ministers of Eadred's court and quietly bringing in his own friends to create support; there were resentful looks in some quarters, but they did not appear to be, as yet, mutinous. Eadwig, was after all, the natural choice, the eldest of the brothers, sons of Edmund, heirs to the Wessex dynasty.

And now he had a wife. There would soon be more heirs of his line. If one of those disasters befell him, Edgar could, at present, be promoted as deputy king. The sooner a son, the better, but there were also advantages in having a brother. Eadwig was already considering that Edgar, when he was just a little older, and with the right assistance, could take over responsibility for rule in Mercia. That would leave him, Eadwig, with the title of King of all England, but lighten the load a little. Edgar could call himself king in Mercia if he wished; as long as the treasure of the realm remained with Eadwig, locked up alongside his father's tomb in Glastonbury and counted regularly by the abbot of that place.

The abbot of that place. Dunstan. Eadwig frowned and let Aelfgifu go. She rearranged her hair and tucked the still-bound plaits back under her brightly-coloured wimple. Dunstan was a necessity; he had become ruler in all but name in recent years, together with Athelstan Half-king and his sons. Dunstan and Aethelwold had developed a partnership of power which dominated the workings of the court; Eadwig had squirmed under their tutelage for many years. Now he was free, surely, of their unpleasant Godliness, of their certainties? And there was Grandmother, forever hovering, asking how he was, what he was thinking, what he was doing, even what he was eating. How was his wife? Was she submissive? Eadgifu had not chosen her, he had made sure of that. Aelfgifu came from north of the Thames, from lands in Mercia. Grandmother had wanted to bring him a bride, chosen by her, from Kent or central Wessex.

Eadwig looked at his wife. It made sense, to him, to take a Mercian bride, one who had been pushed forward by her own mother and who shared his own love of laughter and sex. She was an antidote to the dour Dunstan and a challenge to his grandmother. She was wealthy enough in her own right; there was no suggestion of lowliness. Her only fault was that she had not been chosen by the court, but they would get over their antipathy, in time. Soon there would be children, heirs which all in England could see were meant to be. There would be fun trying to make them and celebrations when the inevitable time came. The young people had already discussed the names of their children-to-be; Edward, for a boy, Aelswith for a girl. They were traditional in that, but as for the other traditions of the court… they could go hang.

Eadwig took his wife by the waist and threw her on the bed. Their squeals of delight rang through the halls.


Dunstan paced the chapel of St Mary. The Kingston stage was set for yet another Wessex coronation; the enthronement stone had its garlands. On the walls, the spears and regalia of former kings, all of whom had been enthroned here, as well as the most important relics of the nation, were witnesses to the anointing of the new king, Eadwig, heir of Ecgberht, heir of Cerdic, heir of Alfred. There had been much labour in writing the form of coronation; the choir had new pieces to sing which it had taken two weeks to learn; flowers and wreaths, bells and incense, candles and robes, had all to be ordered, refreshed and paid for. Both archbishops were in attendance; Oda, upright but becoming infirm in his mind, Wulfstan, carted in from Oundle, as a necessary adjunct to the anointing. He looked incapable of standing, but had been given a wooden support to lean against at the appropriate time. There were candidates for both archbishoprics amongst the monks and priests in attendance. Lesser bishops would covet the lands and holdings and position held by these two elderly gentlemen. Aelfsige, bishop of Winchester, a favourite of Eadred, was a middle-aged man who might be seeking higher office. He would add to the reformers' strengths and counter any demands by the new king and his friends.

As expected, Eadwig was late to appear for his own coronation. He would be deliberately late, Dunstan thought, for his own demise. He would keep the devil waiting, if he could. Where was he? Of course, cavorting with that wife. He had not left her side since the betrothal at Christmas. On twelfth night, last night, he had still not desisted in his attentions. The feast had been embarrassing. Eadwig laughed, danced and ate only with Aelfgifu, the queen, the new one. Two active queens of Wessex was one too many, history had shown.

Dunstan glanced across the aisle of the chapel to see how

Eadgifu was taking the delay to proceedings. Badly, it seemed. She was tapping her foot and her hand was shaking above her knee. Dunstan knew this was a time of trial for her: Eadwig had already talked of giving some of her lands to his wife and to others, who were not friends of Half-king. What would he give away next? Who were these friends who might take control of the court? Not his, that he could be sure of. However, all was not lost. Aethelwold was a friend of the family, if you could call it that, of Aelfgifu's mother, that harlot. Aethelwold might be able to open a door to change the heart and mind of the young king. But Aethelwold had not endeared himself personally to Eadwig in his youth… a pity that he had thrown him onto that dung heap for refusing to learn his Latin lesson. Cock of the Heap, Aethelwold had called him; and Dunstan had, now and then, had occasion to call him worse names, for his own good.

It was too late now to change or alter the character of the youth; he was king, earlier than he and Aethelwold had expected. Dunstan had brought the best of healers and medicines to Eadred at Frome in his last months in an effort to extend his life; prayers had been redoubled since the summer to alleviate his illness. Just a few more years and Edgar could have been brought forward as a potential king instead of Eadwig; but he was too young to do so now.

Aethelwold and Half-king had suggested to Eadgifu that the boys could perhaps share the kingship. Eadwig was a lazy boy; he would not mind allowing others to do his work, as long as he held the title of king. In time, Edgar could move into a position, perhaps, to challenge Eadwig for the crown, but this must wait until he reached a more mature age.

There was a trumpet fanfare. Eadwig had at last arrived. Dunstan looked around from his position near the altar. What daring! Eadwig had that woman on his arm and was walking up the nave with her, side by side. He twitched and looked across to Aethelwold, who had also turned. They exchanged glances. This was not in the script. Was Eadwig intending to seat his wife next to him while he was being anointed? What was his intention?

The two arch-reformers nervously waited for Eadwig and Aelfgifu to reach the altar. There were many witnesses, supporters of the young king, who anticipated, perhaps with fore-knowledge, the coming ritual. Eadwig reached the stone on which he would be crowned. The crown itself, made larger for him in recent days and known to fit his head, sat on an emerald cushion by the holy rock. There was a cushion on the stone which would provide comfort for the new king and an embroidered cloth of silk and gold thread covered its basic qualities. The magic stone of enthronement of many Saxon kings would be the seat for this new, maverick, youngster. Would he appreciate the solemnity of the occasion? Would he step alone to the throne of his forebears or insist, in public, on his wife being anointed too?

If Dunstan had had nails to bite and ill-discipline, he would have paired them to the quick in these moments. Aethelwold looked surprised and then glowered as Eadwig and Aelfgifu, still hand in hand, reached the stone of enthronement. The two archbishops' mouths hung open. There was a pause as they stood before it. Eadwig waved, yes, waved at Dunstan and grinned. Aelfgifu turned and curtsied to Eadgifu who exploded in rage, mouthing a silent expletive. Eadwig dropped his wife's hand. More had been said in these moments by body language than could have been expressed in a family conclave of an hour's length, though that would come later.

The young queen, Aelfgifu, moved to the side and sat beside Eadgifu, two queens of Wessex, together. Aelfgifu crossed her legs, relaxed. Eadgifu sat bolt upright, leaning slightly away from her daughter-in-law.

The jezebel and her mother, seated near the back of the chapel on a high seat, sat straight-faced. A new order was coming, was already in charge. There would be difficult days for Dunstan ahead, and for Eadgifu, coming to the end of her single tenure as woman-in-charge-of-the-doings-of-the-court.

Distrust and suspicion entered hearts and minds. Those who had risen to power under Eadred and while he was ill, felt a psychic cloud descend upon them. The inexperienced and unwise, the young, had taken over the court. The middle-aged and old were being moved to one side, to behind the pillars and posts of the many palaces of Wessex, to dusty corners where they would be expected to wither in frustration, no longer central to the feasts, not influential in the nation's affairs, not advised or advising, but still present, like a grumbling pain.

In the back row of witnesses, placed where Eadwig had demanded, Half-king sat next to Edgar. The young atheling and his adoptive father exchanged looks as, simultaneously, Eadgifu stiffened, Dunstan took a step back from the holy stone and the young queen nervously coughed.

Was this the pattern of the future? The sidelining of the old order in favour of the new? Of a woman, ruling with a man, not Dunstan and Eadgifu in partnership, but this new, active, youthful pair? What would happen to the nation so competently built during the last reign? Better a sick king than this…imbecile. And this imbecile's vapid wife and her mother.


The ceremony of crowning had, in the end, gone smoothly after the initial consternations of those most closely involved in the changeover from one king to the next. God had deemed the young aetheling suitable for kingship; no thunderclap or extinguishing of candle-light had occurred during the service; no one had fallen over; no sparrow or pigeon had darted across the timbers of the roof. The infirm archbishops had done their duties as practised beforehand with Dunstan; they would soon be in their beds. Wulfstan was already on the road back to Oundle. It would be the last time the archbishop of York was seen at court. Dunstan felt relief. Oda seemed determined to remain at the feast in the evening, despite being tired. He would sup a little, he said, before retiring for the night.

The assembly, larger than the chapel had accommodated earlier in the day, was taking their seats on benches in the hall used on these royal occasions. Thegns and earls took their places, guided to the appropriate place in the hierarchy of souls of the nation of England, jostling among themselves for a spot higher, if possible, than the one they had been allotted. Arguments broke out between some of the younger guests; wine had already been drunk.

The crowd settled down. A colourful section, set apart near the dais, gave the noble women of the court a good view of proceedings, well away from the more noisy and physical male members of their families. Young girls, being pressed forward as marriage potentials, sat on another, separate, table.

'They are like flowers,' Aelfgifu said, as, to applause, she entered the hall with her husband Eadwig, hand in hand, side by side. She was wearing jewels in her uncovered hair. Was it a crown? Dunstan, in charge of these proceedings as well as the earlier enthronement, stared. He was to give the prayer before the meal. Was he to ask God's blessing for the wife, as well as the husband? Who had designed and made this preposterous head adornment? It had not been constructed at Glastonbury, that, he was sure of. He would have heard of its making. He examined the young queen as she went by to take her seat - with the king, not with the other women. There was much gold. It went around the head. The hair was dark; chunky jewels gleamed in it. It was as near to a crown as he could have devised, a feminine crown. Had Eadwig stolen some of the treasure to make his wife such a thing? Had some of the old kings lost their jewels to this brazen young woman? Would she keep such a thing? And wear it again? Dunstan looked at Eadwig. His crown was the one he had altered for Eadred, there was nothing new about it. Athelstan had worn it first. The radiant gold spikes of sunlight which emanated from the head of the anointed king were as he had designed, with nothing added; Eadwig had accepted tradition here, at least.

The feast began. There were swans, roasted, their necks a delicacy, their livers a treat. There were suckling pigs, enough to feed a thousand, whose scraps would go to the poor of Kingston later. There were eels and carp for the bishops, cooked in the way that

Archbishop Oda was known to favour and there were stuffed cabbage dishes for the abbots, Dunstan included. The kitchens at Kingston were famous for their ability to produce, simultaneously, many dishes for nobility. Accompanying the meat and vegetable dishes were edible platters of browned bread, followed by dates, figs, apples and, for the high table and ladies, oranges. Mead, wine and ale flowed.

At the end of the meal, while the floor around the benches and tables was being brushed and the crumbs collected in leather pouches for those waiting outside the gates, a coin being added to each, the speeches began. Dunstan, as master of ceremonies, introduced the new king to his noble subjects. He was full of praise; this was the beginning of a healthy, new dawn. The old king had been regrettably ill for many years, but there was vitality in the air. King Eadwig and his lovely bride (here Aelfgifu bowed) would rule a fresh court, full of hope and order, with God's guidance.

Archbishop Oda was persuaded to stand and to say a few words in praise of God's England and its new king, before being allowed, after a few stuttering sentences, to sit and then to slump. His nose almost touched the table in front of him. He was not alone. The alcohol which had flowed with the meal had made many drowsy, on the female as well as the male tables. The children present, too, had had adult-strength mead and had quietened.

The top table, notably the new king and his closest friends from Glastonbury, had not tired. There were giggles and laughter, particularly after the archbishop's speech. Others stood to pay their respects to Eadwig and his bride. Dunstan managed the time each had to say their piece. Men bobbed up and down, eager to give praise, in hope of winning a reward. At such times the king's purse was known to be open; the start of a reign brought about the inevitable jostling for position. One man could step on another's head, so to speak, in climbing the pole of hierarchy. Words said would be remembered, good or ill.

The business end of the feast continued. Dunstan commanded the floor, managing the speakers. Many more, notable names of the midlands of Mercia and thanes from Northumbria, were yet to be allowed their time in the light. He turned around; something seemed strange to his ear. The giggles between speeches on the top table had ceased. The archbishop had lain his head on his arms alongside several of the older prelates. There were fewer heads on the table where the king had been.

Eadwig had disappeared. So had Aelfgifu. Dunstan wheeled round. So had the mother-in-law, that jezebel. Everyone else was in place. Eadgifu, too, in the same moment as Dunstan, had noticed that Eadwig had abandoned his post. She signalled to the abbot, pointing at the king's empty seat. Dunstan waved at a noble to pause his speech, which had just begun and was likely to be long.

'He's disappeared. Gone off with that woman.' One of the younger bishops got up from his bench and whispered to Dunstan, while the hall began to sup.

'Gone off with them both, it looks like.' Dunstan spotted the empty space where the young queen's mother had been sitting.

'What shall we do? It is most discourteous to leave before the speeches are over.'

Dunstan looked at Archbishop Oda, who was now snoring. There was no advice to be had, there. He must act.

'Come with me, bishop. There are a few moments when we might bring him back to the hall, while there is a natural break in proceedings.' Dunstan noticed that some were exiting the hall to visit the latrine. 'They will be back in a few minutes. Eadwig is probably paying an ale visit, himself, but the ladies, too, on their own? We had better go after him, in case he is drunk and needs assistance.'

Dunstan and Cynesige, bishop of Lichfield, one of the younger and more alert of the clergy and one whom Dunstan could trust, tossed their silk capes onto the benches where they had sat. They exited the hall, feeling the blast of cold air from the frosty scene beyond the doors, and hurried to the king's quarters across the yard. There were candles in the window and the sound of laughter, male and female, coming from inside.

Dunstan used his staff to knock on the door of the chamber. He was infuriated. Eadwig had become obsessed with Aelfgifu; he had been like a raving animal since his first introduction to her, and to her mother. He was uncontrollable in his lust. He was aware, from his own, long ago, youthful emotions, how far astray a young man could be led by his wanton needs; but this was too much. Again came the sound of a woman's laugh, a knowing laugh. Were they laughing about him? There was more than one female voice; not just the girl, then, the mother, too. They were all inside, cavorting.

The abbot of Glastonbury saw the devil's face on the door before him, grinning at him. He pushed at the door. It opened. Dunstan and Cynesige fell into the chamber, over-balancing as the door gave way. More drunken laughter, this time in unison, emanated from the three people who were on a large couch, the king between the two women. What was happening? Surely Eadwig would not dare to…the crown, which Eadwig had been wearing during the feast, lay on its side, on the floor. The diadem which Aelfgifu had been wearing was still on her head. Eadwig was kneeling beside her, fondling her hair, laughing and hugging the older woman at the same time, doing what seemed to be obeisance to womanhood, to the power of sex.

Eadwig's face fell from inebriated delight to anger as Dunstan lunged at him. He stood and turned quickly as the older man, his tormentor in so many scenes of tutoring, the man who had struck his hand many times with a stick to enforce learning, who had placed him in corners of rooms, facing the wall to learn his manners, who had said that Edgar, his brother, was the better student, seized him by the ear.

The women beside him on the couch screamed. Eadwig slapped Dunstan's hand away. Aethelgifu shrieked.

'Get out! Get out of here you old goat! How dare you burst into the royal chamber!' Aethelgifu hissed, her face turning from the loveliness of early middle-age into a face of hatred. This was a man who would deny her widow's rights, her rights as the mother of the new queen; her rights as the favourite of the new king.

'Come with me. Now.' Dunstan made a grab again at Eadwig, who recoiled but fell forward, pushed by his wife. He reached and this time held onto Eadwig's ear. He pulled the boy, drunk and now laughing, towards the door, picking up the crown, which was still rolling on the floor, where it had been flung down by Eadwig. He put it, askew, on his head and marched the boy king, with Cynesige following, out of the chamber and back across the courtyard to the main hall doors. He let go of Eadwig's ear. The young man looked sheepish and rubbed it, smiling insolently.

'You are a disgrace. Your company expects you to honour them with your presence at such a time. You are rude, insolent, absent and tardy at the best of times. You should not be king. Edgar should rule.'

This was a statement too far. Eadwig sobered up, not so much at the words, but at the face of his abbot of Glastonbury, his disciplinarian. He woke up to the threat which, years before, Eadred had tried to spell out to him at the sawpit at Frome. He realised that too much power had been handed this preacher, this unholy teacher, with his claims to see angels and devils, with his worthy purity, with his self-denial, with his celibate state. Dunstan was jealous, jealous of the natural ability of youth, of the power to attract the opposite sex, to enjoy their company more than the company of his chief advisors, even his close friends in the court. This was an assault on his new kingship, the worst attack on his character and abilities. He would show him what real power would do.

'Get rid of him!' Aethelgifu quickly recovered from the shock of being found in the royal chamber. The abbot's behaviour, condemning her and her daughter and others for their natural qualities of joyfulness and vivacity, was beyond bearing. She had seen him looking at her and her daughter, seen how he whispered to that other priest, Aethelwold and spoke loudly to the deaf archbishop. She had heard how she had been described: *strumpet, whore, jezebel*. She was well aware that she was the object of disapproval, that her son, Aethelweard, was in receipt of poisonous remarks by followers of Dunstan, that moves were afoot to remove her from the king's inner circle. 'Get rid of that treasonous priest!' She cried again, pulling her wimple over her head.

Dunstan heard the screams, the fury. No woman had ever pierced his heart and mind like this. Not since his decision, many years before, to reject the idea of marriage, to put aside the girl who would have married him for the priesthood, had he felt the full force of his own emotions. But emotions, she had heard him say, were the enemy of control. Control! Aethelgifu watched as emotion, so long held at bay, crossed the face of the abbot. Her enemy's face was purple, flashing orange across the temple. His lips moved. She did not hear what he said. Eadwig pushed himself against Dunstan. His face looked down on that of the shorter, stouter man. They stared at each other. Foam speckled Dunstan's mouth. Eadwig spat on the ground beside Dunstan's feet.

They were quiet words, the words of the commander, of a boy become a man. The menace of youth, realising its powers, its strength, pushed like a metal weight against the abbot. Aethelgifu, her daughter now by her side, watched as the priest received a blow from which he could not recover, not a physical blow, but the blow of insolence and rejection. Dunstan's lips moved in reply. There was a threat, that was clear. Excommunication was the ultimate sanction for a king deemed to misbehave; could that be what Dunstan was applying to this handsome young man? Would he dare? How would Eadwig respond?

'What is Eadwig saying, mother?' Aelfgifu watched as the two men, equal in status in the kingdom, each vying to reduce the other, stood apart, like two stags readying themselves to lock horns for a second time.

'It doesn't matter what is being said. Look at what he has achieved!'

The two women watched as Dunstan turned away from Eadwig, brandished a fist towards them and marched off, away from the hall full of feasters waiting for the final speeches, away from the kingdom of England which he had helped to create and to keep.

*When the appointed time came round, he was by common consent anointed and consecrated king by the assembled nobility of the English. On the very same day, after the king's ritual installation and anointing, his lust suddenly prompted him to rush out to caress these whores in the manner I have described, leaving the happy feasters and the seemly assemblage of his great men....they went in and found the royal crown, brilliant with the wonderful gold and silver and variously sparkling jewels that made it up, tossed carelessly on the ground some distance from the king's head, while he was disporting himself disgracefully in between two women as though they were wallowing in some revolting pigsty....as for the king, since he would not get up, Dunstan put out his hand and removed him from the couch where he had been fornicating with the harlots, put his diadem on him, and marched him off to the royal company, parted from his women if only by main force.*

The Life of St Dunstan, 21.4

## St John's Monastery, Frome, Autumn 988

'WHAT HAPPENED NEXT? Nonna?' Algar squeezed the old man's hand. This part of the story of Wessex was crucial and he wanted, needed to know how the trouble at the feast of Eadwig's coronation ended.

Nonna coughed and sat up. 'Where was I? Oh, I appear to have dozed off again, very sorry, my lad. But if it happens again, go to my journal. You'll find it all in there. And where my own notes run out, you will find my copy of Aethleweard's recollections useful. They will take you up to the present king's time. But, mark you, his views of Eadwig are not the same as others.'

'What others? Who do you mean, Nonna?'

Nonna did not answer. He shrugged and blew his nose on a rag.

Algar would have to read the histories for himself, and decide who was right, who was wrong.

Reading a second-hand account of the doings of kings and Church and the battles between them was one thing; hearing from one who witnessed most of the events of the tenth century at court was another. Nonna must stay awake; Algar was now conscious of becoming a repository of truth, whatever that was. He had realised Nonna's court reputation for fairness. Uncaring of wealth or influence, Nonna had been a witness to the history of the making of the nation of England, an England which was under threat from ambitious Vikings once again. The Vikings were not lovers of books. Nonna's histories could be destroyed in an instant of blood and flame. A new chapter in the story of England would be written, in Danish, but not if he could help it. Algar prompted Nonna again, this time with a cup of honeyed water.

'Go on, Nonna, what happened after the sparring at the door of the palace at Kingston?'

'Eh, oh, Kingston, yes. The scene with Eadwig and Dunstan. I heard a commotion outside the feasting hall and went to look. Abbot Dunstan, as he was then, and the king were staring at each other. The king's mother-in-law and his wife were dishevelled, looking out of the private chambers. Their painted faces were smudged, their hair awry. Eadwig was drawing his knife and then thought better of it. Dunstan turned to the women and raised his crucifix against them, saying something I do not wish to repeat.' Nonna stopped and drank.

'What? What did he say?'

'No, I shall not say. The truth is, I have forgotten all the words spoken at that moment; they were so abominable. But when emotions run high, men say anything and regret it later.'

'Did Dunstan have cause to regret his words?'

'No doubt. The women, particularly the older one, screamed at him and at Eadwig to do something. Violence was being incited, I believe. I shut the feast door behind me to keep out curious parties and to limit damage. There were a few quieter words spoken between

Eadwig and Dunstan and then Dunstan marched off into the snow. Eadwig rearranged his clothing and crown and went back to the feast. The women went back to the private quarters. I caught up with Dunstan at his tent. He was hastily preparing to leave. I asked him what happened and he told me. He said that Bishop Cynesige would tell me how he had been approached, as former tutor, to fetch the king back from his loathsome tryst, as it had become evident that that was where he had gone, and that as a result of the embarrassment felt by the king and his wife, he, Dunstan, was now exiled, again.

'As he was by Eadwig's father! Dunstan must have upset so many people?'

'Archbishop Dunstan, to you. Yes, he inspired hatred as well as love. Dunstan came to believe that he was doing the will of the Lord, you see. It was ever his failing. He could not see the difference between his own will and that of heaven. He thought they were the same.'

'What happened to D…the archbishop?' Algar had difficulty in seeing the old monk who crept in corners at Canterbury, coughing and spitting, as anything other than a spiteful elderly man, jealous of younger men and their family lives.

'He went to Ghent. I had letters from him. I kept him informed, as did others, of the progress of the reign.'

'Then Eadwig had his way, with his wife, I mean – no I do not mean that – with what he wanted to do in the kingdom?'

'Yes. He wanted change. You know he was not liked by the archbishop, who had watched him growing up and tried very hard to train him for kingship and to be aware of the laws of God as well as man. It turned out that Eadwig preferred the laws of man.'

'But Eadred, the old king…?'

'He had been ruled for several years by Dunstan. He was too ill, you see, to carry out many duties, and he became very weary at the end.'

'Who went to battle for him? He is said to have won many wars.'

'He had Athelstan Half-king to lead the men in war.'

Nonna thought of the young Eadred, when he and Edmund had been in their youth, delighting at the poetry and feast of their elder brother Athelstan's court. What times in Cheddar they had had, and at Frome. Nonna had been married then, married to a black goddess of Hywel Dda's retinue, a dancer and singer. What days they had been! Leofa had shared them with him and Dunstan had been a close compatriot. Now one of his friends was in hell and the other about to go to heaven, in fear of his last days being disturbed and hastened by those who could see that he was destined for sainthood. To be dismembered alive by bounty hunters was not an ideal way to die. Dunstan had an armed guard constantly by his side, ready to defend his corporeal body until after his soul had departed. Yes, Eadred had not always been ill; there had been fun, and laughter in the early days of Edmund's reign, until the shocking assassination at Pucklechurch. Assassination? That is what it was being called. Was it murder? Was it an accident, a result of too much ale and wine? It depended whose notes you read.

'But how did Eadwig manage to rule, with Dunstan, I mean the archbishop, gone, if he was as important as you say?'

Nonna yawned. 'There were many men, myself included, who were skilled at the business of government. Dunstan had put them in place and the daily round of work continued. But a few changes were made at the top of government. The witan changed in character. The new queen had many admirers and a large family. They took the place of some who disliked the fresh order and yearned for the old. Aethelweard the historian was her brother, you know.'

Nonna's eyes were closing again. Algar tried to stimulate the old man's mind. 'But what happened to the old queen, Eadgifu and to Half-king? Wasn't he King Edgar's adopted father?'

Nonna opened his heavy eyes. 'Haven't I told you before? The old queen had favoured Edgar for many years. Eadwig had many times heard her crooning over him. It was said that Eadgifu would even do away with her older grandson one day, if she could push

Edgar forward. And, of course, Dunstan and Aethelwold were in favour of Eadwig's early departure from the succession, though they never announced that in public. Dunstan was more frank with me, and I could see what they meant. Eadwig was a disruptor. When he became king, everything changed and not all for the better. The old queen, God rest her soul, was angry with Eadwig once she learned that Dunstan had been exiled. She, more than anyone, knew what he had done to assist Edmund and Eadred during their reigns and she wanted the unaltered continuation of his abilities during the next. She hated the new queen and her mother, that was clear. In order to calm things at court, Eadwig banished his grandmother to Amesbury, where she languished for several years.'

'Until Edgar came to power?'

'Yes. But Eadwig did not stop there. To punish his grandmother for perceived hurts, he dispossessed her of her lands and made her a pauper. He did the same for Dunstan's possessions.'

'And Half-king?'

'His wife had recently died. He announced that he had had enough of the troubles of government and war and went promptly off to Glastonbury to become a monk. He died shortly after.'

'So Eadwig had a clean slate for his reign? Nonna?'

The old monk's eyes had closed again. Algar touched his shoulder. Nonna's eyes opened and he resumed his tale. 'I can hear you, you know. No need to poke me. Clean slate? More or less, but he kept many of the old nobles in their positions. The witan membership remained largely the same. And he made many land gifts to win over those who might have grieved over the removal of Dunstan, or who would have preferred Edgar.'

'And Bishop Cynesige of Lichfield? Wasn't he a part of the scene when Dunstan fetched Eadwig by the ear?'

'He retired to administer his see. He did not appear at court again. Now that is enough. I am exhausted.' Nonna's face crumpled. His eyes closed firmly and he placed his hands across his chest. He snored immediately.

Algar went off to find the notes made by his old companion and those of Aethelweard, the brother of Eadwig's queen. Was it true, what he had heard about Eadwig, that he was despised by the Mercians, that he had destroyed the wise and sensible progress of reform in a spirit of idle hatred, replacing experienced courtiers with ignoramuses like himself to whom he took a liking?

Who was right? Whose truth should prevail?

# St Peter's Abbey, Ghent, Flanders, August 957

'ABBOT WOMAR, I wish to return to England.' Dunstan had been dreaming again. 'My flock at Glastonbury need me. They cannot finish their songs without me. They pause in their prayers; they neglect their souls. Some are conspiring to keep me away. Others have written to plead for my return.'

Dunstan was supping with his Benedictine saviour, Abbot Womar. Exile by Edwig a year before had not caused him to be washed up, dead, on a beach, like Prince Edwin so long ago, but delivered safely by the fishermen who had taken him across the sea from the coast of England, away from his country, away from his remit. Womar's monks, stationed on the coast in local churches, had delivered him to this well-appointed abode. His time in St Peter's Abbey had not been wasted; he had learned much. This was how a true Benedictine establishment should function. He and Aethelwold should be able to forge ahead with their plans at last. The Abbey of Fleury and its ideas had extended its tentacles of reform to Ghent; now they were poised to leap, with Dunstan, across the waters to England.

Something in England had changed. Letters had flooded across the sea to him in St Peter's, informing him that Edgar had formally taken over the role of sub-king, or was it king, in Mercia. There had a been an uprising. The popularity of Eadwig had been short-lived; too many had suffered a loss of land and income at his hands, as he sought to consolidate power with his chosen friends. The thanes of Mercia had had enough of the handsome young king and his in-laws. They were threatening to make Mercia independent once more, to pit the younger brother against the older. Aethelwold, reporting from Winchester, confirmed what others were writing. This was Dunstan's chance. Edgar would give him safe haven. The tide of opinion could be harnessed; reputations, once tarnished, could be destroyed. Eadwig could be ousted, or worse, from his remaining position in Wessex, at the hands of…who? Someone. Someone would be willing to do a deed which would endanger his soul. Someone could be paid. Everyone had his price. God would forgive, if the act was deemed necessary, for the nation's sake.

Abbot Womar was well aware of his fellow abbot's position and wish to carry out what he perceived as his duty to establish the reform of monastic life in England. In Flanders, Benedictine reform had been completed some years before; Fleury had influenced development of thought far and wide. Only England entertained stubborn defenders of the old ways. The Pope needed someone to strengthen the church's power; under Eadwig much that had been achieved under Eadred had been reversed.

Womar bit into his baked carp and swallowed, removing a bone from his mouth and carefully placing it on the ort plate in the centre of the table. Beyond the high table forty or so other fish eaters were similarly tackling their fare. 'I could relish a change of air. What do you say to my accompanying you to England?' He pushed the remains of the carp, its tail fin hanging off the wooden platter, away, and tore off a piece of brown bread from a long roll. He smothered it in butter and honey. 'That's better. Do the clergy eat meat in England?'

Dunstan smiled. 'We do penance with our fish, Abbot Womar, as you do here. But meat eating is allowed, on feast days for the saints, except, of course, in Lent, as you do here. But there may have been lapses…'

'Lapses not just in food fare, eh?'

'No, not just in the table. Priests are marrying, even bishops have their concubines…'

'And it is all your king's fault?'

Dunstan paused. Was it fair to blame everything that seemed rotten in England on the youthful man who ruled in Wessex and no longer in Mercia?

'I am of the opinion, and it is only my opinion, of course, though my prayers are sometimes answered in the affirmative, that the English king has incurred the wrath of God.' Dunstan waited for Womar to respond. The wrath of God applied against a king meant only one thing, doom. He continued as Womar munched on his bread. 'You might ask why. He has married a woman close to his bloodline. That is, as you know, against the law.' Dunstan took a portion of bread and smeared it with honey. He chewed as his fellow abbot considered the case against Eadwig.

'How close is the woman to him?' Womar swallowed. Consanguinity was a thorny problem for kings; heirs of the flesh could be born deformed, demented, or worse, female.

'Close enough. They have a great-uncle in common.'

Womar considered. 'Alfred's brother was her great-grandfather? That is not too close, surely? Most of the court is related to the line of Alfred, is it not? Even yourself?'

Dunstan coughed up a mouthful of bread. 'That is not the point. The concubine has had two pregnancies. One was a female child which died shortly after birth and the second was a miscarriage. God is displeased with the coupling. They should be separated. Archbishop Oda has written to tell me that this is what he intends to initiate.'

'But will the king be willing to give her up?'

'It is clear that I must hasten to Mercia to support Edgar at this time. If he is likely to become king...'

'Is he?'

'It is evidently God's will. I have dreamed of it.'

'What will then happen to the king, or to the queen? If she is well connected, will that not be an obstacle to your...God's plan?'

'She will be well treated. Her mother's death has left her with wealth. She may marry again if she wishes.'

'Your dreams have carried you far, Dunstan. Your farsightedness will restore the Pope to his rightful place in the English court. When do you leave?

'Tomorrow.'

'Then, God speed. I will follow you when you have restored the true faith to your land.'

'I will write, today, to Edgar in Mercia. I am going to my destiny. I am ready.'

God was on the side of the righteous. Dunstan was coming home.

*Eadred's successor in the kingdom was Eadwig, and he for his great beauty got the nick-name 'All-fair' from the common people. He held the kingdom continually for four years, and deserved to be loved.*
The Chronicle of Aethelweard

## Penkridge, Staffordshire, January 958

THE ROBING ROOM was cramped; Edgar and his royal apparel filled the space. The stout young king of Mercia, his full-length cloak, and the voluminous under-garment with its gold edging created a door-jamming spectacle.

'No room to swing a cat. If I put out my arms I can touch the walls. I need more space than a cupboard in order to transform into a king.' Edgar grumbled. The space he was allotted for his dress, the land he was allowed to govern, Mercia, was not enough. He expected more.

Then there was the crown. The old crown of Aethelflaed, which had been cut down from former kings to fit her as Lady of the Mercians, had been enlarged again, with an extra spike of sunray on its circle of gold. It lay on a cushion in a recess, too high for Edgar to reach and only just within reach of his aide to the bedchamber. It was heavy and the aide nearly dropped it as he stretched up for it. He rescued the symbol of Mercia's power from its shelf and placed it deferentially on Edgar's head.

'Let's get out of here. Has the abbot arrived yet?'

Edgar's nobles, revived from their lethargy during Eadred's reign to a fresh anticipation of grandeur and influence in the doings of England, were expecting the arrival of Abbot Dunstan of Glastonbury from Flanders. Dunstan, unpopular with the court of Eadwig, was a new champion for Mercia and for Edgar. In him the festering hatred of Eadwig amongst Mercians could find a unifying voice, or so it was hoped.

Edgar emerged from his robing cupboard to be greeted by the assembly of thanes in the palace of Penkridge with a mighty roar. This witan would be the first of many which would seal his fate and that of his brother, the so-called king of Nowhere, which once, such a short time ago, was the land of England. Divided between the followers of Eadwig, robbed from the families who had supported Eadred and Half-king, the strength of the nation had been severely reduced. The young queen's family seemed to own half the nation; unworthy thanes the rest.

Or so it seemed, to the gathering in Staffordshire on this winter day in the heart of Mercia, amongst a partisan crowd with, at long last, their own king once again.

And with their own powerful abbot, a defection from the dominant Wessex, fresh from his exile and willing to support the cause of their king, Edgar, to become king of the English, not just of Mercia. Hand in hand, Dunstan and the ageing queen-grandmother Eadgifu walked down the length of the hall towards the king, now seated on a chair which resembled a throne, on a dais which resembled the royal prerogative of anointed nobility.

There were more roars of approval as generations of the might of England met on the dais; Edgar stood, his cape flowing around him, his short stature seeming to grow to fill his robes, his crown balanced on his bright head, looking like, but unlike, his brother, the king. The three turned to face the hall, lifting their conjoined hands, sending out a wave of glitter; the costumes of each shone with gold in the candlelight.

Two kings now reigned in England.


'We must pluck out the thorn.' Eadgifu wrung her hands. The stress of being landless and penniless as a result of being dispossessed by her own grandson Eadwig had resulted in souring her relationship with him. In old age touchy, always rehearsing her woes, she had lately learned that her reliquary of St Radegund had been tampered with. Along with other well-rehearsed grudges, she blamed this on Eadwig. The younger servants, employed for her by Edgar, had learned to be careful of her moods. She expected to be free of asking for aid from her son in the near future; Dunstan had returned from exile.

Abbot Dunstan, newly made Bishop of Mercian London, was anxious to return to his brethren in Glastonbury. He felt more generous than many towards the king in Wessex, despite his year-long expulsion. Eadwig's first child had recently died. God had dealt him a terrible blow; was it a relief that the child had been female? After greeting the queen-mother, he studied her across the hall, seated with her servants. She was animated. The bruised eyes might indicate mourning, but he knew that the old woman's character was too complicated to dwell long on the loss of a family infant. She had for two years remained silent in her father's old home in Kent, nursing the wounds of rejection and financial loss which she had received from Eadwig. Her own flesh and blood had thrown her to the wolves. The desire for revenge was causing those sleepless nights and gaunt face. Alone with the queen-mother after the ceremony and feasting, Dunstan folded his arms and sat back in his chair to hear her grievances and plans to rectify her position. Edgar would inevitably play a large part in those plans.

'We must pluck out the thorn.' Eadgifu muttered again as she crossed the floor of the small hall at Penkridge. Her long earrings swung as she faced Dunstan. The abbot took up a pen and tried to sign a document. This was the third sweep of the room by the ancient matron.

'Eadwig may yet surprise us, I feel…' Dunstan, a pragmatist, tried to see both sides in an argument. He had benefitted from his time in Ghent, made many new friends and contacts, who would be useful for the future, if there was to be one. The bishopric of London was helpful, and that of Worcester, too, but the greatest prize was yet to come. Oda of Canterbury was growing old and weary; Some said that he was losing his wits. It would not be long before he was replaced, but the choice of successor would be in Eadwig's gift. As long as Eadwig was king of England, there would be no chance for himself to rise, or for Eadgifu to reclaim her possessions, or her pride.

'If he surprises us, it will be with a child who is male. That disaster must not occur. God has not smiled on him. He can only produce females, that is clear. He must not be allowed to breed again; a monster will result, a monster who will take after his father, a fiend who will keep us away from Winchester, from saving the country from evil practices. You know I am right, Dunstan!' Eadgifu sat down suddenly at the table and grasped Dunstan's writing arm, causing ink to fly.

Dunstan looked the queen-mother full in the face. He had witnessed the determination of this wife of the first Edward over the years; at one time he had felt himself in love with her and that she had returned his affection; now they were complicit, both effectively exiles from England, cast out by the bloodline of Alfred, as though they were common criminals. The crazed look in Eadgifu's eye confirmed his own decision; prayers the night before had revealed that Eadwig's days as king of England were numbered. He must not be allowed the chance to father a son, a corrupt being. The throne might forever be out of reach to those who could see the right way forward, the only way. Edgar must replace him, but how?

The hunt on the outskirts of the gorge at Cheddar was going well; the huntsmen had stirred a fine buck and it had been followed long enough, becoming tired after an hour of chasing, weaving and standing with front foot raised, nostrils twitching. Across streams and moor Eadwig had chased his quarry, thrilled with concentration on the goal of cornering and killing the beast. Now he had him. He raised his spear for the kill.

Suddenly, out of the still spring air, there came a gust of wind.

It seemed only to hit the king as he dismounted from his horse and steadied his arm, the quivering animal before him, exhausted. He stopped, with the spear above his head. He looked up and around. The deer snorted and began to rise for a last dash to freedom.

'Throw it now!' A courtier yelled at Eadwig. 'He is going again!'

But Eadwig had become mesmerised. His focus was on the wind which blew about him.

It was not a wind from the damp moors to his west; it was from heaven, he knew. And it blew strong and against him. He dropped the spear and clutched his stomach. What pain was this?

# Frome Palace, February 958

'THERE WILL BE another. Many more. You are both young.'
Aethelgifu tried, but failed, to console her daughter.

Aelfgifu leaned over the cradle. It had been a difficult and
painful birth; no wonder the child had died. The tiny form looked
asleep, wrapped in what would have been a christening robe, ready to
be placed in a tomb.

'And your child will be a boy, next time.'

'Perhaps.' The imperative to produce a male heir for Wessex
and for Eadwig had become clear to the young woman who was
being forced to admit failure. There had been a miscarriage before, of
another female child.

Would there be a third chance, this time a successful implanting
of the male seed of Wessex? Archbishop Oda would confer with
his priests; there would be prayers and divinations; texts would
be consulted; dreams would be interpreted. Sometimes, Aelfgifu
thought, it seemed that the church was peopled with magicians and
wizards, rather than God-fearing clergymen.

Dice were falling around her, against her and Eadwig; the
gamble which was the throne was losing him the kingship; losing her
the chance to become the mother of the nation. Her grandmother-
in-law and the evil Abbot Dunstan were playing their game and they
were winning.

'Eadwig must be told. Do that, Mother, will you? When he
returns from the hunt?' It was too soon after the birth to think of the
ramifications of this second failure to produce a living male heir. For
now, she wanted sleep. Tomorrow she would hear what Archbishop
Oda had decided would be her fate. She would be asked to retire to
a convent, or to one of her holdings in Oxfordshire. Eadwig would

need a new mate, a new queen to provide what was necessary.

The men would decide. Sleep, and a burial tomorrow, were what was required, for her, now. Sleep, and a retirement in easy comfort. She knew what Oda would say, what the court would say. Consanguinity, the too close bloodline of Eadwig and herself, both descended from the kings of Wessex, was at fault. That's what he had been suggesting after the miscarriage; that's what would now take hold in the mind of the court as the reason for her failure. What would Eadwig do? He was young; he would soon find another to his taste. Perhaps her sister…

# Part Two

## Edgar the Peaceable and Edward the Martyr

## Nonna's Diary, 960

I FIND IT hard to describe the events surrounding the death of Eadwig. The handsome prince was only nineteen years of age; his wife only seventeen. She was declared barren by Archbishop Oda and removed from the court. By this time Eadwig had had failures of policy enough to be convinced that, after all, his wife's family had interfered too much in matters of state; God's judgement was that there had been many bad choices. In 959 he was looking for a new bride, but, mistakenly, continuing to ignore the requests of the strengthened Mercian contingent. They were beginning to insist on a greater role for their king, the young Edgar. There was sword-waving, threats of revolt. England looked as though it would split into two smaller countries instead of one empire. The work of many kings, Edward, Athelstan, Edmund and Eadred, would be undone. Civil war would ensue.

There was an interview between Bishop Dunstan, Queen-mother Eadgifu and King Eadwig to find a way forward. King Edgar stayed in Mercia. Eadgifu, naturally, wanted her land holdings returned to her. Dunstan, promoted to be bishop of both Worcester and London in Mercian territory, by Edgar's gift, demanded his former position as chief advisor to the realm. Eadwig looked crestfallen, defeated. There had been deaths of significance; Archbishop Wulfstan had died in his cell at Oundle, as had Half-king, while consulting the master builder in the library at Glastonbury. Archbishop Oda of Canterbury was on his death-bed. The politics of the new nation had altered; the royal family was divided; England was almost at war with itself.

I took notes at the meeting of the adversaries. The young bishop of Wells, Byrhthelm, Eadwig's choice to be the next Archbishop of Canterbury, stood between them as they entered from opposite doors of the hall at Winchester and then ushered them to the great table where intimate discussions took place between chief ministers and the family of Wessex. I saw Eadgifu bristle at the sight of Byrhthelm, who was dressed in robes which would have graced a coronation. Dunstan frowned. They took their places at either end of the great slab of beeswaxed oak which reflected several sour faces. Straight mouths and angry eyes glanced along the table to the occupants of the ancient chairs, on which generations of the house of Wessex had planned war and strategy. The table became a silvery map of England; who would dare to carve it up?

Candles were lit. The dark surface of the table became like a pool of water where thoughts could be divined. The smell of wax, both on the surface of the table and in the candles, became a remembered scent for many years. I remember that scene now, as I write, and will always do so when I sit at an old oak table to write my notes. It was so short a time before Eadwig went to his maker, unwed and without an heir.

To my eyes, the young king was hail, though he was depressed. He had always been an active and energetic person, full of optimism. What was his fault? Why did his family dislike him so? I have often wondered what set them against him, but I see from my notes that he was a difficult child. He would not learn what Dunstan deemed he should, what his grandmother required. He was not biddable. He had made mistakes, as any young king might do; but these could have been redeemed, with the right advice.

No physical blows were landed, but the discussions had a certain outcome; Edgar, not present, but represented by his grandmother, would become the official heir to England. No sons of Eadwig, legitimate or otherwise, would inherit the crown. Documents were signed to this effect. Like Athelstan and Eadred before him, a promise, backed up by an oath, was made. Eadwig would concede that he would, henceforth, rule as a caretaker king in Wessex. How long his role might last would be up to God.

Within three weeks, Eadwig was dead. Edgar was declared king of all England, an empire once again.

# Abingdon Abbey, Spring, 960

'IT WAS WILLED by God.'

'We will say a prayer.'

'For forgiveness?'

'For that, and also for grateful thanks.'

'You will thank and I will be forgiven.'

Aethelwold and Eadwig's widow, Aelfgifu, knelt in the chapel dedicated to St Aldhelm, a dark recess off the main nave, newly painted in bright colours. A life-sized figure of the saint, cloaked in blue silk and holding a harp, gazed towards heaven.

Aelfgifu had retreated to the comfortable surroundings of her estate nearby; divorce from Eadwig had become a necessity, that was clear; the union had not been blessed. Her pregnancies had led to failure of the worst kind: expectation followed by the production of female young. Both infants had died; God's will was clear.

They muttered prayers. Aethelwold was quietly triumphant. He gave thanks for the generosity of Aelfgifu, which had enabled the nave of the new church to be decorated and peopled with reliquaries of the highest order. His own income had trebled, thanks to her gifting him lands which her mother had left to her in the previous year. The she-devil, Dunstan's bane, had died in great pain. Aelfgifu, formerly labelled by many as a strumpet of Eadwig's making, or her mother's, surprisingly became a sober recipient of doctrinal instruction from Aethelwold. She was becoming a vowess.

There was much to forgive; Eadwig's wife had been royally entertained by grandmother Eadgifu in the months preceding Eadwig's untimely death; the two women, both queens, had buried their enmity and come to an agreement.

Whatever that agreement had been, the shift in influence and power from Eadwig towards Edgar had been dramatic. Courtiers agreed that the young king had become morose, had clutched his stomach several times in public and had taken to his bed during the day. It was thought that he had had a recurrence of the same affliction as his uncle. There had been an episode in his childhood; this could be the same. He continued to travel, visiting the shrine of St Oswald in Gloucester, in the hope that the saint would heal his affliction. It was considered that he should travel to Frome for treatment there, but it became clear that Eadwig could no longer mount a horse. He worsened rapidly, before the healers of Frome could come to him, though Dunstan had summoned them.

The young man died alone in the royal chamber at Gloucester, with only his hunting dogs to hear his cries. The bells of New Minster at Winchester, his grandfather Edward's foundation and where he was buried, tolled his demise to the nation. The rites accompanying Eadwig to his heavenly father were novel; royal funerals were becoming colourful, lengthy affairs. With the direction of Dunstan, the musicians and singing were remembered for many years, the introits used again to accompany further deaths in the family of Wessex. They were heard again at the coronation of Edgar, years later, in Bath and at the funeral of Eadgifu, the grandmother-queen. She still had time left to her, time which she used well and enjoyed, her lands and income having been restored by her favourite grandson.

*Eadwig had through the ignorance of childhood dispersed his kingdom and divided its unity, and also distributed the lands of the holy churches to rapacious strangers*

Aethelwold

# From the Notes of Nonna

MERCIAN BELLS IN restored midland churches throughout the land rang for three days, deafening the cocks and cattle in the fields. Edgar, the seventeen-year-old handsome prince, king already of Mercia, had acceded to the throne of England. Now he needed a wife, to produce the line required; Alfred's Wessex blood would continue through him. He was released from the requirement of deputy or caretaker kings not to marry and was now expected to do so and to produce male offspring.

He was not unwilling. In Mercia he had had the pick of starry-eyed maidens. But the first act of the new king was to reward his chief minister and to alter an instruction of his dead brother.

Brihthelm, proposed as the next Archbishop of Canterbury by his King Eadwig the Fair, was preparing to travel to Rome to receive his pallium from the pope. Messengers were sent to his palace in Wells to request that he should not go; there had been a change of plan. The disappointed bishop was informed that the new king had made a different appointment; it had not been unexpected, such was the nature of the division of opinion between the princes in terms of the proposed reformation which was gathering pace. Brihthelm had not vehemently opposed the direction which Dunstan and Aethelwold were taking and which was becoming clear to all, but neither had he assisted it. It was clear that King Edgar had someone else in mind.

It was not difficult to guess who: the former abbot of Glastonbury, the bishop of both Mercian Worcester and London, who had hardly taken up his duties in the roles, was to be the new Archbishop of Canterbury.

Dunstan was now the unassailable reforming leader of the church in England, the pope's representative in the land. There would be no exile, no more hurried packing of books or accounts at the whim of an offended king. The all-powerful archbishop was to dwell in the hallowed monastic community of Canterbury, at one with its extensive library, for nearly thirty years more, in charge of the direction of the state, of the direction of England's history. The reign of Dunstan, some called it. Others afterwards had such power, but none held it for as long as Dunstan.

# The Archbishop

THE LORD HAD bestowed on me the title; the seats of London and Worcester were bypassed, as I hastened quickly onwards towards Rome and the Pope. I retained control of my old monastery, Glastonbury, and whenever I felt, as I do feel now, that I was placed above my learned compatriots in the Church, the thought of that lowly old church in the damp fields of Somerset brought me remembrance of where I had begun. All men are born equal but by diligence and patience may rise; those roots in the Somerset fields became my tether, prevented my pride from becoming greater.

The position was not undeserved; the archbishopric had been, I must confess, my aim, in order to further reform. I had endured much at the hands of incompetent or wilful kings, but the lessons learned had stood me in good stead. I had friends as well as enemies, at home as well as abroad; King Edgar supported me in all that I meant and mean to do; Edgar was not the poor scholar that Eadwig had been. Words written down would become rules to be observed, in Edgar's time as king. Lord, preserve his life!

And now, in this Spring of 960, I am at Lucca, only two weeks away from my goal, the palium. This is the first time I have travelled with such hope in my heart, knowing that I will be well received in Rome and rewarded on my return to Winchester. No longer an exile, reviled by my enemies, I go and return in glory. The travelling has been glorious; I have seen many churches and monasteries in Francia which echo the establishments which have begun to be built in my homeland. The great beauty of churches raised in stone and wood to the glory of God and the strident bells of many religious edifices declare the land to be His; crosses raised on hilltops and mountains claim a crushing defeat for the devil. Against the backdrop of the cloudless sky they sing out order, control, lawfulness, sending a challenge to the bandits who would beset travellers. To see that everywhere the signs of the heathen are held at bay, that even the taverns no longer nourish evil, that the individual households have symbols of the Christian faith upon their doors as I pass by at this Whitsuntide, gives me hope for the coming millennium crisis. It is clear that England's fate is joined to that of Rome; the binds which include us in this magnificent hegemony of Christendom are those which we must nourish and pursue.

Lucca is my last resting place before Rome; the peach trees blossom and new corn springs up in the fields; the warmth in the air is like nothing I have experienced nor will again. There is so much beauty, both within the churches and without. I cannot visit them all, but the cathedral of St Martin with its labyrinth sculpture holds me spellbound. I would choose to live forever in its shadow, if I could, though my duty requires me to return to Winchester and to Canterbury. This cathedral, more than any other, gives me fresh ideas for the structures which will come in my own establishments and perhaps for the reconstruction works at Glastonbury.


Here another miracle, and which convinces me further of my rightness in my new role, occurred. As we approached Lucca in recent days, my retinue, which had been eating and drinking well, suddenly found that it had no stores left. The wine had been drunk, the food had either disappeared or gone mouldy. Granted, we had travelled swiftly and there was some exhaustion which had led to excess; but my steward, the fool, would not hear me when I told him that God would provide; that what little he could find must be eked out to help us to reach the fortified city which we could see in the distance across the plains. He groaned and moaned and wrung his hands, even grew angry with me for wishing to pray for sustenance; the manna would not flow from the sky, he insisted. He said that we had travelled too fast and been uncaring in our provisions for the journey, whereupon I reposted that the preparations had been his remit, not mine. I had been too generous with food, he said, to beggars on the road, to monks in their monasteries. We parted in unfriendly terms, I to my tent and he to the campfire. No-one ate that night.

I prayed. Vespers comforted me. I was upset at the steward's rejection of my faith in God; but shortly afterwards he brought visitors to me. My prayers had been answered: the emissaries of an abbot in Lucca, who had been expecting us, had come towards us along the road to greet us. They had brought food with them! There were gifts as well, which were loaded onto the pack animals. We continued on our way in the morning, into the city after two days, sustained by the fare which had been brought us. I forgave the steward, who offered his apologies. He served me well on my return and eventually entered a monastery.

Rome changed me. I was captivated, as so many had been before me, by the sights and sounds of the magnificent city. The church of St Peter, though in need of external restoration, was internally a vision of heaven, with the Pope as its gate-keeper. John XII was a handsome young man, as I had been told. He feasted me well and was fulsome in his greeting; only later did I hear that he had fallen from grace. God had deserted him; it was said that he should never have become pope.

Such young men, heirs merely by right of bloodline, should not be groomed by others to command such wealth. There should surely be a system for choice among candidates. I myself have trained and urged self-control of several young men destined to become king in my own land; I have done my best with the material to hand, but it has not been easy. You cannot put an old head on young shoulders, it is said, though I have tried to inculcate wisdom while battling many personal demons. The immature John XII, a disastrous youth, unable to control his flaws, almost ended the institution of the papacy. My successive kings in England have not been as gross; which leads me to wonder if those born to wealth and position and responsibility should not automatically be excluded from leadership, unless they prove that they have ability. Where the position is allied to the church, I have many misgivings, more so, perhaps than in secular kingship.

But the raw material of humankind is flawed. Self-control must be learned, or taught. The rod must be a part of that learning, for who otherwise will choose the harder way?

Aethelwold was right to cast the aetheling Eadwig onto the midden and to take rods to the backs of the renegade canons of Winchester, even to cause his novice to plunge his hand into boiling liquid; discipline is required. How much discipline is a debate which will continue to exercise the church courts. Edgar's kingship is promising, though recent events have caused me disquiet. How should I act on my return, palium in hand? The letters which I receive tell me of disturbances at a nunnery and the king is accused of lechery. Will Edgar give me as much trouble as his forbears? Dear Eadred, if only you had survived for more years. But I must not doubt that God demanded that his servant join him in heaven.

# From the Notes of Algar, made October 1014

THE TIMES OF the king, Edgar, were barely remembered by my friend and mentor, Nonna. He told me that Dunstan, as archbishop in Canterbury, though busy with the works of reformation, held Edgar, still an inexperienced youth prone to the vagaries of a young man, as merely a signatory to the laws and secular pronouncements required by the witans. Edgar, vain and a great follower of the hunt, trusted his chief advisor, as well as his former tutor, Aethelwold. Oswald, who had become bishop of Worcester in the place of Dunstan, rose to prominence then. He spent years at Fleury Abbey in France, learning the best means of promoting Benedictine reformation and returned with Abbot Abbo from there, full of zeal. In these times great things were done to hasten the nation towards full understanding and submission to the requirements of the Church as well as to the secular laws. These were peaceful years, a golden age which men said later they had never again thought to see. Alfred's great grandson had achieved a flowering of art, architecture and erudition, which Alfred, cowering in the mists of the summerlands, could only wish for.

Of course, it was claimed that God, and St Cuthbert, smiled on the young king. In those days the church to Cuthbert was built and dedicated at Wells and a relic was brought there. The former king Eadred had first proposed it but the stones were laid by his nephew. Dunstan designed the church and prepared a sanctuary for the relic, to which many flocked. The revenue of the church increased greatly as this and other great stone churches grew upon the face of the land throughout Wessex. The law demanded that services should be attended and so Peter's Pence multiplied. Coffers were sent daily on their way to Rome, brimming with the coin provided by the poor, but also with indulgence payments for reducing the time spent in purgatory. There were other taxes, too. The royal coffers also swelled. Edgar grew rich and when the time came for him to meet his maker, England, which had known no wars in his time, was one of the wealthiest countries of the western world. The navy, particularly, grew in strength as a result of investment and was the envy of all those whose countries bordered the seas. Edgar, as well as the hunt, spent much of his time circumnavigating his realm, personally inspecting the outer edges of England and, with foresight, ordering defences and men to be placed where they were deemed necessary.

In Winchester, Dunstan and his office of scribes and taxmen laid a heavy hand upon the income of the peasants, creating tythe barns to hold golden corn, both for seed and for milling, and building windmills to grind it, supporting commerce and managing the coinage. He did it well. Still there were problems: Edgar, a man after all, complicated the succession by his lust. I will come to that later.

Thieves met with a terrible justice, more so than in the days of Athelstan; they could be blinded, their hands and feet removed, their ears and nose lopped off and their heads scalped. Less stringent were the ordeals for women regarded as witches; the dunking stool was in use across the land. The populace was in fear of tighter laws and the coming millennium. Punishment meted out by the ministers of the land was terrible, but God's was surely worse. The people were successfully subdued as a result of these strictures. Peace resided over the hills and fields throughout the land. Even Mercian thanes lay quiet, content with the preference of the new king, who gifted to them that which had been lost under his brother Eadwig.

It seems that the great achievements of Dunstan in supporting the fledgling king and carrying out the will of his grandmother, Eadgifu, allowed the young man to relax from his duties. In the early years of his reign, the short and stocky king took to chasing his ideal female form. His fancy unfortunately took him to the convent of one Wulfthryth. Wilton Abbey had educated her; she was handsome, even in the virginal clothing which nuns must wear. It was no hamper to the king, who wanted her for himself. She could not escape his attentions; Edgar is said to have stolen her corporeal body, though not her soul, and taken her to one of his palaces, despite her remonstrations. This offence, breaking his own laws, was one not easily forgiven by his family, or by Dunstan. Nonna told me that this act of lust carried out against the good woman was one of the reasons why Edgar did not receive full anointing for many years after his accession; like Athelstan before him, who did seven years penance for his assumed part in the death of his brother Edwin, he was made to do many years' atonement for his crime.

Edgar's seed produced a daughter, Edith, with Wulfthryth, who, with her mother, and after the remonstrations of Dunstan and Aethelwold, returned as a baby to Wilton, where she grew up and became revered as a saint, along with her mother. She died when I was a child, learning at the feet of my master Nonna, and her shrine is still visited by many pilgrims at Wilton Abbey. Edward, the first great-grandson of that famous queen, Eadgifu, was born at about this time to Edgar. He was half-brother to the holy Edith and became a saint in his own right. Two saints were therefore the scions of Eadgifu. Along with the kings she had bred, her blood had produced these miracle-workers. In these years she could rejoice, as her life was coming to a close.

In the year that Edith was born, there was another significant birth; the great enemy of England, source of many trials, King Harald Bluetooth of Demark, took his servant Tove to bed and seeded Swein Forkbeard, the bane of Wessex and England.

The births of Edward and Edith occurred in 963, when Edgar the king was maturing into his kingship and when Dunstan had his hand on the tiller of the nation. King Aethelred was also of this generation, born to the Peaceable Edgar in 968 and his third wife, Aelfthryth. These three siblings, born to Wessex, brought both holiness and disaster to our land, one a saint, one a martyr and one a fool.

# The Palace of Winchester, Autumn 963

'So where do those arrangements leave Edgar? He is wifeless.'
'Over a barrel.'

'You mean, King Dunstan rules?'

'I would not go so far as that. But Dunstan chose his queen long ago. She is ever the woman in power. Look, here she comes. I hear the clip-clop of her shoes. She has the child with her. I hear the lighter feet of a child.'

'Princess Edith? The illegitimate one?'

'No, she is at Wilton in the care of her mother the nun. I mean the other bastard. The aetheling Edward.'

A blind household servant and the ageing clerk, Nonna, sat on a stone bench placed against a wall in the great hall as a small procession, led by the grandmother-queen, went by on its way to the New Minster for a family service. A small child, held firmly by his great-grandmother's hand, tripped along, excited to be in a place dripping with atmosphere and power. The old men had become friends recently. Nonna had become reacquainted with Ninian, whose seeing eyes had witnessed some of the same events as himself in Wessex's past; Athelstan's weary demise, Edmund's unfortunate death, the unhappy digestive struggles of Eadred at the supper table.

'I have been in Wales for so long; you will have to bring me up to date.' Nonna had recently returned to Winchester. The court had become more formal, he thought, with its requirement for regular attendance at church services; daily life was ruled by the Church and by the growing fashion of consulting relics when making decisions. Things were different in the palaces and hunting lodges of Western Wessex and in the halls of the Welsh kings; they were more relaxed. Clothing mattered in the old palace surroundings of Winchester;

status was declared by heavy brocaded over-garments for the women of the royal house, queens and maids alike; for the men, linen trews and long cloaks, in all weathers. The cloaks were regularly replaced by new; the holes made by heavy brooches and hanging emblems caused ripping.

Bells rang for the start of the service as Eadgifu's retinue disappeared through the great door and crossed the short distance to the New Minster. Edward's church had become a second home to the ageing queen; her husband's spirit was there; Edward had been a greater king than his father, Alfred, to her. Dead for nearly forty years, she kept alive, and would do so for as long as she breathed, Edward's legacy: his will of iron. Her own will had become fused with his; he visited her at night, standing at the end of her bed.

'The trouble with women…' the blind courtier began as the hall door closed behind the long skirts and cloaks of the retinue.

'Sssh.' Nonna counselled with a finger to his lips. In this place it was entirely possible that the walls could hear.

'But where will Edgar put his seed? He will need another son, at least, to secure the dynasty. The queen-mother is said to be against him choosing for himself. You know where that might lead.'

'Where? Little gossip reaches Pembroke.' Nonna had heard a tale about a young woman at Wilton Abbey being abducted, but had not heard the details. Was she a nun? If so, the public must not hear of it. That would be another secret to add to the locker room of Wessex. This was a chance to recover a few years-worth of information. He had seen little of the boy-king Eadwig during his reign and had escaped to the Welsh court on the pretext of improving his Welsh, as the relationship between Eadwig, his grandmother and Dunstan had become fraught. Winchester had not been a pleasant place to be, then. Edgar was becoming known in court circles as the saviour of England, after the so-called depredations of his brother. The rumour-mill had slighted Eadwig's reputation; the words written by witnesses of his time as king were decisively against him. 'The Peaceable', they called Edgar. 'The Foul', some called Eadwig. As with Dunstan, so it was with Eadwig; people either loved or hated him.

Nonna thought and then said aloud, 'Edgar the Docile'. He was taking a risk; there were spies aplenty in the palace; Dunstan's troops were spiders in the corners, the fire-dogs by the hearths, the animals in the stables; they were everywhere, or he had a remarkable facility to hear and see behind as well as in front of him. Nonna suspected that Dunstan had ordered holes to be made between rooms in all palaces in order to place a young spy in each to overhear what nobles and kings discussed when out of his own earshot. The reams of notes on paper in the scriptoriums were witness to that. The new art of writing had brought about a method of surveying the higher orders as well as the lower. Edgar's men and women, Edgar included, could expect swift punishment from the men they had allowed to take charge of the land. Dunstan could discipline with penances which could last years. Edgar still awaited his coronation and would continue to wait until judged to be free of sin. No former kings had had to wait for so long to be crowned.

Nonna prompted the blind courtier. 'Was the girl, Wulfthryth, a novice?' Edgar's lapse from probity would be considered the lesser crime for the abduction and rape of a novice, than for a fully-fledged nun. He hoped for the former, for Edgar's sake.

'Neither. She was being educated at Wilton, but had not taken vows. Though I hear that she did so, after giving birth.'

Nonna winced. It was bad enough. The Church would demand penance. A young girl, in the care of Wilton Abbey, unless she was willing, should not have been available for any man, let alone an aetheling of the royal house of Wessex, to be taken by persuasion or force from the well-guarded abbey. This was not a desirable start to Edgar's rule. No wonder Dunstan had insisted on waiting before consecrating him. The ceremony of anointing at Kingston-on-Thames, which had been carried out for all the remembered kings of Wessex, had been postponed. The king was that in name only, until his lesson had been learned and penance duly understood and experienced. Perhaps seven years, which Athelstan had endured, would be enough; but Edgar had form; he had already bedded Aelthflaed Eneda, called the White Duck, and fathered, God be praised, a son on her, before raiding the dormitory of Wilton and abducting Wulfthryth. His bastards were said to have littered Wessex. One day, when his ardour had cooled, Dunstan had promised, Edgar would be given an anointing such as had never been seen before in the kingdom of the Saxons; he, Dunstan, was in the act of designing it and he, Dunstan, would ordain when it would be held. Where it would be held had been decided: it would be at Bath, to celebrate the coming together once more of the nations of Mercia, Wessex and Wales.

'Hush. She's coming back.'

The familiar clip clop of the queen signalled her re-entrance to the hall, with several wimpled nuns in attendance, who picked up her train. The small child, still excited, trotted at her side. A lazy ginger cat sat up by the fireside and yawned. Eadgifu stopped abruptly, making her followers bunch up. She went to the cat and tickled it behind the ear, crooning, and then went on her way again, passing into the private rooms reserved for her.

The blind old courtier grasped Nonna's arm. 'She limps.'

'She is old, like us, dear friend. The bells will ring out for her, as perhaps, for us, as we pass. We shall not see the millennium. Nor will she. But do you not hear the jangle of her jewellery? She is restored in wealth and will use that to alter the course of history yet, mark my words.'

Nonna stood up. They had seen and heard what they had come to see; womanhood in the land had reasserted itself; children had been born to Edgar from whom the nobles could choose their future king; Dunstan was right, choice was necessary. Dunstan might choose his prince, but Eadgifu would still have the choice of his mother.

# Wilton Abbey, Summer 966

'I WILL WEAR the brown and gold.' Eadgifu pointed to the open cupboard. She was feeling a little better; the rays of sun after the storm had cleared the view to the river from the window and bestowed cheer in her soul. 'And the yellow stole with it. And bring me the large gold earrings and my best brooch.' She would not be travelling to Winchester in anything other than her finery; no road thief would see her in dour work-a-day-clothing. This was one of the few occasions in her old age when she could shine, perhaps not as brightly as before, but then, at sixty-six, what woman can command any scene? Her years at Wilton in retirement had brought about a wish to blend into shadow; only today and for the next few days at Winchester, when the royal family were gathering to honour her husband's foundation of New Minster, would she blaze with pride, pride at having been the wife of King Edward, pride at having given birth to Edmund and Eadred, pride at being the grandmother of Eadwig and Edgar, pride at being the great-grandmother of Edward and Edith.

There were new additions to the family, too: another grandson, Edmund, was in the cradle and another child was on the way. Edgar had wasted no time in procuring a fresh queen after his dalliance with Wulfthryth; Aelfthryth was a fecund choice. Abbess Wulfthryth had chosen not to accompany her to Winchester; she would remain at Wilton. Eadgifu and Wulfthryth had become good friends; Eadgifu had the care of the little ones, who were to accompany her on this journey to meet their royal relatives in the great hall of England's capital city and to join in the ceremony of baptism for Edmund. Wulfthryth had chosen, or been persuaded, never to leave the confines of Wilton Abbey. The archbishop, she heard, was not unhappy with what had occurred between her and Edgar. She was aware that others would be glad that she had decided to take holy orders. Dunstan and Eadgifu had taken the small child Edward under their wings; they would place him where he deserved to be, at the heart of the nation. His tutors were Dunstan's monks; there would be no repeat of the Eadwig disaster.

'Bring the boy in.' Eadgifu, dressed and ready for the journey, beckoned to the nurse who stood at the door with a child attached by a harness to her hand. 'Edward.'

'Grandmama.' The child, released from the grip of his nurse, walked towards the grand dame, trailing a twisted silk ribbon. He stopped a few feet away from her, in awe of the glittering jewellery and tall person of the aged queen in all her finery. He had not seen her like this before. Usually, she wore the uniform of a bee-keeper.

'Great-grandmama, I am very old, you know. Come here, little prince.'

The fair-haired boy, dressed as a princeling with gold edged tunic, blue cloak and sporting an ornamental dagger, went straight to the skirts of his great-grandmother and looked up at her face. He saw the creases and determination in the face of the woman who had guided and witnessed so much of the rise of Wessex. She bent over and smiled at the boy.

'This is the best age,' Eadgifu murmured, smoothing the boy's head. 'But where is your headband, my little aetheling? We should find a crown for you.'

'A crown, Grandmama? But my father does not have one, does he?'

Eadgifu lifted Edward with a grunt. He was getting heavy. 'Angels must wait for their crowns, but you are an angel already and deserve yours.'

'When will Father have his, Grandmama?'

'Soon, my prince. When the archbishop decides. You will see him crowned soon.' Eadgifu lifted the plump boy and sat with him on her lap.

'Today?'

'No, not today.' Eadgifu looked into the eyes of her bloodline. How soon would he question the deliberations of his elders and betters? How soon would he begin to display those family characteristics which had bedevilled the kings of the past, that temper, that inability to be told? But perhaps he would have a debilitating illness, like Eadred, which would make him malleable. She could not wish illness on her great-grandson, but it would make things easier for him if he could be softened sufficiently to receive instruction without trying to thwart it. How like Edmund he looked! The flecks of gold in the blue pupils were the same, the facial features uncannily like, but so many years had passed since Edmund had been a child in her arms. Perhaps she imagined the likeness; perhaps she was feeling the claw of death on her shoulder which made her sentimental. She shook herself and put Edward down. He ran over to a lurcher and started to play with it. Surely Dunstan would be able to cure the character of this prince, make him a ruler to respect and to do the right thing; would teach him to ask for advice, rather than try to dispense it? The boy was hale; the material with which to work was good and there would be others who would be alternatives, other future legitimate sons of Edgar. She put a hand to her heart. There it was again, that fluttering. Never mind. What would be, would be. Edward and his brother Edmund, named for her own son, hero of many battles, they were the future. Dunstan would secure the kingdom with her progeny, her legacy, her's and Edward's.

All was safely in the hands of Dunstan.

# New Minster, Winchester, 966

THE PROCESSION, HEADED by Archbishop Dunstan, followed immediately by the bishop of Winchester, Aethelwold, swayed sedately along the nave, pausing to make the sign of the cross at wooden effigies of saints and stone statues of former kings. All of the history of the land of Wessex, of the recent past of England, was hung on tapestries and banners, etched into capitals. In the dark recesses reserved for relics of saints, there were bedecked altars and more wooden effigies, some dressed like the distinguished occupants of the pews and stools, some in mail coats, ready to do battle for the nation. At an altar with an effigy of St Cuthbert, the leaders of the procession bowed, followed by the royal family and its chief retainers, who did likewise.

The king, Edgar, and his new wife, Aelfthryth, Eadgifu the old queen, and Dunstan continued to the font while the remainder of the congregation sat on benches or knelt. Two brothers of the young queen moved to be behind her. Aelfthryth held her newborn, Edmund. The aethling Edward, his half-brother, was ushered to the font by a man-servant. He could not quite reach the font edge and was lifted up to view proceedings.

The christening of Edmund was the main reason for a family gathering of a kind which in former years had been common, but in recently, owing to the penance and shame of Edgar, had been neglected. This would be a turning point, Eadgifu thought, a return for Edgar to the fold of righteousness, of right thinking and some wisdom. At twenty-two, he had had enough adventures with women. Seeds had been sown. He could now be expected to do as he was bidden by those who knew best.

The ceremony of naming began. It was to be hoped, Eadgifu

thought, that this fresh prince would have fewer strong characteristics than his namesake; less anger, more adaptability. Perhaps it would not matter; he was the second son to Edgar, after all, though it would be as well to tutor him with the rod as his brother Edward. Eadgifu glanced at Aelfthryth. She was pregnant again, she knew, but was not yet showing. The slim girl gave her child to Dunstan to bathe in the holy waters. Eadgifu looked at the congregation. Sitting behind the bishop of Winchester was the former wife of Eadwig, Aelfgifu. Aethelwold had insisted that she be invited; Edgar, too, had pleaded for her presence. The grandmother-queen had no qualms; she had had little to do with her elder grandson during his reign; HE had made sure of that. If he had succumbed to wet weather in the hunt or to an undesirable mushroom in his meal, she did not care. But to see Aelfgifu given a front row view of the business of royalty was galling.

Eadgifu felt nails being hammered down in her coffin. Many had already been placed there. Edgar was too forgiving, perhaps forgetful, a bad sign.

'In the name of the Lord, I name you…' Dunstan was splashing water onto the head of her great-grandson. Edward, namesake of her husband, builder of this church, and Edmund, hero of England, her son, would take their places on the throne, perhaps one after the other. She would not see another reign, nor, perhaps would Dunstan. He was getting old, like her.

The service continued, in thanksgiving for King Edward's foresight in building and financing this magnificent church, this royal focus. The king who had ushered in the century before the millennium became the centre of attention for the congregation; prayers for his soul were released in the air, choirs and musicians sang and played in his blessed memory. Not sainted, but revered, Edward, Alfred's son, lay sleeping in his own niche, next to his mother and father, listening to the voices of his descendants, to the makers of his beloved England.

# New Minster, Winchester, 968

A NOTHER CHILD, ANOTHER christening. Aelfthryth carried yet another boy child in her arms. The gathering of royal descendants of Edward was almost as numerous as two years before.

This boy was to be called Aethelred, after Alfred's brother, who had reigned before that great king. Who knew whether he would be deemed as material to rule? But like the brothers of Alfred, who had all ruled before him, he might, in unforeseen circumstances and as God willed, sit on the throne one day. Now there were three legitimate boys born of Edgar, securing the bloodline of Wessex.

As before, the family and godparents approached the font. As before, with two young boys, the baby's brothers, looking on, Dunstan took the naked child from its mother and held it over the holy waters, praying. The baby started to cry, feeling insecure in the thin, bony hands of the archbishop. He thrashed his legs and arms, trying to feel for solidity, but there was none. Dunstan lowered the child into the water, whereupon it immediately defecated. The holy waters turned brown. The child wailed loudly. Hurriedly, the archbishop muttered the naming prayers and fished the child out and handed it to his mother, who wrapped it in golden cloth.

'He needs attention,' Dunstan muttered to Aelfthryth.


'I fear there will be consequences.'

Dunstan and Aethelwold were having rare moments of rest after the service. 'It does not bode well. I have Christened many children of the royal family; not even the girls have let themselves down. Crying, yes, that is to be expected, but this…is too much. The boy will be an embarrassment for life.'

'It is certainly an embarrassment, but perhaps not for long; the child cannot be to blame, surely, for fouling the font?' Aethelwold sympathised with the wretched child. He had had episodes in his early youth which could be counted, depending on whether the counter was friend or foe, as accidents or conspiracy; in his view they were mistakes made when the guardian angels, who should have been alert, were for some reason looking away.

'Grandmama, what do these animals mean?' Edward, aged six, ran a finger over a door jamb of the main hall of the great palace of Winchester. He traced the line of a serpent as it crawled upwards on its wooden pole, reaching up beyond the boy's reach and then returning down to meet itself at his eye height, dissolving into its own mouth and retreating, weaving in and out of its own body, once again to the top of the door. 'The snake doesn't end, Grandmama! It goes on and on, look!'

Eadgifu was resting after the service. The younger boys were being bathed in the old nursery which had been Eadred's private room many years before. It had been restocked with bookshelves and desks for the instruction of young minds. There were no new female children to cater for, as yet. They would be cared for separately, perhaps at Wilton, where the old queen had endowed the school. Edith, Edward's sister, was currently a pupil there. Eadgifu waved a hand at her eldest great-grandchild. He was a curious boy, always noticing things which she had for many years ceased even to see. 'What? The carving? Serpents biting their own bodies, going nowhere are everywhere to be found, Edward, if you look. Come here.' She drew the boy to her. 'There is a serpent on your head band. Let me show you.' She took the boy's filet from his head and turned it around in her hands, showing him the details of convoluted twistings of gold and silver. She let him follow the eyes, legs and tail of another long-legged animal as it snaked along the filet and then returned to its starting position. 'No ends, you see.'

'But why, Grandmama? Why no ends?'

There was no easy answer. The six-year-old was at the stage in life when to notice something new, which occurred frequently, prompted the 'why' question. 'Let us suppose,' she felt less tired, more inclined to examine a detail which she had taken for granted over such a long lifetime. She had been in the company of unending snakes and serpents all her life and had barely had time to regard the details of the wood sculptor's work. She paused and began again. 'Let us suppose,' she wondered why she had never thought to ask this question herself, 'that this is a symbol of…'

'Of what, Grandmama?' Eadgifu had taken too long to finish her sentence. It was happening often, these days. The younger set were quick to point out her increasing slowness of speech. It was not the speech that was at fault, she thought, just that there were so many thoughts to gather to say what one meant. And in old age, the unintended, unguarded thought which was spoken in haste was a danger. It was better to be slow, or silent, and thought to be slow-witted than to say the wrong thing.

'Of the never-ending skein of life,' she said.' Was this right? Was it life which was being talked about by the carvers, those wood-lovers who seemed to be philosophers, who had kept the same symbolism in vogue for centuries?

'But Grandmama, why does it bite itself so viciously?'

*I don't know*, was the answer which Eadgifu wanted to give. But Edward had awakened a curiosity about the serpents which performed their amazing tricks on doors, on crowns, on arm-rings, on tattoos. Anything metal, anything static. Swords, daggers, belt buckles. Always, there was the snake. Why had she not thought about it before? 'It is a very Saxon symbol, very ancient, Edward. It is a sign of the English, of Wessex and our very old bloodline. As for why it bites itself and has so very circuitous a way of reaching its own beginning, I cannot say.'

'Perhaps it is for each of us to understand it in our own way, Grandmama?'

Eadgifu was genuinely startled. She knew the boy was bright, but this conception of individual responsibility and awareness was fresh in all her experience of royal children. 'Yes,' she said and looked at Edward closely as he gazed at the convoluted snake, again running his finger up its body and down where he could reach it. The snarling mouth as it bit into itself and began again on its endless journey seemed to have captivated the child. She returned to her chair, feeling both elated that she had an intelligent scion, likely to become king one day and fearful for the lad, whose brightness might be dimmed, not by herself, because she knew she would not see the boy grow to manhood, but by others, a generation of observant courtiers, yet to grow themselves. Children, who would challenge another child, bring him down a peg, or worse. Would Dunstan be there to aid him? The years were passing quickly, the bells were tolling. She was tired. She sighed. To go to Edward, that Edward, her husband, who called to her from the edge of the bed in a nightly cry, *Come, my bride,* was all she now desired. And sleep. Wilton, her resting place, called.

Edward, weaving the snake's navigation of itself in the air before him with his forefinger, stepped lightly towards his dozing great-grandmother. He was, on the whole, a quiet, careful and loving child. That would change as he grew, but for now he was mindful of the requirements of the old. Grandmama was old, Archbishop Dunstan was old, so was Bishop Aethelwold. Most of the people with which he had to deal were well past the age of playfulness. It seemed that large numbers of years were accompanied by anxious care. He did not wish to grow up, therefore. He could not do other, though, than ask questions. In order to be a prince or a king, one must enquire, it seemed to him. He stood by his aged relative's side. She was breathing heavily, her eyes shut, but he knew she was awake.

'Grandmama,' Edward put a hand gently on the old woman's arm. Her bracelets stirred and jangled. She opened her eyes. 'Grandmama, why is Father not yet crowned?'

*Questions, questions. But sooner or later these must be answered, unless a child is extremely dull, or convent-bound. Would the lad understand the meaning of penance?* 'What do you know about penance, child?'

'It is a sort of punishment, isn't it? Like when I chase your cat and pull its tail and you tell me to go to bed, or when I spill something and make a mess and I am told to clear it up?' Edward played with the bracelets. There were snakes, here, too, in miniature.

Eadgifu opened her eyes. There had been moments of dreams, of the elder Edward standing beside her, yet again. Blissful longings. She looked at Edward the younger. Yes, the grey eyes were the same. All those years of breeding, and her Edward had returned to her in child's form. She had reached the stage in life when to grasp at dreams, when reality easily crossed over into the dream world, was a state of normality. Semi-awake, she smiled at the child as he played with the bracelets, revolving them around and around on her thin arm. 'Yes, a form of punishment. Your father is doing penance, as many kings do, to demonstrate that they are sorry for doing something wrong. When the archbishop decides that he is free of guilt, he will crown him.'

Edward was very interested. He would be king someday. What did he need to avoid doing in order to receive his crown? 'What did Father do, Grandmama? And who is punishing him?'

The boy was acute, Eadgifu thought. How could she explain to him what Dunstan had thought necessary to placate the court, to keep his own, Edward's, legitimacy whole? There had to be a noticeable punishment for the abduction of a girl in holy orders and her impregnation. Wilton Abbey had been shocked by Edgar's unruly and excessive behaviour in singling out a desirable but vulnerable pupil. Wulfthryth had been wooed, not raped, she had claimed later, after her return to the abbey. Edith had been born at Wilton, a pretty child, destined by order of Dunstan to remain there. 'It was about your sister, Edith. Your father acted wrongly with regard to her - against the law. He had to be punished.'

'The archbishop made the law?' Edward was becoming rapidly familiar with the powers of Dunstan. 'What about my step-mother and her husband? Was that against the law, too, what my father did?'

*How much does he already know?* 'The archbishop was not keen on that arrangement, either. Edgar, though he is your father, is not above the law and nor should you be, either.'

'What happened with my step-mother, Grandmama?' Edward was now seriously involved in getting as near to truth as he could, sensing that helplessness of all children born long after the secrets and sins of their family have been committed. The family tree was not merely a list of facts which could be rolled out across a large table; the family misdemeanours could also be spied. Penance was a serious business; it kept kings, like Athelstan in the case of his half-brother, Edwin, as he had heard, under the thumb of law-makers, at the beck and call of those who were powerful in the church. He saw Dunstan, in his mitre a few hours ago in the church service, as a mountain, immoveable, and recognised that the length of years of his power in conjunction with his great-grandmother had made him a permanent fixture, one which he would have to negotiate himself as a young ruler, unless God took him to his own.

*The boy is motherless. His own mother is dead. His half-sister is in a convent with her mother, never to be allowed to escape. Are all stepmothers wicked? Was I? Aelfthryth is content, for the moment, but she has two fresh aethelings at her bosom. Edmund and Aethelred are bound to be pushed forward. Edward may never know the truth of this matter unless I tell him now.* Eadgifu was in a hurry to tell those dearest to her what many others would not wish to hear. There was little time. Choosing her words carefully, and aiming for simplicity and clarity, she told the tale of the marriage of Edgar to Aelfthryth.

The boy's mouth hung open as he tried to grasp the concepts of lust, jealousy, and murder. It was a fantasy to him as yet, but later the story would return as he repeated it, to his own discomfort. It was hardly credible that adults could behave in the way described by the old queen. But she did not appear to be lying; he could believe her. Were stepmothers really as wicked as he had heard?

'And so, your father had to be punished, you see. He would

have been crowned sooner, but the archbishop added a few more years to his penance.'

'Then when will he be crowned?'

'Dunstan has said that there will be five more years. Your father will then be the same age as Our Lord when he died on the cross, for us. Things will settle down, you will see. Meantime, the archbishop is making many arrangements for the ceremony, to be held in Bath.'

'Not Kingston, Grandmama?'

'Not Kingston. We must look to the west, Dunstan says, and to Mercia. Wales, too, will be represented there. The hot springs will be utilised to give all the visitors fresh bathing water and there will be many conversions.' Eadgifu paused. 'I shall not be there.' The elderly queen was glad to steer the conversation away from Edgar's marriages. With the benefit of hindsight and foresight, she could read that the new aethelings now playing in the nursery would give her favourite child, Edward, some difficulty in achieving his natural right as eldest son. It was inevitable. The children born to a second or third wife, as in her own case, would try to take precedence, particularly if the mother was anointed.

'Not there, Grandmama?' Edward could not imagine a family occasion of importance without the presence of the aged queen.

'No. I shall be in Heaven.' There was little she could do about it. She would soon be buried on the banks of the Wylye river beside her rival, Edward's second wife, whose own sons had been usurped by Athelstan and then by her own. Eadgifu had a greater empathy, at the end of her life, with the disappointments of others. They would hold hands beneath the sod. Edward's first consort, unanointed, uncrowned, illegitimate, would not be there with them. That was something.

Edward had been warned.

# Bath Abbey, 11 May, Pentecost, 973

THE DAY WAS beginning well; the early dawn light had been greeted by a cacophony of bird trills, wheezes and clucks; geese and cocks, held in a thousand coups and awaiting strangulation, joined in, their last cry to the world.

Edgar stretched, looking out of an open window to the river below. He could afford to feel satisfied. He had proven that he could take many years of penance, could be patient. The navy was in order. He had made a recent foray along the southern coastline. There had never been such an array of splendid ships, built from the great forests of oak, manned by the finest sailors and soldiers that a peaceful England could provide. The shipsokes had done their job, the defences of the kingdom were well financed and managed. No Viking army would dare to attack the shores of the mighty land of England. No Norman lord would harbour their ships in his estuaries and havens. Deals had been done, polite threats had been made. Trade had flourished, pirate attacks had waned. Dunstan could look at his years with Edgar with satisfaction, the best times of management of the kingdom. Edgar, still in his night-clothes, turned to face his chief advisor.

'Sign here, my lord.' There were always papers to sign. Endless reams had accumulated in the royal palaces, mostly in Winchester. The manufacturers of ink and paper were becoming rich men. Dunstan put ten copies of the same document on a table in front of a not unwilling Edgar.

'Who are these going to?' Edgar could sign his own name and much more besides. His right arm was weary with penning what his archbishop gave him to write, but his time with the navy had given him some respite. 'The people I am to meet in Chester?'

'That's right, my lord. Each king will have a copy.'

'Do we know how many of them are going to be there?'

'At least six, possibly more, depending on who is available. I have written to Kynath, king of the Scots, Malcolm, king of the Cumbrians, Maccus, 'king of many isles', Dufnal, Siferth, Hywel, Iacob and Iuchil. There may be unrest in some of their states, but I am hoping that there will be a sufficient number.'

'For the rowing, you mean? Or are we going to execute them? Have you changed your mind, Dunstan?' Edgar sat down and began to sign the documents. He did not need to read them; the archbishop would have carefully considered what needed to be done.

"No, my lord, not execution. They will all be bringing you gifts and other tokens of their friendship and submission. The oars on the ship will be decorated with their names. They will be able to take them home.'

'And put them in their straw palaces along with the scalps and other signs of their barbarity?'

'Exactly so. There will, of course, be a feast at which you will demonstrate your magnanimity. They will be able to appreciate the might of your crown, the superiority of Wessex and England.' Dunstan gathered up the signed documents.

'Are we giving them anything other than oars and a few trinkets?' Edgar splashed his face in a basin. *How reliable his servant was!*

*How easy the king was to manipulate!* Dunstan regarded his king in his short shirt. He looked unshaven, of course, but that would soon be altered. He had a paunch; well, what middle-aged man had not, unless he was a labourer or slave? What he did not have was the care-worn look which successive kings of his acquaintance had worn, and some had died of. If only they had done his bidding, as Edgar was doing. Athelstan's blue-bagged eyes at the end of his reign came to mind. 'The documents are promissory notes. They record the presence of the various kings at your coronation gathering in the north and are the culmination of many years of negotiation; these are treaties of good faith, my lord, created and worded to bind.'

'And to bind me?' Edgar waived away a servant who had entered the room to help him to dress. Edgar could manage the undergarments on his own.

'There are certain obligations of the overlord, of course. But the peace which is now ours is born of the good organisation...'

'And the excellent navy patrolling the shores, let's not forget.'

'Exactly so, my lord.'

The relationship between this king and his chief minister had flourished. The business arrangement suited them both well. Dunstan had the power; Edgar could approve or object to his proposals, but over the years of submission to penance, Edgar had been shown time and again that his archbishop's mind was superior to his own in terms of decision-making. That left him with more time to spend with his beloved navy.

Another servant entered from behind a curtain. She curtsied and brought a bowl of steaming water. A barber followed her to the table and stood waiting for Edgar to sit for his shave.

'Is the queen awake?' Edgar enquired.

'Yes, my lord, she is dressed,' the servant replied.

'And the boys?'

'The aethelings are being dressed now, my lord.'

'Bring Edward to me when he is ready.' The girl curtsied again and retreated.

'Have you decided on your heir, my lord?' The choice of official heir was one matter on which Edgar could not be broached. There would be an announcement today, at the crowning ceremony. Dunstan did not want a nasty surprise. Would it be Edward, son of a consort, or Aethelred, son of a wife? It was a pity that young Edmund had died, but, at least, the choice was clear. An older boy would be preferable, but either would do; Aethelred's mother was proving to be as formidable as the old queen, Eadgifu, had been. She was long gone, holding hands with Edward in heaven. The four-year-old dead prince would comfort her; they would converse with her own son of the same name. Dunstan could imagine well the conversations between the family of princes, kings and aethelings.

'Queen Aelfthryth has a preference...'

Naturally, Aelfthryth had a preference. Her own surviving son, Aethelred, would be her choice. The malleability of Edgar was proving difficult in this respect; the queen had a personality. But a choice of heir could be changed; preferences mutate, availability can alter. Perhaps a promise made at such a juncture need not rule out suitability at a later date. Edward was eleven; Aethelred only five. Dunstan appraised the man now wearing his trews. Did he look vulnerable? No, the ageing weight of care had been taken by him, Dunstan, in order to produce a reign of length. Fifteen years, it had been, since Edgar took over from that scapegrace, his brother Eadwig. During all that time there had been peace in the land, thanks to him, Dunstan, and perhaps to the departed queen, Eadgifu. From the look of Edgar, there would be many more years of progress.

And now he would have his crown to wear, and two sons to choose from as rulers after him. The nation was never before so settled, so safe. It was a golden time. If only the millennium could be navigated as the English navy navigated its waters; there was still that to overcome. In religious terms, Dunstan was agitated; in statehood, he could see the Wessex line stretching out for many years, enforcing law-making peace, the language of the English being spoken everywhere, kings rowing their English overlords on mighty rivers for centuries to come; Christendom and the Church becoming the foremost admirals and commanders of the ship of England and the world.

'Edward is the elder,' Dunstan interjected. *Aethelred is not my preference* he thought but did not say.

The bells of Bath abbey began to peal, drowning the bird song. The cooks and butchers began the process of preparing the feast after the ceremony of crowning; geese and cocks were silenced. Below the palace, on the ground before the river, white feathers flew up.

# Chester, July 973

THE EDGES OF the Dee were lined with travel-tents and stalls selling food; musicians and entertainers pranced between groups of men and women and their families; beyond ropes and nearer the water's edge, the nobles of northern England and Wales looked on as a swan-prowed rowing ship, oared by men wearing silver and golden head filets, steered by knowledgeable sailors of the region, commandeered by a drum-beating black slave, passed sedately by on the inflowing tide. The ship appeared to stay in one place, the tide was so strong. For several minutes the craft remained static as the young and older men, none of whom were accomplished oarsmen, struggled with the heavy oars. There was splashing and swearing in foreign tongues. One young man fell forward as his oar slipped from his grasp. All were sweating and dishevelled.

At the stern, seated on a high platform, looking at ease with the watery conditions, sat Edgar and his eldest son, Edward. Welsh, Cumbrian, Scottish and English onlookers on the banks of the Dee nearest to the town centre watched as the struggle against the tide continued for the allotted minutes of humiliation of the regional commanders. After what seemed hours to the oarsmen but was in reality only fifteen minutes, the drum beat faded, a horn was sounded and the oarsmen were allowed to turn the boat towards the shore and the waiting company. There was laughter in some quarters, silence in others.

Edgar stepped ashore, the first to return to his family and courtiers. Edward followed, also accustomed to boats, ships and water in general. He had accompanied his father on several sailings along the south coast and was familiar with tidal changes and challenges. He was disappointed not to see the Dee's bore, but he had witnessed and even ridden the mighty bore of the Severn, which many had not. He thought of himself as a sailor. He would be soon in charge of England's navy, as his great-uncle Eadred had been many years before; the sea and the tidal rivers had entered his dreams. He felt most alive when in the company of sailors and their crafts. There were cheers from the majority of onlookers as Edgar reached the striped tent which held royal refreshments; there would be prizes, too, for the oarsmen, who now, bedraggled and hot, began to leave the swan-prowed boat. They trudged up to their individual tents, out of the view of many of their supporters. They tried, as they went, to straighten their clothing and to adjust their head-dresses, which ranged from light crowns to feather and foliage, according to their tribal customs. All began to drink ale, heavily.

'The boy is growing in confidence,' Aethelwold remarked to Dunstan.

'Yes, he is learning the ropes well.'

The two chief ministers of the crown of England, Dunstan, resplendent in the same robes which he had worn at the coronation in Bath, could afford to bask in the outcome of their vision of England: one maintained by taxation, and ordered by the lawyers of the church. The state court system allowed the church, with impunity, to insist on monetary restitution of any crime; theft on a large scale had been reduced to manageable proportions; exile of renegades of the court had preserved a fifteen-year reign of relative peace, both within and outside the borders of Wessex and England. The lords of Mercia and Wessex had learned during this period, not to love one another, but to work together for the improvement in income for all. The defences of the realm were intact; the navy was the best the world had known; the army fyrd less so, but the hundred system of raising men was under review. Within the next two years of taxation, if no plague or drought or flood disturbed the planning, it would also be well armed, equipped and manned.

The two men, dressed in ornately decorated cloaks reaching from their necks to their feet, despite the warm weather, were meeting for the first time in many months. Aethelwold had lost weight; Dunstan was greyer.

'What has become of the Duck?' It was an opportune time to catch up with news of the royal family.

'I hope you are improving in health, Aethelwold. We cannot do without you in Winchester. The Duck was at Bath for the coronation. She was accompanied by Eadwig's wife. Both looked well. Has Eadwig's widow, Aelfgifu been helpful to you in Abingdon?'

'She has. Her recent monetary contribution enabled me to finish works there.'

'Finished for now?' Dunstan knew that building works never ended. There was always some defect or need.

Aethelwold smiled wryly. 'For now. Eadwig had some uses in bringing Aelfgifu to us and your words to her have stirred some guilt which makes her generous. I am grateful.'

'To me, or to her?' Dunstan moved towards his companion in the Church. His body moved round, but his cloak remained facing forward.

'To both of you.' Aethelwold, not usually aware of subtle differences, detected a slight change in Dunstan's attitude towards him. The time in which he had been ill in recent months had not assisted their partnership. He changed the subject of conversation as they watched the king and his son climb the grassy bank and disappear into the main entertainment tent. 'I hear that the ceremony at Bath was a success, but of course, it would be, there were so many years in the planning. I congratulate you, Dunstan, on holding Edgar off for so long. And it makes perfect sense for a king to be anointed, like the follower of Christ on earth should be, at the age of Our Lord when he gained his own crown.'

'Of thorns. Yes, but it was not too difficult to postpone Edgar's coronation; he was well aware of his own misdeeds and the need for penance. This ceremony celebrates the birth of Our Lord, Edgar the beginning of his ministry. Bath? It went well. Aelfthryth behaved herself and Edward was hailed as the aetheling heir.'

'Is the queen causing problems? Of course, there is no Queen Eadgifu to guide her. The court misses the old queen. Were the music, the banners, the prayers, all devised by you?'

'With a little help from my monks at Glastonbury, of course. I cannot claim all the credit.' Dunstan picked up a tinge of jealousy from Aethelwold. 'Let us join the others.' *It is Aelfthryth who is creating this rift. This is a new situation which must be managed.* For the first time in their long careers at the courts of many kings, the two churchmen felt a splinter fall between them. They walked towards the main tent where the royal family were already eating. Edgar, Aelfthryth his wife, now anointed queen, and Edward were seated in a row. The younger prince Aethelred was on Edgar's knee, being given pieces of roasted chicken as though he were a lap-dog.

'Thirty is a sensible age for a king to find his feet. You have trained him well, Dunstan.' Aethelwold felt the need to continue to compliment his friend.

Dunstan bowed slightly, further increasing the gap between them. 'I am hopeful that that is to be the pattern for the future, after all that has happened and that we have witnessed during these past fifty years of our service. Edward will be a fine king, in time, but meanwhile Edgar has learned his lessons and will be a good servant of the crown for many more years, it is to be hoped. There will be no need for a regency of any sort.'

'No, indeed, none. But what if Edward has a mishap? There is now only Aethelred to take his place.'

Aethelwold and Dunstan looked with different eyes on the familial party. Edward was tucking in to his chicken with gusto, Aethelred, *the boy who defecated in holy water,* was sprawled, content, on his father's knee. The family scene was idyllic. Edgar, the newly anointed king, and his sons, were supreme, in command of themselves, their army, their navy. The chief minister of the land could survey his work and congratulate himself. Dunstan had dedicated his life to the forging of this time of peace in the kingdom, sweating and bleeding as much as any of the sub-kings who had been seen to groan and perspire as they oared their master.

Two princes, two aethelings, to come behind Edgar, what could be better? Both were bright boys, but from two different mothers. Dunstan knew who he preferred, the one who did not defecate… but Aethelwold had the tutoring of Aethelred and had a growing preference for him.

Two different mothers…a regency? No. look at Edgar, now. He's laughing, eating, enjoying himself. There was no sign of disease. There were surely many more years to come of this chastened, sane young man. Athelstan had lasted until well into his forties; Edmund had had potential but his life was brought to an early end; Eadred had been a sick man; Eadwig a hopeless teenager, with all the faults that an over-confident boy can have. Edgar had been trainable; Aethelwold had done a good job with him. Edward was his, Dunstan's, charge and was proving to be somewhere between Edgar and his grandfather Edmund in character. His temper flared, reminding him of the hot-headed Edmund, but he was good with his books and responded to quiet times in a library. Emerging into his teenage years, Edward had promise.

Dunstan, despite his optimism, felt a niggle growing in his mind about the succession. He looked at Aethelred, sitting on Egdar's knee. Father and son enjoyed each other's company. A favourite was in the making, one which he suspected Aethelwold, Aethelred's tutor, of encouraging. Two princes. That bother, the choice, was the culprit, as choice often was. Dunstan grimaced and groaned, in contrast to the happy, triumphant scene.

'Your back, is it giving you pain? Do you have an affliction?' Aethelwold enquired.

'No, just old age, my friend, just old age.' Dunstan shuddered, feeling the weight of the future.

There would be no ceremony to mark the third year of Christ's ministry. Edgar would be dead.

# Nonna's Diary for 973

I, ALGAR, READ the notes made by my old friend, Nonna, as he lay sleeping. I wanted to know more of the ceremony at Bath which crowned Edgar, as devised after long years' management, by Archbishop Dunstan. It was a long way to look back, from 1016. Those were the golden days of simplicity, of comfortable consideration of the nation's internal affairs. Compared with recent years, the almost smug congratulation of ministers and bishops now jars with what we know came next. The peace of Edgar did not last. It died with him, despite all that the archbishop had done and tried to do to shore up the beginning of the reign of his son, Edward.

Two sons. By different mothers. What a recipe for disaster that was! One, Edward, the holy, the martyr, as he came to be known throughout the land. The other, Aethelred, forever lambasted as a failure, though his reign was many years the longer of the two. Perhaps all those who reign for many years receive opprobrium. The written record of the nation's dismay at Aethelred's reign, at his lack of ability to deal successfully with the Viking onslaught at the turn of the millennium, has heralded the ending of Wessex might and possibly of the demise of England. The dire warnings of the Archbishop of York, Wulfstan II show how the nation toiled and groaned under the weight of first Thorkell's and then Swein, the king of Denmark's assault. Could any king, born the second or third son of any queen, have done more than try to pay off the Viking army? Gold flowed from our coffers, yet still it ravaged at will, deep into our countryside.

But in 973, as Nonna remarks, there was peace in England. The evil intent of Swein had not yet emerged. No doubt, as he stood as a boy on the bleak sands of western Denmark, looking out across a grey sea, he dreamed of commanding armies and ships, of taking another's crown and with it the farmland and workforce of England. In 973 the foul Danish boy was the same age as our prince, Edward. Both were becoming young men, both capable of inspiring and leading their own nations, both earmarked for success, that kind of success which breeds more.

But in the summer of 975, while at sea, Edgar died, leaving Edward, at fourteen, the youngest teenage king that England had known for more than a hundred years. Aethelred was a young boy of seven. His mother's favourite, Aethelred was deemed too young to rule, despite protestations, recorded by Nonna, from her, who argued that as she was the only anointed queen of Edgar, her son should take precedence. Edward's mother, Aethelflaed, The Duck, had been a mere dalliance, she claimed, though The Duck had been an ealdorman's daughter. She was no longer available to argue for Edward; the convent enclosure had wrapped around her in silence. She was as one dead.

But what of the ceremony at Bath? Nonna was there. It was a fabulous display of might and wealth, he says, only equalled by that displayed at Chester shortly after. A poet composed these lines, which my old friend has recorded:

The Coronation of Edgar:
Here, Edgar, ruler of the English,
Was consecrated as king in a great assembly
In the ancient town of Ache-man's city –
The warriors dwelling in the island also call it
By the other term Baths. There was great rejoicing
Come to all on that blessed day,
Which children of men name and call
Pentecost Day. There was gathered,
As I have heard, a pile of priests,
A great multitude of monks, of learned men. By then had passed,
Reckoned by number, ten hundred years,

From the time of birth of the illustrious King,
Shepherd of Lights – except there remained
Twenty-seven of the number of years,
As the writings say. Thus nigh on a thousand years
Of the Lord of Victories had run on when this befell;
And Edmund's offspring, bold in deeds of conflict,
Was nine-and-twenty years in the world when this came about,
And then in the thirtieth was consecrated prince.

We who live in the early years of the eleventh century after
Christ, with the end of England seeming close, with our Wessex
bloodline lost, with so much of the land, both south as well as north
of the Thames, ravaged by the infidels, fear that the prophecies of
doom are unfolding as the paintings in our churches predict; little did
we know in 975 what would unfold, what terrors were to come.

It all began, like a fresh fern leaf unfurling, with Edward.

# Winchester, July 975

L IKE THE ARGUMENTS over succession, there were always disagreements about burial place. The kings of Wessex, having little choice in their involvement in court politics while alive, had firm views on their final resting place. Their surviving kin, particularly their wives, had preferences about where they would lie on their backs, looking to heaven, rotting in the soil. It was an area of their lives over which they thought they could have some control, but which often caused argument.

It was important to send a message of unity. The royal family of Wessex could demote an unpopular scion by overriding his wishes and allowing or decreeing burial in a far-flung place; Athelstan had himself wished to be buried in the abbey at Malmesbury, perhaps wanting to lie nearer to his Mercian origins. The royal family, wanting to garner saints amongst its number, always argued for the Old Minster at Winchester, central, certain, Wessex. There rested the remains of Alfred and his son, Edward. Many of the ancient conquerors of Britain were buried there, a memorial in cartilage and bone of the English incursion into the ancient land, a record of their lineage from Woden, from the old pagan gods. Only the convoluted snake on door jambs, daggers and jewellery remained to remind of those ignorant times.

Burial with your ancestors, in a place revered by your descendants, that was an ambition of royalty. With the passing of Eadgifu, the old queen, whose rule in this department had been absolute, the choice of site was, for the first time for a long time, in dispute.

Edgar, crowned only two years before he died, one year short of the age at which Our Lord had assumed his seat in heaven, had shown some independence from the wishes of his grandmother, who had argued during his life and hers for a memorial chapel at Winchester. The archbishop had heard him say, however, that he wished to be buried with his father, Edmund, at Glastonbury. Having lain in state at Winchester, it was logical to the court that he should be buried there, but Dunstan, who had taken the important decisions of the realm for many years, persuaded the council to allow a lengthy traverse across country, stopping to let the people kneel at the passing hearse, to Glastonbury.

It was good propaganda, a propitious welcome to the new king, the fourteen-year-old Edward, who rode with the corpse and took part in the burial ceremony as Edgar was lowered into the grave. Dunstan could count at least two of his kingly charges safely buried at Glastonbury, to the benefit of the abbey.

Dunstan and Edward stood by the grave, watching it backfilled.

'I suppose I must take up my duties on return to Winchester. What is my first task?' Edward wiped a tear away. 'Archbishop?' He had grown used to being separated from his father in the days of the new queen. Her son, Aethelred, had become the light of his father's eyes, replacing Edmund, for whom many tears had been spilled. Since young Edmund's demise, found dead in his crib one morning, Edgar had never been the same. He clung to his youngest child. Aethelred was charming. Edgar had doted on him. He had blithely sentenced criminals to death while Aethelred sat on his knee, or played with a pig's bladder at his feet.

Dunstan realised that Edward had addressed him. He had been deep in thought. 'Task? Yes, there will be many tasks. But, my prince, there are many men in many scriptoriums throughout England who have been put in place to make your work easier. Decisions will come, as they must, to any king as you are about to become, but they will not be a burden, I promise you. Together we will continue the excellent work of your father.' Dunstan put an arm around the boy. Why was he not weeping? 'We should return to Winchester immediately. Your mother will be anxious.'

'My stepmother Aelfthryth has her son Aethelred to comfort her.'

'She will be in mourning for a month. We must make haste to convene the witan to confirm your status.'

'Will she want Aethelred to take over Mercia, do you think, Archbishop? Do I have to share the throne as my father did?'

These were pertinent questions. The queen would want a say over the position of her son. The kingdom had been divided before; it could happen again, but not on his watch, the archbishop thought. He had worked too hard to bring the nation together and to keep it whole, during the last fifteen years. Much had been achieved. Edgar, unaccountably, had died when he should have lasted many more years, should have given certainty of tenure to the archbishop's ideas in his own fading years. But the plan of thirty years of Edgar's rule, which he had mapped out in the counting house of Winchester, taking the nation beyond the dreaded millennium, had been ruined. The pliable ruler had been snatched away by God, he knew not why, nor, unusually, had he been able to prophesy his passing. Dunstan had done all that he could to ensure that God was on his side, and Edgar's. Despite the lengthy penance and the celebration of enthronement on the anniversary of Christ's birth, there had been rejection. Perhaps all was done at random. Perhaps Nonna was right, that doubt was healthy. Had God abandoned him, the Archbishop of Canterbury? Dunstan had cause to wonder. It was not often that he entertained pernicious doubt. It came to him like the onset of an illness.

Riding back to Winchester from Glastonbury, with an eager and untroubled Edward, unconscious of the troubles ahead, Dunstan sought for signs from hedgerow birds, from over-arching oak branches, from sounding bells of churches, from anything, as he approached the centre of Wessex and English power, the city of Winchester, but nothing of significance came to him. His thoughts turned dark. He was sixty-five. How many more years would he have to ensure that the laws and aspirations which he had designed, with so much labour, would be carried out? How could so young a boy as Edward, though a promising youth, continue with purpose and strength? What if he, Dunstan, were to die today? Would Aethelred then become king in name and his mother Aelfthryth his regent? How would that look in the annals of Wessex, that a child, ruled by his mother, who had defiled the baptismal font, should rule, incompetently, through a woman?

The cortege approached the gates of Winchester. Dunstan sat up on his horse. His thighs and legs ached; his head throbbed. The possibilities and probabilities of the coming hours and days surged in his brain. He glanced at Edward. The boy had straightened his back. He was adopting the pose of a man approaching his patrimony, but care had settled on his shoulders like a weight of mail. The boy looked back briefly over his shoulder to the setting sun as the gates closed behind him.

He had aged, too.


*And here Edward, Edgar's son, succeeded to the kingdom; and then immediately in harvest-time of that same year, the star comet appeared, and then in the following year came a very great famine and very manifold disturbances throughout the English race. And Ealdorman Aelfhere ordered very many monastic institutions to be overthrown which King Edgar earlier ordered the holy bishop Aethelwold to establish.*

Anglo-Saxon Chronicles, 975


'Aethelred is too young. I will not have it.' Dunstan was livid. It was the first time he had shown anger to his bishop of Winchester. He wagged a finger at the face of his reforming compatriot.

Aethelwold had learned from his former abbot-master not to give in. Only the king could remove him from his office. Edward would be ruled by Dunstan; but Aethelred would be ruled by his mother. And Aelfthryth trusted Aethelwold.

Dunstan lowered his arm and slapped his hand on the table in front of him. It was clear to him who should be king after Edgar.

Why was it not clear to Aethelwold? He felt pain in his hand. So many years of decision-making, so many years of contending with the traumas and inadequacies of royal families and their chosen lightweight admirers, so many seas to navigate with a boat hardly large enough to ride a Dee bore, let alone the crashing waves of the troubles of England and its fledgling shires. He thought of the golden day, two years before, when the triumph of his time with Edgar at Chester had seemed a prophecy of continued success, everlasting peace. Since then, his foresight had failed him. Now, with the body of Edgar freshly in the grave at Glastonbury, and his hopes that the king might be sainted and revered as a pilgrimage draw dashed by refusal letters from Rome, Dunstan felt that his own days were drawing to a close. He even found himself wishing to retire to a scriptorium on a permanent basis. There was much of the history of Wessex and its kings which he wished to annotate. He estimated that three years were all he needed for the work, if he kept at it night and day. But would his body hold up? When would the diseases which accompanied old age strike him? He tried to estimate his time on earth, but his prayers proved fruitless. In his dreams he was again young, with all the time before him in which to alter things, in which to do good, to defeat evil, but since Edgar's death, his prayers, based upon the hope of his dreams, had not been aswered. God was looking away.

'Edward is illegitimate.' There, Aethelwold had used the word. 'The Ealdormen will not accept him.'

'His mother was not anointed, true, but she was an ealdorman's daughter.'

'He forced himself on the nun.'

'For which he did penance.'

'She gave birth.'

'To a sweet child, Edith. I have met her. She has promise.'

'As a saint?'

'Yes. But before you argue further,' Dunstan nursed his hand, feeling calmer, 'I want to remind you of the coronation and the visit to Chester. You were not part of the planning, which I regret, but we earned the good will of the people, resting their fears about the coming millennium, with making Edgar wait until the anniversary of Christ's birth. Edgar understood the requirement, Edward, too. Aethelred was too young to understand.' He sat down. If he could not persuade Aethelwold, his old ally, of the rightness of Edward to be king, he was wasting his time. He felt the familiar headache begin.

The table slapping had not been wasted, however. Aethelwold could understand bodily pain. He had never before seen Dunstan affected so much that he hit anything. Dunstan had been unwilling to apply the rod to Eadwig when he was a child. The rod had been spared, and disaster had occurred. 'Edward is like Edmund.' This was Aethelwold's last shot.

Like Edmund. Both men reached back into their memories of the hot-headed young man, heir to Athelstan, who, they had decided over the years, had brought about his own demise. If it had not been Leofa who killed him at Pucklechurch, it would have been another.

'He will not be another Edmund. I have him in hand. And he is not regarded as illegitimate by many at court. If he is illegitimate, then so are most of the children of the families who now give their support to the monasteries - your monasteries.'

'If Edward has children of his own, will they be regarded as legitimate aethelings? What happens when Aethelred has a family of sons? Will Aelfthryth his mother use her connections to stir civil war?'

Aethelwold had a point. Dunstan was silent. The trouble of choosing at Edmund's death had been difficult; at Edgar's it was worse. Then the choice had been between a full brother or a child; now it was between an 'illegitimate' or a 'legitimate' half-brother. Civil war was, indeed, on the cards.

Dunstan rose from the table and wrapped his cloak around him. 'I will go to the Old Minster to pray. I suggest that you, Aethelwold, do the same.' There was the cloud of doubt. It was spreading itself again throughout his being. Had God deserted him? He needed a sign.

# Cheddar, September 975

T HE HUNT WAS fast and furious. Men chased the boar on horse, on foot, in carriages, brandishing spears, arrows, poles and walking sticks. The living thing, which must die, skirted the gorge edge, unwilling to enter the narrowing chasm, uncertain of the brush cover beside its entrance. It dashed across a stream, heading for a small patch of woodland and lay, panting, behind a row of sedge reeds. Its snout could be seen by the huntsmen who had caught up with its desperate flight and now relaxed into killing mode, rather than chasing. They understood the beast; it would lurch out sooner or later. They had time to surround and to stop its escape. There would be game for supper.

Dunstan and the young king Edward, one in a carriage and the other on a horse which was slightly too large for him, but which he handled well, caught up with the chasers. Edward had been with the foremost huntsmen and had hoped for the kill, but had diplomatically offered it to his chief huntsman. There would be other days, other kills. The air was gusting, the clouds clearing. It was a fine day for a hunt.

'Did you ever kill a wolf in these parts, Archbishop?' Edward was spending his first time as king away from Winchester with Dunstan, visiting Glastonbury and the family estate at Cheddar. Dunstan had become his main source for information about the past. He had visited his father's and his grandfather's tombs and witnessed for himself the state of the Benedictine reform movement as demonstrated by the monks of Glastonbury. He understood enough of the resistance of some monks to the reform; Ealdorman Aelfhere had described how things used to be. He had tried not to repeat in his mind what Aelfhere had called the archbishop. It was derogatory. He looked at Dunstan, who had plumped up a cushion in his carriage and was lying back, looking a little green. Travelling did this to him. It was a long way from the cloisters of St Augustine, Canterbury and the past week had been tiring, but necessary. Edward had to be introduced to his land and patrimony.

'Not personally, no, but in my youth, there were wolves here, living in the gorge. You will have seen the pelts on the walls of the palace, though some were brought by Hywel Dda of Wales as tribute. They are the larger ones.'

'And bears? Did you see bears?'

'There were no bears here, only those brought by the dancers. There is something I wish to talk about, Edward, while we are waiting for the boar to emerge. He will wait and watch for his moment of escape; the huntsman will be sure to cover his dash. We will be safe here.'

'I am not sure that I want to be safe, Archbishop, but nevertheless…what is it that you wanted to say to me?' Edward dismounted and climbed into the carriage, leaning against Dunstan, who did not recoil. This was a young man who operated, like his mother, the Duck, with touch. Hugs and kisses were endowed on friend and foe, alike. The boy smiled. He was disarming, but Dunstan was becoming used to the young man's charm. He noted that, though much slimmer than him, Edward was growing taller rapidly and was equal to himself in height. The pleasant youth and vigour were beginning to be a comfort to the ageing courtier. It was a pleasure to be with Edward. He wished he had more time to enjoy the lad's company. Edward beamed at the archbishop.

'It is about the future. Have you given thought to your heir?' Dunstan caught the downturned mouth of Edward. 'Of course, the future and your own demise must seem impossible to imagine, you are so young and strong. But these things must be thought of.'

'I suppose they must.' Edward stopped smiling. He leaned forward, detaching himself from Dunstan, who sat up. In the distance, the huntsmen waited for the drama of the boar's escape, spears raised. 'Archbishop, who do you suggest should be my heir?'

'Your brother Aethelred will naturally wish to be acknowledged.'

'Of course. I love my brother dearly, you know that, Archbishop, but what about my own children? Should they not take precedence?' The boar had still not broken cover. There was expectation in the air. The wind had died down, the sun was shining. Over the gorge there was a dark grey cloud, moving slowly, ominously, eastwards. It began to rain. Dunstan pulled a curtain over the side of the carriage. A strong gust blew it inwards.

'Your stepmother will wish Aethelred to be named and presented as aetheling. She will naturally desire no less. We shall have to do this at the Winchester witan next month. There will be other serious matters to discuss there; Bishop Aethelwold's monasteries are under threat, but we should begin proceedings with Aethelred's sworn submission to you as his liege lord. Otherwise, we may have trouble in that quarter.'

'You mean, my stepmother will start a revolt? Surely not, Archbishop?'

'Aethelred loves you as a brother, but is too young to overrule his mother. The bishop of Winchester has been strict with the reforms in his monasteries. I fear he may have gone too far, too fast. In order to restore order and to save the work that has been done in the eastern monasteries, we must give Aethelred the status which his mother requires and which will act to quell the insurgents. You do not wish the bishop of Winchester to lose his position, do you?'

'No, Archbishop.' But Edward was not sure. The growing rift between Dunstan and Aethelwold was clear to him and he knew it was important, but he had limited ability, being a fun-loving and friendly young man, to suspect conspiracy. To entertain suspicion was as yet foreign to him. All he knew was that Aethelred was a charming boy, a friend to him and playmate. He repeated his question. 'But what about my own children? Wouldn't they take precedence?' What about a future wife. Edward had begun to select the beauties available to him from the convent schools. He was aware of his father's misdemeanours. He would not raid the schoolrooms, but wait for a matron to select a few desirables. All the ealdormen's daughters were educated in the convents; Wilton was possibly the best source. His sister Edith would ensure that a beauty with not too many brains would be found.

'For now, Aethelred must be given precedence. Things may change. When you are married and children are on the way, then, if a boy child is born, we will change the name of the heir.'

'My stepmother will not like that. Aethelred would be disappointed.' Edward was beginning to realise the thorns which were contained in his crown. It is difficult for a youth to imagine the fears and expectations of others and to circumvent personal hostility. 'Archbishop, do I have enemies?'

'Not enemies, Edward, but there are things afoot which demand an older head than you, at present, have. Do you understand?'

'I understand that you are on my side, and I thank you for it. The boar! He has broken!' Edward jumped up, rocking the carriage.

The matter had been broached. Before the witan in Winchester, Dunstan could now form the inevitable battle lines. Aelfthryth and Aethelwold on the one side, himself and Edward on the other. Could he look ahead to prophesy what might come to them all in the months to come? Would the misguided anti-reform movement, which caused shouting matches and sometimes worse, in the eastern monasteries and in the corridors of the palaces, be placated by the certainty of Edward's coronation? Would those who wanted Aethelred as king and his mother as regent, be satisfied with taking second place in the land? Would there have to be another split in the nation, with Mercia separating from England?

God was still behind the cloud of Dunstan's doubt. Dunstan could see dimly what must occur at the witan, but he felt unsure of his position. Torrential rain suddenly fell. The boar had been speared. The kitchens would be pleased to present the meat, festooned with the head and snout, on one of their wooden platters. There would be feasting and fun.

The rain made the huntsmen hurry to return to the palace. Dunstan would go to Glastonbury to review the works. Had the ealdormen of western Wessex joined the ranks of the anti-reformists? At night, the clouds had gone; he looked at a full moon. A streak of light caught his eye.

*Oh. God, help me.*

The comet had come, and then the harvest failed.

# Nonna's diary, St John's Monastery, Frome, September 976

THE SWALLOW FAMILIES had the barn almost to themselves. A fast-reducing heap of grain against the inner wall was being shovelled by two dark-skinned slaves into sacks. The few sacks already filled which were awaiting collection for distribution to the markets looked pitiful. Work would stop at midday; there was little for the barn slaves to do.

I walked with Dunstan around the monastery site. He wished to check on progress, taking an inventory of what was needed, what was wanted. I told him that the monks were in dire need of fresh financial input; but there were so many similar places which wanted the same. The days of the oldest missionary monasteries were numbered, even those which were founded by the holy St Aldhelm. Our Frome relics were few and little valued; even the staff of St John was failing to attract pilgrims and the hospital was more popular than the church. There were always the sick and lame to care for and lepers were in abundance. It was being mooted that they should attend and be cared for at separate foundations in Selwood forest, but as yet these had not been funded or become more than paper ideas.

Dunstan could see that this near-empty barn might well be replicated across southern Britain. In September it should have been full. The summer had been dry. From May to the end of August there had been no rain. Then the floods came and spoilt what little crop had grown. We walked around the barn and along Behind Town, picking our way between puddles and heaps of mud thrown up by carts. The urchins of town were looking pinched; the lack of grain and grass had had an effect on the animals normally kept for fattening; half of the local domestic beasts had been slaughtered before their time. Access to freshwater fish had become difficult; carp threshed and died in the shallow monastic pools. Carts made their way slowly through the mud from the south coast, bringing occasional barrels of salted fish, but they were quickly taken up by the wealthier patrons of the court and church.

Bread was the problem, and ale. There was little to keep the hungry at work and little to offer them in safe drink. Even the springs of Frome, usually so abundant, had become mere trickles until recently. Man could keep living, if he foraged, but the navy and army needed more. It was the beginning of severe worries for the well-being of the nation and made us vulnerable.

Dunstan was uneasy. His own foresight told him that the winter ahead would have little bread and meat for the troops and navy. The season of harvest was the worst on record. He would be to blame, he felt.

Other matters weighed heavily on the first minister. Ealdorman Aelfhere of East Anglia had attacked Aethelwold's refoundations in his territory. The Mercian ealdorman was taking his revenge on Aethelwold for casting out the secular canons and replacing them with what he regarded as zealots, Benedictine reformers. Dunstan told me that he would have done what Aethelwold had done, but with less haste. The violence of the canons' eviction had been repaid with a similar approach by Aelfhere. Dunstan feared that Mercia would break away from the king's and his control. He admitted wishing for heaven, or hell, to open and swallow the ealdorman, he did not mind which. That happened, not long after, but Aethelwold, meantime, had to watch as his monastic building projects were torn down and their lands redistributed among the supporters of the rebellious Aelfhere.

Dunstan was distracted by the multiplicity of problems. I had never seen him so down-hearted. He could not see a way forward, he said. The people would starve, the monastic reform movement was threatened, the queen was being obstructive over Edward's coronation. At least she was pro-Aethelwold, as was Eadwig's widow, who joined her in voicing support, in the palace halls as well as the sewing-rooms, for the Benedictine reform. She felt, despite Aethelwold's antipathy to women in general, that he offered the better chance of furthering her educational ideals. Aethelwold was not averse to separate establishments of teaching in the convents; as long as men and women mixed as little as possible, he was supportive. He could not rule the marriage bed, but in these years the retirement of widows to convents became common; Aelfhere would have had them remarried forcibly. Land ownership was the root of the problem, not only that, but also the ownership of peasants and slaves working on it and legally attached to it.

The archbishop told me that he felt blindsided, too, by his affection for the young King Edward. He had never displayed any favouritism, to my knowledge, before, with other aethelings. He had fairly dealt with the material which was handed to him in the bloodline of Wessex. He was telling me how much he thought of the boy, as if he was his own grandson, and of how he held in esteem the boy's mother and his stepmother, now ensconced at Wilton. Edward's sister, Edith, was a beautiful and bright child, like Edward. He saw them as full-siblings, he said, not the half-siblings which they were. They were like twins of different genders. He had had much to do with the education of Edward, who was on the cusp, with his advice and help, he said, of being independent enough to rule by merit in his own right. He was adamant that Prince Aethelred was not ready in any way, how could he be? Besides which, Aethelred's mother had too powerful a faction behind her. He whispered, looking round to see if anyone was near, that he feared that Aelfthryth's closeness to Aethelwold and her anxiety for him and her son had coloured her view of the best arrangement for the nation. She could only see what was best for her, he added quietly.

At this point, the aetheling Edward himself appeared, striding up the Portway with two companions, with hawking birds on their wrists. Dressed in autumnal colours of gold and green, with his companions similarly garbed, he gave the lie to the dreadful season of want which was about to befall us. He had been visiting the palace, reviewing its decrepit state and praying in the room where Eadred had died in 955. Dunstan hailed him, his mood lifting instantly, and they began talking together in Latin. Edward winked at me as he saw me, no doubt with my jaw dropped, conversing fluently with his chief advisor. No wonder Dunstan thought well of the lad.

No wonder his stepmother the queen was jealous.

It was after this meeting that Dunstan asked me to accompany him to Canterbury on a permanent basis. He needed me there, he said, to begin the task of editing the histories. We were both getting too old to be chasing around the country with much younger kings, he said. My days at court were over. I would retire to the scriptorium of the most magnificent library at the heart of the making of the history of the English people, though Malmesbury and Glastonbury would challenge that, in time.

As we made the long journey eastwards, Dunstan continued to air his fears for the immediate future. He needed a sign, he said, from God, that he was doing his will. Or was he doing his own? It soon came. A comet's bright pass brought it, which Dunstan interpreted as a positive omen. Surely, now, the nation would settle on his choice of Edward as king.


Despite the positive omen, things were still undecided at the next Winchester witan. It was clear that two factions, led by two equally wealthy and determined ealdormen, could not, or would not, agree on the succession. It wasn't merely land-holdings which were at stake; each side was blood-related to some part of the royal Wessex dynasty and each thought that their personal claim to disrupt or promote their candidate for king was valid. Aethelwine, who derived his power from that great man, Athelstan Half-king, had his base in east Anglia. Naturally, Aethelwold, with his intense interests in the abbeys and monasteries of the east, was his man. He supported Aethelred and the queen. Aelfhere was the magnate of the west. He and Dunstan favoured Edward. Civil war was but a week away.

The witan was a bruising affair; neither side would give way to the other and the arguments for and against the two princes were equally maintained. Both Dunstan and the queen, who, as anointed sovereign was able to be present, used time and again the same arguments for their respective choices. Time and again the roars from the opposing camps shouted down the opinions which became, as a result, more strident. Swords had been left at the palace door, or they would have been used. Dunstan left the meeting after two hours with a grim expression on his face. The queen retired to her chambers with her family and retinue, the doors to the private apartment slamming closed behind them, keeping out those of us who could have offered mediation. We were no closer to settlement of the nation; the two boys no nearer to wearing a crown.

The great hunger then set in throughout the land; it staved off the crisis as men concentrated on eking out what grain was available. Government quietly continued as before, ealdormen having their possessions to manage, their reeves to instruct. The want of food and income brought men to their senses.

By February 977, Edward was crowned. Dunstan could rest at last. But he still had doubts that peace would hold. Once the crisis of famine was past, the quarrels between the earls began again during the following summer.

# Calne, Wiltshire, February 978

'AELFHERE, WHAT IS your case?'
Aethelwold, fully robed in his role as bishop of Winchester, thumped his staff on the planks of the upper room over the inn which was being used to accommodate the ealdormen and their chief supporters. It was like a court of law. The matter of the succession had been physically settled by the grand crowning of Edward, though the camp of Ealdorman Aelfhere of Mercia still grumbled. Aethelred, the king's half-brother, had been declared heir to the throne, but that did not, either, satisfy his mother. Dunstan was forced to hold an emergency meeting of the chief councillors in the north Wessex town of Calne. The pressing matter of security of the recently endowed monasteries in the east was a major concern. Aethelwold demanded to hear the justification for the continuing raids on his foundations.

'Speak,' he repeated. 'Why have you attacked my monks?'

The answer was obvious, but the question needed to be asked and noted by officials. Nonna scribbled fast, making the written account of both sides; civil war had been averted so far, but there was tension in the air.

Ealdorman Aelfhere shifted his feet. The confines of the room, with only a steep and rickety stair to the ground floor, made him feel trapped. He took a deep breath, looked at his followers and began his defence of the land-grabbing and monk-defying in which he had indulged since King Edgar's death.

'Because I do not like you, nor your reforming ways!' Aelfhere pointed a sturdy finger at Aethelwold. It was a matter of personality. Either you wanted more religion, or you did not. The reformers wanted the former, for all.

From another table there was shouting. Ealdorman Aethelwine of East Anglia was brandishing his fists. There was a rush of heavy bodies across the narrow room.

Uproar ensued. Hatred of Bishop Aethelwold spilled out across the room. Aelfhere's camp jumped to their feet. Dunstan remained seated at the table, governing the room and procedure. There was a cracking sound, then part of the wooden floor gave way. Near the one large window, a group of councillors tumbled through a gaping hole, their tables and chairs crashing after them. There was the sound of screams and shattering glass. Nearer Dunstan, the beams shuddered and snapped, causing more men to lurch and hold onto whatever seemed stable. Much was not. Dunstan's table swayed and rocked. What had caused this sudden collapse of the floor of the meeting house? It had seemed safe enough when they had entered it an hour before, but perhaps more well-fed men and the seating and heavy tables required for the business to be conducted had weakened its structure. The rain of recent weeks may have played a part.

Dunstan hung on to the tottering table. He felt that he would plunge, as Edmund had nearly plunged, into the abyss at any moment, and join the yelling and groaning men on the floor below. He could see them, bloodied and mangled, amongst the broken beams and plaster. Balancing with difficulty on a large beam which remained stable, Dunstan looked behind him. The floor had given way near the stairwell. The melee had been too much; the whole wooden structure, several centuries old, was in danger of complete collapse.

Guards rushed to assist the injured, removing slabs of plaster and broken beams. Screaming continued. These were the sounds of battle, but perhaps worse bloodshed had been averted by the floor's collapse. Men had been prepared to fight; the confusion and emotion reminded Dunstan of the description of Edmund's death at Pucklechurch so many years before, which Nonna had told him about. Chaos, confusion, that was how wars came about. Lack of discipline, the inability to hear another's side.

But look, now, here he was, the Archbishop of Canterbury, the only man left standing in this scene of carnage. All the others had tumbled to their deaths or to broken limbs. Even the opposing ealdormen had disappeared, fallen into the abyss of their own making. Aethelwold, too, had gone with them. Was this the end of things? Had the millennium come sooner than expected?

The yelling subsided into moans; the dust cleared. The building itself swayed. A ladder was propped against a wall. Dunstan shuffled towards what had been a doorway but which was now a gaping hole. He managed, with help from a young guard, to climb down to the timber-strewn grass below. Guards were busy assisting the living to their feet. Bishop Aethelwold had survived, thank God, and he could see the ealdormen, shaken and covered in dust, limping away, arm in arm, both men having sustained what looked to be broken limbs. Aethelwold was sitting up in a pile of wattle, having fallen on a straw-filled midden. Others were not so lucky; by head and foot they were being lifted from the mess of splintered wood to a grassy knoll nearby, where they could be named, and counted. Blood from shattered limbs lay in pools. Dunstan looked up at what remained of the building. Had there been an earthquake, like those he had heard of on his journey to Rome? Why had this accident occurred? Was it the comet which had foretold disaster? Why had he not seen that this would happen? Yet the famine had been overcome; the harvest had been good. The people would not starve, the tythe barns were full again. Plenty had returned, but not, it seemed, goodwill.

There was only one explanation for this extraordinary circumstance; he, Dunstan, Archbishop of Canterbury, had been given a sign, the sign he had been waiting for. Of all the magnates of the land who now groaned and lay broken in this place of Calne, he alone had escaped unscathed.

God was evidently on the side of Reform and angels sat on his, Dunstan's shoulder. Doubt was dispelled. Edward was the rightful king.

**978.** *Here in this year all the foremost councillors of the English race fell down from an upper floor at Calne, but the holy bishop Dunstan alone was left standing up on a beam; and some were very injured there, and some did not escape it with their life.*

Anglo-Saxon Chronicles

## Corfe, March 18, 978

'I T WILL BE my brother's birthday soon. I am satisfied that the defences at Wareham are in good heart; I am allowed a day away from my duties, surely? Am I not to have any joy in my youth?'

Edward was feeling kingship heavy on his shoulders. 'I want to hunt. I am going to. This heathland should harbour some game. Anything will do. I need hard riding.' Edward grumbled to himself, but he was light-hearted.

There had been tedium at Wareham. The sailors of the fleet had been inspected; the ships counted. Every rope had been accounted for, every sail and oar. Lists were for Dunstan's perusal. Detail was to his taste. Edward rode slowly northwards with his retinue across the sandy wastes of Purbeck. There had been a re-enactment of Alfred's defeat of the Danes in the shallow off-shore waters at Swanage. A service of thanksgiving had been held at the church there. Now he was free to let his youthfulness run wild, for a few days, until his return to Winchester and Dunstan.

Half of Edward's retinue, with the carriages of travelling equipment, set off for Winchester. The remainder, his close companions, remained with him and began to beat the undergrowth to put up game. Ground birds scattered, squawking, from behind ferns and thorn bushes. A hare sat up and began to bound away. Edward and two of his friends followed it on horse, chasing eastwards as it ran towards the rising sun.

The chase continued in a flurry of hooves and yells. The hare was taken after a zig-zag chase and despatched quickly. Happy and fulfilled, Edward realised that he was in sight of the great hall on the mound of Corfe, where he knew that Aethelred and his mother were spending time. It had been his intention to call there to check on his relatives; they had withdrawn somewhat from court life since his accession. Dunstan had advised him to make sure that they were content. What did Dunstan mean, *content*?

Edward had not seen his step-mother and half-brother since the Christmas feast. Surely they had no reason to feel neglected? *Do not neglect your close relatives*, was all that Dunstan had said. There was the gatehouse, only a mile away. Here was a fine hare to present to Aethelred. The boy would be glad to view and skin it. Edward would show him how. It would be an excellent chance to be close to his heir, and anyway, the boys were fond of each other. He turned his horse towards Corfe, indicating to his companions his intention of going there. The three young men rode swiftly, feeling hungry and full of life, outsprinting each other as they went, their horses young, like themselves.

As they reached the gap of Corfe, the hall straight ahead on its huge knoll, a trumpet blew. The outer gate in the wooden palisade opened and several tall figures walked out, with hands on hips, to view the approaching horsemen. There had been recent sightings of Scandinavians passing below, traders on their way from the coast to Wareham and further inland, but also a few weapon-totting warriors, which had caused concern to the household. Aethelred had cried himself to sleep on many occasions at the thought of the possible incursion of blood-thirsty warriors. He had heard many tales by the fireside of his family's past travails with Vikings and the gory details had not been spared him. His ten-year-old sensitivity had not yet been hardened by a youth's experience and his mother kept him away from other boys of his own age, who, she thought, tended towards cruelty and bullying. They called him The Stinker. That was Dunstan's fault, Aelfthryth thought, and she had told him so. The incident in the font had not been forgotten, nor Dunstan's remark upon it.

The queen joined her guards at the gate, a tall figure in comfortable clothes, holding a trowel in her hand. She whispered to one of the guards, who walked down the slope of the knoll to the trotting horseman who was now in front of his companions, who hung back, seeing that the queen was present. Edward rode up to the single guard, who was the queen's steward and known slightly to him.

'Hail, Edfrith, I have come to see my brother. Have you ale at the gate to quench a hunter's thirst?'

'My lord, I have a horn at my side which will give you a small drink; there is more inside the hall.'

Edfrith gave his horn to the gasping youth. As he leant forward to take it, Edfrith jabbed with his knife into the boy's throat. Edward jerked back in surprise and horror. He put his hand to his throat. It spurted blood. An artery had been severed.

Wheeling his horse around, he careered down the slope to the bridge towards his companions, who galloped towards him, seeing the distress of both rider and horse. Edward began to lose consciousness; one foot lost a stirrup and the other became entangled in leather strapping. He slipped sideways off the horse. It careered on, past Edward's companions, across the heath, dragging its heavily bleeding rider until it could go no further. The dead hare hung, swinging, at the saddle as the horse came to a halt, foaming and heaving, where Edward's companions caught up with it. It was too late to act to save the young king; the blood loss had sealed his fate. He opened an eye to view the sky for the last time, his face and body broken and bruised. His foot was released from the strapping. He breathed out and was gone.

# Winchester, March 978

'YOU DID NOT foresee this, Archbishop.'
Aeldorman Aelfhere, leaning on a crutch, sat down heavily on a bench and winced with pain. His leg was healing, but he felt that his death had been hastened by the disastrous experience at Calne. He took a more pessimistic view of life now that he knew that God had decided that the two great earldoms in the land should be amicably reunited. And now there was this terrible news of a death of a certain and hopeful youth, Edward.

'No, I did not.'

Dunstan had gained much from the Calne episode of disaster. Clouds came with silver linings. It had brought many who would have made war in England against each other see reason and step back from the brink.

'Perhaps my abilities are leaving me, Aelfhere.'

Perhaps they were. He was getting too old to take on more responsibilities. Aethelred, the stinking child, would be king. Such a short time had passed since Edward had been crowned and anointed. Aethelred's crowning ceremony would take place at Kingston. The boy and his mother had achieved their goal. The boy- king could not be held accountable for his brother's death, and his mother was well protected, both by her son and her well-armed supporters. Dunstan could not bear to think of the destruction of the noble and well-educated Edward. After the ceremony, he had decided, he would definitely retire to the scriptorium at Canterbury. The histories of the Saxons could wait no longer.

Another limping man entered the room to join them. Ealdorman Aethelwine had a smile, to accompany the broken arm and sprained ankle received at Calne. He did not need a crutch;

a young boy provided support. The boy's mother, Aelfthryth, accompanied them, closing the door behind her.

The boy-king Aethelred and Ealdorman Aelfwine sat on a bench beside each other and opposite Dunstan and Ealdorman Aelfhere. The gathering of former foes in the old royal nursery, instigated by the arrival of Danish intruders on the southern shores, had become an imperative; the old adage that a common enemy would draw foes together had been voiced by none other than the boy who was set to be king. The disaster of Calne had been followed by news of Danish raids at Southampton. There had been deaths.

'So it will be at Kingston, then.' The queen commanded, rather than asked. 'When can the anointing be arranged, Archbishop?'

Dunstan gave a noticeable shudder. The former kings, Edmund, then his son Edgar, reasonably well-trained and physically strong, died young. They should have given him more time to view the line of accession. Assassination had come to Edmund; an unexpected illness following an immersion in sun, wind and rain, had done for the other. Edward, the best hope of the family for all of the century, had been snatched by evil intent. And the perpetrator of that intent now sat opposite, smouldering with smug contempt. The queen-regent sat by her son, upright, darkly handsome and determined. She reminded Dunstan of Eadgifu, though not in looks; this was a tall woman, unaided by heeled shoes, with a long almost black single plait appearing, unadorned, beneath the short wimple; her jewellery was modest, her clothing practical. Aethelwold could find no fault in her. In Dunstan's eyes, she was a witch.

The widow had grown in influence since her husband, Edgar's, death and the loss of her first son, Edmund, in infancy. Aethelred was her one chance to prevent forced remarriage and to keep the land and power which she possessed. She knew the sequence of events in her grandmother-in-law, Eadgifu's life; with Edward out of the way the inevitable falling-out between step-son and step-mother which would have occurred had he lived was prevented. Sitting opposite, breathing hard, was her enemy who would have achieved her dismissal from court; Ealdorman Aelfhere was only half the man he had been, since his fall at Calne. Her enemy was visibly broken.

'At Kingston, yes.'

Dunstan, resigned, confirmed the wishes of the queen. Kingston on the Thames was where most of the Wessex kings had received the all-important anointing as the representative for the nation of God's will. It made the queen secure, so long as she had the goodwill of her son. And that was certain, as long as he was a minor. She had time on her side and Aethelred was a sentimental boy, fond of his mother. He wore black still for his brother and father; both had been great losses to him. He still cried every night at his bed as he prayed.

The battle had been won; Aethelred was king and soon to be anointed and unassailable as ruler. The crown would be his and all that came with it. The land was again united; there was no other choice. The child Aethelred and his competent and murderous mother would rule.

Papers were brought in by Nonna. The plans for the coronation were finalised. Mercia, Wessex, East Anglia and Northumbria would unite beneath the head of this new faction of energy and determination. Aelfthryth had done what needed to be done. She was now both queen and king, in all but name.

**Later the same day**

'It is insufferable. She will rob the treasury of the funds needed to shore up the defences.'

Aelfhere and Dunstan shared wine after the meeting with Aethelwine and the widow-queen. They had moved to an inn behind the Nunnaminster. They sat beside an open hearth which blazed and spit from its wet logs.

'She will ruin us.'

'And perhaps the country, my friend.' Dunstan took a large gulp from his cup. He preferred wine as a soothing help-mate instead of ale or mead; his tastes had changed since his trip to Rome. 'There is no alternative, Ealdorman. We must accept that it is God's will that

Aethelred will rule.'

'But you did not foresee this, nor want it, Archbishop. Do you think Aethelred will avenge his brother Edward? Though perhaps it is too soon to expect that he will act…'

'Aethelred will not act against his mother. How can he? I doubt that he will ever take sides against her. Perhaps, when he is grown, he will take steps to sideline her; I have a plan, which I may not live to see, though you might, or your sons.'

'Go on.'

'Edward must have some miracles attached to his name. He must become a cult. That way, if nothing is done to act against the queen, at least the swell of pilgrimage and popular feeling will keep her in check.'

'Can you arrange for that to be done, Archbishop? Edward's body has not been found. How do we find him; how is a reliquary to be made available for the public? Indeed, can we be sure that he is dead?'

'I have heard from my shore watchers that flame has been seen. A pillar of fire.'

'Like the burning bush of Moses?'

'Something like that. I have had scouts looking for the body, scouring the area beyond Corfe. They say they have found a burnt area which has recent digging beside it.' Dunstan looked around. The high-sided settle on which they sat offered reasonable protection from other ears. 'They have found charred remains.'

'That must be Edward!'

'We will assume so. There is little evidence attached to the corpse to prove it, but it is likely. The remains have been burnt beyond recognition.'

'The bastards! Give me a guide. I shall take Edward to a fitting burial place.'

'I hoped you would take on this challenge, my lord. I have a guide ready to take you south to the spot. On a good horse you should reach there within two days. Take the remains to Wareham and begin the rumour of his finding.'

'You mean, display them and use the town-crier?'

'Exactly. Use the maximum of propaganda possible. The flame of Edward's pyre will illuminate the nation!'

# Part Three

## Aethelred the Unready and the Viking Kings

*In the year of our Lord's incarnation 979, Ethelred, son of Edgar and Elfthrida, obtaining the kingdom, occupied, rather than governed it for thirty-seven years. The career of his life is said to have been cruel in the beginning, wretched in the middle, and disgraceful in the end. Thus, in the murder to which he gave his concurrence, he was cruel; base in his flight, and effeminacy; miserable in his death. Dunstan, indeed, had foretold his worthlessness, having discovered it by a very filthy token: for when quite an infant, the bishops standing round, as he was immersed in the baptismal font, he defiled the sacrament by a natural evacuation: at which Dunstan, being extremely angered, exclaimed, "By God, and his mother, this will be a sorry fellow."*

William of Malmesbury, *Deeds of the Kings of England*

## The Castle of Corfe, Dorset, March 18, 978

'HE IS DEAD, Aethelred. That is all you need to know.'
'But how? How did he die, mother?'

Aelfthryth considered that at least her son, Aethelred, the only one left to her after the death of the child Edmund, who had so much promise at the age of four until disease had robbed her of his life and their future, had not yet come to the question 'why', nor was likely to continue to that most difficult question of all, 'who'. This was some relief. Aethelred was not a child who had shown a great deal of curiosity about private family matters, as yet, though he was an emotional child, and cried easily when he perceived cruelty. He was silently weeping now. He had been fond of Edward, despite his tendency to lose his temper. Edward had not been an example which she wished Aethelred to emulate. What mother would?

They were in the inner hall of the wooden palace on the mound of Corfe, gateway to that stubborn realm of Britishness, Purbeck, which had been partly quelled of its pagan character and refusal to accept the Roman church ways by Aldhelm and later Alfred. The port of Wareham, scene of so many excursions and incursions on the Dortsetshire Frome river, lay landwards beyond the fortified palace, controlling the ingress of merchants, smugglers, and those who might wish to disturb the land or avoid the taxes. There had been recent reports of Viking activity. Their ships, not entirely peaceful, were being geared up for war instead of trade. An optimistic ruler might ignore these signs; Edgar's queen had other priorities; her son, her bloodline, should rule unopposed. The threat from the northmen could be attended to later. Meantime, Archbishop Dunstan would ensure smooth passage for Aethelred, a physically strong child, unlike the deceased child Edmund had been.

'How? He was thrown from his horse.' Would that satisfy the prince who was now becoming breathless, panicky. Aethelred was gasping for air. Aelfthryth pulled him towards an open window. She had seen this before. Edmund had gone this way. Aelthelred should not. He would be kept in the dark. This was all for his own good. The boy burst into loud wailing.

'W-what happened, Mother?' Aethelred tried, but failed, to control his breathing.

Aelfthryth put an arm around her son. 'It was for your own good.' The mother tried to comfort the son. His first serious lesson in the politics of the nation and in the requirements of kingship seared into Aethelred's brain as he fought for breath.

'My...my own good, mother? What was for my own good? What do you mean?'

Aelfthryth had said too much, she realised. She held the boy close; he had been fond of his brother and perhaps realised too well that the falling from a horse was a common and not always accidental disaster. What should she do? Aethelwold should be brought in to distract the boy, perhaps, with a complicated piece of translation, or prayer in the chapel.

'You will learn what I mean, in time. Aethelwold!' Aelfthryth shouted for the priest who she knew was in the next chamber. Aethelred's breathing was returning to normal, but he continued to weep with great gulps.

The door opened and Aethelred's tutor entered the room. Startled by the high-pitched shout from Aelfthryth, he had abandoned his writing and still held his pen in hand, dripping ink onto the floor.

'What can I do for...' Aethelwold began. He quickly saw what was needed; the boy who should be king needed discipline, not coddling. He picked up a large unlit candle from a table and approached the cowering Aethelred, brandishing the stick. 'Cease that sound, prince.' The voice was deep and stern. The candle, raised in his hand, looked like a lance, to Aethelred. It fell upon his shoulder. The boy cried out.

'Don't hit him, Aethelwold.'

Aelfthryth was too late. The Church had chastised the king, which is what he had become, in the moments between joy at his brother's arrival at Corfe and his mother telling him that Edward was dead. The boy-king's questions would be asked and answered when he had words to pray and voice to speak, in times to come. Aethelred would remember and punish those who had caused him misery on that memorable day in March, 978, anno domini.

# Burrington Combe, Somerset, October 979

'AND YOU TELL me that men lived here before Christ? In these caves? How could they survive in total darkness, without the light of Christ?' The elderly ealdorman Aelfhere moved towards the mouth of the cave, peering past the shrubby undergrowth which almost completely covered its entrance.

The Abbess of Shaftesbury, not much younger than her companion, was on a fact-finding mission in the western shires. The abbey had recently conducted an audit. The result was not inspiring. Herleva needed to impress. It was not difficult. Aelfhere knew little of his nation's history, or that of the people who had lived on the land before the arrival of the Cerdicings. He was one of the last of an illiterate generation which had discarded anything but the spoken word of gentlemen and poets. His rival, Aethelwine of East Anglia, was illiterate too.

Herleva could feel sorry for the men who were her equals in the disposition of goods and lands, but her educational inferiors. She joined Aelfhere at the cave mouth, using her staff to brush away the browning ferns. 'I have spent some time, while I was younger, and before I became abbess, in learning what I could about the early days of life on earth. The mouth of the cave, which you see before you, was once a burial place.'

Aelfhere took a step backwards. Herleva touched his arm and waved her staff at the dark cave entrance. The practices of faiths of ages past and present stimulated her. She was occupied with studying the religious texts of Islam, wondering what, if anything, the peoples of the Book had in common, but today she was able to share some of what she knew of the pre-Christian era, strange as it was, with the Ealdorman of Mercia and West Wessex.

Ealdorman Aelfhere was discomfited but recovered. The abbess led him nearer to the cave entrance. Horrified, but in awe of the old woman's courage, he allowed her to unlock the potential of his energy to the benefit of Shaftesbury, of her abbey. Herleva's intention to impress the old soldier had succeeded. They stood together, peering into the chasm. A small sliver of light dropped through boulders into shapeless darkness. This was a unique opportunity, Herleva thought, to fuse together the energies of Church and state. The convents and monasteries of the east were still recovering from depredations against Aethelwold's foundations. Pilgrims were eagerly looking for new sites to visit. Money flowed with them, jingling in purses at the saddles and belts of a moving, seeking people, anxious to relieve the burden of care which they carried and the fear of the fast-approaching millennium. Pilgrimage during Edgar's relatively peaceful reign had grown in popularity; together with the accentuated requirement of purchase of indulgences to offset purgatory liabilities, it had become fashionable and required by anyone who wished not to spend his or her soul's entire time in the never-ending waiting room to heaven. Dunstan had planned it well; the doom paintings appearing in the new-build churches and the tales of devil and angel at war in their stained glass had informed the imaginations of the entire nation that their future repose was at stake. The years rapidly reducing before the time of the millennium had done the rest.

Some abbeys had prospered from the new religious activities of the nation, while others had done less well. With the growing confidence of Wessex, pilgrimage was beginning to focus on royal-born saints and less on the traditional favourites of previous generations. The Church encouraged this new trend. Few former kings and queens were suitable contenders for sainthood; most had been marked as flawed humans in life; not many had been regarded as holy. Even the pious Alfred had somehow escaped sainthood, his body lying corrupted in his tomb at Winchester. An occasional check on his remains had proved him not worthy of relic theft; he would be able to rest, entire. In the past, foreign queens from long ago, such as Radegund, had satisfied the public, but longer journeys and unsettled times had made travel for health or wealth to far-flung abbeys unattractive. Archbishops could afford to go to Rome when collecting their palliums, for which there were expenses. Parts of relics of many saints were available in England, brought from far-off lands, but a fresh generation of pilgrim-goers required something new. Herleva had something in mind.

'Men have retrieved some of those who lie here, you know. I have seen them. There are the remains of wolves and bear, too.'

'Spare me, Madam. My mind cannot encompass this, this nightmare of darkness which is not ours.' Aelfhere was dough in Herleva's hands, he knew it and she knew it.

The pair turned away from looking into the opening to hell where the bones of countless, unknown pagans lay. Most of them would rest, deep in the cave, shrouded in their mysteries, for many centuries yet. The emanations of ghostly breath flowed into the air behind the old man and woman, like tendrils from a magician's wand. Aelfhere shuddered.

'It is our breath.' Herleva had noted the descent of cold air during the last hour. Sunset would soon occur.

Aelfhere, removed several feet away from hell's aperture, attempted a grin. 'Not the ghosts of the past, then, Abbess?' Both were pragmatists. Religion was her profession and was a means to an end for him.

'The past has an effect, Ealdorman. The people love a story or a mystery. Why not give them what they want?' Herleva took his arm.

They made their way over rock and shrub to the waiting carriage, which would convey them both to Glastonbury. The palace at Cheddar was at present closed off for repairs.

'Dunstan thinks that it is high time there was another saint in the royal family. It would bolster our case. Edward is available. Edburga will never be allowed to leave the Nunnaminster, in full or part.'

'Edward? He has been laid to rest in Wareham.'

Aelfhere handed the abbess into the carriage, putting a blanket around her legs. She brushed him away.

'No need to assist me, thank you. Yes, Edward. The church in Wareham is an unsuitable setting for the son of a king. No other of his relatives is entombed there and besides, he is growing in popularity amongst the poor. They go to Wareham and leave their prayers and offerings. They should be focussing their attention elsewhere.'

The carriage, driven by a driver and two horses, set off down the darkening combe, emerging eventually into the last of the autumn sunshine. She continued with her plan. 'It would mean exhumation, yes, a grisly business, I know, and no doubt those who have been laid to rest do not wish to be resurrected in such a manner, but I understand from my contacts that Edward has been shifted before.'

'From the marsh where he was intended to be hidden, yes. The foul murderers. Not even a decent burial was given to the young man. And he of royal blood.'

'And a crowned king. He should not lie friendless at Wareham. I propose to bring him to Shaftesbury.'

Aelfhere swung round to view the abbess. Yes, by the look on her face, she meant it. She meant him to exhume what was left of the sixteen-year-old king and to transport him many miles inland to the large but impoverished abbey on the hill. The street called Gold had waned in its remit of transporting money there, of late. Perhaps the abbess had had a good idea. Gold could again flow to Alfred's foundation.

'It could not be done covertly.'

'I have thought of that. Boldness will have its reward.'

Of course she had. Aelfhere sat back, wrapped himself in blankets and listened.

Weeks later, a retinue of soldiers of Wessex, Aelfhere's brothers and Aelfhere himself, dressed as a magnate, resplendent in filet and fur, made its way over seven days to Shaftesbury, stopping regularly to receive the rapt attention of villagers and townspeople, making much in its progressional pomp of the importance of this new saint, about whose body many miracles were claimed. Here was a soul which could save a generation from the doom which awaited each and everyone. Thus, Edward the Martyr joined his grandmother, Elgiva, Edmund's queen, in sainthood. As recently deceased saints of the royal family, they began to draw crowds. Coin rapidly returned to Gold Street.

The first part of Herleva's plan had been achieved. There was more. Politics were an interest, as well as religion and faith.

# Wilton Abbey, January 980

'I TELL YOU, this is our only chance. The abbess is for it. We cannot have more of the queen-mother's rule. She is ruining the nation.'

'I told you that that would be the case, yet you did not listen. Aethelred's reign is doomed. Which abbess? Here or at Shaftesbury?'

'Both. Herleva is keen. Wulfthryth may be persuaded.'

Archbishop Dunstan and Ealdorman Aelfhere had met often in recent times; Dunstan had still been unable to retire; weariness had to be pushed aside; things were afoot which even he had not dreamed of. Edward the murdered king had been taken, with seven days of pomp and ritual, from Wareham to Shaftesbury. He had been laid to rest with a service of dedication designed by the archbishop, the last great ceremony of his life. It had nearly killed him, accompanying the charred remains in their temporary reliquary from the south coast to be received and laid to rest by Herleva at Shaftesbury. But the job had been done; the deceased Edward was now actively performing miracles; the poor and sick believed in his efficacy. He had become 'the martyr', an essential mainstay against outward or inward threats, or simply against the coming apocalypse. The day of his death, March 18, had entered the church calendar. Aethelred and his mother smarted and wept. Their involvement in the murder or their intention to promote it brought a wave of questioning propaganda to the palaces of England; the regent was feeling guilty, while admitting nothing. She had done her best for her boy, had done what was required.

Aelfhere had been the prime mover of the translation of the body. He and Dunstan had physically suffered on the slow journey north from the coast. The inns and tents on the way had been uncomfortable; the cost had been enormous. But it had been worth it; the church at Wareham, where Aelfhere had at first taken Edward, had benefitted by the boy's ghostly presence and Shaftesbury abbey was in receipt of fresh income. The populace had a new, young saint to revere. A new set of relics and reliquaries of all kinds, real and fake, became big business which the monasteries and abbeys could manipulate to their advantage. Workshops in monastery grounds enlarged, equipment and materials were sourced from afar to make new stock; everyone benefitted from the craze which was Edward the Martyr. Most important, to ealdorman and archbishop, the regency of the mother-queen was held in check. Breathing space had been achieved.

Dunstan and Aelfhere reached Wilton abbey gate and dismounted. It had not been an exhausting morning's ride but the roads were filthy and their cloaks were caked. Both elderly men were unashamed to use the mounting block. The heavily metalled gates swung open and they led their horses into the courtyard. There was no visible gateman. They were expected; promises had been made to Abbess Wulfthryth at Herleva's suggestion. Shaftesbury and Wilton abbeys, both female foundations, had long assisted each other in angling for a major share of the proceeds of the revenues of the land; their enemies, though they were never openly called that, were the re-established and new all-male houses which had come into being in the north and east since the Viking wars of the early part of the century. The pacification and Christianisation of the north and east had been a triumph, but the revenues of the south and west had been suffering as a result.

Wilton's cheerful orderliness under Wulfthryth was famous. The two men were ushered into a guest-house and politely admonished to remove their outer garb for cleaning. Boots were taken and replaced by soft slippers. Ale, cheese and newly baked bread were offered alongside a cheerful fire.

'She will take her time.' Dunstan wished to slow proceedings; Aelfhere had been anxious to the point of madness to get to Wilton, to carry out what Herleva had planted in his brain. 'You know, she will resist this.' He ate carefully, examining each mouthful. There were new pains in his stomach. The riding had exacerbated the aches of old age.

Aelfhere, excited, gulped at his ale. 'Abbess Wulfthryth was once Edgar's queen. Her daughter and his should take precedence over that measly youth Aethelred.'

'Measly, perhaps, but legitimate.'

Dunstan again recalled the event in the font at Aethelred's baptism which had so affronted him, but his pragmatism put his fears to one side. 'Wulfthryth was not anointed as queen, at any rate, not by me. And there is the small matter of Edward's mother…' Aelfhere needed a brake applied, he thought.

'Edgar left complications for the royal succession. It is up to us to sort it out. Edith is the elder child. In Mercia we would accept a woman as queen. Alfred's daughter Aethelflaed did a good job, so why shouldn't Edith, too, with the help of her supporters?'

This had been the repeated theme during their long ride together. 'You are harking back too far, my friend. And where there is a legitimate male to be taken as king, there are few who would submit to a woman…' Dunstan wished to believe that there was some happy outcome for the project which was Herleva's brainchild, but he had lived long and seen too much. He put down his mug of ale. The stomach pain had receded. Perhaps he had been hungry. Only his head now throbbed. 'The abbess's secretary is here.'

A young nun with red cheeks invited the freshly cloaked travellers to follow her to the abbess's quarters. Wulfthryth, unlike Herleva, never left the convent, being either content with her short affair with Edgar as giving her enough spice to contemplate, or outraged at her abduction and determined to protect herself and her daughter at all cost; Dunstan was never sure which. The slippered walk, along torch-lit stony corridors, passing the occasional high window which let in light but afforded no distracting view, seemed as long as the morning's ride from an uncomfortable and disreputable inn. The guest footwear which the men had been given gave no support to their arches, which by the time they arrived at the great door to the abbess's office, were aching. Aelfhere rubbed a foot. Dunstan limped a last step towards a closed door. The red-cheeked nun sang a short stanza of the abbey's prayer manual. She turned to the guests.

'The Abbess prefers that we do not knock.'

A hand bell rang from inside the room. The door swung open wide, like the gate, as if by an invisible hand. The abbess stood a few feet from the men, her arms folded across her body, her dark red dress dominated by a heavy waist chain and keys which swung slightly at her side. An ivory cross adorned her throat. She looked like the statue of a saint, as though she had not moved for hours, but had rapidly crossed the room in the moments before, hearing even the softest of steps in the corridor beyond. She bowed to Dunstan and Aelfhere.

'Gentlemen, come in. I trust that you have received refreshment?'

The two guests bowed in return. This was a woman who had earned respect in Wessex for her forbearance in not denouncing Edgar as a lecher, for retreating to the confines of the convent as a respectable woman should. She had been violated, had accepted her fate, remained in the convent and brought up the king's daughter Edith in the protective cloister to avoid the attentions of men, grooming her to be wary of the world beyond the walls of the women. Yet she had been a queen, in name, at least, for a short while, and was conscious of it. Her daughter had royal blood, of the purist kind. She was a Cerdicing, like her half-brother, the dead Edward and the boy, Aethelred.

'I want to get straight to the matter. There is no time to waste.' Aelfhere moved to the indicated table and chairs. 'Your daughter must be queen.' He began to babble.

Dunstan sat next to Aelfhere, touching his arm lightly. It would not do to rush Wulfthryth. The ex-queen stood at the table's end, looking down at her guests, two old men, important in the world outside her abbey, but subject to her rule, here.

A dark shadow beneath the window at the far end of the room moved forward and revealed itself as a slight figure, dressed in her mother's similar raiment of dark red, shot silk. Her head was bare, her hair parted centrally into two long golden plaits held behind her ears. She smiled at the men.

'I am Edith. Must I be Queen? Really?' The girl sat opposite the visitors, quietly examining them. The men looked away. This was incipient holiness, they knew.

Dunstan was the first to speak. As archbishop, he was used to being knelt to; but this young woman made him feel that he needed to kneel to her. 'Princess, and Your Highness, we have come to make a plea to you both to respond to a tragedy of our times. Your brother, Edward, Princess, was foully murdered in Corfe by agents of the queen, the present queen, as you know.'

'So we have heard, Archbishop. We are listening. Go on.'

Wulfthryth sat beside her daughter. Her silk skirt rustled with the richness and volume of material. Both women wore expensive rings and bracelets, gifts, no doubt, of a guilt-ridden Edgar.

Dunstan began again. Wulfthryth's gaze was like that of the abbess of Shaftesbury, perceptive, inquiring. 'It is common knowledge that news comes unfiltered to the gates of Wilton and is understood by those within. You will have heard the rumours. It cannot be proven that the queen killed Edward, though regret may assail her soul. In the circumstances it would be irregular, if not sinful, for a child whose mother has been accused of regicide to take the throne.'

'As you say, the queen's guilt has not been proven. We, my daughter and I, mourn the loss of Edward; Edith was fond of her brother and he her. On a personal level, we have suffered a great loss.'

Aelfhere spoke. 'And Wilton Abbey has suffered a great loss of income due to the queen's interest lying elsewhere.'

Wulfthryth was silent. A bell clanged for a call to prayer from somewhere outside the room. She poured wine from a crystal decanter into glass goblets. Edith offered the ruby red liquor to

Dunstan and Aelfhere. The men drank thirstily, despite their earlier ale. Red wine was a rare offering in a convent. There was an expensive swish of silk as the abbess again turned to her guests.

'You have travelled far, my lords. This nation has journeyed through waters which are dark and tempestuous in recent years. I fear my royal husband's legacy left choices for the next ruler which those who have to govern the land have found too difficult to resolve.'

'But…' Aelfhere began, but was halted by another tap on the arm by Dunstan.

Wulfthryth frowned. Interruptions were not welcome. This was her domain. 'Undoubtedly Edward was the rightful king, but death seals the issue. Surely the ealdormen of the nation will require leadership from a male? That has always been the case.'

'Not always, Abbess. In my Mercian homeland, you will recall that we had a queen who ruled alone.' Aelfhere put down his goblet and covered it with his hand. 'No more, thank you.'

'Aethelflaed of Mercia? The Lady of the Mercians? But she was an unusual personage. And those were different times. Wessex and Mercia were…'

'At loggerheads, yes that was so, Abbess. We regarded her as a queen, the daughter of Alfred, the wife of the lord of the Mercians, who had been our king. Everything changed when the old king Edward took away our princess Aelfwynn, but we had great respect for our special Lady, while she lived.'

'Ah, yes, I heard that the princess Aelfwynn was perhaps taken by Edward to Shaftesbury. Abbess Herleva has no doubt cooked up this plot.' Wulfthryth stood and walked around the darkening room. Edith remained still, seated by the fireside, awaiting her mother's instructions. The abbess lit a half-used candle from another and brought it to the table. 'Though it is, perhaps, an idea worth contemplating. I see why you, at any rate, should think so.' She threw a meaningful look at Aelfhere. She would be referred to, ever after, by the excitable ealdorman, as "the woman in red".

'Gentlemen, I see why you are anxious to offset the

arrangements which may come into being by the regency of the new queen…'

'Queen-mother,' Dunstan interjected. 'She would not necessarily be my choice as regent.' He felt he had to make it clear that he would not object to a fresh view of the succession.

Wulfthryth continued. 'Edith is mindful of the millennium. She prays for her soul and that of her subjects. She is already queen, a queen of the hearts and minds of the populace.' She looked at Edith, who had remained silent. 'She will remain here, as will I.'

Aelfhere groaned. There was despair in his voice. 'It is morally imperative that Edith should come out of the abbey, into the world and take her place at court. The throne is rightfully hers. She is the elder of Edgar's surviving children.'

'And be killed by the queen or her agents as Edward was? I do not think that would be wise.' Wulfthryth remained calm; her eyes engaged Aelfhere's.

'We would protect her. We now know the extent of the queen's malice and determination to have the crown for Aethelred. The boy himself is blameless. He is too young to be aware of her schemes.'

Edith spoke at last. 'And how would you protect a monarch who travels the country of necessity, reviewing troops and navy? How would I be able to carry out the duties which have become so necessary to kingship? I am a woman, as you can see. I cannot do what Edward might have done, or that my brother Aethelred may do.'

'And the walls of Wilton are high, and thick. Edith could rule as queen from here. Her throne is here, within the confines of Wilton.' Wulfthryth was clear, adamant. The two women had thought of the possibility of this deputation. Their course was clear. Edith would pray for her country to remain whole, would do her duty from within the solid safety of the walls of Wilton abbey. She would not become subject to the laws of men, in the man's world beyond them.

Dunstan had had enough. He brought proceedings to an end. 'The queen-mother, then, will have her way. She will be regent. Her eastern monasteries will continue to receive a greater share of the revenues of the land. Shaftesbury and Wilton will suffer. Is this your wish, Madam?' He was almost as anxious to persuade Edith to exit Wilton as Aelfhere, who leaned on the table, head in hand.

'Edith will not leave Wilton abbey. She will be queen while living here or not at all.'

'I will never leave this place.' Edith turned around as though dancing, her skirts rustling, her arms swinging.

'Forgive us, Abbess and Princess, we thought that as neither of you have adopted the habit of nun, that you were open to the idea of entertaining a return to court, where I believe you should be...,' Dunstan spluttered. His brain hurt.

'We remain here. As Aethelred has already been crowned and anointed, I believe your suit is in vain. The die is cast. He cannot be removed except by the will of God. Thieves and murderers lurk beyond our walls. And do not judge us by our dress, Archbishop. We are devout. My daughter is devout.' Wulfthryth and Edith both stood up. The interview was at an end.

# Shaftesbury Abbey, March 18, 981

'THERE HAS BEEN another raid.'

Even at the festival marking the Great Martyrdom, fairgoers, having witnessed the relic parade around the town and thrown their coin to the collecting carriage, were abuzz not only with the reinvigorated awfulness of the death of Edward the short-lived king and the unfairness of his removal from rule, but also by the rumours of fresh Viking activity on the coast.

Two stall-holders in the main street conferred. One sold honey buns, the other purses and leather goods. Placing food and utilitarian item stalls near each other had proven profitable. Pilgrims had always more to share when at a fair associated with a saint. What income could be snatched from the jaws of the abbey would keep the stall-holders in meals for many months.

'Where, this time?' the seller of buns was not convinced that she needed to be worried about activities by pirates in small groups so far away.

The leather seller, anxious to engage his compatriot in conversation during a lull in trade, continued with his news. 'Southampton again. But they came further inland, this time.'

'How do you know?'

'The abbey porter heard the abbess discussing it during her daily walk. The wind was playing havoc with her veil, and she stopped to curse it and to express some dismay at the pirates' movements in the hearing of the gardener. She is getting worried.' The leather man was a bright, bearded craftsman, younger than the bun-maker, active in the community, interested in supplying leather goods to the abbey. He had been awarded a contract for buckets in recent months. He had had speech with the estate manager. 'I know the abbey people well.'

'Then you also know about Bradford?'

The bun lady also had her contacts, of the female kind. Things leaked through convent walls. Her contacts were students, who bought her buns on the few occasions they were allowed beyond the abbey walls. They came to her at her house in Gold Hill.

'Bradford? Where is that? What about it?'

'Bradford-on-Avon. The girls tell me that the nuns here are worried about their relics. They want to take them further inland, to Bradford on the Avon, or somewhere like that. They say that there is going to be another war. They want a lock-up in north Wessex which is going to keep things safe. This may be the last time that we have the fair, until things improve.'

It was annoying to the leather man that the bun-lady, who had no interest in politics, and little apparent skill except in encouraging others to eat too much and pay highly for the food, had information of the outside world which trumped his own. Nevertheless, this was interesting.

A single bored traveller passed the stalls, interested neither in buns nor leather goods. Music started up in the area outside the abbey gate; dancing had begun. A flock of gaily dressed girls ran by, followed by a barking dog. The leather man folded his arms. Customers would return, later, hungry and anxious to spend more coin. Meanwhile the weather was fine, and warm. He could wait. He moved across to the bun lady and picked up one of her offerings, throwing a small coin into her plate of change.

'So things, if they are as you say, are getting interesting. Not a return to the bad old days of King Alfred and Edward, do you think?'

The bun lady looked as though she knew more. 'It may just be a rumour. But the girls seem to think that they may be moved north as well.'

'The whole school? There are some expensively-dressed girls in the school, with rich parents. I suppose the nuns might think that they want to protect them as well as the relics…'

'From Danes, obviously. It would not do to allow the flower of

English womanhood to be snatched and held to ransom, or worse…'

'But to Bradford-on-Avon? Why there?'

'For the protection of St Aldhelm, whose church is there. And also because the abbey hopes to own land there.'

The leather man was amazed at the amount of inside knowledge held by the bun lady. 'But Bradford is many miles away, how many I don't know, but at least a day's ride, surely?'

'That is beyond my ken. It is in another shire, near to Bath, I think. A small place, out of the way, the girls said. They don't want to go there. One told me that she feared the journey. She had heard that the pirates are inland, on the roads. They fear they could be taken.'

'Better here, then, inside the walls, surely? I'll have another of those.' The leather man took another bun. They were small and sweet, not filling.

'I have heard another thing from the girls. They say that the former queen's daughter is dying.'

The leather man choked on his bun. 'King Edgar's daughter, you mean? The nun at Wilton? The one they say is going to be made a saint?'

'Edith, yes. She has a chill and is not likely to live, they say.'

'How far is it from here to Wilton?' The leather man spat out the piece of bun. He had had an idea. What a happy chance he had parked his stall next to this woman!

'Not far, we could get there in a day. We could share a carriage.'

'Done.'


'Mother, what is the news of Edith? Don't lie to me. I heard one of the nuns talking about her.'

Aethelred, aged thirteen, had large ears, which he was learning to use. Hidden beneath luxuriant golden hair, they were proving to be a useful aide for a maturing king who would like to shake off a mother's influence. He stood, taller than his tall mother, at the reliquary to Edward near the altar of Shaftesbury abbey. A bell rang and they knelt on embroidered cushions.

Aelfthryth hissed a reply. 'I never lie. Don't say that. I do not lie to you. You did not ask. Edith has died. She is with her father, in heaven.'

Perhaps, in this public place, there would be no screaming, no tears, no recriminations from Aethelred. He was learning self-control. 'It was nothing to do with me.' Aelfthryth crossed herself and bowed her head as the prayers began. The archbishop, assisted by Bishop Aethelwold, Aethelred's tutor, began the prayers.

They were lengthy, like all the services devised by Dunstan. The eighteenth of March had become a solemn day, a day for all throughout the nation to remember and ask the martyred king for his aid for illness, for wealth, for retribution against their enemies. Aethelred stood up, as Dunstan beckoned to him, to give the eulogy. He faced the congregation. His voice had broken recently; there had been no squeaking or booming; the change had been gradual and natural, but for those who had not seen him since his coronation at Kingston, there was a significant difference. His height, too, was noticeable. He was becoming a man. The congregation looked from queen-mother to king and back again.

Bishop Aethelwold turned the pages of Aethelred's script, balanced on the ornate lectern. The boy spoke well and clearly, as tutored. His voice reached the back of the church, where thanes and their wives heard the voice of a boy becoming a man. They watched the veiled widow queen. Her back stirred. Was she uncomfortable? Did she think that her days of regency were coming to an end? Did the young king possess the character to put his mother to one side, to make a government of his own choosing? Would he uphold the changes in land-holdings which Edward had made in his brief time on the throne? Or would he continue, as Edgar had done, to push forward with the Benedictine reform movement? Aethelwold turned another page. The speech was coming to an end.

In the back row of the church, there were murmurs. There had been no mention of revenge for Edward's death. Three years had passed since his murder and only prayers were being offered for his soul. Three years since the events at Corfe had reigned in the ambition of many nobles to usurp the Church's power over the land and people. Three years since the opportunity to reverse the influence of Archbishop Dunstan had been lost, through the death of the young hothead, Edward. He might have been Dunstan's choice for king, but he would have broken free of that pernicious influence, in time.

But time was what Edward had not been given. It was known that Aelfthryth found her step-son Edward loud, angry and uncontrollable, not like her son, the mild-mannered, sweet Aethelred. Kings seemed recently to have come as alternate characters; one would be energetic and brash, hot-headed and uncontrollable; next would come his son or nephew, meek and biddable by contrast. Usually, the more subservient man was the longer-lived.

Aethelred concluded his speech. Bishop Aethelwold removed the text from the lectern. The queen-mother stood up and walked towards her son, turning to face the congregation. Aethelred coughed. He had more to say, and began to speak, unscripted. 'I feel I must apologise for...' he began.

Aelfthryth grabbed his arm. The boy-man resisted and deftly, lightly, brushed her from his person. The reminder of his mother's domineering character had been enough. It was the last time that Aethelred tried to apologise for the death of Edward, but not the last time that he wished that he had.

# Exmouth, Devon, March 982

THE TIDE WAS going out. Drifting with it, the two heavily-laden pirate ships moved rapidly downstream. On the foremost ship, bearing the white-tailed eagle on its prow, amongst many fair-haired men, there was one who was exceptionally tall, bright in his youthfulness and singled out even more by the glittering metal on his arms. The arm rings declared that this was a young man of great strength, of battle experience, of unusual connections. A king's son.

Swein sang. The others in the boat chorused a swaggering response to his love-song. Mermaids heard him and dived deep. There had been no injuries to his men; the raid had been well-planned, well executed. Tribute had been paid; the cowering English had watched him arrive, prepared to submit and filled sacks with coin, ready to hand over all that they had to prevent murder. The Danes had only to roar, wave their swords and look ferocious and the people on the coast gave in. It was almost too easy.

The eighteen-year-old Prince of Denmark had already had three years of solid adventures abroad; he was a veteran amongst veterans, none of whom were over the age of twenty-five. All were becoming rich men. The rich pickings in England had replenished themselves; where the booty had been robbed in former times, there were now villages and townships prepared to hand over all that they had without a fight.

Swein began a new song; it was the death song, the glorious Valhalla of the warrior, an old song, which was sung less often in these days when the Christian god had been encountered by so many men, but old things, traditions of the seafarers, were treasured. The words might reek of a bloodthirsty past, but they reminded the young men of the difference between them and their prey; like mice faced with the torments of a cat, the English were fearful of death and dying and could anticipate their fate. The work of casting the shadow of fear over the English nation had been done by their thoroughly pagan forefathers; the dark intent of rapidly moving warriors, not born of the land, not fixed by it to its crops, its taxes, its rules, had born fruit for their descendants. What was the sound that the English made? Wailing and gnashing of teeth, sitting ducks, all. Swein came to the end of his song as the ships met the waves of shore and exited the Exe.

It hardly mattered where they went next; it would be the same. There would be beacons lit, yells and screams and then, perhaps after burning a hut or two or killing a cow, the sailors would be met by the local headman bearing the sacks as usual.

The ships raised sail; there was still room in the hold for more coin. They travelled westwards, tacking and rowing, to the next Devon village. On the headland to the south, smoke went up to announce their coming. More sacks were being hastily filled. This would be the last encounter for this spring; after this they would go to Normandy to settled friends to drink, delight and rest. Then back to Denmark. King Harald Bluetooth would be pleased to see his son. The wealth of England drained eastwards across the sea, making those still in Denmark daily more interested in the possibility of doing more than just raid. East Anglian Danes now commonly spoke English, like their rulers; it was only a hundred years since their coming; they had become accustomed to the roped-in, tight culture of the southern English, while retaining their own language at their hearth and their own customs brought with them from the low countries. Half the nation of England were mongrels, if they would look at themselves, not something they liked to do. The Wessex dynasty's rule was waning; the English were English no more. What if a Danish king should offer to rule instead?

Swein began to let an idea grow in his mind. What if…?

# Winchester, August 3, 984

M OTHER AND SON were again at prayer. There had been so many funerals to arrange or to attend in recent years; ealdormen had been dying like flies. Aelfhere, duke of the first order, had gone to his father in heaven recently, and now Aethelwold, the bishop who had steered so much of the life of southern and central England, helpmate and confidante of Archbishop Dunstan, had entered the list of expectant sainthood.

Queen Aelfthryth and King Aethelred were in the crypt of the Old Minster, watching as the corpse of Aethelred's tutor, the charismatic Bishop Aethelwold, was lowered into his specially-prepared tomb, directly below the high altar. The queen-mother wept; she had more awareness of the past than had her son, who looked to the future. He was sixteen. Both were conscious of the change which would occur, marked by this remarkable man's death. For one, it was an ending, for the other, a beginning.

A heavy stone, marked with the simple inscription of Aethelwold, Bishop of Winchester, was slid across the top of the prepared tomb. A monk stepped forward to sweep the tomb cover with his cloak, scattering dusty debris. He finished the act by kneeling to kiss the engraved name. The bowed figure of the Archbishop of Canterbury, Dunstan, moved to the young king's side and put an arm around him. The queen-mother continued to weep. Other women stepped forward to comfort her.

'She was not like this when my father died,' Aethelred muttered. 'Thank you, Archbishop, I shall be alright.' Aethelred moved away from Dunstan. The archbishop had become accustomed to the young man's right to rule, but Aethelred was in the process of becoming his own man. The time had come. Losing Aethelwold, as he felt the tearing of the strings which bound him to his mother, as he felt the urgings of interest in producing his own family, marked a significant change in his life. There would be no more telling him what to do. No more priests, with Mother standing behind them, urging them to tell him how to act, what to say, what to sign. No more.

The king had become what he was destined to be. His mother, Aelfthryth, that night, was asked to leave Winchester. Aethelred selected his bride from a list offered to him in previous days. They were all noblewomen, all suitable. It hardly mattered what they looked like. He found one of obvious advantage; he had been listening, after all, to advice given him by Dunstan.

'Choose a woman of the north. That way you will cement the northerners' allegiance.'

Aelfgifu of York, then, it had to be.

A new family of Cerdicings was beginning; Aelfthryth the old queen would be ousted from the intimate royal circle. A new queen would take her place. Permanently.

# Algar's notes, 1010

MY MENTOR'S DIARY and extensive writings have given me dreams, not all of them pleasant. My youth and imagination is dominated by his clear testimony and histories of the Wessex family in particular, of the twists and turns of political and religious life throughout the last century. Nonna was a witness to the marvellous and tortuous events of the century which came to be thought of as the last before Judgement, but after all the fearful expectation, the terror did not come to pass. The end of the millennium has come and gone and a new century has begun, overseen by the wise judgements of The Wolf, Wulfstan, our Archbishop of York.

Those who are wise will listen to what he, Wulfstan, has to say; he has a historian's mind and knows what Nonna also perceived: that the British many centuries ago and now the English have allowed the enemy in, weak as they are, lacking in will, forethought and sufficient guile to act beyond the coming days. In panic the English wriggle on the hook of a disaster borne by the throne of Denmark, on a hook of its intentions, which are to claim, not just the shoreline but the whole of Britain for itself, as Eric Bloodaxe once tried to rule the kingdom of York.

What comes in the future, no-one can tell, but a call for prayers to be redoubled have been demanded by the king and the archbishops; God's assistance has never been more required. But will he hear our prayers or favour the Danes'? The Danish are a Christian nation, too. The devil sides with someone, but who? Aethelred may prevail but much is uncertain.

Returning to my notes and to Nonna's account, while I was still very young and hardly aware of the world around me, the troubles began in earnest. In the year 988, after Aethelred had come to his senses and readmitted his mother to his inner circle, the severe attacks on our island defences began. Exeter was again sacked. The old Archbishop Dunstan succumbed to his final illness, leaving the mortal coil and our king with all that promised to be another onslaught on our nation, one which could not easily be dealt with. The queen-mother was restored to her position near the throne, outshining Aethelred's wife, Aelfgifu of York in all things; she was too often pregnant with the king's children. Aelfthryth took each babe immediately into her care to ensure that each son was well versed from his earliest days in the necessary thought patterns required to enable the royal dynasty to succeed; six sons were born in quick succession and two daughters joined their brothers in the early years of Aethelred's reign.

The bishop, Aethelwold and the old archbishop, Dunstan, were much missed; their steady advice could not be heard by those, early in the reign, who were determined, with Aethelred's assistance, to overthrow what had been achieved by their dogged insistence on reform in the Church. Had the enemy a face? Reports, which came daily to court in the time after the archbishop's death in 988, brought news of a man who was ever present in the most serious of raids; Swein of Denmark became a name to fear. The navy did what it could; I watched the growing dismay of the court and overheard conversations as I grew older and more involved with taking over some of my former mentor's work. My voice broke early and I was spared the fate of other boys who were destined to join a choir; Nonna's name was synonymous, by this time, with goodwill and useful aide to memory and I took on his mantle of assistant to the court, not in interpretation; that was not my talent, but in making records. Perhaps in time my notes will be read by those who look back to this terrible period from a point of peace. Wars and destruction come in waves, that I can tell from my old master's writings, they catch fire and burn themselves out. Perhaps I shall live to see the restoration of peace in the land, perhaps not. What I am sure of is that corruption of the soul, of the nation's soul, can occur and was doing so at the time that first Aethelwold and then Dunstan died. The world was not the same after their passing; the nation of England and the Wessex line was in mortal danger. Many men have died or been injured in the last years, though we are well into the new century; many men, who, they say, will not grow old and suffer the illnesses and disabilities of advanced years; but would they have preferred to do so, I wonder, surrounded by their families? I suspect that they would have.

A new face came to the scene as Aethelred reached his maturity and played with his children, the little kings, as he called them. Eadric Streona, as he came to be called, the Greedy, I could see, moved gradually and subtly towards the throne. Aelfthryth, the queen-mother, occupied with the babes in the nursery, was not able to warn her son of the dangers of an ambitious man; but he would not have listened. It was enough that his mother was one step removed from the considerations of ruling, being wholly concerned with the next generation. He made his choices alone, before Wulfstan, who became Bishop of London in 996, could advise. Eadric Streona, the ambitious one, like a snake winding itself around the feet of the king, raised his head to his lap and hissed there, poisoning the king's mind, charming him into fateful decision-making, all to benefit himself.

Had Aethelred died as a young man, as so many of his forbears had, there might have been a reckoning, but Eadric and the king, after a few years, became as one. The snake had his prey in its mouth and was sucking him in. Aethelred looked out at the threats around him, saw Danish ambition grow and made a decision, a rash choice, no doubt aided by the snake. Serpents can change their minds and alter their prey, and Eadric did so, but not until later. Aethelred and he hatched a plot to bring England back from the brink, from the Danish threat.

The night of the long knives became their plan. It brought about the downfall of the nation and ultimately the end of Wessex.

# Canterbury, May 20, 988

'WHAT HAVE WE lost in the passing of this old white-haired man but a fanatical zealot, whose back-side was dumped in a duck pond, who beat the walls of the cloister every night while on the rampage against devils? We may sleep in peace, at last. The nation can breathe deeply, knowing that it is released from the constant carping and correction of its ways.'

The deputy librarian of St Augustine's could think aloud, for the first time in his work at the monastery. He had accompanied the body of Aldhelm, years before, when Dunstan had removed it from Malmesbury to Canterbury. It had been a mistake which he could not undo. Malmesbury had not been as completely controlled by its leading theologian as had St Augustine's. He sat with his companion, a lay clerk, on a stone ledge on the sunny side of the cloister. The body of the former Archbishop of Canterbury, chief prelate of the land, lay in state in the nave behind. It was assumed by the living world that he would not hear words spoken of him, but the lay clerk was not entirely sure of this.

He agreed with the librarian about the relief from the severely imposed mindset of entry into the order in Canterbury. It was the reason why he had remained a lay clerk. They had had exchanges before, in the quiet of the cloister. What was the hearing capacity of a soul yet to ascend to heaven? What was a ghost able to do? Did it hover over the body, and for how long? These were questions which they would come to later, when the corpse had been laid to rest in its carefully designed tomb. Dunstan had surveyed the works in recent years, finding comfort in the knowledge of his mortal remains being firmly enclosed and guarded, forever. 'But we should not criticise our leader, the ruler of so much in this century. He has left us before the time which we have all come to fear; the millennium is upon us without Dunstan to protect us. The Bible's Revelations tell us what is coming. And he is not far away from this place. We should be silent. He will become a saint, you know, in the fullness of time.' The lay clerk shivered as a cloud passed overhead with its own attached gust of wind, as though forces beyond their ken were at play and attending to their conversation. He put a hand on the deputy-librarian's arm.

The deputy-librarian, though, had a grievance about a criticism of his work by the dead archbishop. Words said, grudges held, last long in the mind, for some. 'We should voice our opinion meanwhile. He is not in heaven yet. It would be as well if he had not stoked that fear of the millennium. For so long, so many years and through so many reigns of kings, Dunstan made sure that the 'right' way was followed. There was no room for thought or reason. The cloister-bashing episode should have told us that he should be locked away, but no, he was too much revered. And the times that we had to rescue the diaries and histories from him when he scrawled on them, 'correcting' them, as he said. He defaced much of importance. We are well rid. We will be able to encounter the millennium with a new archbishop. The king is open to reason; he will find a way to see us through the thousandth year. Dunstan's staff will swing no more against the cloister walls -see the pock-marks over there where he hit the wall in anger- or against us.'

'Perhaps. But don't you think that Dunstan's madness was a sort of holiness? And he did have good ideas. He steered the nation admirably through the reign of Edgar, and put up with duplicity and anger from many other kings who thought they knew best, the histories tell us so. England is the wealthier for Dunstan's careful charge of the treasury, surely?'

'Thank heaven he had little to do with the treasury in recent years, or the madness in him would have sent us to war, or want.'

'There will be an inflow of pennies to the coffers because of him, especially while he lies on view. The pilgrims will want to snatch sight of him before he is laid to rest.'

Matters turned practical. The two friends were on the committee for the arrangement of affairs for viewing by pilgrims. The influx was likely to be huge; arrangements for hygiene, food and bedding had to be thought of; strict plans had been put in place well before they were needed. The fields beyond the abbey walls could accommodate many thousands. Large latrine pits were being dug while they sat in the sunny cloisters. The lay brothers and their helpers were getting some good exercise.

Meanwhile, Dunstan, on a bier in the nave of the church, waited to be moved closer to the high altar. His time in purgatory would be short, only the time, perhaps, that it took for the brothers of St Augustine's to consider that the body had been exposed for long enough. The service of thanksgiving for his life would take place in two days' time, after which the tomb would be covered. Between now and then, four monks stood guard as pilgrims filed past on their knees, praying and weeping. They had believed Dunstan when he warned them, many times, of the effect of the millennium. Belief was the anchor which Dunstan had impressed on them. And now their protector, who should have been with them during the coming trial in only a decade's time, was gone before them to that better place. A better place, but not a safer one. Even those who had passed through the gates of heaven already, who might, in times past, have considered themselves secure from any future ill, would be tipped out of their final resting places, emptied onto the stones and grassy knolls of their naves and cemeteries and be made to stand before the anti-Christ. The sorrow of the loss of their former archbishop and their own unacknowledged fear that a promised afterlife was unbelievable led to an outpouring of emotion and a clawing at the silk cloths which draped the bier, in hope that parts would come away in their grasp.

Some clawed with small knives in their hands, concealed by long sleeves, eager to take a portion of the sacred decoration. Occasionally a youth stood up, anxious to reach nearer to the holy body, eager to touch or to take a more intimate sample of the soon-to-be saint. The guards allowed a single glance into the bier, and then motioned the perpetrator back down to his knees. Negotiations were ongoing about the relics which would be available; it would not do to have any part of the vision of the new saint disturbed, despoiled, or stolen.

The year 988 came and went; Aethelred and his wife continued to procreate, Swein continued to enjoy sea-eagle flurries, fleeting, teasing nibbles at the edges of England and Wales, coming ever closer to a fully-fledged idea of the possibility of kingship over a nation which employed so many of his countrymen as mercenaries, becoming aware of the history of the place, which had become weaker, over years, at the end of the Roman rule. The Saxons had conquered the Britons. Swein could read. He knew it had happened before and could, again.

# Cheddar, Summer, 995

'LOOK, FATHER, A big bird!'

It was the first time that the young Wessex clan had visited Cheddar. The wonders of the summer, the flocks of geese and ducks over the still flooded levels, the reeds as tall as a man, the smell of sea and river combined, the bright, gorse-clad hills around and, to cap it all, the excitement of the gorge and all that it stirred in the imagination, impressed themselves on the boys. Aelfgifu of York had done her work, though she would not yet retire; five boys had been achieved from her loins in quick succession, Aethelstan, Ecgbert, Edmund, Eadred and Eadwig stood in a row, holding each other's hands, looking into the bright sky, where a sea eagle soared. It flapped low over the royal residence, crying a call which seemed to say 'I am, I am, I hunt, I am king, I am.' The small boys, tugged by the eldest, Aethelstan, dashed to the safety of a nearby barn. The bird, having examined the potential prey, rose up on its chosen thermal to the hill above, searching for hares on the gorge plateau.

Aethelred laughed. He enjoyed the company of small children and these boys were fine examples of the Wessex line, all blonde, all strong, all intelligent. The youngest, Eadwig, had curls which shone in the sun like the convoluted carvings on the timber walls in the nearby palace; he would be the best of them, the doting father thought. Aethelstan was serious and wise beyond his years; he would be a good king, one day. Between them, the lads, if they remained friends, might make a wondrous team, kings and earls of many lands, perhaps beyond these shores; why restrict ambition to England alone? With good lads like these, the army and navy would be well led, tutored by English monks, trained by Viking mercenaries. The nation would be in safe hands.

And another son, no doubt, was on the way. The next would be called Edgar. If another was allowed by God after that, then Edward. All the kings of the line of Wessex would be reincarnated. All their qualities, improved and refined, would be resuscitated in the bloodline of himself and Aelfgifu. There had been no deaths of any of Aethelred's and Aelfgifu's young children; all were hail, there were to be many more, that was sure. Aelfgifu was still young; at twenty-seven she had many more child-bearing years left and Aethelred loved her dearly. She had been married as a political expedient, but the formal arrangement had blossomed into a mutual attraction. Nevertheless, there had been no anointing of his queen. There would only be one anointed queen during the lifetime of Aethelred's mother, she would make sure of that.

Aelfthryth and Aelfgifu, queen-mother and queen consort, emerged with a young girl into the sun from the barn, where they had been observing milking time, having heard the squeals of the children as they ran for cover from the eagle. Aelfgifu was heavily pregnant; Aelfthryth, tall and straight-backed, towered over her. Edith, a shy child, sucked her thumb, in awe of her father. The boys ran to their mother and grandmother as Aethelred caught them up. Edith hid behind the copious skirts of her grandmother. It was too dangerous to play with her brothers.

'It was a wild eagle. Probably attracted to the tame birds. It had its eye on my little kings, but look at Eadwig; he would be more than a match for its supper!' Aethelred laughed and pointed at his youngest son, leaning into the protective arms of Aethelstan. 'He is the smallest but chubbiest of them all!'

'Perhaps his hair caught the eagle's eye. See how it gleams!' Aelfgifu surveyed her brood. How lively, how handsome they were, and loving the unfamiliar experiences of this palace by the fowl-hunting grounds, so far away from Winchester and so like the coastal area of Yorkshire which she had known in her own childhood.

Grandmother Aelfthryth, though, was concerned. The boys had been allowed more freedoms since arriving in Cheddar; the family were intending to take a break from the cares of the nation for several weeks; unruliness, she could predict, might become a problem. Fresh air was all very well, but it could lead to unusual temptations and character development. Eadwig, particularly, concerned her. The baby of the family had yet to understand the position of his namesake in history, but when he did, there might be trouble. She had seen it before. Heroes can become villains and be copied. If only Dunstan could be here to guide the boys, and so many of them. All would need a good tutor, but she had not yet found a suitable replacement for Aethelwold or Dunstan, none with the force of character necessary to guide and control this extensive, bright brood. She could not do it all, though this had been her task, of late. The nursery at Winchester palace, was once again, the training ground of eating, playing, sleeping and study. Little beds lined the walls and desks occupied the centre of the room. The communal table allowed for lessons to be taught and learned and lectures given; Latin had been mastered in part by Aethelstan; the others were beginning to grasp the readings and writings put before them, except for curly-haired Eadwig. Here, at Cheddar, there were no facilities for indoctrination; the fresh air was what was required, Aethelred insisted, when challenged by his mother; and that, at Cheddar, was what the boys were getting.

'Weeeeeargh!' Edmund, the third boy, emulated the eagle, dashing around the compound with arms outstretched and finally ending up on the edges of the horse midden beside the stables, where he slipped on urine and fell headlong into the wet straw. There was a loud tut from grandmother Aelfthryth and a silent dash to help her son from Aelfgifu, with a murmur of remonstrance, as she picked up Edmund. The boy let out a loud scream and started to cry as he saw blood on a grazed knee. The moments of familial sunshine were clouded as the other boys started sympathetic bawling.

'Fresh air, eh?' The queen-mother took Edmund roughly by the arm and hauled him off to a nearby water butt to douse the filth from the child. The cold water made him yell again. 'Three more days like this and they will become untameable.'

'Three more days of heaven, then you may return with them to Winchester, Mother. But I shall stay here to receive our guest. He wants the hunting and has not been here before. I want to impress him.' Aethelred swung a small child over his shoulder, stopping the cries, which turned into squeals of delight. The other boys jumped at their father, begging to be tossed about in a similar fashion.

'Who is he, anyway, that he should be able to keep you from your affairs in the capital?'

'You may not have met him, Mother, but he is one of the new thanes who have attended the witan in the last year. His name is Aethelric.'

'From where?'

'From Herefordshire. A Mercian.'

'Ah, the Mercian offensive?' Aelfthryth finished cleaning off Edmund with a splash of icy water on his face. The boy ran off to join his brothers who by now had turned their attention from their father towards the cockerel on the dung heap and started to chase it. It ran around the cobbled yard, followed by small children, screaming, this time in joy.

'Yes, the Mercian offensive, as you call it.' Aethelred smiled. His mother was astute. She hailed from the eastern parts of Mercia, which were accustomed to the dominance of Wessex. Herefordshire was in the wild west. Diplomacy was still required, even after all these years, when dealing with those born of the Mercian soil.

Aelfthryth shrugged. 'I am glad I shall not be here to see the grovelling.'

Aethelred could take sharp words from only one person, his mother. He, too, shrugged. His mother was like that. 'There will be no grovelling, Mother, only diplomacy.'

'That's what you call it.'

'I do. And Aethelric is bringing his sons with him.'

'More children?'

'More children. I understand that he has six boys. I do not know their ages, but older than mine, I think.'

'And when did you say they are expected to arrive?'

'Perhaps tomorrow...'

'Then I shall be gone tomorrow. Edmund must come with me, at least. Aethelstan might stay, he is more sensible, but you must promise me to send the others as soon as possible. Look at them! The sooner they are in the schoolroom the better. Aelfgifu, come, let's go in.' Aelfthryth grabbed Edmund's arm again as he ran by after the cock, which was making a din. She marched off, holding Edith's hand, with the pregnant Aelfgifu waddling behind her. 'I hope the next one is going to be a sensible girl, like Edith, here.'

Aelfgifu nodded. The next daughter would be hers, named for her, kept by her. A little mini-me. Someone to cuddle, someone to sew with, someone to comfort. Someone who would find the schoolroom, as she did, an uncomfortable place to be.


'And I thought, as well, that perhaps we should review the numbers of Norse in the navy. I do not want more Norse than Dane. There has to be a balance, or they may start fighting amongst themselves. And there is the question of cost. There needs to be a thorough financial review. My father Edgar promised that each sailor would be guaranteed a pension and that a son could automatically fill his father's shoes. The navy has become more expensive than I would wish. It soaks up too much revenue. What do you think?'

'I am a landlubber, lord. I know very little of the affairs of the sea. Shropshire and Herefordshire are far from the coast.'

'But you are good with money. I have heard you in the witan. You have a fine grasp of the workings of the treasury. Now come on, don't be modest.'

Aethelred and Aethelric and the eldest of the thane's sons, an intelligent looking lad of fourteen or so, sporting down on his chin, wandered over to the stables to prepare for the hunt. It would be a good day for fowling. Cheddar was renowned for producing easy and varied prey and the birds available here were the best in the land, trained exceptionally well by the raptor-keeper who travelled with his wards to all the outlying palaces.

Aethelric the thane put a foot into a stirrup. The raptor-keeper handed him up a hooded marsh harrier. 'I should need to be working alongside one of your admirals. Eadric, here, my lad, could be trained up to help me. He has a fine brain for figures.'

Aethelred and the boy settled themselves onto their horses and grasped the reins. They were each given a bird; a male sea-eagle wobbled on Aethelred's arm and a small hawk on the boy's. Eadric had evidently done this before.

The hunting group moved off out of the gated enclosure, with other thanes and their birds following. The company was modest; these were guests of the witan who were becoming closer to the king, who he wanted to please and who wanted to please him. Overnight the tented area for visitors and their families had mushroomed; there would be feasting to complete the visit, an enjoyable display of diplomacy. The Mercian contingent and their Wessex counterparts would renew friendships, hopefully. There were matters to discuss besides the navy; the entire financial situation needed to be reviewed. Edgar's well-run empire of England, which had been overseen by Archbishop Dunstan, had been giving concern. No-one grasped the affairs of the land as well as he, it was being said. The population had grown, the army and navy had become even more dominated by foreigners; they demanded high fees for their work, and so the burdens of office had grown. Without war, or the threat of war, the grumbles of the witan and treasury officials had multiplied; war kept them quieter; emergency exacted compliance.

Compliance from the witan was what Aethelred most needed, at this juncture. The gold in the treasury was reducing at an alarming rate. *Bring back Dunstan* was often a prayer which Aethelred made, as he tossed in the early hours.

Meanwhile, the boys and their sister had gone back to Winchester with their grandmother and mother. Even the eldest, Aethelstan, had been taken from him, but he would see them all again in a week's time, in the gloom of the nursery schoolroom, no doubt. And there was the confinement of Aelfgifu to look forward to, which would not be far away. His sixth son, he was sure it would be another boy, would be welcome. He loved babies and young children, liked to play games with them. Hide and Seek in the palace at Winchester was a favourite. He looked across the path to the mere at the boy who accompanied them, Aethelric's son Eadric. In six or so years his own eldest son would look like that, upright, calm, accomplished on a horse, intelligent. He noted light grey eyes, which returned his gaze. Financial intelligence and order attracted Aethelred, who was always on the lookout for useful talent, someone to replace the dead Archbishop Dunstan.

Eadric felt the gaze of the king and looked at him. The look was one of controlled interest, of understanding. There was something about the boy which was compelling. It was not his good looks; they were sufficient to cause any girl to look at him as a potential partner, even at his young age. There was something else; pride, perhaps, no bad thing in a youth. Self-knowledge of his abilities, perhaps. Aethelred could not quite understand what it was that made the youth so attractive to him.

Eadric observed the man, the king, riding a few yards away from him, beyond his father. The movement of the horses, as they walked, afforded many moments to observe their surroundings, the people who journeyed with the group, what they wore, how luxurious were their hunting trappings, how good they were at their day's task, controlling the birds of prey and successfully catching the wild birds. A suitable number of kills would lead to being given a privileged place next to the king at tonight's feast. Eadric, as he looked, saw a man, who happened to be a king, a tall, handsome man in the prime of life, capable, modestly decorated with sparse but rich jewellery, his eagle clutching a leathered arm being held firmly in place despite its weight, a strong man. But there would be weaknesses, which the boy could discern, having been born with special insight. In time he would find them out. He was not called Eadric Streona for nothing.

# York, Autumn 999

WORCESTER, LONDON AND York. How could a man manage the bishoprics of all three at the same time? And yet it was possible. Others before him had done it. Dunstan was one. Perhaps he would, too. 'I am The Wolf,' he reminded himself aloud. 'Wolves are capable beasts.'

Bishop Wulfstan toyed with his notes. The legal proceedings of the last witan needed careful editing. The land holdings of the north were complicated; Danes who had been settled for many years competed with the demands of the English who had been in the region the longest. The Norse newcomers demanded what they called fair dealings. Often, proceedings were further complicated by the suits of British families, who had tried to recover lands taken from them centuries before, but their efforts were losing energy in these years. The old kingdoms of Elmet and Bernicia were fast becoming the subjects of fairy-tales and poetry, home to dragons and dwarves. Northumbria had swallowed and encompassed them, making of them a kind of mystical undercurrent, but one which, nevertheless, even in the law of the current century, existed. Old names die hard and in the north three, sometimes four, languages were spoken, all with varied accents born of time and separation by valleys and uplands, a melting pot of peoples, the old tongues and the new remaining distinctive, holding onto the past and remaking the future anew. The soup of culture changed character slowly, its flavour, though, unmistakeably mongrel, unmistakeably northern.

Could Wulfstan, born in East Anglia, raised in Peterborough monastery, which had been restored by the unsainted Aethelwold, brought up in the strict form of Benedictine thought and practice, taught to read and write by the age of four, adjusted to a regime of prayer and work, both physical and literate, contemplate the additional burden of the archbishopric of York? There were some who were pushing him in this direction, seeing in his orderly mindset a force for control and an eye for detail which the rebellious north required. Required, that is, for the successful rule by Wessex of this rugged and rain-swept part of the kingdom. The present archbishop, Ealdulf, was looking for a suitable successor; his nomination could provide an excellent introduction for the young man, already known as The Wolf because of his tenacious abilities in a court of law. He knew he was the favourite, but could he adjust to life being spent principally in York, away from royal action in Winchester? Away from his beloved Ely? Wulfstan mused on the competition. No, no-one else was as well qualified, as well suited, as well, let us say, indoctrinated as he to oversee the affairs of the north. He prayed, he asked for forgiveness for his weaknesses, which he knew were many, he asked for God's guidance.

Ultimately, he knew, casting the eyes of his mind around the court of Aethelred, that he was the man for the job.

And here he was, trying for size the throne of his namesake, Wulfstan, who had been such a trial to Wessex earlier in the century. Was the hard stone archbishop's throne stained with indecision, with corruption, even? Would the treasonable character of the old archbishop, condemned by Saint Dunstan and others, infect his archbishopric if he sat here? No, he did not need to pray on this point. The carvings on the arms of the throne, a dog on one side and the other the face of an old toothless woman, held silent memories of past decision-making. The Wolf placed his hands on both creatures. Would they speak to him? They remained dumb. His namesake had sat here, pondering his fate, brewing treachery.

Wulfstan knew that his own upbringing and experience in public life were beyond reproach. Bishop Aethelwold had taught him well at Peterborough and later at Winchester. The work of subduing the north had largely been achieved in times past; all that was required was a quick and clever mind, one used to intricate legislation, to keep things in order. Diplomacy came naturally to him. And then, the archbishop's palace in York was a splendid house; the conversion of the Danes in the old kingdom of York and their ability to manufacture, by energetic trade, a surplus for investment in fine buildings and the arts in general, had ensured that York itself had become a centre for innovation and worth. The hovels of English settlers had been razed; the Danes and recently the Norse had erected wood and stone buildings, both private and public; the treasury building alone had cost hundreds of pounds to design and construct and its gate and walls ensured that taxes were well and safely stored for investment by the Danelaw authorities. The guards, all Danish or descendants of Danes, were well trained and capable of defending the chest of coin and gold against intruders, including of their own kind; theft, of items large or small in value, was discouraged by severe penalty. Order had a smell; it was wholesome. York was in good hands, albeit those still deemed by the south to be foreigners.

The penalties for theft, which Wulfstan had often handed down to thieves in London, were severe, but agreed to be fair by all freemen; the nation which had groaned at Athelstan's decrees earlier in the century were accepted as the common rule and highway muggings had declined, easing north-south travel and trade between Wessex, Mercia and Northumberland. Edgar's reign had enforced Athelstan's rules and now Aethelred continued the control, making the harsh repercussions of stepping outside society's requirements less likely to be given out in the courts. Thieves with hands removed and hangings of juveniles had become less frequently seen in the south, though there were still examples of severe justice meted out to offenders here in York; beggars could be seen at the market, struggling with their wares, clutching heavy bags of carrots or the like with their handless arms, or squatting, sometimes, on sacking and beseeching passers-by to buy their wares, their footless legs sticking out in front of their bodies, their stumps a reproach and warning to all.

There was no time to consider the messy past, the turbulent life of his namesake, Wulfstan, Archbishop of York during the reign of the king's great-uncle Eadred. He was safely stowed away at Oundle near Peterborough, his northern origins wrapped and permanently contained in the stone sarcophagus in the crypt, the high thorn hedge of the monastery a barrier to ingress or escape. Monks and souls were kept in order at that southern place; there would be no martyrs made there, in that firmly supervised centre of Benedictine reform. If only more were like it! Oundle had the reputation of being a leading light, continuing the excellent work of its re-founder, Aethelwold. Peterborough and Abingdon, of course, focussed the character of the former Bishop of Winchester into their prayer and outreach; few in East Anglia and the midland shires of Mercia could unravel, if they had wished to, the works set in train by the energetic Aethelwold and few would dare.

How far away, though, York was from those informed and controlled centres of excellence. Could he bear to be parted from his fellow students, now becoming abbots and masters of libraries, in the rich south? Wulfstan had prayed, nightly and often during the day, at his writing labours and in the midst of the more tedious court cases in which he was involved, for an angel to give him a sign of what he should do. He tapped the head of the old lady. Old Woodenhead, he called her. *Come on, tell me your secrets.* But she remained silent.

The north had its attractions; there was challenge here; the bulk of the mixed population was Christian of sorts, but monastic life was little reformed and underfunded. Even Hexham, the revered Wilfrid's foundation, had been neglected. Monastic life was the foundation of a Christian nation; its beliefs and tenets were fundamental to the system of government and taxation, to peace and the ability to live with others unlike yourself; the polity of the nation required, as had been shown over many years and through many reigns, to need a firm hand, a bishop's, or an archbishop's.

What about the personalities who played their parts on the stage of York? Could he cope with them? He had had some forewarnings. Some of his contacts in York had reported on the character of the Ealdorman of Northumbria, Aelfhelm. He was a Mercian, put in place after his predecessor, Thored, had failed to control Norwegian incursions. Aelfhelm was, at least, familiar with religious requirements, having been brought up in Northamptonshire, though his ability to toe one line, far away from Winchester, was in doubt. Any man, in charge of such a faraway and diverse region such as Northumbria, might be expected to have difficulties; Aelfhelm, though, would do for now, according to King Aethelred, but he was not sound. *Was he, Old Woodenhead?* He was known to enjoy the company of Danes, royal Danes, and his older children were often to be seen about York, laughing, with Danish youths. This was part of the remit of the archbishop, as told to him by the king himself, in confidence. Watch the ealdorman. Watch that man.

Earls this far north had always to tread a fine line between the requirements of successful trade, which needed the support of the Norse, and the control of ambition by Danish or Norse upstarts, of which there had been many. Religious strictures to keep the peace had to be enforced. The memory of the partnership between Wulfstan, the traitorous archbishop and the Norse king Eric Bloodaxe had not been forgotten. No power comes easily; could he, the modern Wulfstan, The Wolf, wield this power with success? It would be required. It was a sacrifice. But Aethelwold had trained his monks well in the art of sacrifice. Physical pain could be born; hours of study and prayer were the norm; starvation during fasting was not an unwelcome friend.

Aelfhelm was one problem; the Norse and Danish elite were another. Did he have enough of the natural gift of diplomacy, not to say the language skills and stamina to encompass frequent discourse with these? Notable amongst them were the Danish woman, Gunhilde, who was the sister of the latest man to sit on the throne of Denmark, Swein. Her husband was the influential ealdorman of Devonshire, Pallig Tokensen. Danish influence was growing strong in the nation, even as far south as Devonshire; no longer confined to East Anglia or Northumbria, the Danish influence in the navy in particular gave Pallig his influential base in the natural harbours of the south-west. The navy was by this time almost entirely made up of sailors imported from Scandinavia, or descended from Scandinavians. Well-paid and happy in their ships and stupefied with drink when onshore, they were ready to fight, and acted as a human shield to prevent more than small, unimportant raids by their Norse brothers, the pirates.

Old Woodenhead received another decisive pat on the head. Wulfstan had made up his mind. He could not refuse the responsibility offered to him. Gunhilde and Pallig spent most of their time in York amongst other family members, he had heard. He had yet to meet them. Tonight, at Archbishop Ealdulf's banquet, he would.

# The Archbishop's Palace, York, Autumn 999

'AND HOW IS the old place at Peterborough? I have not visited in years and am not likely to until I go by in my coffin to Ely. Is the abbot a reformer in spirit? There will have been changes since Bishop Aethelwold's death, that is to be expected, but I hope that the abbot has held firm against any reversals of the correction which we have witnessed in recent years?'

Two men, one young, the other, not old, but prematurely aged, passed between an avenue of young oaks on the outskirts of the city, which led to the palace.

Archbishop Ealdulf of York, with Peterborough firmly in his heart and forming a strong midland base for his interests, despite having been in the north for eight years, was counting his days before returning south, in a coffin or otherwise. He regarded his chosen successor with an air of desperation. He felt hemmed in by the energetic Norse culture which was bursting into flower around him in York. It was overwhelming. The newly arrived royalty of Denmark had brought with it a vibrancy which could not be denied. And more visitors were expected, some intending to stay. Letters from Winchester in reply to his own reports had come to expect an iron hand, wielded by him. But he was not that sort of personality. Retirement was the only solution. Death would be a release. Diplomacy wearied him. Perhaps the younger Wulfstan would do better.

'It thrives, Archbishop. It continues to send out its graduates to positions in government at all levels; I myself am one of them, but of course you know that.' Wulfstan walked beside the older man; Ealdulf had become stooped in the few years since he had last met him; he needed a stick to walk and looked pale. 'You will no doubt be glad to return to the safety of its walls.'

'And to an English ambiance, my friend. These Scandinavians are too hearty for my liking. But you are young and have studied the language; you might be better able to take them in your stride. You will see what I mean tonight, at the feast. They are indefatigable. They dance and carouse all night. Such a noise they make! You would not think that they have been baptised.'

'All of them?'

'The ones that matter.'

'Pallig and his wife?'

'I carried out the immersion myself, but you can never tell how deeply the experience affects them. There is an immoveable under-current of their culture which they display in all that they do. They swear constantly, even in meetings with me, as though peaceful speech is unknown to them. They blaspheme, but I cannot continually call it into account. Their children are the same. They run screaming obscenities through the city.'

'At least the obscenities are in their own tongue, Archbishop?'

'In English, as well. They have picked up acquaintances and language from our own youths, who have largely forgotten their mother tongue. But now, with Gunhilde and Pallig, they wave Danish flags and talk of insurrection.'

'Is it youthful enthusiasm for a lost cause, do you think, Archbishop, or something more troubling?'

'That I will leave to you to discover. Meantime, we have the millennium to worry about. Though I am of the opinion that these youths envisage that they are the antichrist which has been foretold and that there will be an overthrowing of English rule in the north. They look back to the days when Eric Bloodaxe ruled here. Many of the flags sport an eagle, a symbol of Eric. And they want Gunhilde to be their queen.'

'How likely is Gunhilde to try for a separate kingship, or queenship, of York, do you think?'

'It is not unlikely. But you will see for yourself, tonight, what sort of woman she is.'

'The daughter of Harald Bluetooth of Denmark is likely to be a character, I suppose. Does she take after her father?'

'You mean the teeth? She is beautiful, I suppose, and has long nails. Her face is comely. Perhaps she is a bird of prey, rather than a fanged serpent. There is cunning there, certainly, and her husband stays silent when he is with his wife in company.'

The men approached the outer palace gate, leaving the peaceful tree-lined avenue and passed through to the courtyard beyond.

The bell for afternoon prayer was ringing. They shook hands and went to their rooms to prepare for prayer in the church. Behind the solid walls of the palace no Norse swearing could be heard. Both men braced themselves for the evening of entertainment and diplomacy to come.

Ealdulf turned round as he approached the stairwell leading to his rooms. He waved to Wulfstan, who was entering the cloister. His face showed agony, of spirit as well as body. 'Wulfstan, shall we see the end of this madness, do you believe, in this coming Christmas tide? Or will we all be swept away by the end of the world?'

Wulfstan could not answer. There was no answer. None could foresee what would befall the nation, all nations, Christian or pagan, in the coming days of doom which were now so near. All he could do, all Ealdulf could do, was to try to prepare his soul.

# Winchester, December 31, 999

'DOUSE THE BRAZIERS. We will await the end in darkness.'
Wulfstan, Bishop of London and Aelfric, Archbishop of
Canterbury, nodded agreement to the king's command. They had
been brothers at Abingdon and Ely, Aethelwold's men, brought
in as believers in the coming doom to their high positions. The
reformers had control of York, too, where the archbishop, educated
at Peterborough, would lead a similar retreat of Northumbrians to
basements and crypts. It might be the last command of Aethelred on
earth and the last time they, as representatives of the church in the
south, had to hear a secular order and to action it.

The royal family joined the churchmen on their knees at the
altar in the crypt of Old Minster. They were surrounded by the bodies
of the Wessex clan. They would rise, anew, after the Antichrist had
finished with them. Pledges had been made, offerings promised. The
former kings, Alfred and Edward, would return to earth, alongside
their ancestors and descendants, all of whom crowded the tombs
and walls of the ancient church. There was confusion about what,
exactly, would happen as the candle burnt down to midnight. There
were many questions, which the youngest royal children, in the
previous hours, had asked. Was the candle-time reliable? The gently
flickering flame increased anxiety. There were no clear answers, even
from the highest-placed churchmen of the land. Archbishop Ealdulf
had remained in York to sit out the anticipated end of the world.
In churches and monasteries all over the land, crypts were full of
their elite, living and dead, cowering in the depths of their ancient
institutions, some maintaining that they needed to light candles
to see and understand what was inevitably coming to them, others
preferring total darkness, as in Old Minster. Poor men and women,

unable to shelter within holy ground, sat in their hovels or lay down on the mounds of their forefathers in graveyards, anticipating the end. Large flakes of snow had started to fall silently on the gardens and grounds of Winchester palace, carpeting the earth in an indifferent, beautiful glaze.

Three days of fasting had made things worse. The run-up to the remorseless ticking of the clock had been a time of strain and madness; lack of food and urgent prayer had produced collective disproportion. The terror of the Antichrist was such that many said that they preferred to end their lives in the present world, wishing to remove themselves from the shock, which would occur, of the destruction of all they knew and all that they did not. Plague had made them gloomy; too many had seen the horror of that devil-produced curse; this would be worse. Better to leave now than to remain, desperate, burying the bodies of their children in worm-infested pits.

The royal family, made up of so many children, knelt and closed their eyes, waiting for the awful moment. The younger ones and the girls huddled together, inching closer to their mother, who was again heavily pregnant. Aethelred and the older boys held firm, their lips moving in silent prayer as the seconds ticked by.

They heard, or thought they heard, a distant bell ring. Afterwards, it seemed that the men, women and children heard different things; some fainted, falling forward onto the stone paving before them, others whimpered in fear as the bell sounded the end of the world. Would it happen at the first bell, or the last? Six, seven, eight times the bell sounded. Nothing happened. The darkness became a shroud around them; even the bishops were silent, though Aelfric could be heard to puff in panic. Was it worse if nothing happened, or if it would? The twelfth bell sounded, and then there was silence. The queen and the nest of female children clustered around her fell forward, joining her husband on the floor, where he and the boys had already forged a protective heap against assault. In the darkness their bodied mingled, adults with their brood, crying in terror and relief.

Moments of silence, as the family held their breath. The world had not ended. Wulfstan lit a candle, struggling to use his strike-a-light. He was not convinced that the prophecy was incorrect, but perhaps the calculation of the number of years from Christ's birth had been the wrong formula; was it, after all, to be calculated from his death? Stunned, the royal family remained huddled on the floor for many minutes, blinking at the light shed by the candle. Gradually the brave amongst them restored their positions to that of prayer and thankfulness.

They had been saved, this time; but there were many travails to come, many Danes to kill, many anxious moments in the dark nights of December, when the Antichrist, that mocking devil, might yet arrive. They moved out of the crypt to a new millennium, to a snow-covered world; changed, but in a most marvellous way, into one of wondrous beauty.

# Algar's notes, 1004 AD

IN THIS YEAR I have begun my work at court. My old master, Nonna, taught me well. Perhaps I will add my notes to his own, to make a heap of newsworthy accounts of the actions and events in Winchester and further afield as they occur. I cannot be as close to the kings as Nonna was, but he trained me to have keen observation and particularly to be watchful of the influence of the royal ladies at court, whose cares and vengeful spirits, he told me, could have an effect on the politics of the day, not to mention on the mood of the kings and courtiers they are married to. Doubt was no bad thing, but the moodiness of a less successful king spelled disaster. I was trained to remark on both, informed by my master's acuity at understanding the currents and eddies of the recent past.

Aelfgifu, Aethelred's queen, bearer of so many children, was not one who could be suspected of political interference, despite being born in the north, in York. She was, after all, the daughter of the Ealdorman of York, Aelfhelm, whose roots were Mercian, a trusted Midlander. Her brothers were liked at court and were frequent companions of the king in the hunt. Aelfgifu, gentle creature, given over entirely to the mothering of the next Wessex generation, which she did so well, died giving birth to another son, named Edward, by his sorrowful father. The child expired with her, in 1002. Aethelred was grief-stricken. Winchester and its inhabitants, where the queen had died, was coated in black material for weeks. Doorways were surrounded by blackened reed. The nation was sent into mourning for its queen.

The royal family locked themselves in Winchester palace, excluding all apart from essential servants and slaves. Aethelred briefly appeared, with his eldest sons, to visit the Old Minster, where his wife's body lay. Correspondence and diplomacy ceased for several weeks; I played chess during that time with monks from Abingdon, who had been brought to Winchester to refresh the library and to do corrective work. We waited while the king recovered and watched as he buried his queen, his Aelfgifu, his great love, in the crypt where he had spent the night of 999, awaiting the end of the world. This was the end of the world for him, he said loudly and with tears running down his cheeks.

The children, too, cried, as was expected of them. Their champion, their mother, who could forgive anything and everything, had passed away. Their grandmother, Aelfthryth, had declined and died suddenly in her convent retreat at Wherwell. Dying shortly before the millennium, she had gone before them all, avoiding, for the time being, retribution for any involvement in the murder of her stepson at Corfe.

Life continued. Gradually, the black reeds were removed and the royal children emerged into the sunlight, to play or to practise with wooden swords. The older boys were noted by the lookers-on as becoming young men; Athelstan, Ecgberht and Edmund were fine boys, with the fair hair of their line and the determination of their ancestors, without the obvious signs of illness which some of them had suffered and which led them to an early grave. Their noble mother of York had bred out any contagion of the flesh and perhaps had given them, in her devoted nature, a good start in retaining and developing a loving constitution and mutual brotherly admiration. All had their own talents which were being nurtured; languages for one, religious piety for another, music for another. All were good scholars and the delight, in their different ways, of their father.

Gradually the talk of the court centred on another wife for Aethelred, who sorely missed his helpmate. There were discussions, in the king's presence and beyond it, of suitable brides. It was considered, that, as there were no sisters of the old queen, who Aethelred would have preferred, having a taste for nostalgia and replication of that which he had lost, that he should look to the continent, as long ago, Athelstan's sisters had been successfully married to continental rulers. This had brought benefits to England, including the rich gifts of relics. Courtiers discussed the possibilities while I took notes. Letters were sent to foreign powers requesting details of princesses who might be willing to marry a thirty-four-year- old king who appeared hale and who wished to complete his family. A child called Edward became his desire, and another son, Alfred, if God could grant it.

The general discussion focussed on one notable character, a potentially fertile eighteen-year-old daughter of Richard the Fearless of Normandy. Emma was brought to England and delighted the king by her beauty and youth. She brought with her the great connection of Viking support; diplomacy ensued between the opposing shores of the channel, much of it in favour of protection for our land from pirates and especially from the forces of Swein Forkbeard, which had troubled us for many years and which were becoming more serious.

The new queen liked what she saw of the riches of England and took to the king as a duck will to water; independence from her Norman family breathed beauty into her. She flourished in the loving environment of her husband. She quickly became a capable manipulator of the will of court, which made her, before long, as she quickly gave the king what he most desired, another son and then another, as powerful a force in the witan as any man there. Her foreignness, and particularly her Viking roots, however, caused concern amongst the West Wessex people, who had suffered from Swein's attacks. They were mollified by Aethelred's insistence, however, that she be known in England by the old queen's name, Aelfgifu.

So, Emma/Aelfgifu, produced an Edward and an Alfred to add to the royal nursery. But before she could do her duty, in the same year that Aelfgifu died and she was brought to England to fill the king's need, a circumstance occurred which blighted both her life and that of Aethelred's. The nation reeled from the results of a vicious attack on the Danes in the north, particularly those who held rich holdings here. The St Brice's Day Massacre was the event which those who survived it said was like the coming of the Antichrist, for them. And Aethelred, in his distress at the loss of his queen and the assault on his shores, authorised it, and received, rightly, the blame. This unwarranted attack, I feel, will be our nation's undoing.

# Winchester Palace, September 1002

THERE WERE NEW grey patches of hair amongst the gold on the king's head, a grizzledness in his pallor. His shoulders had drooped; there was a loss of confidence, a loss of interest. Or so Wulfstan, not long into his role as the Archbishop of York and anxious to go north to his own palace, thought.

There was more than this, though, he considered, as the inner circle of Aethelred's court sat around the oak table in his consulting room, soaking up the atmosphere of past decision and indecision, where the very walls breathed Wessex pomp and grit, its fear and need for control. A bell at the nearby Nunnaminster struck the hour. There was a dramatic silence as the thanes and ealdormen present considered action.

'Things have come to a pretty pass,' one man ventured to break the cacophony of the bells of various churches which all began to strike twelve times.

The obvious needed to be stated. The king's court had to act; it could not put off decision-making any longer. 'They have drifted,' the thane repeated. 'Things, I mean.'

The faces of the six courtiers present looked at Aethelred, sitting at the head of the table. Was he going to snap out of his gloom? His wife had died over six months before; his newborn son, Edward, had died with her; it was an unfortunate tragedy, but there were so many other sons for the king to enjoy, so many daughters, too. Not many men had been blessed as had Aethelred with such an acceptable family life and the wherewithal to enjoy it. All children born to him, except for Edward, had survived birth and childhood as yet; the king must have thought that he was especially blessed by God; it was understandable that this blow to his heart had caused thought, doubt, and depression.

Aethelred leaned towards his new archbishop. Wulfstan heard him whisper in his ear. He leaned forward to respond. What was said, the others could not hear, but as Aethelred stood up, he appeared to have new blood in his cheeks. His shoulders went back and he stood up straight. He had made a decision. The Danish question would be settled, once and for all.

St Brice's Day it was. The enemy would experience something of what they had meted out to Englishmen. The thirteenth day of November in the year 1002 would never be forgotten by the aggrieved English or by their foes in the north, in the south, in the east. There would be no more Danegeld paid to assuage the barbaric north men. The piratical Swein would be sent packing back to Denmark.

The next week, Aethelred married Emma of Normandy, who became his new Aelfgifu, Queen of the English. He had chosen a Viking queen to offset his barbarian enemies. The north men of Normandy would bring their forces to defend the channel from their own Viking brothers. Only time would tell if the decision made to kill Danes on St Brice's Day would deliver the desired blow to their fortunes. Wulfstan went north to his cathedral with the plan to execute an uprising of Englishmen. The killing of pagans was allowed; the lawcourt of the king and Wulfstan's legal mind would find a way to assuage the guilt of planned extermination.

St Brice's Day dawned in the late autumn of the year which had seen the death of Aethelred's queen and the descent of the king into a morose sadness, neglecting his duties. With the intended massacre, his spirits rose; the horror of the grave would be visited elsewhere; God had intended him to seek revenge for the loss of his love; this he was sure of. Let Swein tremble.

Within a month of the massacre, Emma was pregnant. Edward was reborn.

# Exeter, Devon, November 13, St Brice's Day, 1002

THE WALLS OF the Roman-built town of Isca Dumnoniorum, the last Dumnonian city to be captured by Saxons, were still sound. They towered above the streets of the port which thronged daily with economic activity; longship traders of the Norse, flat-bottomed shore huggers of the British, and Danish warships jostled in the river estuary. Today was no different. This was a Tuesday, market day, another day in the post-millennial sparing by God. He waited patiently in the sky above, the clouds of early winter obscuring his plans. All those below waited, now sure that they would have some years before the anticipated arrival of the Antichrist on the anniversary of Christ's death. Some said that 1033 would be the end of everything, but many who had Viking blood, whether Dane or Norse, were not convinced. Christianity, to the outsider, and there were many amongst them, had its troubling contradictions, too many, it was said. Exeter was a hotbed of doubt. The bells of the city churches might ring out each day of the week to call each man to work and prayer, but on Sundays, when they called them to sink to their knees to offer prayer and adoration to a god who wished to keep their kind at bay, caused the population of Isca, born almost entirely of Scandinavian heritage, to raise their eyes to heaven and remember their former commitment to the wisdom and valour of Odin.

The bells rang out today, as the market stalls were assembled and Scandinavian tongues mingled in the streets. Cooperation, give and take, had brought about a stable Viking culture in Isca; like that in York, it flourished. In the comfortable halls of rich merchants and the home of the Ealdorman of Devon, Pallig Tokensen, coin was being counted and cellars filled with goods. In the yards of each large house, barns were now full of salted carcases and wheat; poultry spilled out into the alleys in search of grubs, sheep from the nearby hills were herded into hurdles for sale and immediate slaughter or to sell to supplement breeding stock. Cocks crowed, dogs chased them from dung heaps, washerwomen scrubbed at travellers' clothes, pilgrims from the interior of old Dumnonia queued at the south doorway to the minster church of St Peter and St Mary to breathe the air of relics deposited there by the generosity of the former king, Athelstan. Old women with padded kneecaps prepared to bend their frail bodies to the stone-paved floor of the nave to enter chapels, harbouring cold stone effigies and tombs, to lay their bodies in line with the corpses of their revered saints; old men prepared to offer coin and bits of cloth to adorn the doll-like saints who filled crevices and altars in darker corners of the wide nave aisles. The rags would be discretely removed by attendant monks and priests; the coin stowed away in the treasury and sent on, after accountancy had taken its share for the rebuilding of the church, to Canterbury and thus on to Rome.

Pallig Tokensen and his wife, Gunhilde, had little to do with the business of the Church. There was nothing to interest them in the income from pilgrimage; the Church could take its cut from the beliefs of the ignorant, as far as they were concerned; there was more than enough commercial business to make life worth living, being brought in on the ships of traders and being taken away in slaves or more easily portable goods from the hinterland of Dumnonia. Gunhilde sat in a window seat of their dock-side house, one floor above the workings of the market, looking out on the minster church, which was today having scaffolding applied to its north face.

She was a young woman, in the early months of a pregnancy with her second child, her first having died soon after birth not long before. The child, if it lived, would have a claim on the throne of Denmark; she was a sister of Swein Forkbeard, the daughter of Harald Bluetooth. In England, she was the wife of the Ealdorman of Devon, who lounged nearby, his feet, crossed, up on a table, papers of accounts scattered before him, a bearded, handsome man in his mid-twenties. He had just returned from a trip along the south-west coastline with friends of Swein. A little scare-mongering, a little leaping into shallow waves and sword rattling, a few swearing threats, a quick visit to the nearest church on a vulnerable headland and a snatched sheep for supper, back in the ship and home with a few jewels from the church, which had foolishly replenished its coffers since the last time he had visited. He showed the gems to his wife, who handled them with interest.

'And you say they were left with nothing after the last time you visited?' She held a stone, a glowing red ruby, torn out of a crucifix, to the lattice window. The world of the market, its busy people and stalls beyond, glowed crimson. The rosy world made her laugh. She took up a blue stone. 'How stupid these people are to restore, so soon. Where do they get the money?' The blue stone displeased her; the vision of the world, though transformed, was less to her taste. She examined the scraps of silver gilt, torn from the crucifix, which remained attached to the gems in her lap. 'Oh, the Bishop of Crediton, of course. His purse is always full.'

'His purse is full and he is foolish. He thinks that by replenishing the symbols of the Christians that he will keep us at bay.'

'Do you wear masks in your raids? It might be wise. You are expected to protect these lands, after all.'

'The inhabitants of these creeks are like savages; they scramble over their rocks on the seashore like crabs in their haste to get away. Frightened savages. They give us little trouble. We shout a bit and they scamper. I doubt if any of them look back at our fearsome faces or recognise us. To them, we are bearded devils, all looking and acting alike. None of them have ever reported names of my brothers. They cannot pronounce our names.'

'The Cornish cannot grasp English names, let alone Scandinavian. It will be better for them when they learn the language of land and commerce, I suppose.' Gunhilde tied a knot in the material holding the gems and placed the small sack into a chest by the table.

'I prefer to treat them as foreigners. It makes it simpler to use them for slaving. If they start to speak English, we shall have to look further afield.' Pallig recrossed his legs. 'Pass me the wine.'

'Wales, perhaps? But they are Christians, too.'

'The wrong sort of Christian, though. It will be further to take our ships, but I am planning raids from the north coast of Devon, into Pembroke. There will be some easy pickings there; our brothers have not visited for many years. Their guard will be down.'

'Will you bring your captives back to Exeter?' Gunhilde sometimes wished she could accompany her husband on his jaunts. Her blood was thick with the genes of adventure and raiding. Her brothers as small children and she had played often with pretend ship-raids and capture of under-nourished strangers. It was enjoyable, how much you could frighten people, and surprisingly easy.

'No, it's too far from Wales to here. The port of Bristow would be the obvious place to take them. But that's enough about business. A plate of food would bring me strength.'

'Strength for what?' Gunhilde playfully switched her eyes to smile sidelong at her husband. Success had made her fertile and willing for more. She had already conceived plans for the use of the red and blue gems. Together, they reminded her of the old religion, the hot and the cold of the afterlife. A brooch would be splendid. It was easy to twist Pallig around her finger. Fair exchange of goods and services was, after all, in her blood as well as his.

It was midday, and the market was in full swing, but they went to bed, with a plateful of bread and cheese, good replenishing fare, ready on a bedside table for Pallig to feast on when he awoke.

It was the last time that they copulated. By morning, both were dead and the marriage-bed was soaked in blood.

# Cheddar, Christmas 1002

THE HUNTERS RETURNED from the gorge. All morning they had chased, but were unsuccessful, at capturing and killing a determined and fleet-footed stag. Escapees would be found another day, perhaps tomorrow; there were several days earmarked for hunting at this Christmas-tide. There were many reasons to enjoy England at this time. The wretched Danes were cowering in their towns and cities, which they had converted into trading centres largely for the enrichment of themselves. They had been stopped in their tracks, by terror. St Brice's Day had had an effect, one of dampening ambition amongst the Scandinavians. They had been threatening with their careless behaviour, destabilising the economy and drawing resources from the nation's treasury. They liked to hoard their wealth. It had encouraged their idea of a Northern empire, with the capital being in Oslo, or Denmark. It was nonsensical, but, from their point of view, and the English crown's, possible, and a fond ambition.

A severe lesson had been delivered. The St Brice's Day massacre would be remembered forever as a lesson to the upstarts. English men, true to Aethelred and privy to his thoughts and counsel, had organised gangs of aggrieved young men in various cities of Scandinavian influence, no more than five men in each gang, to enter and attack Danes in their homes. They were to use their supposed positions as traders wanting instruction from their masters. Having wielded weapons and used them in confined spaces, where the merchant masters would be at rest and not expecting attack, delivering their blows at the dinner table or in the counting house, these trained men, who had happily carried out orders to kill, had reported deaths not only of lowly merchants, but leaders of Danish trading posts, earls, even, who had been promoted to office as a form of defence against their own kind but had taken advantage of their powerful position to enhance their own and their fellow country-men's riches. Pallig Tokensen was one, Ealdorman of Devon, husband of the daughter of King Harald of Denmark. Blue tooth, blue blood, it made no difference in the appeal for clemency by the young couple. Their throats were slit and life was over.

Eadric rode by the king's side through the gates into the yard at Cheddar. The chase had been exciting, the disappointment of failing to capture the beast and to bring it home was as nothing, compared to the general air of relief and triumph in the aftermath of the massacre.

'And you say that Exeter is now back under our control? The revenues will flow back to Winchester?' Aethelred dismounted.

'Yes, Lord.' Eadric, already dismounted, patted his borrowed horse. The hunter was equal in height to the king's. They followed the horses as they were led to the stables by grooms. 'The lady was dealt with, too. She will not have her fingers in our coin box in future.'

'I heard she was fond of jewels around her neck. She glittered, the one time that I saw her at court. Aelfgifu disliked her. And what of others, elsewhere?'

'In Oxford, York, Lincoln and many other cities, my men ensured that the serpent's head was cut off.'

Eadric had proved himself, in the few short years since they had encountered each other in this same cobbled yard, to be an able enforcer of the king's wishes. The loving family man, Aethelred, was troubled throughout his life by nightmares of Edward's violent death in Corfe and dark requirements to visit evil on someone in retribution, revenge. The killing of a foreign enemy salved his soul. He was happy, the nation relieved. A massacre it might have been, but not by his direct hand. God had wished it, as had his dead brother, Edward the Martyr, in his dreams. He had known few good nights' sleep in his adult life, but recent weeks had restored pinkness to his cheeks, the brown areas beneath his eyes had softened to grey and he felt well and relatively untroubled. He loved to rehearse what had been achieved in one single sweet night of revenge, but he was also mindful of the future. Eadric had carried out the mission; Eadric must be rewarded.

Aethelred dusted his thighs of gorge mud and cleaned his boots on the nearest scraper. What do you give a young man who has carried out your wishes, seen into your dark heart and understood your thoughts? He had hardly voiced his requirements before Eadric had retired from his position as chief advisor in the witan and secretly held meetings, allied with training, of a hundred young men, all English by birth and affiliation, known to be aggrieved with Scandinavian upstarts. In a short time, having discovered the king's will and acknowledged his Christian unwillingness to act, not to say his indecisiveness, Eadric had organised and made plans to send each group of five or six men, posing as exchequer servants, into the cities and towns run by Danish merchants and to cut the throats of their chief men. A sitting man could be approached from behind; any squeamishness would be minimised. Death would be immediate, if done correctly, like killing a sheep, or goat.

It was unfortunate, and it played on Aethelred's mind in his waking hours and was beginning to in his sleep, but the witan had roared in triumph at the achievement. For too long Aethelred had failed to act, in their opinion. Now, over the course of one day and night, the threat of domination of the treasury by foreigners had been removed. There were few murmurs of dissent. Eadric had done well, very well. He moved his chair closer to Aethelred's as the witan members looked on. There was little doubt about who had masterminded the task.

Aethelred, still basking in the glory, had at last turned his thoughts to the thorny question of how and what to give to Eadric. He was too young to be eligible as an ealdorman and the bloody coup had not been seen to happen in open battle. The treasury accounts were bleak.

'How can I reward you?' It was easier to ask the young man than to offer him something which might not be regarded as sufficient.

Eadric was now a marked man, who would do what it took to achieve a goal, that was clear. Aethelred looked at his clear grey eyes with fresh admiration and some fear. To bind and yet to command; there was a balance to be achieved. Negotiation, Aethelred could do. 'Name what you desire. If it is within my power to give it, I will.'

'You have many children.' Eadric had spent many days considering what would benefit him most. He was at the beginning of his climb to power. What would consolidate the steps up the ladder which he had already successfully taken?

'Too many, perhaps, but they fill me with joy.' Aethelred had been ruminating on giving Eadric a valuable relic, one which he would be reluctant to part with, but had guessed that relics were not considered by Eadric to be essential. What did he mean by talking about his children? His eyes narrowed.

'Edith is a fine girl.' Eadric stopped. The idea must be allowed to grow in the king's mind. Marriage to the king's eldest daughter, though she was one of several, would be seen by some as demanding too close an alliance. And the young man already had a wife, and a son, though this could soon be remedied.

'You mean you want to marry Edith…' Aethelred's mind raced. What would he gain, what would he lose? 'My dear daughter Edith? She is of an age to marry…' Aethelred had no wife to ask, no Aelfgifu to consult, except the girl's stepmother, Emma. He reviewed what he had seen of the relations between Edith and Emma. They were frosty, to say the least. Perhaps the girl would be better off leaving court and marrying. And to who better than the young man who so brazenly asks for her hand? And he was unmarried, so far as he knew. And if he was, well, wives could be discarded. He would not ask the question.

Aethelred made a quick decision. The thought of losing Edith would be painful, but Eadric would come closer to him, be tied to him, be useful to him, in future. He sensed the pent-up energy in the young man, willing to do what could be done. Ambition seeped from his pores. If he could command this force, Aethelred could see that it had a place in the story of Wessex. There was nothing to be lost. Edith would mature with this man, Edith would temper his soul, teach him goodness. Edith would bring him into the family, would balance out the quarrels which had begun to surface between Emma and his older children. Emma was strong-willed, livelier at eighteen than she had seemed on first arriving in England. Her temper was formidable; although she was renamed Aelfgifu, she was nothing like her. An equally-strong-willed son-in-law might be what was required.

'You shall have Edith, with my blessing. When shall it be?'

'Why not on Twelfth Night?'

'Next week?' Aethelred swallowed. But daughters must eventually leave the nest; he thought of the smile on his wife's face.

# Caen, Normandy, Autumn 1005

'THORKELL WILL SELL himself to the highest bidder.'
'As will you, my lord?'

Swein, sporting a beard which had grown wider and longer since his sister's murder and now, naturally divided with the uncertainty of beards as they grow, plaited and confined to the upper portion of his chest. He stroked it thoughtfully. The moustache covered his mouth and spread to his ears. His ruddy, hirsute appearance, allied with a balding head, gave the impression of determination and wild excess. Duke Richard of Normandy, himself a scion of the northern empire of ice, looked at his companion and wished he could accompany him in some of his adventures on the seas; but it was not to be. His was a landed inheritance. The management of Normandy was his remit, but he enjoyed diplomacy, while his feet were firmly imprisoned on shore. His hirsute companion was a sailor; himself a soldier.

Swein smiled beneath the moustache. He felt himself superior to his younger host; more experience, more battle-hardiness, less words, more action. And he had achieved much; southern England, the target of so many raids over so many years, quaked each time a Viking trader went into port. Would it bring more than the trade-goods expected, take away more than the English would willingly offer in payment or exchange? Swein felt at ease with Duke Richard. They were both able, in different ways, to achieve their aims; Duke Richard to protect and expand what his father and grandfather had carved out of the former Merovingian lands of France and Swein to revenge his sister's death at the hands of Aethelred of England. Since the start of his sojourn in Normandy, seeing the comfort of Duke Richard's halls and his lifestyle, commanding a swathe of the richest and most productive part of the near continent, his ambition had changed. Denmark, though already his to rule by right, was not large enough, for him, as a kingdom. The projected northern empire of Scandinavia needed to be expanded. England itself was now in his sights. Why not? A crown could as easily sit upon a Scandinavian head as an English one. The old Wessex dynasty was evidently debased. Richard and his ancestors had shown that it was possible to bend a people's minds to his own; they preferred a strong defender to a weak, generous master. More Viking attacks had been stopped by the ruthless family now squatting in Normandy's defences; it took a Viking to understand the ambition of the Viking mind, the Viking greed for more.

The pact between Swein and his Norman host had been easily achieved; Richard had his influence at the English court in the presence there in the king's bed, of his sister, Emma; he needed no more for now. If Swein wished to bite off more than he could chew by assaulting the English state in a concerted attempt to take the crown, well, the deposition of Emma and her two sons by Aethelred could be borne; she could live with him in Normandy and be well-looked after; meanwhile Swein would play his part as leader in the north of a mighty trading nation, with its capital moved from Winchester to York. His half-Viking nephews, the young Edward and Alfred, would eventually play their part in England. Swein had children; Cnut's existence had not escaped him, nor his part in the assaults on England, but Emma's son Edward had the right to inherit, though in this current agreement, Swein could temporarily hold power and glean what he could of England's wealth. Richard's nephew would take the throne in time; meantime, Swein could do the pacifying of the island nation, by force. Cnut's ambitions could wait. The contract worked both ways. Both men smiled and clasped arms, their arm rings clashing.

A scribe entered the high-ceilinged room. He brought parchment, ink and two pens. Swein and Richard had been students in their youth; writing was no longer the preserve of monks. The illiterate pagan past had been rejected, along with its natural detestation of the written word. A seal was applied to their signatures on the document which decided England's fate.

'But what about Thorkell?' Duke Richard had entertained the Jomsviking in the previous month, and Swein was aware of it.

'Cnut will tire of him, I guarantee. He has taught him well, but he is his own man now.'

'But is he your man, Swein? Does Cnut regard Thorkell or yourself as his father? Who will he follow?'

'Cnut will follow me in battle. His training is over. He will do what I require.'

It was a folly of the Viking mind; that a son could be persuaded to do what a father required him to do; generations were doomed to disappointment in their offspring. A crown, once snatched, would be grabbed as it fell afterwards by the nearest, the strongest. It would be caught, as it fell, by Cnut, aided by his right-hand man, Thorkell.

# Winchester, Spring 1006

'I TELL YOU, that man is not trustworthy. Did you hear what my slave in Bamburgh had to say of what he had said?'

Aethelred and Eadric, the king and his understudy, strode along the old hall of the palace towards the king's rooms. They passed the empty nursery. Emma had taken her sons to visit their uncle in Normandy. Aethelred and the palace servants were free, for a while, of the joyful shouts of the two boisterous boys. Business could be done. Aethelred reached the private quarters and opened the door. Eadric passed through. The king's son-in-law had grown in stature politically and in girth since he had become his favourite handy-man.

Eadric was, unlike Aethelred, an irreligious man. He had a conscience, of sorts, but he was less troubled by it than many men. Sometimes he found himself worrying about his former wife and son, but he kept them well fed and secure; they were not suffering, nor without comfort. His new wife, the king's daughter, Edith, was a charming companion and urged him to think of others, which he often did, but not in the way that she intended. Edith was inclined to deny him the marriage bed because of the way that his mind worked, but Eadric could seek comfort elsewhere; he had no qualms.

Eadric continued to build the case against Aelfhelm. 'No, not trustworthy.' What man is, he thought. Aelfhelm of York, ealdorman of Northumbria, had been present at the king's side in the witan for many years. Chosen to be lord of the north because he was not of the north, but from Mercia, Aelfhelm had in recent years become too close with foreign traders. What had started out as a diplomatic mission to attract wealth to English coffers had become a dubious relationship with the Scandinavians. It threatened the treasury. Once again the separation of Northumbria was being mooted, not only by those living in the north and clinging to their language and foreign laws, but by the southern thanes as well. It had been a mistake, after all, to make Pallig Tokenson the ealdorman of Devon. Others who had been handsomely paid and expected to defend the nation had turned against it, to line their own pockets. 'And I hear, through the usual channels, that he has a husband in mind for his daughter.'

'What do your watchers say?' Aethelred grew alarmed. He slumped onto a chair. Eadric remained standing, leaning on the narrow end of the oak table which had seen so much, heard so much, of gossip, plans and secrets over so many years in its time at the heart of Wessex. His belly lay on it. His sword-belt buckle clattered and scratched against the antique surface. He leaned forward to relate his latest information, information which would, he knew, send Aethelred into a welter of dismay and indecisiveness.

'He wants to marry his daughter to Swein's son.'

'To the bastard Cnut? And is it done?' Aethelred was used to hearing about disaster having already been accomplished.

'He's not a bastard. He's the heir to Denmark. I hear that they are betrothed.'

So, the ealdorman of Northumbria, one of the chief ministers of England, had turned traitor indeed. Aelfgifu, born in Northampton but raised in York, was to be the wife of the king of Denmark's son. The blow was unforgiveable. Aethelred rubbed his forehead.

Eadric had spent the previous days discussing the likely outcome of this event with his followers, making plans. He could now present them to the king, to ease his mind. 'My lord, there is something which I can do for you.'

'Another St Brice's day massacre? No, I could not stomach it.'

'No massacre is necessary, my lord. One of my men, Godwine Porthund, a butcher, known as the Town Dog for his tenacity, has orders. He is in my pay and a trusted man. I have his debts. He will be silent.'

'Silent about what? Oh, you mean to destroy Aelfhelm? Is it really necessary?'

'You need not hear the details. I meet Aelfhelm soon in Shrewsbury. Would you wish to accompany me there? The hunting will be good.'

Aethelred shuddered. Eadric was going to kill again. But it was necessary. This was a man, his man, doing bad things, but for the good of the nation. It could not be helped. His own soul was mired in blood; Eadric's doom was to go to hell. Together, they would save the nation and spend eternity in flames; it could not be helped.

'No. Do it alone. Report to me of the success of your mission as soon thereafter as you can. Make sure it is Aelfhelm alone who is... killed. I wish no harm to his children.'

# Shrewsbury, Easter 1006

T HE FOWLING AND hunting were fine; dry day followed dry day. Crops were being sown, flags were flying over the town in the north of Mercia, one of the bases of the new ealdorman, Eadric. His territory stretched from the shire of Chester to Bath; eight shires of the midlands were at Eadric's command, for defence to the west from Wales, for trade, for interference in East Anglia, as the occasion demanded. The name Streona had already been attached to Eadric by his enemies; East Anglian thanes and church authorities referred to him, outside the witan, as The Greedy One. At his hunting lodge on the outskirts of Shrewsbury, Eadric had the wherewithal to entertain the richest men in the land, the king included; the Christmas festivities would be spent in the king's company in the coming winter; meantime Eadric had other fish to fry. The question of Ealdorman Aelfhelm of Northumbria had to be answered.

And here came that man, the chief guest at the Easter feast which would last for many days. Aelfhelm, like Eadric, was a gourmand. More than hunting, he liked to sit at table, sampling tasty and filling tarts, swallowing the meat of many sucklings, the flesh of pike and lampreys and eels, the loaves of honeyed bread and aged cheese, the ale and French wine held in Shrewsbury lodge's large cellar. Aelfhelm rolled off his horse as he came to a halt, with his attendants, in Shrewsbury's main street. Eadric was there to greet him and ushered him into the nearest inn, which flew the flags of both Mercia and Northumbria. An English flag, freshly designed to incorporate both states, flew above the town from the gate of the wooden stockade.

Aelfhelm was without his family, though they had been invited. His two sons and married daughter were still in the north, Aelfhelm explained, witnessing the Christian rituals of Easter in York in his absence. It was a fine thing, he noted, to have a family who could willingly share the burden of power, particularly in Northumbria, where, all knew, English power was still weak. Wulfheah and Ufegeat, his sons, would accompany him to Cookham in the summer, when they hoped to take part in witan proceedings. And what of Aelfgifu, Eadric Streona asked? He had begun to use the surname for himself, especially with those he disliked. He found it instilled yet more compliance. Whispers against his person bounced off him; he found that the more he was hated, the better he liked it.

'Aelfgifu? She and the baby are doing well. Cnut is an excellent father. Swein will grow up as an English lord…'

This was not the time to challenge the obvious delusion and fatal mistake of Aelfhelm in allowing the handfasting of his daughter to Cnut. If he could not see that this was unacceptable to the English crown and that there would be a violent reaction, it was not Eadric's fault. It was typical of so many who had charge of Northumbria to think that they were impervious to the king of England's wishes. Eadric smiled.

'My own family are well; you will meet Edith tonight at the first feast. Tomorrow we shall hunt. I have a fine prospect of rolling hills and woodland for us to search out the best bucks. Meanwhile the table is ready for you to sample the finest eel pie that you have ever tasted and the cheese hereabouts is of a fine quality. We shall have pleasures this Eastertide which even the king will not enjoy, in Winchester.'

'I look forward to sitting down to feast with him later this year. I hear Cookham has fine culinary expertise, too.'

'Indeed, you will taste some exceptional flavours there. But here come the lads with our first meal to refresh you.'

Hunting and feasting went on for days; the two men were inseparable, enjoying each other's company and carousing at night. On the fourth day, though, they separated while riding out, to track a boar. On that day Godwine Porthund did the work for which he had been paid well; Aelfhelm was knocked from his horse by a pole as he passed a ditch; he died there at the hands of the Shrewsbury butcher, the town dog.


*The crafty and treacherous Eadric Streona, plotting to deceive the noble Ealdorman Aelfhelm, prepared a great feast for him at Shrewsbury at which, when he came as a guest, Eadric greeted him as if he were an intimate friend. But on the third or fourth day of the feast, when an ambush had been prepared, he took him into the wood to hunt. When all were busy with the hunt, one Godwine Porthund (which means the town dog) a Shrewsbury butcher, whom Eadric had dazzled long before with great gifts and many promises so that he might perpetrate the crime, suddenly leapt out from the ambush, and execrably slew the ealdorman Aelfhelm. After a short space of time his sons, Wulfheah and Ufegeat, were blinded, at King Aethelred's command, at Cookham, where he himself was then staying.*

John of Worcester, Chronicon ex Chronicis, twelfth century.

# Diary of Algar, 1016

I T WAS IN the years after the dreaded millennium, which had so
entered the minds of all as a year, or years, to be feared, and still is
today, that the king, who has returned to us from exile, having packed
off Swein's body back to his homeland, became too close to his ealdorman of Mercia.

I saw myself how Eadric, who had become known in court
circles as The Streona, the Greedy One, easily twisted the king
around his smallest finger. Even at feasting, where Eadric was in
his element with grandiose ideas of menu and elaborate delivery of
exotic preparations of meats, assisted by his wife, the king's daughter,
who, like her husband, had grown in girth though not in pregnancy,
he seemed to decide matters. He always said 'If your lordship permits,
may I suggest that something is done in this manner', but there was
no real choice for Aethelred; if Streona had decided on a thing, then
that thing would happen.

Eadric Streona, was rarely absent from the king's side during
the time before Swein became king; he carried out atrocities in the
name of Aethelred which many thought would never have occurred
to the king's mind and heart, being a holy man and mindful of the
relics, always at prayer and sleepless at night with the actions carried
out by his henchman in his name; nevertheless it was clear to some
of us that he would have wished to roll back the years, perhaps to the
time before Corfe and all that was done there by another person, for
his own good, as it was said. Of course this was impossible; the king's
soul has been doomed and his heart fractured, by the many cares of
state and recently by the duplicitous association of his handy-man,
Streona, with Swein's son Cnut.

Aethelred trusted his man too much. There were warning signs in what Streona was prepared to do; he was ruthless. As he grew older and bolder, it was clear that he would stop at nothing to feather his own nest. Not content with his extensive estates, some even considered that as the king's daughter was his wife, that he might make a bid to take the crown.

The idea was not preposterous; on the shores of England and inland, as well, the forces of Swein had been rioting and swaggering across the land, marching blithely by the gates of cities, even of Winchester, our capital, in full view of its frightened inhabitants. The countryside was ravaged by fighting and poor crops; famine came to many in those years that Swein chose to try to take the crown; the treasury was emptied to pay him off.

It was at this time, as Swein rode his horse across the south-west, accompanied by a swelling army, that the monastery of Frome, home to my mentor, Nonna, was destroyed. Swein, for a time, camped his army north of Bath at a place which became known as Sweinswick and from there ravaged about, terrifying the populace. When his men came to Frome on one of their sojourns to the south coast, they alighted on the little township and slaughtered all that they could find, men, women and animals alike, driving out the few monks who were in charge of the hospital there and setting fire to the ancient palace, the place where the great king Eadred had died. The largely wooden buildings could not be restored without great expense and, in any case, Aethelred chose to remain in Winchester for much of the time.

It is a sad thing when the buildings which have hosted so much history and have beauty in themselves, disappear in a single firing at the hands of an enemy; the carvings of previous centuries crackled in the flames and were lost. The small stone church of St John remains, though that, too, will need restoration. It will be done, the king has decreed, just not yet. The coffers must refill.

But will this be possible? The king is not young; his older sons are at odds with him and with each other, looking over their shoulders at the sons of Emma, considering their positions. Swein might be dead, but he took and held the crown for a year, completing his ambition to master the kingdoms of both England and Denmark at the same time; now his son, Cnut, no doubt wishes to follow in his father's footsteps, seeing that it can be done; and Eadric Streona has joined him, in open defiance of the wishes of the king.

Streona the greedy, Streona the traitor. Has any Englishman ever been more unfaithful to his people?

# Frome, May 1130

A TALL FIGURE in heavy cloak and high boots tied his horse to a pole at the inn on the south side of the river called Frome, at the bottom of a stony path which led upwards to a cluster of wooden buildings. The tower of a stone church rose up on the hill above the river. Jackdaws and rooks peopled the sky, filling the nests with fresh bedding, attending to their squawking young. A shorter figure, also heavily cloaked against the spring chill, heaved leather bags from another packhorse. As he did so, his hood fell back from his face. The younger man was evidently assistant to the older, taller monk who now strode into the inn. Both had the severe circular tonsures of Benedictine habit, grown fuzzy during travel over their pates.

It was midday, time for repast and refreshment for bones from riding for several days; research was wearying, but essential; William, historian of Malmesbury Abbey, liked to check his information by visiting sites on the ground. You could not trust some historians who called themselves that but made no attempt to concern themselves with details; William had no inclination to leave a legacy of fiction, not fact.

He was on a mission: to restore confidence in a growing readership that what they were absorbing was correct. William was aware that Truth differs from one person to the next, but the 'truth' as promulgated by his contemporary, Geoffrey of Monmouth, in his speeches in Oxford, was, he knew, far removed from reality. The Welsh held a grievance against the writing of history by Englishmen, fair enough, but to deceive and confuse was unforgiveable. If historians and history were to be trusted, the reading public needed to have the facts checked and where necessary corrected. The past was littered with culprits who did not apply diligence. Geoffrey was mangling historical fact and confusing it with fiction. The Mabinogion was his bible; imagination his source.

Not only Geoffrey; others in the years before, stretching back to the far-off Romans, had used accounts and histories to portray dogma and propaganda, to impress the uninformed of the rightness of their views. In religious as well as political matters, the fluent scribe and his dictating master had seen fit to take advantage of the innocent hearer or reader. Reputations of kings had been trashed by the severe use of words; queens had felt the force of trial by no more than a sentence; opponents had been made enemies; opposing views coloured as heresy. Scapegoats littered the writings of those for whom the pen was the mightier weapon.

Geoffrey, that mad canon, had forced his hand; William must now try to correct, as far as he could, the treason and fantasy which the Welsh canon had injected into the firesides of the new middle-classes. The history of Britain? Bah. It was the inside of one man's migraine, no more.

William had come to Frome as part of his mission. This was one of the sites founded by Aldhelm, the great man who had established the monastery which now housed the great library at Malmesbury. Malmesbury's books and records were a treasure trove of England's past; in its dusty corners he had spent many hours, from youth, examining and collating material, indexing and sorting it into a year-by-year account of the formation of the nation. Material from the courts of kings from centuries past had been sifted and rehoused where it had become fragile; for twenty years this task had been his alone. There had been times, in the middle of the night, when he had wished that the Vikings had managed to destroy more of it, as so much had been, elsewhere, but on waking he had realised, each day, what he had to do and thanked God for the task. Now he was in a position to check the information contained in the papers at his abbey, to see it on the ground, and to have a holiday, of sorts.

In the last weeks of effort before he set out on his planned journey, William had made an unexpected discovery, which prompted a change in his journey's direction; he had been going to Winchester but instead headed south westwards to the favourite place of the Saxon king Athelstan. In one of the last places in Malmesbury library cellar and in a worm-eaten wooden chest, covered in cobwebs, William had found several manuscripts and a book. There were other things besides, including a small box containing a brooch with the figure of a horse and rider. The writing was spidery and even more spidery and mouldy were the rolls of manuscript, of a very ancient date, which the chest had preserved. It was clear that these items had been untouched since they were placed there. There was a lock, but the wooden frame for it had worn away, allowing the lid to be lifted with ease. The book was readable; in Latin and the language of the Saxons and sometimes in Welsh, notes had been made, of years which were discernible; the years of the rise of the house of Wessex.

William had found the notes of a monk, Nonna, and the details of the time of Dunstan. Athelstan was there, as were all the kings of the tenth century who succeeded him. The notes faded and became sparse in the time of Aethelred, though a fresh hand had added some notes to the brief reign of Swein. Two hundred years had passed since the first king of England, Athelstan, had come to the throne. Someone had placed these writings for safe keeping in Malmesbury Abbey's library, presumably before the last ravages of the Viking wars. Things had become settled once more since then; Henry the Norman had built on the laws of the peaceable Saxon Edgar; the land had become a place of plenty; historians could now afford to look at the past without fear for the future. The dreaded millennium plus one hundred years had brought nothing with it but relief; the saviour would come, but the fear could now be put off until another seventy years could show on the candle of time. Seventy years? William would not be here. As a child, surviving the millennium plus one hundred year's threat of the imminent arrival of Judgement Day, the innocence which had saved him had given him purpose.

After refreshment, William and his assistant Norbert climbed the stony track to the church. They walked around it, noting the many wooden and stone markers of graves which hugged the south and west walls. The bones of the dead lay amongst the streams of water which issued from the hillside. Not all were channelled; the spring water trickled, or in some cases amalgamated and descended in a rush, pushing aside some of the wooden markers and feeding hawthorn and buddleia bushes. Rabbits, newly liberated throughout the land, had pierced many graves with their diggings, causing small landslides to occur. A particular interest to him was the early missionary monasteries of Aldhelm, established on Wessex's western boundary with Dumnonia in the late seventh century. He wanted to see for himself how much had survived of the famous Malmesbury monk's great works.

In Frome, it seemed that the rabbits had been busy, gnawing at what remained to be seen on the ground. There were robbed trenches where walls of stone had been, now filled with detritus. Anything built of wood had rotted. Where William supposed there had been monastic buildings, close to the church of St John, there were now carpenters' and butchers' workshops. On enquiry, he heard that stone had been moved from the trenches in recent years to rebuild a large tythe barn further up the hill, along 'behind town' as it was called. Further from the church, William discovered cobbled areas with stabling and a large packed-earth rectangular area which had been cleared of former wooden walls which was now mainly used for threshing, or storing raw materials for wood-working. He saw the remains of mounting blocks and in some places, large fireplaces along what remained of a few well-built dressed stone walls.

William asked a woodworker the name of the street which seemed to align with the rectangular area. He was told that this was the Portway, a main way into the town from the old Wessex heartlands. This was the best and most trafficked route for heavy carts into Frome, he was told, avoiding the steep hills of other routes and the bridge across the river, which meandered around the town, was reliable except in heavy rain, when the whole area of the lower market area was prone to flooding. He was told, too, that this threshing and storage area, now under the ownership of Cirencester Abbey, was still known as The King's Rooms.

Jack-by-the-hedge now decorated the cracks between cobbling and packed earth, cats and a small dog sniffed at the middens and piles of old and new building materials. There was little to show for the centuries of feasting and diplomacy which had taken place here. It was his opinion that Swein had started the process of destruction of the royal palace which then was continued by the local inhabitants. Time had done most of the work, and nature was completing it.

William turned away and returned to the church. Outside it, he noticed the fallen remains of a stone cross, being used as part of a grave. There were more parts of it on another grave. There were the tell-tale creatures, beloved of the old peoples, etched on the surface of the stone, like the cross shaft he had been told he would find at Keyford, a village to the west of Frome. Preaching crosses, dating from long ago, before the churches existed, were a common sight in rural communities such as this, but pulled apart and misused in some places, particularly where commerce ruled, as here.

The palace of the kings of Wessex, gone, Aldhelm's monastery, gone. Was there a sadness in this? William and Norbert noted the absence of active religious life, except at the church, which needed renovation work urgently. He could report to the Abbey at Cirencester what he had found, but perhaps it would do no good. There were memories here of what had been, but in one generation, perhaps two, there would be little of interest to see left on the ground, and little interest in the minds of those who had work to do and livings to make.

He had hopes that there would be more surviving at Bruton and Sherborne, where his journeys would take him in the coming days. Aldhelm's mission to convert his own people, while the Celtic Christian Britons gave way to their Saxon masters, had done its job. England in William's time was a firmly Catholic country, looking forward to its future allied with Rome, not to the parochial past, where the answers to many questions lay and would remain.

# Reference

## Discussion

THE PERIOD OF Wessex domination of England from the death of Edmund in 946 to the accession of Edgar in 959 was fraught with power struggles as the Wessex dynasty attempted to consolidate their position as overkings of the whole of Britain. First Mercia and then Northumbria resisted their requirement to subject and annihilate the old British kingdoms of Bernicia and Deira. The Celtic peoples of the north and west were in retreat but retained their own cultures and languages. Into the mix came a fresh wave of wealth-seekers, the Danes and Norse Vikings, with a series of determined leaders including Eric Bloodaxe and Swein Forkbeard.

The collaboration between the Strathclyde, Scottish and Viking rulers which culminated in the loss by them in battle at Brunanburh in 937 to Athelstan and Edmund, changed emphasis. Northumbrian Saxons remained resentful at the southern kings' overlordship and joined forces with Norse leaders to overthrow the yoke of the south. They were assisted by the duplicity (to Wessex) of Wulfstan, Archbishop of York, probably himself a Northumbrian (see timeline), who first threw in his lot with Anlaf, ruler in Dublin and York and later with Eric Bloodaxe. Nearly captured in 943 in a siege at Leicester and imprisoned perhaps in Dewsbury, near Leeds, by Eadred in 952/3, Wulfstan managed to wriggle off the hook of the crime of treachery, despite attempts to have him exiled or killed. That Wulfstan survived to die in his bed in 956 at St Wilfrid's monastery in Oundle, near Peterborough, says much for the position he held in the esteem of the Saxon Northumbrians and suggests that he had a close connection by birth with former Northumbrian royalty.

As with the relic collection by Athelstan of significant saints, we see in the gathering or alienation from the north of totemic, protective heroes or saints by Dunstan and others (Archbishop Oda brings Wilfrid's remains south to Canterbury as Oswald was brought to Gloucester) a deliberate attempt to wrest spiritual power from the north, to weaken its defences. The burning of Wilfrid's monastery in Ripon by Eadred in 948 is clearly meant to add to the dismay of the northerners.

# Glossary

**Benedictine Reform**: A tenth century movement to return the church and particularly monastic institutions to a more 'pure', strict form of Benedictine practice. Dunstan, Aethelwold and Oswald, Bishop of Worcester, were its chief protagonists in the mid tenth century. Kings and nobles were often in two minds about what they preferred. Eadred bowed to the wishes of Dunstan and his mother; Eadwig did not. Edgar was trained by Aethelwold to promote the reformers' ideas.

**Brunanburh, Battle of**: Defeat of Norse, Scots and Cumbrians in 937, probably on the Wirral, Cheshire, by Athelstan and Edmund.

**Caldarium**: warm room for the infirm.

**Cerdicings:** the dynasty of the West Saxons. Cerdic was claimed by his descendants as one of the original conquerors of Britain. He is said to have ruled in Wessex from 519 (about the time of the Battle of Badon), to 534.

**Consanguinity:** marriages in the medieval period could be annulled because of deemed familial closeness. In Eadwig and Aelfgifu's case, the decision to separate them was probably inspired by the growing influence of Aelfgifu's family and supporters, unwelcome to the

Mercian faction who were in favour of Edgar becoming ruler. Eadwig and Aelfgifu were distant cousins.

**Eboracum:** The Roman name for York.

**Exequies:** funeral arrangements.

**Fyrd:** The Saxon Army.

**Haligdom:** Relic room or collection.

**Jomsvikings:** Group of particularly violent Vikings.

**Labyrinth:** at St Martin of Lucca: a labyrinth was the pilgrimage symbol of the Via Francigena, as the shell was the symbol of the Camino de Santiago.

**Lagentium:** Castleford, on the Roman road south of York, near Pontefract.

**Miklagard:** Viking name for Constantinople (Istanbul).

**Palium:** A cloth article of decoration worn by archbishops on top of their vestments and given to them by the Pope or collected by them. It became the norm to travel to Rome to collect the palium in the late tenth century. Earlier on it had been sent. Archbishop Sigeric (elected to Canterbury in 990) detailed his journey to Rome, recording 23 churches visited, on the Via Francigena, his midday meal with Pope John XV and the 79 stages of his homeward journey. Dunstan probably followed the same route, taking the Spring and Summer of 960 to complete his journey to Rome, meeting the Pope in the early autumn and presumably returning before winter.

**Secular priests:** priests who were not attached to a monastic institution and did not necessarily follow the services of the Benedictine order. They might also be married.

**Tanshelf:** Part of Pontefract, Yorkshire.

**Totemic:** (guardians, relics): protective symbols of an area or people.

**Witan:** Saxon parliament

# People and Saints

**St Cuthbert:** (of Lindisfarne) Seventh century northern saint, of vital psychological importance to the Wessex Dynasty, along with St Oswald. Said to remain in his coffin today at Durham cathedral, alongside the head of Oswald. Folklore records that he was offended by a woman who claimed he had fathered her child. The seventh century father of the woman, a Pictish king, decreed that women must not enter churches dedicated to Cuthbert. A rare southern dedication, founded in Saxon times, exists at Wells.

**St Wilfrid:** Seventh century monk of Hexham, founder of Ripon monastery in north Northumbria (Bernicia). Battled successfully with Abbess Hilda of Whitby to establish the Catholic link to Rome at the Synod of Whitby in 664.

## Timeline: Eric Bloodaxe, Queen Eadgifu, Archbishop Wulfstan and Eadred

**885** Eric born. Dies 954 aged 69 at Battle of Stainmore, Pennines. King of Norway and at different times, of Orkney and Northumbria. **885**(?) Wulfstan born. Dies 956 aged 71(?). Brother? or close relative? of Ealdred 1, last Saxon king of Northumbria. Ealdred was a friend of the Wessex court. Appointed Archbishop of York by King Athelstan in 931, held post until death at Oundle. Buried at Oundle,

St Wilfrid's monastic foundation.

**902/3** Eadgifu born to Kentish family. Marries Edward the Elder, son of Alfred, in 919. Mother of Kings Edmund and Eadred and two daughters, Eadburh and Eadgifu. Dies 966(?) aged 63.

**919** Eadgifu marries Edward as his third wife.

**922(?)** Edmund born. Died 946, killed at Pucklechurch near Bristol, at a feast.

**924(?)** Eadred born. Died 955 at Frome. Had stomach problem for much of his life (like Alfred).

**924** Edward dies and his eldest son Athelstan succeeds.

**927** Athelstan makes pact with northern states at Eamont in the Lake District.

**931-933** Eric Bloodaxe is king of Norway.

**931** Athelstan appoints Wulfstan as Archbishop of York.

**934** Ealdred of Northumbria dies, Athelstan becomes overlord. Athelstan creates a one-mile area sanctuary around the minster of Ripon.

**937** Battle of Brunanburh (probably the Wirral, Cheshire), defeat of northern forces including Vikings and Scots by Athelstan and Edmund. Northumbria now part of a united nation of England.

**939** Edmund succeeds Athelstan. Queen Eadgifu, his mother and his brother Eadred play major roles in the rule of England from Wessex.

**940** Eadwig, elder son of Edmund, born.

**940** Anlaf (Norwegian) becomes Edmund's godson and client king in Northumbria and later in Dublin.

**942/3/4** Edgar, younger son of Edmund, born.

**943** Edmund besieges Anlaf and Archbishop Wulfstan in Leicester. They escape by night. Later Anlaf is befriended again by Edmund and baptized, as Alfred earlier befriended and baptized Guthrum, the Danish leader, after the battle of Edington in 878. Edmund becomes overlord of Northumbria.

**946** Edmund killed by Leofa ("a thief") at Pucklechurch. (For the story of Edmund, see *The Gorge*).

**946** Eadred, Edmund's younger brother, succeeds Edmund.

**946-7** Eadred quells an uprising in Northumbria. Anlaf, king in Dublin, returns to York as king. He and Wulfstan make an agreement with Eadred at Tanshelf (Pontefract, west Yorkshire) to tolerate English rule.

**947-8** The Northumbrians are disloyal to Eadred and take Eric Bloodaxe, formerly king of Norway, as their king with the help of Archbishop Wulfstan who invited him, as King of Orkney, to be king in York. Anlaf presumably returns to Ireland.

**948** Eadred again in Northumbria quelling opposition. Burns Ripon including the minster of St Wilfrid, with links, it is thought, to Wulfstan. Heavy losses by Eadred's forces as they return south at battle of Castleford, near Tanshelf. Despite this, Eadred manages to persuade the Northumbrians to oust Eric. The northerners give compensation to the southern king.

**949** The Scottish king raids Northumbria as far as the River Tees, perhaps to aid either Eric or possibly Anlaf. Anlaf returns to Northumbria as king. Eadred does not respond, presumably because this is acceptable to Wessex.

**951** Wulfstan ceases to witness charters at the English court, perhaps because he is supporting Eric.

**952-3** The Northumbrians drive out Anlaf and take Eric as their king again, until 954, perhaps with help of Wulfstan. Eadred invades again and takes Wulfstan prisoner, imprisoning him at *Iudanburh* (site unknown but probably Dewsbury, an important Saxon centre near Leeds).

**953** Wulfstan is in Dorchester-on-Thames.

**954** The Northumbrians expel Eric. Northumbria is dissolved as independent kingdom. Eadred becomes over-king.

**954** Eric is killed at battle of Stainmore, perhaps when escaping north from York, by Maccus, possibly Anlaf's son.

**955** Eadred dies in Frome. Eadwig, Edmund's eldest son, succeeds to the English throne.

**956** Wulfstan dies in Oundle.

**957** Edgar, Edmund's second son, becomes king of Mercia and

Northumbria.

**959** Eadwig dies. Edgar becomes king of England.

**966** Eadgifu dies?

## What Really Happened to Edwin

ATHELSTAN DID 7 years' penance and founded a monastery at
Milton (Abbas) in Dorset as a result of the accidental or otherwise drowning of his half-brother Edwin in 933. He may have felt
the need to assuage guilt. English versions of the controversy have
Athelstan, having been convinced by a cup-bearer that Edwin was
plotting against him, putting Edwin in a rickety boat, with a squire,
somewhere in the English Channel. The boat was said to have no
oars and its sails failed while out at sea. Edwin dived overboard and
was drowned. His squire hauled him aboard and brought the body
to Kent. Athelstan was appalled at having caused the death of his
brother and executed the cup-bearer.

Continental sources, however, have Edwin being taken ashore
in Flanders and buried at the abbey of St Bertin, a few miles inland
from Calais.

Sarah Foot, in her book, 'Aethelstan', covers the arguments. In
this story I have chosen to have Edwin launched and remembered as
having been found at Studland in Dorset.

## Reg's Story
## Mother Herne of Milborne Port

A TALE TOLD to the author by a friend about an old woman,
known as Mother Herne, who lived in woods near Milborne
Port in Dorset in the early twentieth century. He said that she cured
his mother's anxiety over an affair which his father was conducting,
removing 'the black stick' from her and bringing the family back into
harmony. Mrs Wills is described in Charles Whynne-Hammond's
book, Ten Somerset Mysteries (The Witches of Wincanton). Herne

refers back to the Iron Age nature god, Cernunnos. Women (and men) like Mrs wills were common until the twentieth century.

Reg Veale, born 1914 in Stoford, near Yeovil, Somerset, died 1996.

Reg was one of a large family of children, born in a cottage with no running water. His father was a 'rake' who was having an affair with his wife's best friend, who lived nearby. Reg's mother was feeling unwell and anxious, not knowing of the affair. She decided to consult Mrs Wills, as she knew her name to be, who lived on a wooded hill near Milborne Port in north Dorset, not far away.

Reg's mother was wary of going to talk to the old woman and went alone, but told Reg later what had happened. Mrs Wills examined Mrs Veale and pronounced that 'she had had the Black Stick put on her' i.e. bad luck. She told Mrs Veale to go home; she would do 'something' to improve her position.

Mrs Veale returned home and found that her friend had fallen down stairs and broken an arm. While assisting her friend, Mrs Veale learned of the affair and the two women became closer. The affair ended, though Mr Veale might not have wished it to and the matter was resolved, as far as Mrs Veale was concerned.

## Eadred's Illness

KING ALFRED, IN the description by Asser, his Welsh biographer, was said to have suffered from some form of stomach pain throughout his youth and particularly on his wedding night, after copious eating and drinking. The pains still afflicted him in his forties. Asser mentions piles. Eadred appears to have had a similar complaint.

Chrohn's disease or irritable bowel syndrome may have been the problem, and this can be hereditary. Inflammation of the bowel is extremely painful but can be alleviated by strict diet. The contemporary description of Eadred sucking at meat and discarding it at feasts, his hair and teeth loss and 'weak feet' may be symptoms of Chrohn's, which can cause malnutrition. It doesn't seem to have stopped him from leading or organising engagement with Eric Bloodaxe, though a flare-up may have caused him to be passive when Anlaf returned to York after Eric's first expulsion. Another reason for his passivity may be that Anlaf, who was buried in Iona, was by this time (949) becoming overtly Christian and therefore more acceptable to the south.

The story has him being possibly a sufferer of Coeliac disease, which is a gluten-related illness. If he had this, beer and bread, staples of the Anglo-Saxon world, would have been problematic.

## Eadred's Will

EADRED'S WILL IS comprehensive. He must have made it shortly before his death in 955 as he leaves lands to his mother, unless he expected for many years not to survive her, which is possible.

It survives as a document held in the British Library. It smacks of someone facing up to imminent death. He leaves large quantities of gold and silver 'for the redemption of his soul and for the good of his people, that they may be able to purchase for themselves relief from want and from the heathen army if they have need'. The money was entrusted to church leaders for distribution in their areas of jurisdiction. He does not mention his young heir, Eadwig, who may by the time of his demise have been considered less than a perfect choice for king. Eadred tries to enrich his mother, Eadgifu. He is worried about the welfare of his soul; he wanted gold given to 'every ecclesiastic who has been appointed since I succeeded to the throne,' another clue that the will was constructed immediately before his death. He also left individual legacies to each member of his household. The fictional characters, Bica and Hersfig, could have benefitted.

Unfortunately, most aspects of Eadred's will were ignored after his death. He was buried at Winchester with his forbears, but

Eadwig dispossessed his grandmother of her property. Whether Abbot Dunstan ever received his share of the legacy (two hundred pounds) is not clear. After death, the king's body was said to have been deserted by his courtiers.

## Dunstan at Work

**Charter 546 (AD 949),** written by Dunstan, probably at Glastonbury, Source: Sawyers Charters.

King Eadred to Canterbury Cathedral, grant of Reculver minster and its lands, estimated at 26 hides.

*The fraudulent instigator of vices deludes human minds thus with many tricks, now, I say, he deceives, as it were, with the promised courses of a longer life; now he stubbornly entices with transitory things as if they were necessities; in the meantime he also suggests that the stygian punishments of Hell are like trivial and superficial things in order that he might feebly destroy the hearts of wretched men in desire and lascivious behaviour and lead them with him encaged to hell. But holy men in a spirit of foreboding, recognising the bestial ambushes, crowned with the shield of good will unceasingly and zealously bring to an end with holy works whatever they perceive to be earthly in themselves, whereby they are presented with their merits laid bare before Jesus Christ, glowing with the light of splendour most like to a Titan. In celebration of these men the trumpet of Holy Scripture resounding pours forth by re-echoing amongst other evidence these two texts that should be the more readily heard by our ears, 'Blessed are those whose garments are white in the sight of the Lord' and in another place, 'the just shine like the sun in the kingdom of their father'. Filled with love for the sight of this kingdom of the Lord and Father, therefor, where assured nourishment remains for us without doubt, about which the Lord said, 'blessed will he be who eats bread in the kingdom of God'. I, EADRED, KING and sole ruler by Divine Grace of the whole of Albion and chief officer to Christ my king, enthroned forever on the throne of the everlasting kingdom, and with the treasures of transitory kinds granted to me by the Same, in the* *fourth year of my earthly reign following reception of the office, at the church dedicated to His name that cannot be comprehended in the city of Canterbury, Archbishop Oda presiding over the metropolitan see and carrying the keys of the heavenly kingdom over the country of Britain, most humbly and devoutly with a sincere heart am giving that monastery of Reculver, assessed at twenty-six hides within and without with all things rightly belonging to it, whether of shores or fields or marshes, just as the lands are published below, as a right in perpetuity as long as Christianity shall flourish in return for washing away my transgressions perpetually. If, however, anyone relying on the tyrannical power of royal or episcopal – or a man of any – rank should attempt, which God forbid!, to destroy this decision granted by God to me or should sever even a foot of this gift from the aforementioned church, unless he first sweeps away this enormous crime by penance, may he be aware that he has incurred blame for his sacrilege and will be damned by the Lord Jesus Christ forever without any consolation of a reduction. This document was written in the year of the Lord's incarnation 949 with the unanimous consent of the men of orthodox belief whose names can be seen to be distinguished by their written nature below: + **I, Eadred,** with the protection of Divine Grace king of Albion, presiding, marked the top of this charter with the sign of the holy cross I, Oda, metropolitan archbishop of Canterbury, presiding over the royal governance, have marked with the sign of the cross this gift of munificence that has been granted **I Wulfstan**, archbishop supported by the summit of the metropolitan office in the city of York, have written down the cross on this generous gift. I, Aelfheah, bishop of the church of Winchester, have confirmed this gift with the sign of the cross (there follow ten bishops and abbots, then 3 dukes) + **I Eadgifu,** mother of the aforementioned king, with a heart rejoicing at the aforementioned generous gift to Christ have most humbly marked with the corroboration of the mark bringing salvation (i.e., the cross) +**I, Dunstan**, unworthy abbot of Glastonbury, at the behest of King Eadred my lord have composed by dictation this charter of ownership and have written it with the joints of my own fingers. (Then follows the boundaries of the land)*

*Short version: In the year of the Lord's incarnation 949, I, Eadred, king, with the venerable man, Oda, archbishop and father of the whole of Britain being present and Eadgifu, the queen, my mother, have given to the Christ Church in the city of Canterbury the monastery of Reculver with the whole vill and all rightly belonging to it, free from all secular servitude except three: military service and the building of bridge and fortress. And I, Dunstan, unworthy abbot, composed the charter thereupon at the command of my lord, King Eadred and wrote it with my own hand.*

## Relics and Resurrection

THE DIVISION OF holy corpses in the Christian world was being undertaken from an early part of the Church's history. The fifth century theologian Theodoretus, Bishop of Cyrrhus (Greece) 423-457, declared in his Sermon on the Martyrs, that "grace remains entire with every part" (of the body). "Sectis corum corporibus, integra et indivisia gratia perseverat".

No matter how small a holy person's relic might be, whether of finger nail, leg or head, all would be able to live again on the day of resurrection, it was believed.

Not so the unfortunate criminal or political opponent who was deliberately dismembered throughout the medieval period. Hanging, drawing and quartering were not merely physical punishments. They were intended to deny the offender any chance of living again in the imagined Heaven.

## Edgar's Marriages

EDGAR HAD THREE relationships/marriages which are known to have produced children:

Aethelflaed Eneda (the 'white duck'), who gave birth to Edward the Martyr, b.962, d.978,

Wulfthryth of Wilton, removed or abducted by Edgar in 962, who gave birth to Edith (Saint Edith),

Aelfthryth, married Edgar in 964/5 after her first husband, sent by Edgar to view her as a prospective wife, was killed/murdered after marrying her himself. Aelfthryth had two sons by Edgar: Edmund, b.966, d.c.970 and Aethelred, b.968, d.23 April 1016.

After Edward's death at the age of sixteen at Corfe, the ten-year-old Aethelred became king, with his mother as regent.

## Edgar for Sainthood?

WILLIAM OF MALMESBURY, writing in the twelfth century, recalls the opening of the tomb of Edgar in 1052 by the then abbot of Glastonbury, Ailward. He found the body 'uncorrupted' which would usually be the mark of a saint. Instead of reverencing the body, however, it was shoved into a too small receptacle and cut to size. The body reportedly bled copiously, another sign of potential sainthood. Edgar's remains were enshrined with the head of St Apollinaris and parts of Vincent the Martyr and placed upon an altar at Glastonbury. The abbot broke his neck shortly after, William says, as a result of this display of profanity. A blind lunatic was said to have been cured at this shrine, further enhancing Edgar's status as potential saint. William evidently thought that Edgar had achieved saintly status, or at least that he deserved it; he comments that *after his departure, the state and the hopes of the English met with a melancholy reverse.*

It was probably an aim of Eadgifu, grandmother of Edgar, to claim sainthood for her progeny; she succeeded with her great-granddaughter Edith, Edgar's daughter by Wulfthryth of Wilton and Edward, Edgar's son by Aelthelflaed Eneda (the White Duck), who became known as the Martyr. Edward the Confessor, Aethelred's son by Emma of Normandy, also achieved the status of sainthood.

Edgar's remains and those of the others enshrined with him were lost at or before the dissolution in the sixteenth century.

# Edith for Queen?

I N THE LATE eleventh century Goscelin of Canterbury wrote the lives of St Edith (Vita Edithe) and her half-brother Edward (Passio Edwardi). In it he describes how Ealdorman Aelfhere of Mercia, desperate to find an alternative to Aethelred as king, went as head of several magnates to Wilton to try to persuade Edith to become queen. Goscelin says that the magnates offered their own daughters in fulfilment of Edith's monastic vow if only she would leave the nunnery and rule in place of the unworthy Aethelred. This story is rejected by Ridyard as a product of the eleventh century hagiographical imagination, but, taken with Dunstan's apparent aversion to Aethelred at both his baptism and coronation, there may be truth in the story. Aelfhere would certainly be opposed to Aethelwine's and Aelfthryth's wish for power as regents for Aethelred.

It was Aelfhere who brought the body of Edward the Martyr to Shaftesbury for reburial. It is likely that the abbess of Shaftesbury, Herleva, played a part in this and perhaps she had an interest in promoting Edith, too. She may have considered that Aethelred's mother, who had estates in the east, might divert funds to east Anglia which would otherwise have come south and west to Wilton and Shaftesbury.

## The End of Frome Monastery

W ILLIAM OF MALMESBURY, a historian on whom we can rely, visited Frome in the early twelfth century. He was looking at sites associated with St Aldhelm, who founded the Saxon monastery at Frome in the late seventh century.

He says:

*He (St Aldhelm) also founded (besides Malmesbury) another monastery near the river which is called the River Frome. We can read about it in the charter of privilege which pope Sergius gave to both monasteries. This church, which he built in honour of St John the Baptist, still stands there today, surviving and living on after many centuries. The common opinion is that he founded also a third monastery at Bradford-on-Avon, and this seems to be confirmed by the name of the town occurring in the course of the charter, which the then bishop gave to his monasteries, and being written in an ancient script. The little church dedicated to St Lawrence, which he is said to have founded there, exists to this day. But although the church survives, both monasteries, at Frome and at Bradford, have followed the fashion of mortal things and disappeared, leaving only an empty name, although it is hard to decide whether we should blame the fierce wars with the Danes for the destruction of these great buildings or the rapacious altercations of the English. Only Malmesbury lives on, still packed with monks, its buildings still beautiful.*

William of Malmesbury, Chapter 198 *Aldhelm's Monastic Foundations*, The Deeds of the Bishops of England, trans. David Preest, Boydell Press 2002

# The Ruin

Wondrous is this stone-wall, wrecked by fate;
the city-buildings crumble, the works of the giants decay.
Roofs have caved in, towers collapsed,
barred gates are broken, hoar frost clings to mortar,
houses are gaping, tottering and fallen,
undermined by age. The earth's embrace,
its fierce grip, holds the mighty craftsmen;
they are perished and gone. A hundred generations
have passed away since then. This wall, grey with lichen
and red of hue, outlives kingdom after kingdom,
withstands tempests; its tall gate succumbed.
The city still moulders, gashed by storms....
A man's mind quickened with a plan;
subtle and strong-willed, he bound
the foundations with metal rods – a marvel.
Bright were the city halls, many the bath-houses,

lofty all the gables, great the martial clamour,
many a mead-hall was full of delights
until fate the mighty altered it. Slaughtered men
fell far and wide, the plague-days came,
death removed every brave man,
Their ramparts became abandoned places,
the city decayed; warriors and builders
fell to the earth. Thus these courts crumble,
and this redstone arch sheds tiles.
The place falls to ruin, shattered
into mounds of stone, where once many a man,
joyous and gold-bright, dressed in splendour,
proud and flushed with wine, gleamed in his armour;
he gazed on his treasure – silver, precious stones,
jewellery and wealth, all that he owned –
and on this bright city in the broad kingdom.
Stone houses stood here; a hot spring
gushed in a wide stream; a stone wall
enclosed the bright interior; the baths
were there, the heated water; that was convenient.
They allowed the scalding water to pour
Over the grey stone into the circular pool. Hot…
…where the baths were
…that is a noble thing,
How the…the city

## The Sermon of the Wolf to the English (extracts)

D EAR MEN, UNDERSTAND that this is true: the world is in haste
and it approaches the end, and because it is ever worldly, the
longer it lasts, the worse it becomes; and so it must necessarily greatly
worsen before the coming of Antichrist because of the sins of the
people, and indeed it will become then fearful and terrible through-

out the world.

Here too many in the land, as it may appear, are grievously stained by the stains of sin. Here are murderers and slayers of kin and killers of priests and persecutors of monasteries....

And the English have been for a long time now wholly without victory and too greatly disheartened through the anger of God, and the Vikings are so strong by the consent of God that often one puts flight to ten, and sometimes less, sometimes more, all because of our sins.

And let us often reflect on the great judgement to which we all shall come, and earnestly save for ourselves from the surging fire of hellish torment, and earn for ourselves the glories and the joys which God has prepared for those who do his will in the world. May God help us, Amen.

## Boxes of Bones

SIX MORTUARY CHESTS containing the mixed bones of 23 individuals, thought to be the remains of late Anglo-Saxon kings, princes, bishops and a queen, kept for many centuries at Winchester cathedral, are being investigated at Bristol university. Radio-carbon dating has confirmed the late Saxon dates of most of the remains, though they include early kings of Wessex as well as later. The names on the caskets provide some clue to their occupants:

William Rufus (11), son of William the Conqueror,
Emma, wife of Aethelred and Canute,
Cnut,
Edmund Ironside,
Eadred,
Eadwig,
Aethelwulf, father of Alfred (died 858)
Ecgbert (died 839),
Cynewulf (died 786),
Cynegils (died 642),

Bishop Wini (died c. 670),

Bishop Aelfwyn (died 1047).

There may also be the remains of St Swithin (died 863),

Harthacnut, Cnut's son and

Richard of Normandy, another son of William.

The 11th century remains of two unknown teenage boys were also found, presumed to be members of a royal family.

The bones were disturbed in the 12th century by the building of the present cathedral and relocating and again during the 17th century English civil war, when some of the long bones were used by Cromwell's Roundhead soldiers to smash stained-glass windows. An exhibition of Winchester cathedral's role as a royal mausoleum was mounted in 2019.

Athelstan was buried at Malmesbury, Edmund at Glastonbury, Eadred at Winchester, Eadwig at Winchester, Edgar at Glastonbury, Edward the Martyr at Shaftesbury, Aethelred at Old St Paul's Cathedral, Aethelwold (bishop) may be part of the boxed remains, Dunstan was presumably buried at Canterbury. Swein's body was embalmed and returned to Denmark.

Alfred was originally buried in the Old Minster of Winchester, but his remains and those of his wife and children (Ealswith and Edward) were later moved to Hyde Abbey (just outside the walls of Winchester) and were lost when a prison was constructed on the site in 1788. The convicts who were put to work constructing the prison scattered the bones. Part of a pelvis, recovered in 2014, is thought to be from Alfred or his son Edward.

## Aveline's Hole, Burrington Combe

HUMAN REMAINS OF fifty individuals dating to the Mesolithic period in Britain (the bones were dated to be approximately 10,200 years old) were found in Aveline's Hole, a cave mouth, in 1797. Only the remains of two individuals survived a bomb during WWII.

# William of Malmesbury (c.1095-1143) and Geoffrey of Monmouth (c.1100-1155)

WILLIAM AND GEOFFREY were twelfth century contemporaries. William was based at Malmesbury Abbey and Geoffrey at Oxford. The second and third decades of the twelfth century, in the reign of Henry 1, William the Conqueror's fourth son, saw a rise in historical investigation among clerics or priests with a view to establishing truth or to popularising myth and legend, the story of the land of Britain. William would surely have sneered at Geoffrey's works (The History of the Kings of Britain, published c.1136). William's main works, *Deeds of the Kings of England* and *Deeds of the Bishops of England* were completed by 1125.

William, educated and tonsured at Malmesbury, is taken by modern historians to have been the more reliable of the two as an historian. The term 'flights of fancy' could be applied to Geoffrey's approach. William would have had access to a considerable store of earlier material at Malmesbury on which to concentrate his attentions, including a lost account of the life of Athelstan, considered to be the first king of a united England. He makes comments about the Wessex and English kings which seem to be based on now unrecoverable records. The account of events at the baptism of Aethelred, which only appear in William's work, indicates that Dunstan had foretold that his reign would be a disaster, which suggests that the ageing archbishop had been, perhaps with hindsight by himself or his biographers, a supporter of Edward the Martyr, Aethelred's murdered teenage half-brother, as king. On Aethelred's accession in 978 as an eleven-year-old, there must have been psychological conflict between Aethelwold, bishop of Winchester, who was a close associate of Aethelred's mother, and Dunstan, probably only resolved with Aethelwold's death in 984.

After Aethelwold's death and before Dunstan's in 988, Aethelred asserted his own authority and independence by acting against the interests of some of the reformed monastic houses, which Aethelwold and Dunstan had so vigorously promoted. Perhaps Dunstan was aware of Aethelred's preference towards undoing the work of the reformation of monasteries and wished to preserve his interests by favouring a more sympathetic Edward. The disappointment of Edward's early death (978) must have been a considerable blow to the archbishop, only assuaged by Aethelwold's and Aelfthryth's (Aethelred's mother), continuing control of the young king.

William gives us clues to the motivations and events which shaped the politics, both of church and state, in the years preceding the millennium, and can be relied on to relate notable circumstances. The unfortunate occurrence at Aethelred's baptism may well be a fanciful picture of the king who has become in later times to be regarded as ineffective, thrust by history into the naughty corner along with King John, but it seems quite likely. That an evacuation in a font by a baby should be seen by later historians to be symbolic of disaster, shines a beam of light on the medieval mind and also on Williams's support for Dunstan's position.

## The Comet of 975

THIS WAS PROBABLY Halley's Comet, which appears every 75-76 years. It was seen in 912 as reported in the Annals of Ulster and was probably the comet shown in the Bayeux tapestry. William of Malmesbury reports a comet in 989, which may be the same as the 975 sighting, with misunderstanding of the date. The 975 sighting coincided with a famine in Britain and with the death of Edgar. Comets were regarded as portents of good or ill.

## The Fear of the Millennium

THE REVELATION OF St John, in the Apocrypha of the Bible, spells out the disaster likely to occur at the end of the first millennium after Christ's birth. In no uncertain terms, the fate of the world is portrayed in descriptive terms likely to concern the faithful, if believed to be true. Several verses outline in detail the vision of John:

'Then out of the sea I saw a beast rising. It had ten horns and seven heads. On its horns were ten diadems, and on each head a blasphemous name. The beast I saw was like a leopard, but its feet were like a bear's and its mouth like a lion's mouth.'

The vision of fearsome beasts is extensive as is the exhortation to bow down to the creator. The implication, if used from the pulpit, is that those who wish to be 'saved' should do the will of the speaker. The message would have been driven home as the millennium approached, with prayer and fasting required by all in the hope of offsetting total disaster. In 1008 AD three days of prayer and fasting, when only bread and water could be consumed, were legally required by everyone to prevent Viking onslaught. Punishment and fines were imposed on those unwilling to do so.

## St Brice's Day Massacre

A ETHELRED AUTHORISED THE killing of all Danes 'living in England' on the 13<sup>th</sup> November 1002, St Brice's Day, having been informed of a plot to kill him.

St Brice of Tours, 370-444 AD was Bishop of Tours, a contemporary of Augustine of Hippo.

38 skeletons of young men were found during an excavation at St John's College, Oxford in 2008, who may have been some of the victims.

Swein Forkbeard's sister, Gunhilde, is thought to have been killed, which may have influenced him to plan further assaults on the English crown.

# Places

**Eboracum:** Roman name of **York**.

**Lagentium:** Roman name of **Castleford,** near **Pontefract,** Yorkshire.

**Dewsbury**: may be the site of Archbishop Wulfstan's incarceration in 953. Said to be Iudanburh (site unknown) or Jedburgh in differing translations of the Anglo-Saxon Chronicles. Most likely to be Dewsbury on etymological grounds. Dewsbury was an important Anglo-Saxon centre in Yorkshire.

**Jorvik:** Viking name of York.

**Tanshelf:** modern **Pontefract,** near Leeds, Yorkshire. Tanshelf and Kirkby, pre-1066, were independent areas in what became Pontefract (Broken Bridge, named after Anglo-Scandinavian resistance to William in 1069, when they destroyed the bridge over the river Aire to prevent him moving north to York. He was intent on what became known as the Harrying of the North.

# Further reading

Anderson, Poul, *Mother of Kings*, Tom Doherty Associates, New York 2001 (fiction, on the theme of Eric Bloodaxe's life)

*Anglo Saxon Chronicles*

Bede, *A History of the English Church and People* (8th century)

Burkitt, Annette, *Flesh and Bones of Frome Selwood and Wessex*, Hobnob Press 2017 (King Athelstan)

Burkitt, Annette, *The Gorge*, Hobnob Press 2021 (King Edmund)

Byrhtferth of Ramsey, *The Lives of St Oswald and St Ecgwine*, ed. Michael Lapidge, Clarendon Press, Oxford, 2010

Crossley-Holland, Kevin, *The Anglo-Saxon World*, Boydell Press 1982

*Domesday Book, Somerset,* Phillimore 1980

*Egil's Saga,* Penguin 2004

Foot, Sarah, *Athelstan,* Yale University Press 2011

Foot, Sarah, *Monastic Life in Anglo-Saxon England c.600-900,* Cambridge University Press, 2006

Gittos, Helen, *Liturgy, Architecture, and Sacred Places in Anglo-Saxon England,* Oxford University Press, 2013

Goold, P A, *King Eadred of Wessex,* Proc. Somerset Archaeology and Natural History Society, 142, 1999 pgs 317-327

Hesse, Herman, *The Glass Bead Game*, Penguin 1972, first pub. 1943

Higham, N J, *The Death of Anglo-Saxon England,* Sutton 1997

Holland, Tom, *Athelstan,* Penguin 2016

Keynes S and Lapidge M *Alfred the Great, Asser's Life of King Alfred,* Penguin 1983

Lapidge, M and Winterbottom, M, *The Lives of St Oswald and St Ecgwine,* Oxford University Press 2009

Oxford Dictionary of National Biography

Page, R I, *Life in Anglo-Saxon England*, Batsford 1970

Reader's Digest, *Folklore, Myths and Legends of Britain,* Hodder and Stoughton 1973

Rex, Peter, *Edgar, King of the English,* Tempus 2007

Ridyard, S J, *The Royal saints of Anglo-Saxon England,* Cambridge University Press 1988

*The Chronicle of Aethelweard,* ed. A. Campbell, Thomas Nelson and Sons Ltd 1962

*The Earliest English Poems,* Penguin Classics, 1966

Whynne-Hammond, Charles, *Ten Somerset Mysteries,* Countryside Books 1995

Williams, Ann, *Aethelred the Unready,* Hambledon and London, 2003

Winterbottom and Lapidge, *The Early Lives of St Dunstan,*

Clarendon Press 2012

    Winterbottom, M and Lapidge, M, *The Early Lives of St Dunstan*, Clarendon Press, Oxford 2012

    Yorke, Barbara, (ed) *Bishop Aethelwold, his Career and Influence*, Boydell Press 1988

    Yorke, Barbara, *Wessex in the Early Middle Ages*, Leicester University Press 1995

# Acknowledgements

I WANT TO thank my family and friends for their encouragement during my years researching and writing about the people and England of the tenth century. I have enjoyed every minute. If I have helped to interest just one person in this little understood, pre-Norman century, I will have done my job.

www.ingramcontent.com/pod-product-compliance
Lightning Source LLC
Chambersburg PA
CBHW030550020726
47494CB00005B/1552